DESERT KING'S SURPRISE LOVE-CHILD

CATHY WILLIAMS

THE INNOCENT'S PROTECTOR IN PARADISE

ANNIE WEST

MILLS & BOON

First Published in Great Britain 2021
by Mills & Boon, an imprint of HarperCollins*Publishers* Ltd,
1 London Bridge Street, London, SE1 9GF

www.harpercollins.co.uk

HarperCollins*Publishers*
1st Floor, Watermarque Building,
Ringsend Road, Dublin 4, Ireland

Desert King's Surprise Love-Child © 2021 Cathy Williams

The Innocent's Protector in Paradise © 2021 Annie West

ISBN: 978-0-263-28270-2

11/21

DESERT KING'S SURPRISE LOVE-CHILD

CATHY WILLIAMS

MILLS & BOON

CHAPTER ONE

CROWN PRINCE ABBAS HUSSEIN glanced cursorily at the
pristine paperwork on the conference table in front of
him and signed with a flourish.

There was no need to check anything. Due diligence
had been done by his fleet of lawyers, several of whom
were around the table, already packing away their computers, ready for the flight back to Qaram.

Behind him, flanking either side of the closed door,
two bodyguards had been patiently waiting for the end of
the proceedings. It was a little after seven in the evening,
freezing cold outside and, like him, they were probably
looking forward to a return to sunnier climes.

He straightened and absently glanced at his watch. At six
feet four, he dominated everyone in the room and none more
so than the CEO who could not have looked more joyful at
having just sold his hotel. It had once been a firm fixture
with minor celebrities but now, like an ageing has-been film
star, it was in desperate need of a revamp and a new role.

It was a mutually beneficial sale for both parties and
added to Abe's choice portfolio of boutique hotels, a sideline to the serious business of running his country, a
small but wealthy and powerful kingdom.

He had been here in London for three days of non-stop
work. Frankly, he could think of nothing he wanted more

than to return to the comforts of the five-star hotel where he had rented one entire floor to house his personal entourage, so when Duncan Squire suggested that he take a little time out to enjoy some of the savouries they had made especially for his benefit, he had to stifle a groan of pure frustration.

'My chef is excellent. She's spent some time creating delicacies for you and your staff.' Clearly in awe of the much younger man, Duncan half bowed and took a step back as he said this. He avoided bumping into the wall behind him by only inches.

'Of course.' The bath he had been envisioning would have to wait, as would the stack of emails that had piled up during his absence from Qaram. His father, after a health scare four years ago, had firmly retired from active duty, convinced that he needed to rest in defiance of everything both Abbas and a team of highly respected consultants had said.

He pottered now, enjoyed tending to his orchards and tracking down art to add to his already bulging private collection. It was a sedate pastime and, in truth, he seemed content enough to retreat from the world and its demands. Unfortunately, it meant that the weight of running the country now fell squarely on Abbas's shoulders so time out was not a luxury he could afford, not when there was work to be done.

He frowned, dragged his thoughts away from his father and the discomfiting notion that having lost him once, many years ago, to the isolation of grief after his wife had died, he was now losing him again, this time to the fear of his own mortality.

He would do as required, politely pick at what was on offer and make his getaway as quickly as he humanly could.

Surely they couldn't still be signing on dotted lines? She'd been buried down here in the bowels of the hotel kitchen for the past couple of days, sending up drinks and snacks, and Duncan had faithfully promised that this would be the last day of working overtime.

Georgie looked at the clock on the kitchen wall, registered that it was nearly seven-fifteen and gritted her teeth with frustration.

She cast a jaundiced eye at the staggering array of delicacies she had spent the entire day concocting. They ranged from several different types of hummus to mini sliders and smoked salmon rolls with caviar. No continent had been left untouched because, as Duncan had repeatedly told her from the very first moment royalty had decided to buy the hotel, she had to pull out all the stops—because the way to a prince's heart might very well be via his stomach.

Georgie was less concerned about the Prince's stomach than she was about the fact that she needed to get back to her apartment and was so tired of hanging around, sending stuff up and making sure everything was picture-perfect. She had yet to meet the Prince, but she was already sick to death of the man.

Now, as she picked up Duncan's urgent summons to the conference room with the last of the tasty morsels she had prepared, Georgie stifled a sigh and eyed the unwieldy trolley that she would have to shove into the elevator because there was simply no other way of delivering everything that had been prepared.

Ever since she had started working at the hotel, she had seen the upsides. For starters, Duncan had employed her at a time when she would have struggled to find work and he had bent over backwards to be accommodating. The members of staff had warmly welcomed her. It was a small hotel in a niche part of London and the people who worked there were all young and creative and lively and Georgie had built up a fantastic rapport with them all.

But, realistically, Bedford Woolf Hotel was on its last legs. Its quirky, theatrical flamboyance now felt dated, belonging to another, more innocent, era. It lacked the refined sophistication of its newer, brasher neighbours. There was also no air conditioning and the décor needed drastic surgery—some lightly applied make-up wasn't going to do—and there was a certain desperation to the old-world charm Duncan had spent the last couple of years trying to cultivate.

Everyone, herself included, was overjoyed that some rich prince, from a country she had never heard of, had paid handsomely for the place and the fact that he would be keeping every member of staff on was a massive bonus.

So who was she to moan about delivering a bit of food before heading home?

She glanced at herself in one of the ornate mirrors in the corridor on the way to the lift, saw her reflection staring back at her, serious, thinner than she used to be, her brown eyes enormous in her heart-shaped face and her cropped hair spiking up in all directions, always determined to do its own thing. She was twenty-six years old and sometimes she felt absolutely ancient. Right now just happened to be one of those times.

Usually, she wore jeans to work. Why not when she was usually wrapped up in an apron? But in keeping with Duncan's mantra to them all to be *neatly attired*, she had forfeited casual today in favour of a navy-blue skirt and a white blouse and a pair of flat black pumps, which made her feel a bit like a flight attendant who had somehow lost her way and ended up in a kitchen, in front of a stove, slightly dishevelled with a few suspicious smudges of grease in unexpected places.

She spun away from the mirror and briskly made her way to the lift.

It was a heavy-duty contraption that slammed shut on her and shuddered its way up two floors to where the conference facilities were located.

Head down, Georgie knocked on the door and pushed it open, her face flushed with embarrassment.

She wasn't accustomed to front-of-house duties. Those were usually the domain of Marsha, who was tall, beautiful and chatty.

Georgie, always quiet and contained, enjoyed the kitchen, where she could concoct dishes and play around with food, leaving the patter to those who were more adept at it.

Opening the door, she was immediately aware of *people* and a lot of them. Lawyers, accountants, two beefy guys on either side of the door and, of course, the Prince himself, who had his back to her and was staring through the window.

She barely saw him. She just wanted to ditch the trolley and head for the bus stop but then Duncan spoke. He asked her to explain what was on the heavy silver three-layered trolley.

Georgie drew breath, looked up and two things happened at once.

The man by the window slowly turned around and she, in turn, glanced in his direction, eyes drawn to him because he towered over everyone else in the room.

The Prince.

His bloodline was stamped in the regal arrogance of his bearing and the cool, controlled command in those deep, dark eyes.

He was so tall and so ridiculously striking—his face chiselled perfection and forbiddingly beautiful.

So sinfully good-looking and so terrifyingly *familiar*.

Georgie blinked and knew that while one part of her brain was telling her that he just couldn't be the guy she thought he was, there was another part of her brain pointing out that his was a face that, once seen, could never be forgotten. Yet how could this be the same man? How? *Buying* a hotel? Not *working* in one? *How?*

She knew that everyone had stopped talking and she could feel eyes boring into her. Duncan nervously said something but it was just white noise because the only thing she was aware of was that man by the window, staring at her in silence.

Disbelief, incredulity and shock roared through her with the force of a freight train and, like a computer suddenly overloading on too much information, her brain made up its mind to stop functioning altogether. Her breathing became shallow and panicked as she began to hyperventilate and, with a gasp, she felt herself doing something she had never done in her life before.

She fainted.

When Georgie came to, she was on a sofa and surfacing to consciousness like a patient emerging from a coma. Where was she? *What was going on?*

Her brain was foggy. It seemed, from what she could see through half-closed, still-dazed eyes, that she was in one of the hotel bedrooms with its familiar décor reminiscent of an old Penguin classic novel. Cream walls with burnt umber dado and picture rails displayed framed classics by Virginia Woolf. The sofa on which she now found herself was the same burnt umber as the woodwork.

She vaguely knew that, by registering what was familiar, she was putting off acknowledging what made no sense.

'Here, drink this.'

If Georgie had been in any doubt about the identity of

the guy who had caused her to black out, then his voice killed all those doubts stone dead. She would have recognised that distinctive drawl in the middle of a crowded bar. It was deep and dark, with just the merest hint of something smoky and exotic.

It was a voice that had haunted her dreams for so long. In her head, she had played and replayed so many scenarios where she would hear that voice, turn around and walk towards it as unerringly as she once had.

She would be in charge—calm—not lying on a sofa with her skirt hitched up one thigh and struggling to get her thoughts in order.

She wriggled into a semi-sitting position and breathed raggedly as her wide and still disbelieving eyes collided with his.

'You!' She fought back the prickle of tears. 'It can't be. What are *you* doing here?'

Everything was in freefall.

Time slowed. She couldn't tear her eyes away from his and, in a sickening rush, she was not just seeing into a past that had come and gone years ago but into a future that was irrevocably breaking down in front of her.

A unit. *Her* unit. Tilly and her. A team of two, because that was what happened when you had a child and the dad was nowhere to be found. When the dad had disappeared without leaving a trace of himself behind.

Except here he was. Tilly's dad. Gone from the scene for years. Back now...and *a prince*. She stifled her terrified whimper but there was a rushing in her head and in her veins and she felt dizzy and nauseous.

Memories broke their banks and came at her in a surging flood. And to her horror, not all those memories were toxic. Intermingled were other dangerously unsettling ones of languorous nights spent together, their naked bodies merging into one with a sense of belonging that had felt so very right at the time. But it *hadn't* been right. It had been *all wrong* and she had lived with the devastating consequences of misreading a situation, had dealt with them, made peace with them. And now...

Now everything was in freefall.

'You know what I'm doing here.' He sounded as shocked as she felt. 'I'm buying this hotel.'

'I can't believe this is happening.'

'Believe it or not, nor can I.'

Abe had regained his self-control at speed but for a few seconds, as he had turned round and seen her, the shock had surely equalled hers. Never had recall been so vivid. The breath had left his body and the walls of the room had closed in until there were just two of them in a confined space, the only other intruders his memories of a past now gone.

He had seen the horrified incredulity in her eyes and it had mirrored his, but he was a man for whom emotion was always rigidly disciplined. He had broken eye contact, begun moving smoothly towards her, powered by some sixth sense he never knew he possessed, somehow instinctively predicting that she would faint and already knowing that he would make sure the room was vacated so that there were no witnesses to the conversation that would take place when she awoke.

'Where is Duncan? Where's everyone gone? How did I get here?'

'You should drink that water, although I can always get you something stronger. You've had a shock.'

'You haven't answered my question! And I don't need water! I need... I need...'

I need to find out what is going on.

The guy who had vanished into thin air four years ago hadn't been a prince. He'd been an ordinary guy, a guy she'd fallen head over heels in love with, just *an ordinary guy*. Her mind grappled desperately to fit pieces together that just made no sense and underneath the chaos and confusion was the blistering realisation that life as she knew it was over. They shared a daughter. This wasn't a bad dream and nothing was going to be the same, if only he knew.

'How can you be *a prince*?' she whispered. 'It's not possible!'

'This is a long conversation to have here,' Abe said tautly. 'I never thought I'd see you again but now that our paths have once more crossed, I should tell you that I am not the person you probably thought I was.'

'Oh, you've got *that* right.' She swung her legs over the sofa and was assailed by a sudden attack of giddiness. Everything in Georgie raged against being here.

Hatred, bitterness and the sour taste of all of her shattered illusions ripped into her with such ferocity that the four years since they had last seen one another could have been four minutes.

He'd gone. Left her. Walked away without a backward glance and with no forwarding address. No telephone number. No point of contact. Just disappeared into thin air, leaving her to struggle with a love she hadn't asked for but one that had swept her away with the force of a tsunami. Leaving her pregnant and alone.

She'd been a notch on his bedpost.

Through her devastation, that simple truth had been unavoidable. He'd used her and then, when he'd grown tired of her, he'd walked away and he'd left no clues behind so that she could trace him—and, oh, how she'd tried.

'You haven't changed,' Abe said on a rough breath, only the slight deepening of his tone advertising the fact that he was as shaken as she was.

'I don't want to be here.'

'There are people waiting outside. I have given them orders not to enter but they will be wondering what's going on.'

'I have to go.' She pushed herself up and brushed aside his hand when he moved to help her to her feet.

More than that, she had to think.

'You can barely walk in a straight line.' He raked his fingers through his hair and brought the laser intensity of his focus back to her ashen face. 'Where do you live? Allow me to get you back to your place.'

'No!'

Abe was startled by her vehemence but then how could she be anything *but* angry with him? Bitter?

Unwittingly, his dark eyes roved over her face. She really hadn't changed at all. She still had that *something* that had once fired him up against all odds and held him captive. She was so slight with a slender, boyish frame and short, dark hair that framed an intensely pretty, heart-shaped face. Her eyes were a curious shade of light brown with flecks of green and her lips were full, the perfect Cupid's bow.

Even with those huge, almond-shaped eyes pinned resentfully on him and her mouth downturned with simmering antagonism, Abe could still feel the unwelcome intrusion of a libido that had been all too dormant for way too long.

He gritted his teeth, vaulted upright and sauntered to the window, from which he stared down at wet, dark bustling pavements and street lamps fuzzy against the steady rainfall.

He was here on business.

He wasn't going to complicate anything by trying to recapture what was in the past. That door had been firmly shut and he wasn't going to reopen it. He couldn't.

Even though she was still the biggest test to his resistance that he had ever had. It wasn't just the way she looked, so different from the women he had always dated in the past. It was who she had been. Irreverent, outspoken in her own special, reserved way. Intelligent and challenging. Strangely shy and yet not afraid of holding her ground. So she hadn't known who he was back then, hadn't felt the need to be subservient, but even now she knew he sensed that in that respect she had changed very little.

She had burned a hole in his life. So different from any other woman...

They had shared a scorching affair and his last truly liberating one before his father had fallen ill and the course of his life had changed for ever.

'Wait here,' he said on impulse.

'Why?'

'We should talk.'

Georgie stared at him in mute, resentful silence but she stayed put even though every instinct in her was telling her to run away as fast as possible.

'I need to get back home.'

'Fifteen minutes is all I ask. I return to my country in two days' time, after I've sorted the last remaining legalities of the hotel purchase. The way we parted company last time... Let's at least clear some of the air before I head back to Qaram.'

Georgie wondered what he could possibly say to her that could clear the air. But of course, even now, things would seem straightforward to him. He didn't know of the beautiful life they had created between them. He didn't realise that nothing was straightforward any more.

In the days and weeks and months after he'd left Georgie had gradually come to accept that he just hadn't felt the same way about her as she had felt about him. He hadn't seen her as 'relationship material', for want of a better description.

As she had tackled huge changes to her life she had never, ever foreseen, she'd looked back and assessed what she'd missed at the time, in the heat of the moment. They'd never discussed the details of their lives, never shared their surnames. They'd adopted a 'live for the moment' philosophy that had suited her at the time and would have worked if only she hadn't ended up wanting so much more.

Now a few more things fell into sharp relief. The way the one-bed flat that she'd been renting when she'd first arrived in Ibiza had always been used as their base. She'd had no idea where he'd lived and he'd been adept at swerving around awkward questions. She'd assumed that he worked at one of the many hotels that lined the long strip of beach because he'd never denied it. He'd had a cool air of self-assurance that had made him seem so much more mature than his peers, but she'd just put that down to the fact that he was from another country and had been brought up differently. Although, in retrospect, those were details that had also been kept from her.

Now it made perfect sense, all those missing bits. He was a prince and she was a pauper and she was *never* going to be relationship material for him.

Was that what he was so keen to talk about? Did he want to justify his disappearance?

He reappeared in the middle of her agonised deliberations and she blinked. It was frustrating that she still couldn't seem to look at him without being intensely aware of his sexual pull even though she knew that it was that damned innate magnetism he possessed that had sucked her in in the first place.

He dragged a chair over to where she had sat once again on the sofa and leant forward, forearms loosely resting on his thighs.

'What did you tell them?' Georgie asked flatly. 'I don't want any gossip circulating about me. This is a small place. People talk.'

'I told them you were still a bit shaken, probably run off your feet preparing for this visit. I said that I blamed myself for the situation and, that being the case, I would take a corner seat and stay while you gathered yourself. Least I could do. The less fuss everyone makes, the better. I assured your boss that once you were less woozy, I would ensure that you were safely delivered back to where you live. I assure you that there will be no gossip.'

'You were always good with words.'

'I never lied to you.'

'No?'

'Perhaps I would have told you the truth, but the fact is that I never enjoyed the company of a woman the way I enjoyed yours and to have told you who I really was would have put an end to what we had. I was selfish and greedy and I wanted you for as long as possible.

'And then you left and didn't spare a thought for me,' Georgie said bitterly. 'I suppose, given what I now know—that you're royalty—it wouldn't have occurred to you that I might have had feelings, that I might have been hurt at being used as a rich boy's plaything and then discarded without a second thought.'

Abe flushed. 'We had fun, that's all. There was always going to be an end to it and I thought you understood that.'

Tears stung the backs of Georgie's eyes because how differently had they viewed the situation. Had he used her? Not in his eyes, clearly, because they had just been having fun, two ships briefly crossing paths on separate journeys to other destinations.

In his case—to rule a country and run around buying hotels. In her case—to face a life that had been utterly derailed.

'The least you could have done would have been to tell me that you were going,' she said coldly. 'Did you think that if you'd done the decent thing and said goodbye that I might have become annoying and clingy?'

'I...had to leave suddenly.' He raked his fingers through his hair and sat back.

'How convenient. You could have texted me, but I guess that didn't occur to you either. Why should it? It seems that you are a man who can do as he likes with the click of a finger and that included walking off without a word. I looked for you, you know. I spent ages asking around and in the end I gave up.' She thought of Tilly, beautiful, innocent Tilly, the result of a relationship that never was.

'I was recalled to my country because my father had had a heart attack,' Abe said bluntly. 'It was sudden and there was no choice in the matter. Yes, I could have texted you but there seemed little point. I had to go and I felt it better to sever ties completely, without needless post-mortems. I knew you would move on.'

As he obviously had, Georgie thought with a mixture

of sadness and animosity. People moved on after brief flings. It was always harder when the heart was involved though, as hers had been.

'Your father,' she said quietly. 'Did he recover?'

'In a manner of speaking. Tell me how it is that you've ended up here, working as a chef in a hotel in London, when you had plans to continue with your art, to free-lance as an illustrator. I know you worked in the kitchen at that hotel in Ibiza…did you suddenly develop a craving to change career course?'

Georgie stilled as the present met the past. She glanced at the clock on the wall. Time was ticking by and she had to go. He needed to know about his daughter but…not right now. She just had to work things out in her head first, work past the pain of knowing that he had abandoned her without a backwards glance.

'Things didn't quite work out the way I'd planned. What do you mean when you say your father recovered "in a manner of speaking"?'

'He recovered but has not been himself since that episode.' Abe hesitated and Georgie knew that he was uncomfortable with sharing anything private about himself.

'If you feel embarrassed answering, then please don't bother.' Her head was beginning to throb and she rubbed her temples. 'I wouldn't want to put you on the spot by asking you for any personal information about yourself,' she said somewhat sarcastically.

'He has retreated from public service,' Abe said abruptly. 'Hence the urgency of my departure four years ago. I am his successor and it fell to me to take over the running of my country while he recovered. I had no idea that my role would become a permanent one, as it has. My father has decided, in defiance of everything the doctors have told him, that his life is effectively over. He has always been very energetic but he has lost his ebullience. He is no longer the man he used to be and that saddens me.' He shrugged awkwardly. 'That's of no account. It is what it is. My point is that I had to leave immediately and I knew things would have come to an end for us eventually anyway.'

'I have to go,' she muttered.

'This conversation needs some kind of conclusion. And you're working here...you still haven't told me what happened.'

She shrugged and averted her eyes. She wished she could close them and pretend that none of this was happening.

'This hotel? It's been failing for some time, am I right? How is it...? Your plans... I don't quite understand.'

Georgie reddened because somehow that felt like a personal slight. She wanted to tell him that it wasn't her fault. She surreptitiously glanced at the faded elegance of the bedroom. Scratch beneath the surface and signs of dilapidation were all too visible, and she suspected Abe would have done a lot of scratching below the surface before he decided to sink money into the purchase.

'What were you doing in Ibiza in the first place?' she suddenly asked, and she noted the discomfort on his face as he lowered his eyes briefly, lush dark lashes concealing his expression.

'I was buying a hotel to add to my collection,' he admitted without bothering to dress it up. 'In fact, we met by chance and because of you I ended up staying three weeks longer than I had originally planned.'

'Should I take that as a compliment?' Georgie asked acidly, but even as the words left her mouth she knew that bitterness wasn't going to get her anywhere. 'Forget that. In answer to your question about the hotel: yes.

Things have been rocky for over a year. Longer. It seems that no one is really interested in a hotel that's small and charming, not when they can go to somewhere bigger and better equipped, never mind the fact that this hotel was home to the Bloomsbury set years and years ago. You'll fix everything here and paint over the character that no one is interested in and you'll get bookings by the dozen, I'm sure.' Then she offered a stiff smile. 'I apologise. I suppose I shouldn't be saying stuff like that considering you're now my boss.'

Under any other circumstances, that very fact would have already kick-started thoughts about handing in her resignation, but she knew that once he left the country he would not return, whatever the circumstances. He had left once without a backward glance. He would leave again.

'You may not have realised this, but I have saved your boss the unappealing prospect of having to let staff go. I have looked at the accounts of this place in some depth.' He paused and looked at her steadily and Georgie could feel those dark eyes boring into the very core of her. She was desperate to tear her gaze away but she couldn't and she licked her lips as nervous tension built.

She hadn't realised that Duncan had been planning redundancies but, of course, what choice would he have had? The place had been running on less than half full practically since she had started working there.

'I know how much you are paid. G Curtis—Head Chef. Had I known your surname I might have twigged.'

'You know how much I earn? That…that's none of your business!'

'Of course it is. Everything about the finances of this hotel became my business the second I decided to throw money at it. I know how much you started on here, which was a deplorably small amount, and I know that since then you have had all of two pay rises as you worked your way up the culinary ladder. You had big dreams when I knew you, Georgie. How have you ended up working for pennies in a place like this? Yes, it's charming but, when it comes to career paths, surely you must have known for some time that you were facing a dead end?'

'I...' Her face was burning. She thought about those dreams he had mentioned, the career illustrating children's books she had hoped for... She'd always known it would be tough to start with, but she'd made some connections before...everything had happened. She'd known the road she had mapped out and the one she had ended up going down, working as a chef, had never been on the map.

She felt ashamed and then was angry for feeling ashamed because being a chef was very creative and fulfilling. As Plan Bs went, it could have been a lot worse. Her thoughts were settling into some kind of order now. Perhaps the intense shock had begun tapering off. Perhaps horror had been replaced with a sweeping sense of the inevitable or maybe, deep down, she had always known that sooner or later those conversations she had visited in her head would actually happen because the guy who had broken her heart and stolen her faith in love would return like a storm sweeping in from the sea—a tempest blowing away everything in its path.

She could see the guarded curiosity on his face and resented it. *It was okay for some...*

'No need to explain but...' he hesitated '... I would really like to find out about why you have ended up working here. No, more than that... I want to explain in greater depth, Georgie...why I left the way I did. We all are faced with choices. I would like to explain mine.'

'There's no need,' she muttered sullenly.

'Let me buy you dinner.' He smiled faintly. 'You're thinner than I remember. You look as though you need feeding up. Wasn't Italian your favourite choice of cuisine? Pasta carbonara, if I remember correctly. One last dinner, Georgie, before I go. Wherever you want to go, I will take you. I realise I do not *need* to explain myself, but I would really *like* to. Take this. My card.'

Georgie was busy staring at the embossed card he'd placed next to her. His name. His number. A royal crest. Gold on cream.

'I'll understand if you won't let me deliver you back to...wherever you live. I know that you may feel that my presence in your house is an intrusion when you are obviously still resentful about how things ended between us after all this time.'

'Can you really blame me?'

'There are always two sides to every story.'

'No, Abbas, sometimes there's just the one side.'

'Have dinner with me.'

'So that you can try and clear your conscience?'

'Perhaps I, also, have thought about the past and what we had...'

Her heart jerked, a weakness she knew had to take second place to the cold business that lay ahead of her. She loathed the pathetic, desperate voice inside her that ached for him to tell her just what those thoughts had been.

Had he missed her the way she'd missed him, even when she'd resigned herself to the superficial role she'd played in his life?

'Consider it, Georgie,' he urged softly, rising to his feet but continuing to watch her. 'This time, let us part ways in peace.'

She would have loved nothing more than to have ripped up that card in front of him. Peace? Over dinner? Two adults burying hatchets? Did he think that they would part company with a solid handshake, a *'You must drop by if you happen to be in the area'* and maybe a kiss on the cheek? Did he? How far from the truth that was. Time and events had put paid to any such thing.

She watched in silence as he waited, head tilted to one side, before turning on his heel to head for the door, and as he opened it she caught a glimpse of his bodyguards, waiting outside for him, stoic and incurious.

The door closed with a soft click and she reached for his card, shutting her eyes as her fingers curled around it.

CHAPTER TWO

TWENTY-FOUR HOURS LATER, practically to the minute, Georgie was standing in front of the impressive five-star hotel where the Prince was staying.

There had been no need for him to tell her the name of the hotel because she'd known even before he and his entourage had arrived in London to finalise the details of the sale of the hotel. She'd been told that the food would have to be superb and she had dutifully done her own due diligence and scoured the hotel's menu so she wouldn't replicate any of their dishes when preparing the delicacies for his visit.

Of course, she could simply have called the number on the card, that *very special* card with its *very special* hotline number to the big man himself, but she had rejected that idea because the mere thought of it had made her feel sick.

Such a card was the very thing she had craved four years ago. Now it felt like an insult, something that cheapened her, something dished out with the arrogant pity of a guy who hadn't thought twice about leaving her and now wanted to set the record straight with his conscience by letting her know why.

Poor Georgie, with all her dreams of making it big in the world of illustration and all her high hopes and hard-won contracts... Where had it all gone? Down the proverbial...

Anyway, the thought of hearing that dark, dangerous voice down the end of a phone line had given her too much pause for thought.

Best to take the bull by the horns and just show up at his hotel because her morals were far too deeply ingrained for her to turn her back on what had to be done, even though what had to be done filled her with simmering panic and fear.

She had dressed for the part. Not quite office ready, but certainly not casual. The flight attendant had been replaced, she now thought, heading towards the hotel, by mourner at the funeral of a distant relative. Just enough decorum to pay her respects but no wailing or howling because she hadn't known the relative very well. Black knee-length skirt, black roll-neck jumper—and a black cardigan on top of that because it was freezing—and black tights. Underneath the puffer jacket, she felt she was sartorially equipped for what lay ahead.

It was going to be the most difficult conversation of her life, one she had anticipated having years ago but since then she had moved on with her life, and now she was scared stiff of the unknown because she had no idea where this conversation would take her. She just knew first-hand what loss felt like. She had lost both her parents, so there was no way she wanted Abbas to stroll into Tilly's life, upend it, and then casually walk away again. He'd done that with *her*, hadn't he? Telling him the truth was the decent thing to do, for her the *only* thing to do, but she would need to make it known to him that there would be no room in the equation for someone unreliable and a prince from a faraway country carried the definite whiff of unreliability.

The guy who'd walked away without a second thought would definitely not be the man who was suddenly overpowered with a sense of duty to a child he hadn't asked for.

She would do what she had come to do and her conscience would be clear. He didn't have the monopoly on wanting a clean slate. But when she tried to imagine what she was going to say and how he might react, she felt the sickening twist of dread deep inside her and she had to remind herself that this was about Tilly; this was about their child and his right to know of her existence.

Head down, looking neither left nor right and definitely not behind to the entrance to the Tube and the temptation of flight, Georgie made her way into the hotel.

The call from reception came through just as Abe was about to phone his father.

Georgie. In the foyer of the hotel.

He tossed his cell phone on the leather sofa where he'd been sitting and strolled towards the bank of windows in his suite that offered extensive views of the City of London.

At a little after seven in the evening, it was dark and the city was like a blurry impressionistic artwork, washed out by the steady torrent of rain that had been falling since mid-afternoon.

She'd come. He hadn't realised how wired he'd been since he'd left her at the hotel with his card. Of course, there was no way he could have chased her if she'd decided not to take him up on his offer, but it would have left a sour taste in his mouth.

Seeing her again... Yes, he could understand her antipathy towards him. He'd left. No tearful goodbyes or weeping and wailing. He'd done as he'd seen fit at the time because there had been no way the future he'd instinctively known she wanted would have been compatible with what Fate had chosen for him.

Everything in life came with its own limitations and subclauses and caveats—and his life came with more than the usual amount. Nothing was ever straightforward for him.

When he thought about that snatched moment in time in Ibiza, when there had only been the sea and the sun and Georgie and so much lust there were times he felt he might combust from it, it was like a glimpse of what normal life might look like. Naturally, he had not yearned for what lay outside his reach, but it had been…liberating and he had enjoyed every second of it and seeing her again now brought all those memories flooding back.

He remembered her youthful plans and felt intensely sad that those plans had come to nothing.

Why?

He realised she hadn't gone into any detail but that, in itself, told a story. Whatever had happened, she had clearly been too ashamed to tell him when he'd asked the day before.

He hoped she would confide in him now, perhaps over the dinner he had offered.

Abbas was surprised at how strong the urge was to talk to her, to try and be open with her about why he'd left the way he had, so that she would understand and forgive.

He could only think that some undercurrent of, yes, guilt must have stayed with him all these years and had been resurrected by her sudden reappearance in his life.

But where she had ended up…

He wanted to find out more.

He knew she likely struggled to make ends meet on her salary, her pay enough to keep body and soul together but without any frills. Cheap plonk but never champagne. He'd revisited the hotel's books since seeing her yesterday to remind himself of what she earned. She'd started out waitressing but her talent at cooking had soon been spotted, judging from that first pay increase a mere month after she'd joined, but even in the role of chef she still wasn't making a huge deal of money. The hotel was on its last legs—no one there earned that much because there wasn't enough to do the rounds.

How? How on earth had her dreams crashed and burned so spectacularly? The question kept coming back to him because it made no sense.

If she'd come here because in the cool light of day she really did want to hear his side of the story, then she would know that he wanted to hear hers.

He half closed his eyes and the image of her leapt into his head with graphic clarity.

So damned pretty...so sweetly tempting without ever realising it...

She'd come to talk and talk they would, but what if talking was not her only reason for being here?

He allowed his mind to drift, went back in time and enjoyed the memory of her, her slight body under his, so supple, so elegant and as graceful as a ballet dancer. There was nothing obvious about her and that subtlety had been an addiction. He had been mystified how someone could be so soft yet have such a fierce core, so shy yet sizzle with such allure...

What if she's come for more than just a meal and a heart-to-heart? a little voice insisted on whispering in his head and Abe very firmly closed the door on that notion. He hoped she hadn't because he didn't relish the prospect of gently showing her the door. Because whether he still found her attractive or not, he was not in the market for any kind of involvement, least of all with an old flame.

Abbas was well aware of what he brought to the table. He also knew what he didn't bring, and that was emotional involvement.

He couldn't. Experience had taught him that the whims of emotion would never serve a crown prince. Only a cool head could do that.

But that aside, he'd seen how love could cause as much pain as it could create joy. He'd keenly felt the pain of losing his mother and lived through the horror of his father's anguish when he'd lost his wife. Abbas wasn't really sure whether his father had ever got over the loss of the woman he'd loved so much. He just knew that from every angle, it didn't work letting your heart take over the reins. He'd done Georgie a favour by walking away, he told himself. He'd spared her the pain of realising that he couldn't allow himself to offer her the sort of emotional connection she would have been looking for.

He stiffened at the rap on the door, moving to open it himself before one of the two bodyguards stationed outside could buzz to let him know of his visitor's arrival.

Outside Abbas's hotel-room door, Georgie was trying hard not to feel cowed by the presence of the same beefy bodyguards she had glimpsed yesterday. She was staring straight ahead at the closed door and doing her best to ignore the men on either side of her. In her mind's eye, she pictured Abbas and was dealing just fine with the obedient, cardboard-cut-out image in her head, but when he softly pulled open the door, she felt the breath leave her body in a whoosh.

He was in a pair of jeans and a dark, fitted long-sleeved tee shirt. Gone was the immaculate, hand-tai-

lored suit of the day before. This was more the guy she
remembered and yet, in a thousand crucial ways, nothing at all like him.

Her mouth went dry and for a few seconds, she couldn't
think straight. In fact, she couldn't think *at all*. How could
he still exert such a pull on her senses? When she knew
him for what he was? A creep who had used her. He might
have been summoned back to his country because of an
emergency but, face it, he hadn't seen any reason to tell
her as much because she'd simply been disposable. She'd
reached her sell-by date and he hadn't thought twice about
walking away.

So why the hell was she finding it so hard to tear her
eyes away when her head knew how the land lay?

'You don't look surprised to see me,' she told him,
chin up.

His eyebrows shot up. 'Would you like to come in before we begin this conversation?'

He stood back and Georgie swept past him, breathing in his scent.

'Drink?' He padded barefoot through to a living area
that was bigger than her entire flat.

'Are you?'

'Am I what?'

'Surprised that I'm here.'

He paused and considered her with his head tilted to
one side. 'Not entirely,' he admitted. 'You can take the
jacket off, Georgie. I am no fan of the cold. The heating
is on in here.'

He was still so beautiful, she thought resentfully. So
tall, with tigerish gold-flecked eyes and perfectly chiselled features, stamped with the cool, superior confidence
conferred upon him from his noble lineage.

She removed the puffer jacket and hesitated before taking the glass of wine he was holding out to her.

'That said,' he murmured, 'I anticipated some advance warning… A chance to book a table at a restaurant…'

'Dinner…' she said vaguely.

'Is that why you're here?' He shrugged but his dark eyes were intent under lush lashes. 'No matter. The room service is excellent. Will you leave it to me to order? And relax, Georgie.' He paused. 'We're just going to talk. You don't have to worry that there might be anything else behind my suggestion that you join me for dinner.'

'I'm not,' Georgie said sharply.

'Good.' He smiled. 'Tell me what you'd like to eat. No need for any menu. Whatever you want, they will oblige.'

'The advantages of being a prince,' Georgie muttered, feeling herself flush. 'I don't care. Anything.'

'Okay.' But his voice was cooler now, more speculative. He sauntered over to his phone, dialled what she expected was room service and ordered who knew what. She didn't listen and instead busied herself looking around the sort of expansive, luxurious space that only the ridiculously wealthy could ever hope to afford. Huge, ultra-modern kitchen, huge ultra-modern sunken sitting area with leather furniture, several doors ajar, probably leading to huge ultra-modern bedrooms and bathrooms. Everything, from walls to blinds to curtains, was in varying shades of off-white. It was clearly the biggest and the best the hotel had on offer.

'So…' he drawled, moving to sit on one of the leather sofas and looking at her over the rim of his glass. 'You're here and I am glad you decided to come, Georgie. I need not tell you that I've been curious as to what's happened with you since we last saw one another… Tell me what you've been doing…'

'You know what I've been doing,' she said tersely, edging her way towards one of the pristine white chairs and perching awkwardly on it. Surrounded by this lavish display of luxury, she was acutely aware of the gaping chasm between them. Sprawled on the sofa facing her, he was the epitome of sophistication. He *belonged* against this sort of backdrop, casually elegant and at ease in his surroundings.

She, on the other hand, looked as she felt—out of place and ill at ease.

'Tell me why you ended up where you did. What happened? When I knew you, you were so enthusiastic about illustrating. You were also good at it. I remember the sketches you constantly used to do.'

'Life happened,' Georgie said curtly, heart speeding up and nervous perspiration dampening her upper lip.

Abe nodded sympathetically and she gritted her teeth, willing to bide her time for the moment.

'It has a way of doing that,' he agreed. 'I never expected my father to fall suddenly ill the way he did—the best-laid plans and all that... I also never saw myself taking over as ruler of my country at such a young age but, as you say, life happens and we simply have to adjust and go along for the ride.' He paused, frowned. 'There's no need to look so nervous, Georgie. No one's forced you to come here so I don't understand why you're so tense. Art and catering are worlds apart. Did working at that restaurant in Ibiza kill off your original plans?'

'I couldn't afford to invest in the time I would have needed to get contracts,' she told him jerkily. 'Yes, I had some connections but even with those... I would have needed to be able to financially support myself for a while in order to successfully build my business.'

'Quite,' Abe murmured with an understanding smile.

'I never told you,' she said quietly, 'but I went to Ibiza in the first place to recover from my father's death.' She watched as he registered surprise and she knew why because when they'd been an item, she had been the one doing all the confiding, but she had still been too raw then to tell him about her father's brief illness and sudden death.

Her mother had died when she'd been young, too young for Georgie to really remember much about her. Her father, the local vicar, had been the rock in her life. He had never remarried and so there had been no competition for his attention—it was always just the two of them. He had been a gentle man with a very firm moral compass and Georgie had spent her life striving to please him, to do well at school, then at art college, aware of but not unhappy with the expectations he'd placed on her.

She wondered what he would make of her situation now. Frankly, she worried he might be turning in his grave.

'I had to get away for a while, wanted to throw myself into a lifestyle that could…make me forget.' She waited for him to interject but he remained silent, looking at her with his head tilted to one side. He'd always been a good listener. That was something she remembered. He looked like a playboy, with those swarthy, impossibly sexy good looks, but he knew how to listen. It had been seductive, especially at a time when she had been hurting and vulnerable. He had shown her how to trust again, how to laugh again, how to see that there were always rainbows even if the skies looked stormy. She'd been ready to reveal that final snippet about herself to him, knowing that he would understand, would be there for her, would know just how to wrap her in the safety of his embrace…but then he'd vanished.

'I'm sorry,' Abe said quietly.

'Why?'

'I wish you'd told me.'

'Really?' Past hurt suddenly swamped her   she clenched her fists. 'Because you would have sympathised for five minutes before disappearing into thin air, without bothering to tell me?' She waved her hand and looked away. 'Doesn't matter. I was there…to recover. I needed to get away from everyone and everything. I grew up in a small village where everyone knew everyone else's business. It was stifling after my father died. The kindness, the sympathy…the pity, sometimes. I appreciated that people cared but I needed to escape.'

She shook her head, determined not to let emotion get the better of her. 'Anyway, why should you be interested in hearing all this now? The fact was that I ran away, used some of the money Dad left me to travel. That was how I was able to afford to rent that flat in Ibiza. When I returned, there was just about enough left to buy somewhere small…but there was no way I could contemplate months of living off my savings while hoping to make it big. Illustrating is a competitive business and… No, I couldn't take the chance of striking the jackpot, even though my list of contacts might have been enough to see me through. There was just too much uncertainty in going down that road. It would have meant sacrificing the chance to buy a place of my own and there was no way I could do that.'

She breathed in deeply and gazed down at the black void of a precipice. She had come here for a reason yet she was cravenly relieved when he picked up the conversation.

'Your father's death was unexpected enough to make your world unravel,' Abbas said with pinpoint accuracy, 'as my father's sudden heart attack caused my life to deviate from the direction in which it had been going. Similar situations, in some ways, would you not agree?'

Sitting here, Abe remembered with a pang how easy their relationship had been. He was surprised to learn about her father, but he could empathise because there were always some things a person found difficult to share. When he thought back to the girl she had been then, it made a curious kind of sense because he'd never thought she had the personality of someone who enjoyed the brash party life of that particular strip of beach where she'd worked. He'd first met her when she had blushed her way through an explanation of the paella she had cooked. He had insisted on the head waiter fetching her from the kitchen because the food had been so good and had been amused and tickled pink at her embarrassment.

It didn't sit well with him knowing that he had hurt her, even though, at the time, he had seen leaving as the most efficient way of ending something that had only ever been an exceptionally enjoyable fling. Whenever he'd thought of elevating it beyond that, he'd mentally put the brakes on, preferring to stick to what he knew, to adhere to his usual limitations. He'd known that going off-piste on that front could never be an option for him.

'I never expected my own father to have a heart attack,' Abe confessed. 'He had always been a strong man. The only time I remember him laid low was when my mother died. At any rate, it was a shock to be recalled to the palace out of the blue.' He hesitated. 'I did what I thought was best, Georgie.'

'Best for you, you mean,' she shot back.

'Best for the both of us. I never meant to hurt you. I never made you any promises, Georgie.'

'I'm not saying you did,' she said stiffly.

'My life has always been prescribed,' Abe said flatly. 'As an only child, I was relentlessly groomed to be ready to take over the duties of my father at any point.' He hesitated. 'My father had a very successful arranged marriage. He learnt vital lessons from his own father who had cast his net wide, had mistresses and eventually married two of them. My grandfather had no control over his behaviour and the country suffered as a result. Vital investments in infrastructure were sidelined, business of any sort was put on hold, money was squandered and we lost standing in the international community. It took a long time for things to be steadied and was in no small part due to the efforts of my father, who had the sense to rein in his private life. He married for convenience to a woman who knew the role she would have to play. Love may have come later for them, but suitability was the key factor to his choice of wife and there was never any question that I would have to follow in his footsteps. If I led you to believe that things were more serious between us than they were, then I sincerely apologise to you now.'

'You didn't lead me to believe anything,' Georgie denied. 'I over-invested.'

'You're a romantic. That is a road I have never travelled down and never will.'

'So you've said.'

'Which doesn't mean that I'm lacking in emotion...'

Georgie didn't know what was worse, the message or the messenger. In a minute, he would be reaching for a handkerchief so that she could dab her tear-filled eyes while laying it on thick with the sympathy.

'Like I said, I enjoyed what we had and after what

you've told me… I understand it would have been a tough call choosing between a house and a career.'

'I'm not asking for your pity, Abe,' she said tightly.

'That's not what I am giving you,' he said, slowly rising to his feet before heading towards the well-appointed kitchen and returning with the bottle of wine. 'Pity and sympathy are two different creatures and they stem from two different standpoints.' He sat back. 'Perhaps this is the conversation we should have had four years ago,' he mused. 'Do you think the parting of ways would have been made easier? If you had told me about your father? If I had explained to you who I really was? That there could be no future between us? I am not a believer in retrospective wisdom, so it is good that the air has finally been cleared.' He reached across to top up her glass.

Georgie remained silent. 'No more wine, thank you.' He had ordered food and she'd completely forgotten about it until there was a knock on the door and a trolley was wheeled in and silver cloches whipped up by a fully uniformed waiter. A Chinese feast. Her mouth watered but she reminded herself that this wasn't a social visit. She would eat but she wasn't going to consider it sharing a meal with him.

She helped herself to the food and didn't look at him as she ate. Despite the delicious smells it was emitting, it tasted like cardboard. How could she enjoy any of it when her stomach was churning and her mind was spinning cartwheels?

'The truth is always better than lies and subterfuge.' Georgie knew this to be a fact, but if she had known his true identity she would have run a mile. She might have been innocent, but she wasn't completely lacking in grey matter.

Yet, when she thought about *never* having had him in her life, her mind drew a blank.

Without this stranger sitting opposite her, there would have been no Tilly and Tilly was her unexpected heavenly gift that gave her life meaning.

Was it possible to sift through the strands of your past and pick out the bits you didn't like, or did cause and effect make that impossible?

'You never expected to ever run into me again, but you did, Abe. Maybe you feel guilty at the way things ended. Do you? Is that why you asked me out for dinner before you disappear to the other side of the world?'

Again.

Georgie knew that that was something she should not forget. He had disappeared with no warning. That was the kind of man he was. Programmed to end up with a certain type of woman and she was not that type of woman and never would be.

'Why should I feel guilty? Haven't I explained?'

'It doesn't matter.' She waved one hand impatiently. 'You're right, we can continue going round and round in circles but we won't get anywhere, because there's a reason I'm here and it's not because I feel any need for you to apologise. I don't. What happened, happened.'

Despite the disinterest she was displaying, Georgie had never hated anyone the way she hated him now. For disappearing, for stealing her heart, for showing up and glibly writing off what they had shared as nothing important, for asking her out for a stupid expensive dinner because he wanted to *salve his conscience*. She hated him for knowing what she had failed to see at the time: that he was completely out of her league. She hadn't been playing with a full deck of cards because she hadn't known who he was, how rich and important he was. She felt foolish now for not instinctively clocking what should have been obvious to anyone with half a brain. Even masquerading as Mr Ordinary, he'd still been so sophisticated, so self-assured, so good-looking. There, in Ibiza, she'd actually believed that she was a different person and not the girl next door she'd always been, but if she'd taken a few seconds to stand back, she would have known that there was no way he was going to hang around for ever.

Mostly, though, she hated him for showing her what she wanted to forget, for showing her that he still got to her, that her body could still react to him. She hated him for the dreams he had put in her head that would never have materialised.

'You asked me how it was that I ended up where I did, working at the hotel.'

'Your father died. If I had known that then, perhaps I would have told you who I was, would have—'

'Would have what? That's raking over old coals, Abbas. The past is best left alone. Let me fully explain why I ended up where I did. I could have worked something out with the illustrations if I'd really wanted, used up savings and maybe worked evenings so that there was some money coming in until I made a name for myself. I could have figured something out, but in the end there was no choice for me. Life had other plans in store. You see, I found out that I was pregnant.'

'Pregnant?'

He couldn't have sounded more shocked and his eyes lowered with laser-like intensity to her stomach.

'Pregnant,' he repeated, laughing shakily. 'Yes, I can see how that might have interfered with the future you had planned. And...the baby?' he asked after a brief hesitation.

'A daughter. I called her Matilda.'

'Nice name. And the father?'

* * *

His dark eyes remained pinned to her face but he felt a sudden surge of emotion at the thought of another man with her. *Touching her...inside her...fathering a child.*

He shifted because such raw emotion, springing from out of the blue, was not welcome. What they had enjoyed was in the past and, as she'd said, the past was best left alone. There was certainly no room there to harbour feelings of jealousy because she had moved on with another man. Any lingering sexual attraction he might still feel for her didn't make sense. In his well-planned and well-ordered life, he couldn't afford the chaos of emotion even though, and he was loath to admit it, seeing her again had fired up all sorts of memories and wayward thoughts that made him wonder whether he had actually put her behind him as successfully as he'd assumed.

Georgie didn't answer. Her hand was shaking as she reached for the bag she had brought, fishing out her wallet, from which she carefully extracted a photo to extend to him.

'Tilly is a little over three years old. That's her.'

'Attractive child.' He set the photo on the table next to him and looked across at her quizzically, wondering what it was about her that wouldn't let him shut the door completely on their past. 'But I admit I'm confused. Where is this going?'

Abe genuinely didn't know. For once his sharp brain had hit a roadblock and, search as he might, there were no clues on her face to offer any signposts as to what his next move should be. Why was she here? She'd picked at the food and been uninterested in any kind of catch-up conversation. This had not been the evening he had envisaged but in truth he wasn't entirely sure what he *had* envisaged.

Did she think that there were still the embers of a fire between them that could be stoked back to life? He'd tiptoed around that possibility, then closed the door by telling her that his offer of dinner had contained no hidden agenda, but had he not been clear enough?

Surely she couldn't be playing some sort of long game—it didn't tally with the girl he remembered, who had been so open, so honest and so lacking in guile, but then people changed and especially so when bitterness took the starring role. Had she sensed his weakness? Had she gauged, despite his best efforts, his infuriating temptation to touch what he used to be able to freely touch? He would have to disabuse her of any notion that they could pick up where they had left off, that playing hard to get wasn't going to stir his interest, but, for a fleeting moment, he felt the pull of something so powerful that he breathed in sharply and lowered his eyes, shielding his expression.

'I don't see a wedding ring on your finger,' he said abruptly. Perhaps the father had done a runner.

Had she come here to ask for money? he wondered. But he dismissed that thought as fast as it surfaced. Every instinct told him that this was not a woman with a begging bowl behind her back and every intimate memory reminded him that she had never been the sort to ask for anything.

'For a very good reason,' Georgie said in a low voice. 'Because I'm not married.' She shook her head impatiently. 'You really don't get it, do you?'

'Get what?'

'You probably don't remember but I got a stomach bug when we were…going out. Something I ate.'

'Sardines.' Abe frowned and then smiled and relaxed at the innocuous change of subject. 'I warned you not to have them. You can never trust the quality of the fish cooked in a pop-up restaurant on a beach. You were out of it for nearly two days.'

'I'm surprised you remember.'

'I remember everything about our time together,' he returned, shocked to find it was the truth.

Searching her face, Abe noted the flushed softening of her features and the flare of her nostrils and her sudden intake of breath and felt the atmosphere between them change, and this time the charge was sexual, firing him up and killing all of his good intentions to ignore the chemistry that was still lingering somewhere inside him. He shifted, gritted his teeth against the heaviness of a sudden erection that threatened to be all too visible unless he could manage some of the prized self-control he was so proud of.

Without either of them noticing, the distance between them decreased as she leant into him and he, in turn, edged towards her.

'Georgie…'

'Don't.'

'Don't what?'

'Don't look at me.'

Their eyes tangled and just like that every thought flew out of her head and Georgie was back to the past, back to the way she had felt when he had first touched her, as though she'd spent her whole life in deep freeze, waiting for him to come along and wake her up, like Sleeping Beauty and that kiss, minus the happy-ever-after ending. She'd run away to Ibiza to recover and she had found love, or maybe love had found *her* because she certainly hadn't been looking for it.

She would have turned away, but she could barely

move. Recall of all the pleasure she had had at his touch
slammed into her with shocking clarity and she felt the
tightening of her nipples in hot response. Her tongue
darted out and her lips remained parted as her eyes
dropped to the wide, sensuous curve of his mouth, a
mouth that had once devastated her body and set her
aflame with desires she'd never suspected she was capable of feeling. He had shown her how to feel alive again.
She had always marvelled that he had been attracted to
her in the first place, when she'd known that he could
have had any woman at the snap of a finger, but there
had been no room for doubts or insecurities in her headlong, burning need for him.

Shaken, Abe dropped his eyes, unnerved by his visceral
response to her.

'Why have you come here, Georgie?' he asked softly.
'I realise now that I inadvertently hurt you when I left
Ibiza without discussing it with you; in hindsight, I probably should have told you I was leaving. But you do understand that, ultimately, I would still have had to go. Is
it that you think we may be able to reignite what we once
had? I cannot change the past or the present…or indeed
the future, as it is not mine to command. I have a country
to lead and you have a child to care for now, do you not?'

He clenched his fists, suddenly frustrated beyond all
bearing because, despite every word leaving his mouth,
he *still* wanted her. She was already beginning to make
him long for things that were completely impossible and
she'd only been back in his life for an hour!

'Are you mad? You think I don't know that if you
couldn't contemplate a relationship with me when I was
young, free and single, you certainly would never contemplate one with me now that I have a child?'

Of course he couldn't, but he genuinely didn't understand what was going on and so was clutching at anything that might make a bit of sense. Naturally, in his hunt to find answers, he was looking in all the wrong places.

'I've already told you, I looked for you, you know. Everywhere. After you'd gone. That's when I worked out just how much I'd invested in you emotionally, and just how little you'd invested back. You'd never had the slightest interest in us having any sort of relationship...'

'We *had* a relationship!'

'No, we had sex, Abe, great sex, and lots of it. Ask most women, and they wouldn't call that a relationship. And then you left and made sure I had no way of contacting you.'

'For reasons I thought were sensible,' Abe reiterated, spreading his hands.

'I get it. We came from different worlds. You, a prince...' She laughed shortly. 'It must have been a novel experience slumming it with me.'

'I don't like to hear you putting yourself down,' he said sharply. 'Nor do I enjoy the implication that that's the sort of man I am.'

'But it *is* the sort of man you are!' Georgie cried helplessly. 'That's *exactly* what you did! You would *never* have considered anything serious with me because my background wasn't elevated enough. That's why walking away without bothering to tell me you were going was okay with you.' She sighed with angry impatience. 'It doesn't matter. I wanted to tell you and I couldn't find you *anywhere*. Heaven only knows why I'm here at all, but I suppose I still feel the same way now. That it's important to do the decent thing.'

'Do the decent thing?' he echoed.

'Despite what you seem to think, I haven't actually

come here to have a go at you because you dumped me four years ago. People get dumped all the time. I'm just a statistic. I've grown up a lot since we were last together. And I certainly haven't come to beg you for one final fling! I'm here to tell you that you're a father.'

The silence stretched to breaking point. He was frowning, then he shook his head.

'Sorry but I think I may have misheard you.'

'No, Abe. You didn't mishear anything! I'm here to tell you that four years ago you fathered a child. Tilly is *your* daughter.'

'No! It's not possible...'

The instant the words were out of his mouth, he knew for certain he was wrong, that Georgie would never, ever lie about this. His stomach rolled and his eyes shot to the photo that still sat on the table next to him. Now that he looked closer, he could see that Tilly was so very like him. Same dark hair and dark eyes and smooth olive skin. She was utterly beautiful, and his heart clenched. He swallowed uncomfortably. Georgie must think him an utter fool for assuming she'd taken up with another man the minute he'd left and he'd been too distracted by his own jealousy to put two and two together.

'The contraceptive pill I was taking failed when I had that stomach bug,' she said flatly when it was clear he was unable to convert his thoughts into speech. 'Apparently that's not unusual. After you left and I took a test, I stayed on at the hotel restaurant for a while but there was no point hanging around, knowing that I was pregnant. I had to get back to England and start sorting my life out.'

'I can't believe it's the first I'm hearing about this...' Abe said unsteadily.

'I couldn't find you.'

'I... *Four years*... It's been four years...' He was dismally aware he was rambling incoherently, but couldn't seem to pull a sensible sentence together.

'You don't believe me that she's yours? Well, I said what I came to say and to heck with whether you believe me or not!'

She flew towards the door, grabbing her jacket en route, seemingly unaware that he was behind her, his long strides eating up the space between them.

'You can't just tell me...*this*...and then try to run away!'

Georgie spun around, her eyes filled with tumultuous emotion and resentment. 'Tilly is three years and three months old,' she said in a rush. 'You left a month shy of four years ago. Do the Maths, Abe. And if you still doubt what I'm saying then that's just fine with me! I'm not asking you for anything and I don't expect anything of you either. Believe me, I'm not *that* stupid. I just thought you should know and now you do, you can go back to your royal life...'

CHAPTER THREE

'WHERE DO YOU think you're going?'

He positioned himself directly in front of her and folded his arms. Six feet plus of immovable muscle.

'I'm going home. Where else would I be going?'

'Forget it.'

'Sorry?'

'No way are you going to run out on me without finishing this conversation!'

'What's there to finish? I've already explained what happened!'

'Don't be naive, Georgie.'

'Naive?' She laughed humourlessly. 'Believe me, if I was ever naive, that stopped the second I found out I was pregnant. Having a baby on your own makes a person grow up extremely fast, trust me. And if you knew me at all, you'd know that I would never lie to you about something like this.'

No. He already knew she wouldn't. As he stared down at her, Abe's mind was still reeling from a bombshell he hadn't seen coming. How could he be a *father*?

Fatherhood was obviously on the agenda, but at some vague future point in time. He had returned four years ago to the immediate stress of having to step up to the plate and take over where his father had been obliged to leave off and, since that time, he had given only passing thought to the inevitability of marrying and producing heirs, even though he had been pointedly introduced to several suitable women and even dated one, two years previously.

He'd refused to be rushed into anything. It would happen and it would happen at a time of his choosing and with a suitable woman, also of his choosing. But now? Fatherhood? A bolt from the blue hurled at him from nowhere and embedded into his rigorously controlled life without warning? He was struggling to take it in.

Abbas had grown up with the mantra of the importance of having a cool head when it came to the responsibilities of his position. He'd studied the history books and knew the history of his own bloodline all too well. He was well versed in how things could implode when emotion got the better of measured judgement—what his country needed was calm guidance. He'd watched, alone, from the sidelines as his father had fallen apart and then withdrawn at the death of his mother from cancer, and he'd decided as a small boy that falling in love was a road he'd never knowingly choose to travel. But the visceral emotion that had exploded inside him on discovering he had fathered a child with Georgie, a perfect little girl, suddenly warred with the cool, calm demeanour he'd spent a lifetime honing and the vision of practical duty he'd always pictured lay ahead of him. The impact of the collision felt as if it had just cracked something inside him, and he hurriedly sought to paper over it before it turned into a breach too wide to contemplate right now, when it was more important than ever that his country had the effective leader it needed. So that when duty finally beckoned, he would be fully prepared to control the outcome.

Except, as he eyed the mother of his child standing in front of him with a challenging tilt to her chin, it appeared that, far from being in control of any outcome, he was staring down the barrel of a gun, still clinging to the flimsy hope that somehow things were not as they seemed.

'You're in a state of shock,' Georgie stated as calmly as he wished he could sound right now.

'To put it mildly,' he said in a driven undertone.

'You want to believe that I'm making this all up but I'm not. I know you're probably wishing I'd kept my mouth shut because the last thing you need is...*this*... in your life, but I couldn't do that to you or to Tilly. It wouldn't have been right to keep the existence of your daughter from you. I know how important parenthood is. My father was there for me every step of the way after my mum died. I would never have dreamt of depriving you of at least knowing that you are a father, even if you choose not to do anything about it.'

'No, there is no way I would have rather you said nothing...'

He raked shaking fingers through his hair and stared at her, but he wasn't seeing *her*, he was seeing a future he hadn't predicted, frantically trying to recalculate what this would mean for him and for his country. The ground was moving under his feet, as perilous as quicksand, but even so he meant what he said. She had come to say her piece and, even if she had blown a hole in his minutely planned future, he was still incredibly glad that she had told him. He already wanted to meet his new daughter with everything that was in him. But on the heels of that thought came once again the sudden fear that the walls he'd fought for so long to build and reinforce were in danger of developing hairline cracks that he couldn't allow to worsen, which had him forcibly pulling himself together.

'You tell me that I have a child,' he said, his shoulders straight and his voice entirely steady now, 'and I believe you. But DNA proof will be required. Once we have that, then we can talk further.' He hesitated, cleared his throat. 'The photo. I would like to see it again.'

Georgie's eyes tangled with his for a few tense seconds then she looked away, rummaged in the bag to extract the photo and handed it to him and watched because this time he really *looked*. When at last his spectacular dark eyes lifted from intently studying Tilly's image and rested on her again, they were cool and unrevealing.

'Tomorrow,' he told her in a voice that left no room for her to manoeuvre, 'I will arrange for a DNA test to be performed.'

'Don't you trust me to do it? No, don't answer that. Of course, you don't!'

'This has nothing to do with trust,' he countered quietly. 'Make sure you and…the child, Matilda, are available. I will personally text you to give you the details. Allow me to have your number.'

'Don't think you can order me around!' But her voice wavered because the implications of the situation were beginning to sink in. With the best of intentions she had clambered on board a roller coaster and she was only now realising that she had no idea how far it would go or how fast before she could get off.

But there was no reason why she shouldn't remain in full control during the ride, was there?

Whatever happened, whether he was royalty or not, she, as Tilly's mother, would always be in a position to call the shots.

'This is very far from ordering you around, Georgie. This is about a protocol that must be followed. I am a crown prince and a DNA test is not a matter of choice in this instance, but one of necessity. I hope you can see that.'

'Yes. I suppose so.'

The following day she kept Tilly home from nursery and fudged an excuse to skip work so that she could wait for Abe's doctor to make an appearance.

She had heard the ping of her phone at six in the morning and had read what she should expect and who.

There had been no sentimentality in the message, nothing to set her mind at ease. Practical information was imparted by Abe, and she was told that he would contact her at precisely nine that evening, by which time he would already be in possession of the results.

There was no choice given in the matter and it was hard to cling to the belief that she was in charge when she felt as though she were in the path of a steamroller.

When her cell phone buzzed next to her at nine sharp that evening, every muscle in her body froze.

The results are back. We need to talk.

Yes. Of course.

I will be over in half an hour.

What? Tonight?

Tell me where you live.

You can't rock up at nine in the evening!

Why? Is there someone with you?

No, but I have a child. Remember?

I think it's fair to say that it is a situation that needs to be urgently addressed. Your address?

Taut with consternation and aware of that steamroller gathering pace and moving ever faster in her direction, Georgie rattled off her address and then sprang into action.

Tilly was fast asleep, curled up under her duvet with just one foot poking out. For a few seconds, Georgie looked down at her daughter and marvelled at the absolute innocence. She drew the duvet over that tiny foot, smoothed down the rebellious dark curls and then quietly shut the door as she left the room.

She had only just managed to change into some old jeans and a jumper when her mobile rang and Abe announced his arrival.

Of course, there had been no doubt in her mind that he was Tilly's father but she was still a bag of nerves as she pulled open the door and fell back for him to brush past her.

She didn't have to see his face to sense his heightened, restless energy. It was there in the jerkiness of his powerful stride as he spun round on his heel to look at her as she closed the door to her flat quietly behind her and then pressed herself against it to stare back at him.

He dwarfed the small space. Her flat was tiny and she had gone for it because it had been in a good neighbourhood. Better somewhere small where she felt safe than bigger where walking through the streets with a small child posed a problem.

It was in a pleasant made-to-measure block overlooking the Thames with sufficient communal gardens to ensure her daughter had somewhere outside to play, because the trip to the nearest park was a bus ride away.

'I want to see my daughter,' he said abruptly, his lashes sweeping down to hide his expression.

'She's asleep.'

'I have no intention of waking her,' he pressed.

Georgie nodded. She unglued herself from the door and padded past him up the short, narrow flight of steps where two small bedrooms nestled on either side of a bathroom.

She stood aside in silence and watched as he tentatively approached the low bed and peered down in the semi-darkness.

What was going through his head?

Figuring it out was not beyond the wit of man, she thought. He'd been well and truly dumped in it and he was probably frantically trying to work out damage limitation.

'I'm sorry,' she told him stiffly, after ushering him into the kitchen and offering him something to drink.

Every nerve in her body was alive to his presence. Her back was to him but she was very much aware of him pulling out one of the kitchen chairs to sit. He had tossed his camel cashmere coat over one of the other chairs and when she finally turned to hand him the coffee she had made, she couldn't help but think how out of place that coat looked...how out of place *he* looked. Too expensive, too elegant, too sophisticated for her little kitchen where all the detritus left behind in the wake of an energetic toddler was piled here, there and everywhere.

With the width of the small white kitchen table between them, they could have been adversaries waiting for a fight to begin.

Regret at having told him what he evidently hadn't wanted to hear poured through her like poison battling against the certainty that she had done the right thing, for better or for worse.

Besides, how would it have played out if she had kept Tilly's existence to herself? What would have happened when the innocent toddler turned into an inquisitive adolescent who found out that she had been wilfully deprived of the opportunity to have a relationship with her own father?

Children didn't ask to be born. Yes, there were circumstances that dictated lives that were far from ideal, with absentee parents or parents who just didn't care, but she would never have been able to live with herself if she had made a unilateral decision to deny her daughter the chance of having two parents, even two who were no longer together.

'I wanted to tell you when I found out but couldn't... and when I saw you again, I'm sorry... I didn't think...' She stumbled over her words, shying away from the hard look in his dark eyes. 'You could have been married, for all I knew. Had kids of your own...'

'That would not have mattered,' Abe said evenly. 'The child sleeping in that bedroom would still have remained my responsibility.'

'I'm glad to hear that.' She extended an olive branch because a way forward had to be found, and if they were on opposing sides that was going to be impossible. 'I know a lot of men would find it easy to walk away from their responsibilities to a child they hadn't asked for. I know this might put you in a difficult situation...' She laughed uncertainly. 'It's not as though you're an ordinary guy and I know it'll probably be impossible for you to see much of Tilly, but I won't stand in the way if you happen to be in London and want to meet with her without being able to give me much notice.'

Every word hurt because never in a million years had she ever seen herself in this place, talking to the father of her child the way she would have spoken to a stranger. She had loved this man, given herself to him, *trusted* him and now what was left? The pain of disillusionment. Yes, she was happy that he wasn't going to walk away from Tilly, but it was a dagger through her heart to know that the only reason he was even sitting at this table opposite her was because he had no choice.

And, more than that...what happened now?

Losing both her parents had shown Georgie how desperately she longed for stability. Having Tilly had only reinforced those concerns and yet here she was teetering on the edge of the unknown and her hard-won stability felt as though it were disappearing like water down a plughole.

Trying to be detached, as he was, was the only way they would be able to deal with the situation in an adult, satisfactory manner but she felt sick from the effort.

'You're telling me that you will allow me to play a part in my daughter's life?'

'Well, yes,' Georgie said uncertainly. 'And, of course, if you want to contribute financially, then I won't stop you...'

'That's very generous of you,' Abe responded with just a touch of incredulity. 'I understand that for reasons beyond your control, beyond *our* control, I have been uninvolved in my child's life for the past three years, but I can assure you that the winds of change are beginning to blow.'

'What do you mean by that, exactly?'

'I mean that it is unacceptable for me to only play a walk-on part in Tilly's life. How do you imagine that would work? Realistically?'

'Well, I don't think there would be any need to get lawyers involved...'

'If you had been able to contact me when you found out you were pregnant, Georgie,' he said quietly, 'how do you imagine the scenario would have played out?'

Georgie thought that, had she been able to contact him, it would have entailed a whole series of alternatives that would have made things very different. It would have meant that he was still around or had at least given her his number, which would have implied that he would have wanted her to keep in touch...and that being the case, who knew? They might have actually remained together, had the committed relationship she had craved back then, given their child the best head start in life by being a *family*.

A sheltered upbringing had been her own worst enemy, had deprived her of the defences required to live life as he did—on an easy come, easy go basis before he married someone from the same background and elevated standing as him.

She had had a mighty learning curve since then. Reality left no room for romance and what she was facing now was reality. He was here and they would have to come to some kind of agreement about visiting rights.

'Like this,' she told him. 'Of course, I would have thought it would have been a bit more straightforward because I would have assumed you lived in the same country or else somewhere reasonably commutable, but I would have said what I'm saying now—that I would never stand in your way of seeing your child and would never stop you from helping out if that was what you wanted to do.'

'Participating in my child's life from a distance isn't going to work for me. I can't hop on a plane and visit every weekend and, even if I could do that, I wouldn't want to.'

'What are you trying to say?'

'Do you think it's fair for my daughter to be an occasional visitor to her father? To miss out on her heritage and birthright? Don't forget she's the firstborn child of the Crown Prince of Qaram. She's entitled to all the privileges that come with that. Would you deny her access to the very best of everything?'

Georgie gasped at the implication that Tilly had in any way been disadvantaged. 'How *dare* you? I have worked hard every single day to give Tilly the very best I could! You have no idea what it felt like to return to London, single and pregnant, with all my dreams put on hold, terrified that I wouldn't be able to earn a living!' Shaking at his insinuation that what she had to offer Tilly was paltry in comparison to him, Georgie sprang to her feet and stalked across to the sink, putting some space between them while she gathered herself.

She stood staring out of the window by the kitchen sink, her back to him, hands braced against the counter and taking deep breaths because, right now, she could have hit him.

She froze when she felt the weight of his hands on her shoulders. She turned around slowly, caged in and suffocatingly conscious of his proximity.

Her eyes flickered to the hard lines of his face then

dropped to his wide, sensuous mouth and skittered away before her imagination could start filling in blanks.

'Georgie, that is not at all what I meant to imply. You've done brilliantly under very difficult circumstances,' he said stiffly.

She folded her arms and reluctantly raised her eyes to his face. 'How else could I take it? This may not be up to your standards,' she said tightly, 'but it is *my* castle and I have never stopped counting my lucky stars that I had the means to buy it so that there was at least a roof over our heads when we needed it.' He'd dropped his hands but he was still so close to her that she could feel the warmth of his breath on her face. 'I was alone and afraid, so don't you *dare* swan in here and say you could give her more than I have! She's loved, and she knows it, and that means a lot more than material possessions, even solid gold ones!'

Every single word was a proclamation of how much he had hurt her with his thoughtless words, and Abe knew that her bitterness would be the greatest impediment to what could be the one and only conclusion to this bombshell situation.

There was no choice going forward for either of them but marriage. Anything else was unthinkable. He could not conceivably have a child and commute a handful of times a year to pay lip service to visiting rights. He hadn't asked for a child, but he now had one and there was no part of him that did not intend to be a hands-on father.

But this was not exactly a straightforward situation.

Not only was there the matter of breaking the news to his father and, in ever-increasing circles, everyone else in his country, but there was the even more significant challenge of trying to persuade a woman who clearly hated him that they had to get married.

He would have to be at his most persuasive. He would have to put his natural inclination to get what he wanted, whatever the cost, on hold. In fact, he would have to dispense with that line of attack completely. He had already taken legal advice on what his rights were and, despite his prominence, wealth and royal status, the rights of a mother who had taken on the role of single parent for over three years won hands down in any court of law. Not only had she been the sole provider for Tilly in his absence, but she had tried to find him at the time of her pregnancy and it had been entirely his fault that she had found that an impossible task.

He could, of course, point out the considerable advantages to marrying him—not least a lifestyle of such breathtaking comfort and downright opulence that she would never want for anything in her life again—but he had an uneasy suspicion after what she'd just said to him regarding material possessions that, as persuasive arguments went, she might not be as bowled over by that one as another woman might be.

She had tried to contact him three years ago and yet there had been no financial motivation behind that as she hadn't known who he was, and it would seem there was no financial impetus behind her contacting him now.

How did that make sense?

'Can I ask you something?' he murmured, watching her with veiled eyes. He propped his hands against the counter on either side of her, his dark gaze wedded to her attractively flushed face.

In this moment, he was entirely taken with the strength of his own response to her, bemused by the peculiar hold she still seemed to exert over him. Once upon a time, it had seduced him into staying in Ibiza for far longer than necessary and now...

'You obviously have a problem with me.'

'Do you blame me?' she asked.

'That's a question that could keep us going round in circles for ever. You have a problem with me and yet that didn't stop you from doing what you felt was the right thing to do.'

'Why would it?' Georgie said defiantly.

'Because, and this is just my cynicism winning the argument, a woman with an axe to grind against a guy she thinks unceremoniously dumped her without an explanation could do one of several things...'

Georgie wanted to break free from that devastating gaze but she was spellbound by him, locked into immobility and barely able to breathe.

'What things?' she asked, as the drag on her senses grew more powerful by the second.

'She might decide to have no further contact with him, whatever the circumstances. Alternatively, she might make contact with the aim of using the child as a pawn in a game of payback. More likely, however, a woman might be tempted to see what was in it for her financially, especially when she realises that she's dealing with a man who has the wherewithal to change the direction of her whole life. Yet you fit none of those categories.'

'This is so...hard for you, isn't it?'

'What do you mean?'

Georgie looked down and blinked rapidly. She folded her arms and stared at her feet, jutting in between his legs.

He pushed himself away from her and on impulse reached for her hand and twined his fingers through hers.

He led her to the sitting room and she followed, and

she didn't resist when he gently sat her down on the sofa and positioned himself next to her.

'Talk to me,' he urged as he tried to find some solid ground, however small.

'We don't even know one another,' Georgie said honestly. His fingers were still entwined with hers and she was reluctant to break the physical contact because that physical contact felt good, like a lifebelt in stormy seas. She looked at him, searching for the right words. 'Okay, so we once had a brief fling. But you weren't who I thought you were, and in a way I was pretending to be a different person as well.'

'Explain.' He frowned.

'I'd had a very sheltered life, raised deep in the country. I went to the local village school and then to the local secondary school. The most exciting things to happen were the school dances and a trip to the cinema. It was always my dad and I and it was an easy life with none of the temptations, I guess, that I would have had growing up in the city. Going to university was the first time I really took in what life outside a small hamlet in the middle of nowhere felt like.'

'Frightening?'

'Exciting.' She could feel some of the tension oozing out of her. 'An adventure for a rural girl like me.' She blushed. 'I... You asked how it is that I wanted you to know about the pregnancy even after I found out that you'd dumped me without a forwarding address.'

Abe tilted his head to one side and waited.

'My dad...my dad was the local vicar, Abe.' She laughed self-consciously. 'I never considered not doing what I felt was the right thing to do. You can fight against a lot of things, but you can't fight against your upbringing and, as you can imagine, I was raised with a great many moral codes firmly in place.' She could feel her cheeks stinging with colour. She suddenly realised he was as guided by his own rigid upbringing as she was and she softened slightly.

'A vicar—'

'I didn't tell you,' she rushed in hurriedly, 'because I knew that it would put you off sleeping with me. You'd be surprised how many guys are put off the minute they hear that. When I went to Ibiza, I guess I felt I needed to try and be a different person. University had prepared me for the big bad world out there, but, for the first time, I no longer had my dad to back me up and I suppose I wanted to do something out of my comfort zone. Taking a gap year...working at that hotel...dealing with an everyday life that wasn't planned out...it was all new to me. I was frightened and alone and desperate for *new* to distract me from what I'd been through, what I was *still* going through.'

'A vicar...' Abe murmured a second time, almost as shocked by that admission as he had been by the bombshell baby news.

And now many things slotted into place--from her shy charm, which had bewitched him, to her conviction that he should know about his daughter, without any hidden agenda aside from the fact that she was 'doing the right thing'.

And then several other considerations fell into place and by far the one outweighing all others was his recognition of just how devastated and abandoned she would have felt when he'd left. She would not have had the usual armour in place that many women of her age might have had. She hadn't taken any knocks in her life before, and then he had come along and unwittingly delivered a whole series of them…and just after she'd lost her beloved father.

Guilt and shame that he'd been the cause of even more hurt twisted his insides and he almost couldn't bear it when she continued.

'So I just can't believe that I'm in this place, with a child from a guy who didn't want me, who doesn't know who I am.' She shook her head. 'At any rate, I've managed very well for the past three years, whatever you may think.'

What Abe thought was that never had he felt so badly positioned on the back foot or so determined to make things right for both Georgie and Tilly.

'You make a very good point,' he acknowledged, mind now firmly made up on the only way forward that he could see for the time being. 'We *don't* know one another, but that doesn't detract from the reality that we share a daughter and, as someone guided by having to do the right thing, wouldn't you agree that the right thing would be for us to remedy that oversight as quickly as possible?'

Georgie shot him a dubious look from under her lashes. 'Of course, we will have to be on speaking terms…' she agreed.

Abe swept aside her interruption to continue, levelly, reasonably…but determinedly. 'Tilly has a heritage that she has every right to know, a grandfather who would be overjoyed to meet her, a country which she should, I'm sure you would agree, get to know as it is, at least in part, *her* country too…'

'Yes…well…'

'*Our* duty, Georgie, is to make that possible, wouldn't you agree?' He left the question dangling persuasively between them, challenging the moral codes she lived by, demanding the one and only response she could give.

The sort of half-in, half-out relationship she envisaged

for them wasn't going to work but he knew full well that breaking that news to her right here and now wouldn't be wise. He had hurt her badly, and it was time to put things right in the only way he knew how. He was positive Georgie was already an excellent mother, and he wanted to prove both to her and to himself that he could be just as good a father to Tilly. In fact, the increasing drive to do so kept sending shockwaves deep inside him, and he was forced to keep a tight rein on his self-control. Becoming emotional had never worked well for anyone, particularly his father, and he utterly refused to go down that road himself. It only led one way, to certain loss and pain.

'So the first thing we need to do,' he murmured, 'is to start by getting to know one another much better.'

'You mean…we become friends? After everything that's happened between us? I think that might be asking a lot but I'm willing to keep the channels of communication open.'

'Tilly is only three. Would you be prepared to let her see my country, without you there as chaperone?' He made an expansive gesture with his hands that implied the prospect of that was just fine with him.

'Tilly wouldn't go anywhere without me,' Georgie said, sounding alarmed at the disturbing picture being painted of her daughter ferried out of the country to be surrounded by strangers who spoke a different language.

'Nor should she. So perhaps you would like to hear what I propose?' He ignored her scepticism and carried on soothingly, placatingly…the very voice of reason. 'I suggest you *both* come to Qaram with me, then. It is urgent that I return and, rather than rushing my first contact with my daughter here, on borrowed time, I will be able to devote time and space to getting to know her in Qaram.

We need to work on this as a unit if we are to do what's best for her, as parents. So…are you in agreement?'

He found himself holding his breath, waiting for her response. Everything in him was urging him to make her his wife, but for once, he would have to be satisfied with settling for this small step forward.

CHAPTER FOUR

How could Georgie argue with the calm logic of a guy who wanted to do what was right? She couldn't. So she would go.

She hated to leave Duncan in the lurch and wondered what she should say about taking a chunk of time away. Should she come clean and explain the situation to him? That was an option she dismissed as fast as it raised its head. Why would she do that? Whatever the outcome of the talks she and Abe might have, she would end up back in London and would want to continue with her career at the hotel, irrespective of what financial arrangements were made regarding Tilly. She and Tilly were two separate entities and she was smart enough to realise that, while he would feel duty-bound to support his daughter, he certainly had no obligation to support a woman he had walked away from, whatever justification he might feel he had had for doing so. Nor did she have any intention of trying to squeeze any money out of him for herself.

Yet money would have to be something to be discussed because that was the world he lived in.

They were different people with different dreams, different goals, different *standards*. If there was some ridiculous, lingering physical attraction towards him, then it could be explained away easily enough by the fact that he was her first lover and, as things had turned out, her last. He'd shown up out of the blue and, of course, nostalgia had swept aside the years and deposited her right back to that place where she had only had eyes for him. She hadn't had any experiences with anyone else and so could not call upon a present to help eradicate the past.

She would visit his country because it made sense to do so but she would maintain distance between them, would discuss future arrangements in a businesslike fashion.

He had asked if he could look at Tilly once again as she had slept and had remained standing by the side of the low bed for a lot longer than Georgie had expected, gazing at his daughter intently, almost as though he could will her awake, then he had finally left, having given her a million and one instructions as to what would happen next.

The trip. What to expect. What she should bring with them. How she would get there. The driver…the flight…

She had agreed to meet him in Qaram and so it was something of a surprise when she opened her door the following evening to see him standing outside, minus bodyguards and casually dressed in a pair of jeans and a jumper with his coat hooked over one shoulder.

'Why are you here?'

Acutely conscious of the fact that she was in her pyjamas even though the clock had yet to strike nine, she remained defensively by the door, before relenting and letting him in with a sigh.

'There is something I feel we should discuss before you come to Qaram.' He turned to look at her for a few seconds and she thought she caught a flash of wariness and uncertainty in his eyes, before his magnificent lashes swept down to conceal his expression. When he lifted them his gaze was cool and steady once more, and she decided she must have been mistaken. 'I contemplated waiting until you were there, when things might have been a little less rushed, but, on reflection, I think this is something I really need to say to you before you come...' He shrugged, suddenly looking uncomfortable, and her gaze sharpened. Perhaps she hadn't been mistaken after all.

'What is it? Why are you looking so serious?'

'Let's go and sit down.'

'You're worrying me, Abe.'

He smiled reassuringly. 'Don't be worried.' But he waited until they were sitting facing one another in her small sitting room before leaning forward, forearms resting lightly on his thighs. 'I had hoped that my beautiful country might help me build my case for what I am about to say, but then I decided that not being on home ground might put you in an awkward position...'

'I have no idea what you're talking about, Abe.'

'Yesterday, we discussed...' he hesitated, his eyes keenly on her puzzled face '...in a manner of speaking, a possible way forward for us.'

'Yes, because you want to have a role in Tilly's life, don't you?'

'And yet I am a prince.'

'I haven't forgotten, Abe. How could I?'

He sighed and shifted in his seat. 'I haven't even met her properly yet, but already I know that it will never be enough for me to simply dabble in my daughter's life.'

'What are you trying to say?'

'I would like you to marry me, Georgie. I genuinely believe this is the best way ahead for us.'

Georgie's brain sluggishly absorbed what he had said but refused to break it down into bite-sized pieces. She stared at him, confounded, until he asked gruffly, 'Did it never occur to you it might be an option?'

'Marry you? *Marry you?*' She stared at him wordlessly. No, she could say with her hand on her heart that she hadn't seen this coming. If Tilly had been *his* bolt from the blue, then this totally unexpected proposal was *hers*.

To show up at this hour for a conversation like this? With their leaving for Qaram a matter of a heartbeat away? How on earth could he expect her to agree to *marry* him?

'You need to think about it,' he said, rising fluidly to his feet.

'You're *leaving*?'

'I will see you again in a couple of days.'

'You can't just drop this on me and then walk away!'

'Is that a direct quote from me?' he teased.

Georgie glared at him and he returned her look steadily.

'Yes, that's exactly what I intend to do, Georgie. Leave you to think about this with no pressure. Come to Qaram. Experience what life over there is like and keep an open mind. Remember—if my life is about to change, then yours is about to as well...'

He couldn't have done a better job of sending her into a tailspin.

She spent the next two days feverishly playing and replaying that marriage proposal in her mind. Had she seen it coming? No! But he was right, she should have. How could she have possibly thought that a crown prince wedded to the notion of duty would be happy to accept the role of part-time dad to his own flesh and blood living on the other side of the world?

It didn't help that he refused to discuss it on the three occasions when he had telephoned her.

'When you get here,' he had told her, gently but very, very firmly, 'then we can talk about it. There's still a lot of water under the bridge between us, hence the importance of having plenty of time to consider my proposal.'

Georgie had refrained from asking what would happen if and when she refused. She didn't want to confront that issue over the telephone either. He'd been shrewd enough to have left her mulling over his explosive proposition knowing that she would have to gnash her teeth and wait until they were face to face to discuss the ramifications.

She didn't think anything could stop the ceaseless churning in her head, not even Tilly's excited antics at the thrilling change to her routine, but the shock of being ushered like royalty into a private jet certainly did the trick.

She had been wrenched out of her comfort zone, every atom of self-control and self-preservation hijacked by the astonishing change to every single thing she had ever experienced in her life before.

Tilly was cheerful, inquisitive and blissfully accepting of the deference accorded them. Once in the private jet, which was so luxurious that Georgie had to make an effort to keep her mouth shut lest it hit the ground, she had proceeded to explore every nook and cranny not out of bounds. She blithely babbled away non-stop to the crew, which included two minders and a charming young girl who seemed to have a never-ending array of tasty finger food, which kept appearing at various intervals.

By the time the plane began its descent, Georgie was exhausted and Tilly was asleep. She gasped as the heavy door slid open and the heat assailed her.

Looking around her for some familiar point of reference, her eyes fell on the sleek black limo slowly heading towards the jet.

Abe. It had to be. Relief washed over her as she made her way down the metal steps with Tilly draped over her, softly snoring.

From behind the blacked-out windows of his chauffeur driven limousine, Abe watched Georgie as she emerged from the jet, pink-faced and bemused, with Tilly in her arms.

A sudden wave of protectiveness threatened to overwhelm him. In the space of a week, he had rediscovered a woman he'd never forgotten and become a father to a child he was yet to meet while she was awake!

A beautiful daughter. A woman who would become his wife, if he could just convince her to see things his way. That this was right. That this made perfect sense. A marriage of convenience between two consenting adults, both of whom would put Tilly at the forefront of their lives. He wouldn't make the same mistake as his father by falling in love with his wife, devastating him and their child when she died. No, he would go into this marriage with his eyes wide open, as would Georgie, and, with no expectations of love on the table, nobody would get hurt. It was the ideal solution and he would strive with everything that was in him to bring it about.

He vaulted out of the car before his driver could obey protocol and open the door for him, and walked towards Georgie.

She was in a pair of trousers and a blouse and she looked utterly at sea.

'Abe!'

Abe paused as Tilly, still nestled into Georgie's shoulder, opened her eyes and looked at him drowsily for the first time.

His daughter...his flesh and blood...

He had felt more than a twinge of guilt knowing that the proposal he had left Georgie to mull over could only really have one outcome. Because Tilly was his heir, a princess in her own right. She would need the protection only he could provide. He just had to find the right way to explain that to Georgie.

He had already explained the situation to his father, who assumed that they would be married.

Any guilt, however, was swept aside the minute he saw Tilly. He reached out, displaying a lot more confidence than he felt, to take her from Georgie, so he could hold her for the very first time.

She was warm and soft against him and he breathed her in, astonished at how primal his urge to protect her was. Where his defences were used to being up when it came to the entire human race, this small child had managed to obliterate them simply by being his daughter.

'How was the flight over?' he asked, ushering Georgie into the blissful cool of the limo, relinquishing Tilly to her as she slid in.

'Very smooth, thank you.'

'You must feel out of your depth, but please don't.' He sat back, angling himself so that he could look at her. She looked flustered and uncomfortable. 'It might feel very alien for a while being over here and I'm very grateful that you agreed to come. It was a big step and an important one for Tilly to be introduced to Qaram.'

'Not that she'll have the faintest idea what it's all about.'

'She's here and I'm here and we will have to explain who I am to her.'

* * *

'She's too young to ask questions or understand the answers properly,' Georgie said truthfully. After the bewildering and hasty preparations to get here, she felt drained and there was still so much to discuss. His marriage proposal seemed like a dream, but it wasn't. It was just that she couldn't face talking about it now, when it could only lead to an argument she wanted to avoid on day one. Defences down, exhausted as Tilly sleepily nuzzled against her shoulder, she rested against the seat and closed her eyes. Abe was here, an anchor in this alien environment whether she liked it or not.

'Growing up in the vicarage...' she half yawned, not opening her eyes '... I had loads of contact with young children, especially in challenging circumstances. Parishioners would come, pour out their problems, brings their kids with them and I would play with them, look after them, talk to them. They're very robust. Much more adaptable than adults think they are.' She turned to look at him and blushed at the intensity of his dark gaze. Outside, an arid scenery flashed past but then the sprawl of the city began taking over and her interest was piqued.

She asked questions, sat straighter. There was a minimalist beauty about it. Tall white buildings, glass and steel, as modern as anything to be found anywhere.

'There aren't many people walking around,' she remarked, turning to him.

'You live in London,' Abe said wryly. 'You're accustomed to pavements thronging with people. My entire country has a fraction of the number of people living in London alone and yet it is much bigger. You will never see crowds surging along roads. The intense heat also makes it uncomfortable to be outside for long periods of time.'

'I like that,' Georgie admitted. 'I went to London after Ibiza because that was where I knew the jobs would be. One of the guys at the restaurant I worked at was related to Duncan. He recommended me for the job. There would have been nothing for me in the country but I missed the peace and the quiet.'

'Was it…hectic caring for a young baby amidst the chaos of an overpopulated city?' Abe asked.

'Exhausting. You try taking an infant on public transport. Nightmare.'

Abe felt another stab of remorse that she'd gone through that experience all alone, without him. If he'd been there for her when Tilly was a baby, they'd have been married by now… He made suitably empathetic noises and spent the rest of the trip explaining just how calm Qaram was, how still the dunes were at night, how clear the skies were. The subject of his marriage proposal sat like a white elephant between them, but he knew this was neither the time nor the place to bring it up and he guessed she felt the same. In the temporary lull, he intended to push the advantages of his country as much as he could. All was fair in love and war, even if it was paternal love he was fighting for…

'You could almost count the stars,' he said lazily, noting the way her eyes automatically travelled up to the clear violet skies above them from which stars were appearing as obliging gold studs against deepest purple velvet.

'Sometimes,' he murmured, his voice purposefully seductively soft, 'in the desert, if you listen hard enough, you can hear the movement of the sand. It is like a whisper.'

He knew the heat and the newness of the surroundings were massive points in his favour and before the discussion about his proposal began in earnest he wanted her to think beyond her obvious objections to see a much bigger picture. He really wanted her to agree of her own accord without feeling backed into a corner.

His sprawling staff were waiting for their arrival, primed to expect a companion and her young daughter. If they suspected anything, they were well versed in remaining silent and were all so utterly loyal to him that gossip would have been unheard of. At any rate, they would all discover, in due course, that he would be getting married to her, that she was the mother of his child and a woman with whom he had fallen in love but had been forced to leave until Fate decided to throw them together once again. A story of exceptional romance that would capture the hearts of his entire country, not just his staff. He wouldn't allow a whiff of scandal to be attached to Georgie or Tilly, so for them he'd bear with the image of a man in love.

'Wow.'

Darkness had shielded the splendour of the palace, but it was unmistakable the second they stepped foot through the door. White and marble dominated an entrance hall big enough to host a ball.

'I'll show you to your quarters,' Abe murmured, dismissing the congregated staff with a near invisible gesture. 'You look dead on your feet.'

Georgie nodded, too tired to pay much attention to her surroundings but awed by what she saw as he scooped Tilly from her and headed up one of two impressive staircases.

'Where are our bags? I can't believe you live here...'

'I'm a prince. What did you expect?' But there was amusement in his voice.

'I didn't really give it much thought.'

'Your bags will be delivered to your suite.'

He pushed open a door and stepped aside and Georgie walked into an antechamber that led to a central living area off which were two bedrooms separated by a bathroom. All this she took in in a single sweeping glance.

'My bedroom adjoins yours,' he told her, 'and there's a connecting door. There will be two nannies available day and night. From tomorrow, they will be entirely at your service and would be offended should you choose not to avail yourself of their services.'

'I'm not used to…all this…' Georgie whispered, shorn of her fighting spirit for once. She looked at him anxiously as he channelled her towards the smaller of the bedrooms. Tilly was too sleepy to explore but Georgie could see an array of toys in a wicker basket and everything she might need for a toddler.

She was happy to sit and watch as he slid off his shoes and squatted down to his daughter's level, interacting a little awkwardly, glancing to Georgie often for approval, but he wasn't shying away from the attempt and he was trying hard to connect.

He would have given instructions about the bedroom, she thought, would have predicted that a young child might be wooed with toys and so he had imported them. The soft linen was also child friendly. He'd had just a couple of days but in that time he had obviously given a lot of thought to how a three-year-old toddler might be made to feel comfortable away from the only environment she had ever known.

He'd been *thoughtful* and Georgie sleepily welcomed that.

After fifteen minutes she could hardly keep her eyes open and Tilly had been popped into her pyjamas and climbed into her bed, clutching the stuffed rabbit she had brought with her, her eyes fluttering closed.

'I'll take you to your room,' Abe said and before Georgie could object he had lifted her off her feet and was carrying her through to the second, much larger bedroom.

Georgie wound her hands round his neck and leant against him and closed her eyes. It was delicious being in his arms again, and almost a shame when he gently deposited her on the enormous four-poster bed with its lavish coverings.

She watched him as he went to close the heavy drapes and then he strolled towards the bed and perched on the side.

In semi darkness, with just the light outside filtering through the door, which he had left ajar, he was all shadows and angles and she shivered.

She sat up and drew her knees up and gazed at him.

'We still need to talk,' she whispered. 'When you left, you said that—'

'It's late and I can see you're very tired. Maybe we should talk about it tomorrow?'

'I can't get it out of my head. You asked me to *marry* you, Abe.' She looked at him with feverish urgency, but he was right. She was exhausted and on uncertain footing and this was a conversation definitely best left for when she wasn't dead on her feet. 'You shouldn't have left me to think about it.' She stifled another yawn.

'It was important that you had time to consider what I put in front of you, Georgie. Responding in the heat of the moment would not have been a good idea. If I could have stayed longer in London, we would have had the conversation there, but I had to return to Qaram, hence...' He shrugged.

'I suppose so.'

'Don't think about that right now.' He lowered his eyes, his ridiculous lashes once again shielding his expression, but when he raised them to look at her, there was genuine sincerity in his gaze. 'I cannot imagine what life must have been like for you, coping with a pregnancy on your own, and then a tiny baby on your own. Having to settle Tilly into a nursery so that you could join the workforce and earn a living to put a roof over both your heads and food on the table...' He shook his head, clenched his fists and breathed in deeply. 'It must have been so hard.'

'It was.'

'But you are here now,' he said in a low voice. 'I want you to seize this opportunity to relax and allow yourself to be looked after. Your every need will be unhesitatingly met.'

Having conjured up the memory of how it had felt to struggle on her own and how wrenching it had been to leave Tilly in a nursery when she was only a baby, Georgie found that every word from his mouth tasted like manna from heaven. His voice was calm and soothing and she sighed in pleasure.

'I have arranged for us to have dinner with my father tomorrow evening. He is keen to meet you both.'

Georgie nodded drowsily.

'You don't have to be apprehensive,' he said, correctly sensing her hesitation. 'He...he hasn't been the same since his heart attack but for the first time I saw real pleasure on his face when I broke the news to him about Tilly...'

He feathered her cheek with his finger and she breathed in sharply and closed her eyes. She knew that this would pass, that she was feeling vulnerable and out of her depth and yet...never had she wanted anything more in her life than to touch him. He'd hurt her so much when he'd walked away and had hurt her again when she'd seen him again and realised just how fleeting a reference point she'd been in his life. Not even much of a footnote.

Yet right here and right now, she felt safe with him. How was that possible? She could remember every touch, the feel of his body and the way he'd made *her* body feel. She shut the door on those thoughts but she could feel them pressing to get out.

'Your father,' she whispered, 'I know you say that he's looking forward to meeting us and that he's over-joyed, but he must be disappointed that you've ended up in this situation.'

'I see that you've decided that an in-depth conversation trumps going to sleep.'

He grinned and Georgie smiled back at him. For a moment he was shorn of the aura of power that made him seem so formidable. For a moment, he was the same guy she had fallen for four years ago.

'Well, it feels weird being here, Abe. I've never known anything like this in my life before. A week ago, I was taking public transport to get to work and spending weekends with Tilly at the park, and now... I'm in a palace with nannies round every corner and sitting on a bed that's as big as my entire flat.'

'Bit of an exaggeration there.'

'I wasn't prepared for something like this.'

'Sometimes, life throws you curve balls.'

'This is more than just a curve ball, Abe.' She sighed. 'Your father would have expected you to marry someone who was raised for this sort of lifestyle.'

'You need to stop worrying about that.'

'Easier said than done.' She looked at him. 'I wish

you'd be honest with me. This can't truly be what you wanted for yourself. Me and Tilly on your doorstep...'

'I think she's going to enjoy being here.' He could feel the conversation drifting into territory best avoided right now, especially when her eyes were closing and sleep was taking over. She was nervous and out of her depth and he wanted to reassure her but it was a delicate balancing act.

Fear of the unknown was driving her towards a maudlin interpretation of what she could expect here. He put himself in her position, tried to imagine what it must have been like for her when she found out that she was pregnant.

He tallied the image with his memory of the girl he had left behind, the one who, as he now knew, had just lost her father and been left all alone in the world.

When he'd met her, she'd been shy, hesitant to start any kind of relationship with him. That, in itself, had been a pleasing novelty. With or without his regal status, Abe had never had trouble when it came to attracting women. Any women. All of them. The feeling of having to work to seduce a woman was a concept as alien to him as commandeering a rocket and flying to the moon.

So when she had politely turned down his offer for dinner, he had been intrigued but he had never thought that something begun so casually would end up consuming his interest with such power.

He'd been there to buy a hotel. Serious business for someone intent, not only on eventually running the country when his father retired, but investing in businesses that could bring recognition to Qaram and provide additional wealth to help his people.

Staying with just one bodyguard at one of the most expensive hotels on the island had meant there had been no shortage of women interested in finding out more about him. Having a bodyguard in tow was always guaranteed to engender lots of attention from the opposite sex and he had turned a blind eye to every curious glance slanted in his direction.

Craving a bit of normality, he had ditched the bodyguard for one evening and sauntered into the town to breathe in an atmosphere that wasn't as suffocatingly rarefied as the one where he had been staying.

And there she had been, working in a restaurant.

She had emerged flushed and blushing from the kitchen, anxiously awaiting his verdict on her food and braced for something disparaging. He had seen it written on her face.

And when he had complimented her, she had lowered her eyes and smiled and it had made him feel ten feet tall.

He'd immediately asked her out. Of course he had! He hadn't been going to be hanging around for long and he'd been consumed with an urgent need to see her, to go out with her, to sleep with her.

She'd refused but he hadn't given up and neither had he regretted the pursuit, because he had enjoyed her company more than he could have imagined possible.

She'd…enchanted him.

He hadn't known about her father. When he thought about that now, he could remember that there were times when he had surprised her wearing a lost expression on her face and times when there had been a hyper quality to her that had seemed at odds with her reserved nature.

Then he flashed forward to him leaving, and then to imagining her discovering that she was pregnant.

When he thought about that, something inside him twisted and he suddenly found it hard to swallow. An imagination he'd never known he had fired up with a series of graphic images, heartbreaking images of her searching for him, gradually coming to terms with the reality of his disappearance.

He had been called away, yes. Events had galvanised him into returning to Qaram and that in itself had been a frightening time for him. He had really and truly thought that he had done the right thing walking away from a situation that could never have developed into anything permanent and he'd already been navigating a very fine line delaying his departure more than once to remain in her bed. He'd never done that before for any woman, but he'd repeatedly pushed that thought away at the time. He genuinely hadn't known just how emotionally vulnerable she had been because she hadn't told him about her father's death. Would he have pursued her in the first place, slept with her, if he'd known?

Abe had a sinking feeling he'd have been drawn to her regardless, but it was a moot point anyway.

The fact of the matter was that she was here now and those winds of change he had mentioned were about to blow her ordered world to pieces.

'But you can't really think about that at the moment, can you?' he murmured understandingly, and she stared at him in silence. 'You've been wrenched out of what you have spent the past four years building and now you feel you've lost your foothold.'

'It's…'

'I know. Scary.' He half smiled and glanced around at the magnificent bedroom that made her seem small and wide-eyed and lost all of a sudden.

This was where he'd grown up. He barely noticed the opulence of his surroundings any more. He was accustomed to living in a palace, where rooms flowed into other rooms, where there was so much space that the problem was what to do with it all.

And, yes, had he had an arranged marriage, he would have found a wife whose background would have fully prepared her for this lifestyle. She would have moved in exalted circles, would be acquainted with all the unspoken mores and traditions and customs that would have been expected of her.

No wonder Georgie was at a complete loss.

'And you don't want scary, do you?' he asked pensively. 'You want stability.'

'More than anything in the world,' she breathed with heartfelt sincerity. 'I lost my mother when I was young, but life grew around that loss, like skin growing around an open wound until it scars over and stops hurting so much. When my dad died, my whole world fell apart. Now that I have Tilly, I want to make sure that she has all the stability in her life that I haven't had...'

Abe privately thought that she was making an extremely good case for marrying him, but that was a point he wasn't going to make just yet.

'I understand.' He looked to the door. 'You should try and get some sleep now. Is there anything you need? Food? My private plane is usually well stocked but if there's anything you want...'

'I'm okay.'

'Still nervous about meeting my father?' He smiled, reassuring her, wanting her to have a good night's sleep as free of worry as possible given the circumstances.

It was important she didn't see this as an ordeal. It was also important that he establish a footing between them in which conversation could be had without the past overshadowing everything.

'Where does he live?'

'Would you be alarmed if I told you that he, too, lives in a palace?'

'I would be surprised if he didn't.' She smiled.

'It's smaller than this one, though.'

'I guess it couldn't be any bigger. What on earth do you do with all these rooms, Abe?'

'They're occasionally filled with diplomats, members of state, visiting dignitaries…' He laughed, his dark eyes drifting to her mouth. She had a perfect mouth. He could remember exactly how it had tasted and he wanted to kiss it again now. His pulse picked up a gear and he shifted uncomfortably.

This pull of intense attraction felt even stronger than those recollections of the many times they had spent together in her bed. He was uneasily aware that what was supposed to have been a brief fling had never really felt like that to him, but it had taken meeting her again to really bring that point home. He tensed, but then reminded himself that not everyone shared such an intense physical connection. Yes, that was all it was, amazing sexual chemistry. There was no question of it being anything else. At that thought, his tense muscles relaxed.

'Weren't you ever…lonely?' Georgie asked, interrupting his unwelcome thoughts.

'Lonely?' Abe opened his mouth to deny the suggestion, his long-standing habit of politely knocking back anyone daring enough to try and venture into his private life, but instead he heard himself say, thoughtfully, 'I guess…maybe there was a point in time…' He laughed but when their eyes met, hers were sympathetic.

She didn't say anything and for once he wasn't the one using silence as a means of extracting information.

'When my mother died,' he admitted, 'I was also young. My father took her death extremely badly. He carried on ruling the country, he talked and walked and performed his duties as he always had, but unfortunately I was the one who saw behind that façade and it was tough for a child. In truth, I lost both my parents that day. My mother through death and my father through many months of mourning.' He shook his head, surprised at the direction of the conversation. 'By the time he surfaced, I had grown up.' He slapped his hands on his thighs, ending his astonishing deviation from the straight and narrow. 'Right, then, should there be anything at all you need...' he nodded to a buzzer by the side of the bed '... buzz and someone will bring whatever you request.

She reached out and her slim fingers lightly curved over his wrist.

'I'm really sorry, Abe. Yes, you must have been very lonely indeed.'

They had moved closer to one another. How had that happened? The atmosphere was suddenly heavy with feeling and with a powerful, invisible bond that took them away from the charged present back to the past they had shared.

She trembled and her eyelids fluttered as he traced his finger along her cheek.

Of course, he was going to kiss her.

She *felt* it with every nerve in her body and she *wanted* it with every nerve in her body.

She sighed, mouth parting, her whole body straining towards him. In her head, she had yearned for this so much and so many times but now, as his lips found hers, she realised that no imaginings had come close to replicating the fierce sizzle of electricity that zapped through her.

His tongue invaded her mouth, meshing against hers as he drove her back against the pillow.

His fingers weaved through her short hair and the heavy weight of him against her reminded her of hot, sultry nights when they'd done nothing but make love for hour after hour.

He suddenly drew back with a shudder and vaulted to his feet and, in turn, she squirrelled back up into a sitting position, aghast at her loss of self-control and hating herself for having succumbed to the treacherous demands of her body, seduced by the fact that he had talked to her, really talked to her, for the first time that she could remember.

She wasn't here playing tourist! And she certainly wasn't here as his lover!

She was here to discuss a life-changing future and she was utterly dismayed at how fast she had lost track of that.

She couldn't look at him, but she could feel his eyes boring into her as he moved to stand by the door, looking over his shoulder with one hand on the doorknob.

'Don't forget,' he said evenly, 'we meet with my father tomorrow for dinner.'

'I won't.' Her voice was as controlled as his, thank goodness.

She only realised that she'd been holding her breath when the door clicked quietly shut behind him, and she exhaled long and slow before flopping back onto the pillows and staring up at the ceiling.

CHAPTER FIVE

GEORGIE AWOKE TO sharp brightness pouring through a slit in the thick curtains in her bedroom.

It took her a few moments to orient herself and to work out where she was, in a strange bed in a strange house in a strange country… No, in a strange bed in a *palace* in a strange country!

She was in pyjamas and she took a few mental steps backwards to remember the events of the day before.

She'd left one world behind and stepped into a completely different one, like stepping into that magical wardrobe and being transported to a mythical kingdom.

In all her confusion, Abe had been the one constant and she had clung to him. She knew that Tilly had taken everything in her stride and adjusted with enviable ease to their exalted surroundings before flopping into bed in the adjoining bedroom in their suite.

While she…

She groaned and buried her head in her arms because recall of that searing kiss the night before leapt out at her, gleefully reminding her that of all the stupid, *stupid* things she could have done, passionately kissing Abe had to be right up there.

She'd kissed him and she'd *wanted more*. She'd been

dragged back at speed to where they had been four years previously and every single memory had risen to the surface, firing her up and setting her body alight.

Her response had been a heady combination of buried lust and a surge of dependency on him because he was the only thing in this strange new world that seemed to make any sense.

She had no idea how she'd managed to make her way to the bathroom and actually have a shower and change into pyjamas before collapsing into bed, but she had and now...

New day, new way.

She leapt out of bed, flew into Tilly's bedroom and then all hell broke loose when she realised that her daughter was missing.

She spent five minutes hunting her down, opening and closing cupboards, panic levels rising by the second, before she remembered the all-important buzzer by the bed whereby anyone could be summoned at any time of the day or night.

She summoned.

Within minutes there was a knock on her door and she yanked it open to Abe standing in the doorway with Tilly in his arms and Georgie's first instinct was to pull her daughter away from him and hold her tight.

Tilly responded by vehemently protesting while Georgie glared at a composed and cool-as-a-cucumber Abe.

'What the *heck* is going on?' She tried to keep her voice controlled for the sake of her daughter, who was demanding release, but she was shaking with anger.

'Nothing is *going on*,' Abe responded, looking slightly taken aback by her frantic response. 'Mind if I come in?'

'Yes!'

'Mummy, I want to *play*!'

'Play *where*, Tilly?' Georgie was finding it impossible to contain a wriggling toddler and, with a sigh of pure, teary-eyed frustration, she stepped back, allowing Abe to brush past her before swinging around and pinning her to the spot with his dark gaze.

Georgie fell back. Their eyes met and hers involuntarily dipped to his sensuous mouth, hot colour staining her cheeks as she remembered that kiss of the evening before.

'What's going on, Abe? Why wasn't I called when Tilly woke up?' she demanded in a more restrained voice.

'I thought that you might sleep a little more soundly than you expected and in a new environment, Tilly might not necessarily wander into your bedroom, not knowing the layout of the suite, so I positioned one of my people by the door to the suite and to inform me immediately if there were any signs of a small, curious child on a mission to explore.'

'I should have taken her into bed with me. I planned to but I was so tired.'

She deposited Tilly on the ground and hugged her arms around herself, awash with guilt.

'Go get changed,' Abe said gently. 'I will take care of Tilly while you do.'

'You had no right,' Georgie muttered helplessly, watching as her daughter wandered off back towards her bedroom and the familiarity of the handful of soft toys that had made the journey with them. Through the open door, Georgie could see her happily holding bunny by the ears while sourcing a few more from the suitcase on the ground.

'I am her father.' Abe's voice was reasonable. 'You may not want to accept it yet, but I have every right.'

'She doesn't know you.'

'She knows me a lot better now that I have had a chance to spend some time with her. Go and change, Georgie, and try to stop seeing me as the bad guy in all of this, because we'll never get anywhere otherwise.'

She was still in her pyjamas. Her pyjamas consisted of an old tee shirt with a cartoon character on the front and a pair of stretchy sleeping shorts that left very little to the imagination and she was suddenly conscious of how little she was wearing.

Hard on the heels of that came a surge of heat and she nodded abruptly. 'Okay, but we need to talk.'

'Yes,' he agreed. 'We most certainly do. We will be seeing my father later, and before then we have some important issues to iron out. I have made sure that Tilly has eaten. When you're changed, I will take you to where Tilly has just been playing—supervised, I should add, by two highly qualified nannies, just in case you might be tempted to think that I might be witless enough to not provide the necessary safeguards for my daughter.'

'I didn't think any such thing. Don't put words into my mouth, Abe.'

Important issues to iron out...

Georgie knew exactly what he was talking about. That marriage proposal. It had been put on ice because he had wanted to give her time to digest what he had put on the table but now there was a thread of steel in his voice and she quailed at what lay ahead of her, a complete unknown.

She had spent the past few years struggling to make sure her life was as secure and as stable as possible, that *their* lives, hers and Tilly's, were as secure and as stable as possible. It was all she had wanted. For Tilly to have stability. She knew how disorienting and painful a lack of security could be. Now all of that was up in the air and she felt sick at the thought of how she could try and correct it.

She had a sudden, fierce longing for the routine of her poorly paid hotel job and for her small flat and those trips to the park on rainy weekends.

It might not have been grand, but that life had been *hers*, and now she was scared stiff because it had been ripped out from under her feet.

She hurried off to change, casting one last look at Tilly, who was happily introducing Abe to her stuffed toy collection.

She would need to remember that, whatever his position and whoever he was, he didn't get to have the last word on their daughter. She was Tilly's mother and she had been a damn good parent for the past three years, so she was sure her rights would always trump his in any court of law.

She dressed in a pair of cut-off jeans and a tee shirt and wished she'd thought a bit harder about the sort of clothing that might have been appropriate to wear in a palace, but then she shrugged and decided that she didn't care.

They both looked up as she returned to the huge sitting area, Tilly with a broad smile and Abe smiling as well but his dark eyes rather more guarded.

'Are you playing tea party, Tills?' Georgie ignored the towering alpha male lounging on the ground next to his daughter, his long, muscular legs stretched out in front of him, his body language loose and relaxed.

She could feel his eyes on her, though, as she stooped down and ruffled her daughter's hair.

She was so smooth and soft, her baby skin pale gold and her eyes as dramatic and dark as her father's. When she smiled, there were dimples in her cheeks and she was smiling now.

'Mummy, there's a toy shop here.'

'Is there, baby? Where?'

'I'll show you.'

Georgie looked at Abe, who flushed and looked ever so slightly uncomfortable.

He uncoiled his long body and gracefully stood up, reaching out to tug Georgie to her feet and releasing her as soon as she was standing next to him.

A moment of physical contact quickly withdrawn.

'Well?' she asked as they headed down a marbled corridor wide enough to house sitting areas on either side. Impressive chandeliers interrupted the fresco painting that snaked along the ceiling.

'Perhaps,' Abe said as Tilly skipped along ahead, pausing now and again to make sure she was on the right track and that they were right behind her, 'I should first tell you the sequence of events for today?'

Georgie tensed. 'I know. We need to talk about the whole marriage thing you threw at me before you returned to Qaram.'

Abe winced.

One step forward, two back, he thought with an internal sigh.

Every word she had just spoken indicated that this was not going to be anywhere near as straightforward as he'd hoped. Ha! Who was he kidding? He'd known it was never going to be anything like straightforward persuading this woman to marry him. She really was like no other he'd ever met. He tried to gather his patience, knowing that if he wanted to bring this to a successful outcome, to ensure his child would be safe with both parents to support her, he would have to tread extremely gently.

But he couldn't help feeling it was a frustrating setback after what had felt like a pivotal conversation the day before. He'd thought that they had connected, but now he could feel the tension radiating from her in waves.

Would there ever be an end to her fighting him? To him, it felt as if their marriage was inevitable, but he was clearly dealing with a one-of-a-kind woman who was blind to all the material advantages that would be gained that way.

'We will leave Tilly with Fatima, one of her very enthusiastic nannies.'

'And does she know who Tilly really is?'

'I expect she has made an educated guess,' Abe said wryly. 'Of course, she will breathe nothing of her thoughts until an official announcement is made.'

'Of course not,' Georgie muttered.

Casting a sideways look at her, Abe smiled. He'd always appreciated the way she'd spoken her mind, gentle as she was, and, despite his frustration with her stubbornness, he was glad to see that the years had done nothing to alter that trait. It showed her spirit was just as strong as it had always been.

She could be truthful with him that he was a father because she had a keen sense of what was right and decent, and yet she could argue with him till the cows came home about a marriage proposal that, from his point of view, was as right and as decent as her admission had been. He *almost* rolled his eyes…

'We will have brunch together in the sun room. I have issued instructions. We can then discuss…'

Georgie straightened and stared directly ahead. Tilly

had disappeared through one of the doors. 'The Proposal,' she filled in for him.

'Indeed,' Abe said with a smile. He could practically hear the capital letters.

They were at the entrance to yet another massive space and Georgie stared, mouth dropping open, because when Tilly had said there was a *toy shop* in the palace, she hadn't been kidding.

'What's this?' she asked faintly, turning to Abe, who was slightly behind her.

Ahead the space was dominated by a soft play area worthy of any commercial venture. To one side was a small village comprised of several houses, varying styles and all big enough for Tilly to play in, and outside one of them was a ride-on miniature Mercedes Benz with its own electric charging point. There was a craft area with an assortment of crayons and paper and a sketch pad mounted on an easel.

'I had no idea what toddlers enjoy…er…playing with…'

'So you decided to get *everything*?' she squeaked.

'Actually, I had to restrain myself,' Abe admitted guiltily and was gratified when she burst out laughing.

'I should be really mad,' Georgie teased him, while behind her Tilly was busy picking up where she had apparently left off, under the supervision of a smiling girl who was sitting on a small kids' chair by one of the toy houses that were almost big enough to hold an adult.

'You surely cannot have much more annoyance left in your reservoirs,' Abe teased back.

She blushed like a teenager. Always had. He'd always found it irresistible. She was a glorious rosy colour now and his eyes drifted inexorably to her parted mouth.

He hadn't meant to kiss her the evening before, but

it had felt so natural, and, once his mouth had hit hers, rational thought had disappeared through the window.

He had shot back in time to when he hadn't been able to see her without wanting to rip her clothes off.

He considered what marriage had always meant to him, something he had always assumed would be a formal and possibly sterile arrangement, a union forged for the sake of a country.

He thought now, as he stared hard at her full mouth and did his best to resist the urge to run his finger along that bottom lip, that marriage to Georgie would definitely have its upsides. He might not be able to fully give himself to her emotionally in the way she'd prefer but he would certainly be more than prepared to give himself physically to her just as often as she wanted.

He lowered his eyes and gathered himself.

She might hate him for what he had done, resent him for the position he had put her in, but he had kissed her just once and all that hatred and all those resentments had faded away under the seething passion that still burned between them.

Georgie felt the charge suddenly running between them, a chemical reaction she didn't seem capable of preventing, and she turned away sharply to focus on her daughter and then, for the next half an hour, to get to know the young girl who would be helping look after Tilly, because there was no doubt in Georgie's mind that she would need a bit of help while she was here.

Tilly was energetic and curious, and Georgie had no idea how she could help her daughter explore and run around when she was unfamiliar with the layout of the palace.

Nerves kicked in once again when Abe, who had remained in the room for the entire time, stood up and said something very quickly to the nanny in his native language before turning back to her and indicating the door.

Would Tilly burst out crying? Georgie wondered.

Left alone with someone she had only just met? But attending nursery from a very young age had, by necessity, turned her into a sociable child and there were no tears as the door to the playroom was very gently shut behind them.

Phase three was about to begin, she thought as she followed him wordlessly down another bewildering route. Same marble, different grand paintings and mosaics and balustrades but presumably a different destination.

Phase one had been the introduction of the idea of marriage, which had been followed by phase two, the introduction to his country and the life she and Tilly could have here, and now phase three was about to commence and she realised that, in the tumult of everything that had been happening, she hadn't thought enough about his proposal to consider possibly uprooting herself from everything she had ever known.

It had lain there, on the periphery of her mind, a bridge waiting to be crossed.

The room into which she was ushered was lavish. She could understand why it was called the sun room, because a bank of arched glass doors allowed brilliant light to wash in, diluted by clever use of shutters and very fine muslin panels. It overlooked gardens she hadn't noticed before and beyond that, as she moved to gaze through one of the windows whose shutters had been flung open, she could see the rise and fall of sandy dunes.

The marble here was black and white on the floor and the furniture was white wicker intermingled with upholstered sofas and on a sideboard was a veritable feast.

Her chef's eye appreciated the effort that had gone into its preparation.

They helped themselves to food, the silence stretching between them until she could feel her skin break out in a thin film of nervous perspiration.

'You have had some time to think now, Georgie.' He sat down and dumped his plate in front of him and watched her as she sat opposite him at the glass table.

'But it's all been such a rush...'

'I have stepped back from discussing my proposition,' he said, ignoring her lame excuse, 'because I thought you might want time to think about it. I also wanted time to adjust to parenthood and the reality of having a child. To launch into the nitty-gritty of a marriage proposal seemed...too hasty.'

'Abe.' Georgie sighed helplessly. 'I believe in marriage. I just don't believe in *this* marriage. I really want you to be a huge part of Tilly's life and I know you've said that you can't possibly be a part-time dad, but surely where there's a will, there's a way?'

'Why?' Nothing in his voice betrayed any emotion other than mild curiosity at her answer.

'Because I always thought I'd be married, and married for the right reasons, married for love. I'm as traditional as you are, Abe, but I do recognise that this is the twenty-first century and people no longer feel that they have to shackle themselves to one another because they happen to have had an unplanned baby together.' She looked around her, at the opulence. 'I know I can't provide this level of material comfort for Tilly but there's more to life than that.'

'I agree that money isn't everything, but that's being incredibly simplistic about our situation,' Abe told her quietly, his eyes suddenly intent on hers. 'You told me about Tilly because you felt I had a right to know. Now, you want me to believe that you have our daughter in mind when you out of hand reject my offer of marriage. Are you sure you are not only thinking of yourself?'

'That's not at all what I'm saying,' Georgie protested heatedly. She leant towards him, her slight body trembling with tension. 'I'm saying that marriage without love would be a disaster and you don't love me.'

He closed his eyes and when he opened them she could have cried at the bleakness in them. 'And you say this in the full knowledge that every marriage that starts with declarations of love ends up with living happily ever after?'

'No, of course not...'

'Because there are no guarantees, even if love is involved, are there, Georgie? If my memory serves me right, you told me yourself of the many hours you spent with the children of divorced parents...' Whether parents chose to separate, or it was forced on them through death, the true victims of love, he considered, were always the children. Love hadn't given either his or Georgie's parents a happy ever after, only grief for the remaining adult and child. Perhaps, if coming together to start a family was approached in a more logical way, as he was proposing, there would be fewer casualties along the way?

'Which is just what I don't want for Tilly!' she declared.

'And I repeat, you imagine that love will be a guarantee against that? It won't. Listen to me, Georgie. I have no intention of being a part-time father. I wouldn't want that if I were Joe Bloggs from the house next door and I certainly cannot and *will not* accept any such arrangement given my position. Tilly is a princess in her own right, will be wealthy in her own right, even if you refused to marry me, and she will need qualified protection as she grows up. Can you provide her with that?'

Driven onto the back foot by questions she hadn't even considered, Georgie scrambled to make a case for herself but there was a trickle of doubt in her mind. Surely she wasn't being selfish in wanting love to be a part of the equation? But could love trump Tilly's safety? She shivered at the thought.

'Tilly also has a heritage here that is centuries old and it is one she deserves to know. Not to be *acquainted with* but to *know*. Would you willingly deprive her of that too, Georgie? In your quest to find love?' he asked with a raised eyebrow.

'It's not a crime for me to want a life with someone who loves me,' she protested in a whisper.

'No, of course it isn't. But in this case, surely you agree that your *wants* cannot take precedence over the *needs* of a child too young to make decisions for herself? I want my daughter to grow up *here*, to inherit what she is due, to be safe while she is doing so, and to have the best possible upbringing. Will you stand in the way of that because you crave a fairy-tale life that largely doesn't exist?'

Assailed by doubts on all sides, Georgie blanched. How could the life she wanted, which was one she had been brought up to expect, suddenly seem like a self-serving dream only attainable at the expense of the most important person in her life?

Her heart was thudding. Would she be willing to sacrifice Tilly's future for her own?

'There is no point in going round the houses,' he said, voice flat. 'Tilly deserves the best that life has to offer her and, more than anything else, that means being here and having the unity of both her parents at hand for her.

Together. Married. And the business of love has nothing to do with it!'

Georgie marvelled that he could wipe out something as important as that with a dismissive slash of his hand, but then, as she had just discovered, he was nothing like the warm, passionate man she'd once known. Now, he was a man as cold as the Arctic waters when it came to emotions.

And she had fallen for him. She, with her belief in love and her casual acceptance that her life would follow the same path as her parents', a loving union that stayed the test of time.

She had fallen for him and she hadn't managed to clamber out of the hole she had dug for herself four years ago because she still had feelings for him, even though everything inside her railed against the injustice of that. Wasn't that why she was so conflicted over marrying him? He made her hope and made her yearn for the impossible and she hated him for that. Every second with him was a reminder of the perils of still having feelings for him when he had none for her.

'I will do everything within my power to do what I think is right for my daughter and, by extension, for you,' Abe said quietly, almost sympathetically, 'but, as a matter of interest, can I ask how you would feel if you got your own way on this?'

'Sorry?' She rubbed her temple with her finger, tiny circular motions to relieve the tension.

'Here is another scenario for you, Georgie. In pursuit of an impossible dream, you return to London. Tell me how you would feel when Tilly is old enough to understand that in *your* best interests, you decided to deny her the sort of life she could have had here, and how would you feel when she *does* come over here to be with me and whoever I may marry in the future, a woman who will have a say over how Tilly fills her time, what she does, a woman who will doubtless bond with her and with whom I will make joint decisions about things we choose to do as a family? How will that play out with you? What if, at that point, you still have not found Mr Right? What if, when you wave goodbye to Tilly, you return to life on your own knowing that our daughter will be absorbed in family life on this side of the ocean? What if, by walking away from my proposal, you discover that the very stability you want Tilly to enjoy ends up with me and a new family here, rather than with you over there?'

Georgie stared at him in consternation, for he could have said nothing more destructive to her peace of mind.

She waded through the imagery in her head and surfaced to acknowledge one thing, and that was, however damaging he might be to *her*, his number one concern was, without doubt, for his daughter. Everything he had said was out of consideration for Tilly. She had overturned the direction of his life in the most devastating way possible, but he had not turned away or tried to fob her off with money to buy her silence. He openly wanted to admit Tilly as the legitimate heir to his kingdom, to marry her, Georgie, even though that meant sacrificing the more normal route he would have wanted to take to find his bride.

In other words, he had not baulked at self-sacrifice.

And now that he'd asked, how *would* she feel if he married someone else? *When* he married? Because of course he would. There would be no angst-ridden questions about finding the right woman. He would interview some suitable candidates and choose someone fitting for the role of wife to a prince and he would make it work. Emotions wouldn't be involved and, with a child to consider, the imperative of a wife would be pressing. He was right, while *she* looked for Mr Right, he would simply move on with his life and by Tilly's next birthday would probably be wed and ready for the next phase in his life.

'I don't want to have to fight you,' he said softly.

'What does that mean?'

'I will fight for full custody of my daughter, if needs be.'

'I'm her mother!' But Georgie's blood ran cold. Yes, she knew her rights, but could those rights be undermined by the extraordinary circumstances of their situation? Could he hold the trump card just because he was a prince? And was that something she wanted to risk?

'I would never aim to exclude you from our daughter's life, Georgie, but likewise I would never roll over and give up the fight if you decided to return with her to London.' He sat forward and looked at her urgently. 'I don't want a war on my hands and the truth is that, tradition or not, I would not find it palatable to force you kicking and screaming into a marriage if I thought the whole edifice would collapse in due course...'

'What are you saying?'

'We got along four years ago, Georgie, and we get along now. Drop your weapons and you might find that we rub along very well together.'

She wondered what would happen if she dropped all her weapons and forgave him for the past. What would she open herself up to? For him, putting the past behind them would herald a pleasant future rubbing along nicely. He'd always assumed he would have an arranged marriage and, in the context of an arranged marriage, 'rubbing along nicely' would be deemed a successful outcome.

For *her*, though...putting the past behind her might open up an even bigger Pandora's box than the one already open. How long before the creeping love that had never gone away staged a comeback, as they 'rubbed along nicely' in their marriage of convenience?

That thought frightened her. Could she live a life on shaky ground when all she'd ever aimed for was security? Or had she already gone past that point by entering this royal world?

'I don't even like you, Abe, after what you did...' But her voice was not quite as steady as it should have been and she was frowning, unable to look at him.

'You sound as though you have become so accustomed to thinking like that, that you're finding it hard to let the sentiment go, but you have to try, for Tilly's sake.'

Georgie blinked and focused on him.

She was spellbound by his beauty. He sat there, so coolly confident in every word that left his mouth, and his very confidence was making a mockery of her concerns.

'This isn't my world,' she protested weakly and he waited a couple of seconds before replying.

'If you become my wife, my world will be yours, as it will be our daughter's.' He paused and this time his dark eyes were lazy and speculative and sent a trail of fire coursing through her.

She fidgeted and realised that somewhere along the line she had closed the distance between them.

Suddenly hot and restless, she sprang to her feet and walked jerkily across to the window to stare out at this world he promised would be hers. Behind her lay a fabulous brunch, barely touched, and a fabulous room, furnished with all the regal pomp money could buy. Ahead of her lay splendid grounds and the vast panorama of desert beyond.

She was unaware of Abe approaching her from behind although she suddenly saw his reflection in the floor-to-ceiling glass through which she had been staring. Her heart stopped and then accelerated. She turned around and he was so close to her that if she reached out and placed her hand on his chest, she would feel the beating of his heart.

'Marry me, Georgie,' he said, voice low, dark eyes searching her face. 'Get past your resentments so we can make it work.' He reached to place his flattened palm on the glass behind her, caging her in, eyes intense and mesmerising.

'I am not the enemy...' He paused and his eyes roved over her face. 'In fact, I am very far from that, as that kiss last night demonstrated...'

'That was a mistake.'

'Was it? Truthfully?' he asked huskily.

She knew that he was going to kiss her, and she *knew* that that kiss would throw everything into turmoil...because she was going to respond. Her body was melting and she knew he was right. She couldn't pretend that she didn't find him as compelling now as she had four years ago.

Still, she shivered as his warm lips touched hers and then groaned as his tongue traced the contour of her mouth before delving in to taste her. She clutched at his cotton shirt and tugged him closer so that his thighs were hard against her and nudging between her legs and, oh, it felt *so good*.

He was the first to break apart, but he stayed close, staring down at her upturned face, rosy with passion.

'We don't just get along,' he murmured, 'we have this going for us too, and it is far more than just a bonus...'

CHAPTER SIX

THE SILKY SOFTNESS of his words washed over her, as seductive as an embrace.

What had she thought might happen when she had decided to tell him about Tilly? Not this.

And yet, if she backtracked to that very first moment when she had seen him standing in that room, with his back to her, bodyguards by the door, a tall, dominant figure, a prince…the process of working out just where everything would lead should have begun.

She'd told him that she'd said goodbye to naiveté the minute she'd found out that she was pregnant. You had to wise up very fast, as a single mother, to cope with the demands of parenthood without any support and particularly without the support of the father because he'd done a runner, vanished without a forwarding address.

So what if he was a prince? she had thought when they'd been unexpectedly reunited. She would do what she had to do, do the right and decent thing, and if he wanted some kind of contact with his child going forward, then she would be happy to accommodate him.

On every count, she had completely misjudged the situation.

Had she really thought that she would have emotionally recovered from the devastating effect he had had on her? He'd been in her head pretty much every day for four years. That in itself should have been a vital clue telling her that he was still dangerous when it came to her emotions, yet she had turned a blind eye to that peril and bought into the illusion that she would be able to handle whatever was thrown at her. She had thought that it would be easy because at the end of the day, as Tilly's mother, she would always have the last word.

But Abbas Hussein was a crown prince, which made having the last word a great deal trickier. He was a man of honour and duty and those qualities had come to the fore in his unhesitating response to the situation he had faced.

Surprising? Maybe not. He might have walked away from her all those years ago—and she could almost, *almost* follow his logic in doing that—but the truth was that she would never have fallen in love with someone who *wasn't* decent and honourable.

And that decent and honourable man wanted, of course, to do the decent and honourable thing.

Like finding herself in a maze, she could now look over her shoulder and see that every step she took would inevitably lead her to where she was now even though she'd imagined herself to be completely lost during the journey.

He'd laid out his reasons for marriage with a levelheaded logic that characterised this new Abe that she was starting to get to know. He'd shown her, in small steps, just how willing he was to involve himself in Tilly's life, to incorporate her into his magnificent royal world, even though he had never asked for her to be born.

He had been thoughtful and patient in his handling of the situation, even if Georgie suspected that he had known from the very start where things would end up.

And of course the one thing she hadn't anticipated, but should have, had happened.

She had fallen in love with him all over again and with love came hope and that was something that had no place in her situation.

And now this...

The chemistry between them, a kiss that had sent her soaring into orbit and the knowledge that, although he might not love her, he still wanted her.

Marry him, a voice whispered inside her, *and you'll do what's right for Tilly... Marry him and you won't have to live your life watching from the sidelines as he moves on with someone else... Marry Abe and you can have him in bed with you at night, wake up with him in the morning...*

He was right, they did get along, when she wasn't busy remembering how much she hated him, and she knew that she only hated him because of what he did to her, what he made her feel for him, and not because he was a hateful person. He wasn't. His very response to what she had thrown at him was testimony to that.

'Well?' he prompted, stroking her cheek with one finger and making it impossible for her to think straight. 'Respect...trust...and mutual physical attraction. It's enough for a successful marriage, enough to give our daughter the life she needs and deserves, don't you think?'

'I c-can't think when you're looking at me like that,' Georgie stuttered with utter sincerity, and he laughed just as he used to.

'Good. Maybe I don't want you to think. Maybe I just want you to agree with every word I say.'

'That's the most arrogant thing anyone could ever say!' She gasped but he was still laughing, still looking down at her in a way that was making her blood boil, and she lowered her eyes and smiled reluctantly.

'I suppose it makes sense,' she told him. 'I never thought I would marry someone because it makes sense, but this does.'

I'm marrying him because it makes sense but also because I love him, Georgie thought suddenly.

He would never know that, it was a pointless love that would never be returned, but she knew that if she really hated him there was no way she could ever accept his proposal, regardless of his arguments.

'Could I have something a little less lacking in caveats?' he teased, further lowering her defences.

Georgie looked at him, eyes clear. 'Well, then, yes. I accept your marriage proposal.'

She paused and he cupped his ear with his hand, frowning.

'Why are you doing that?'

'I'm waiting for the *but...*' He smiled, eyes lazy. 'And I am very glad there appear to be none. You're doing the right thing. Give this a chance and I promise you will find in me a husband who will not let either you or Tilly down.'

He curved his hand along the nape of her neck and then smoothed it over her shoulder.

Desire bloomed inside her in a sudden, shocking burst. It was as though, in accepting his proposal, she had mentally freed herself from the business of denying her attraction to him.

He must have sensed that because he drew just a tiny bit closer, his breathing quickened and there was a slumberous look to his eyes as they rested on her flushed face.

'Come upstairs,' he urged, and Georgie made a feeble attempt to tell him not to be crazy.

'I have to go and see how Tilly is doing,' she said, but she didn't pull away as he continued to stroke the side of her neck, his touch so soft and gentle that she almost moaned aloud.

'Of course, you must, if you feel you have to,' he agreed.

But the floodgates had been opened and she didn't want to shut them.

She was going to marry this man and there was no way she could expect the marriage to remain a celibate one. Not only would that have not been feasible, neither of them would have wanted it.

There was a real and tangible pull between them, and deep inside her she felt that was something, *hoped* that it was something that had stuck with him as it had stuck with her.

Excitement flared.

Marriage! So the circumstances didn't quite live up to her girlish fantasies of the perfect situation but, as she had discovered from experience, nothing in life was perfect and as solutions went this was a good one.

'But I think you'll find Tilly is fine,' he murmured. 'Fatima has me on speed dial. If there is a problem, then I will know within seconds. I also have a camera installed so that we can check on her at any time if we feel the need. Fatima knows it's there, indeed was the one to suggest it, so...'

'Your father...what time...?'

'I will perhaps take Tilly over slightly ahead of you, which will give him time to get to know her. I plan on leaving here in...' he glanced at his Rolex '...a couple of hours and my driver will be on standby to deliver you to his palace at six-thirty this evening. It's going to be an informal affair.' He smiled faintly. 'So we have a couple of hours to play with,' he said wickedly. 'Would you like to play with me, Georgie?'

Georgie blushed furiously. She had made love to this

man so many times and had had a child with him and yet, as he looked at her now, she felt like a virgin on her wedding night to the man of her dreams, shy and tentative and yet fizzing with excitement.

'Dare to walk away from old resentments,' he challenged. 'I know you want me. I want you too. And we are to be married...' He smiled and she felt faint and in thrall as he took her hand and they headed upstairs, headed to his bedroom suite, which adjoined hers.

She made a point of peeping in to check on Tilly as they went past the playroom. She wasn't going to rush into bed with him just because he snapped his fingers! Her heart was beating with nervous anticipation but she wanted him so badly. The genie had been let out of the bottle and was running amok and there was no way she could think of shoving him back in.

She felt his presence looming behind her as he lounged indolently against the doorframe while she coddled Tilly and hugged her before the siren call of the playroom beckoned the little girl back, then she turned and looked at Abe, drowning in his dark, inviting gaze.

There was acquiescence as she twined her fingers into his and he squeezed her hand in response.

The atmosphere was thick with anticipation and she half expected him to hurry her to his bedroom, intent on following through but, in fact, he took his time as they headed up the imposing staircase and when he opened the door to his suite, he seemed in no rush to do anything.

He stood back as she walked into a space that must have been twice the size of hers and certainly bigger than her entire flat in London—far bigger.

'By royal command,' she said, catching his eye, and he grinned.

'Command is not a word I associate with you.'

'I'm here, aren't I?'

'Royal consent, shall we say…?' He strolled towards her and then reached for her hands, holding them lightly as he looked down at her. 'That is what this marriage will be about, Georgie,' he said seriously. 'Never command, always consent. I know you feel that you may have been coerced into this position, primed to wear my ring on your finger when you hadn't envisaged that being the outcome when you first decided to tell me about Tilly, but we're both on new territory and we have to consider that our actions from now on will have our daughter as the centrepiece of whatever we decide to do. Agreed?'

Georgie nodded, but couldn't help her heart twisting a little. She would always want to put Tilly first, but wondered if there would ever be a place for her, Georgie, in his reckoning. It would be best not to hope for that, she decided. It would hurt too much when inevitably it didn't happen. So she would focus on making Tilly happy instead.

'And I think you'll agree,' Abe continued huskily, tugging her gently towards him, 'that happy parents are parents who physically enjoy one another…'

Georgie looked at him with wry amusement. 'Really, Abe? I don't think I've ever heard that definition before…'

'You should have.' He looped his hands behind her and then lowered his head and kissed her, long and slow, leaving her trembling for more. 'Don't they say that people who play together, stay together?' he muttered against her lips.

'I think they may have meant racquetball and golf.' She was laughing now, relaxed as she hadn't been since he had walked back into her life.

'Then that is a serious omission on their part.' He led

her through the outer sitting room, which she belatedly appreciated was more personal than the other areas of the palace she had seen. Perhaps he had had a hand in choosing what sort of décor he wanted and had decided to lose the acres of clinical pale marble in favour of the warmer tones of wood, or maybe it was the fact that the silk rugs breaking up the space were more colourful.

Likewise, the paintings on the wall were less austere. There was a clutch of lined drawings that looked very Picasso-like and a couple of abstracts that brimmed with vigour and colour.

And beyond, lay his bedroom.

Her nerves fluttered but she was fired with anticipation. She'd dreamt of him for so many long months and even when the dreams had stopped, he'd always been right there, on the edges of her mind, a constant thought in her head.

She was led into a bedroom dominated by a super-king-sized bed with a velvet headboard that matched the drapes that pooled on the ground. The sun poured through the windows and he moved to shut the curtains, plunging the bedroom into cool darkness.

Abruptly sheathed in shadow, Georgie felt a sharp tingle of intense excitement. Her eyes adjusted to the darkness after the brilliance of the sunshine outside and she caught her breath as he moved towards her, undressing slowly as he did so.

Like yesterday, she remembered the first time she had slept with him, the nerves, the racing, pulsing thrill, the warmth of feeling that she was safe with this man.

Against all odds, she felt the same now.

He was already half naked and Georgie stared in open-mouthed fascination at the ripple of muscle and sinew. He had the perfect shape, broad shoulders tapering to a washboard-hard stomach, and just the right amount of dark hair across his chest. He was all male, oozing dangerous sexuality, and he was *all hers...*

For reasons that were right or wrong.

How had she made it onto the bed?

She didn't know. She must have sidled onto it as he'd strolled towards the window to draw the curtains.

At any rate, she was kneeling on the bed now, hands on her thighs, barely breathing as trousers followed in the footsteps of the shirt, falling onto the floor, leaving him in silky boxers and the prominent bulge announcing that he was as turned on by her as she was by him.

She followed his progress towards her and arched up to meet a kiss that was surprisingly gentle, a simple tasting of one another. She drew her hand softly along his cheek, contouring it and losing herself in the feel of his skin against her fingers.

'You realise,' he murmured, clasping her fingers in his hand and looking at her, 'that we're turning over a new page, and there will be no going back now.'

'What do you mean?'

'My bed becomes *our* bed. We'll get married, Georgie, and I sincerely hope you'll be able to say goodbye to resentments so that together we can begin the process of smoothing over old scars. No more fighting, no more trips down memory lane, no more recriminations. I think we should focus on the present rather than the past, and look towards the future, as a family. We might not be the kind of family you've always imagined, but it will be ours, whatever we make of it.'

He would do his utmost to make both his wife and daughter happy, and he knew the best way he could make Georgie happy was to remind her exactly how good they were in bed. He might not believe in romantic love, but he definitely believed in the powerful chemistry between them. He would make this as easy for her as he could. He remembered his own vast pain when his mother had died, when his father had emotionally vanished, leaving him lost, alone. It had taught him the importance of self-reliance, of containing that which could cause hurt. Love. He would never allow Georgie to step into a place where she could end up hurt because of this marriage, or him, and so he would remind her of what they'd once had between them, and that would be enough for both of them...

'I get that.'

Of course, he was right.

She would have to come to terms with a new page being turned over and if, as he'd said, it didn't resemble the page she had hoped for growing up, then it could have been a whole lot worse.

He'd very graphically painted a worst-case scenario already for her. The one that involved him moving on with his life, absorbing Tilly into it, while she watched from the outside like the little matchstick girl peering through the window to a banquet she couldn't enjoy.

Oh, yes, that was definitely a worst-case scenario for someone who couldn't envisage anyone ever taking her place in her daughter's life.

They got along and they were certainly attracted to one another. Both those things counted for a lot.

She was smiling as he joined her on the bed, smiling as she pulled him down to her to nuzzle the side of his face and luxuriate in the feel of him against her.

'It's been such a long time.' She sighed.

'Long enough for me to want to take my time,' Abe responded unevenly, 'but also long enough for me to suspect that that won't be happening. Take your clothes off,

Georgie. I want to see your nakedness. I want to see the body that bore our child.'

Abe had no idea how he was managing to have anything approaching a conversation because his body was on the verge of exploding. How long had he wanted this? She'd just said that it had been a long time. She had no idea how long it felt as he sat back and watched her peel her top off, revealing small breasts pushing against a simple cotton bra.

He dimly wondered whether a secret yearning for just this moment had been inside him for four years.

Not possible, surely!

But it felt like it as he watched her as she shifted off the bed, elfin and slight, and stood to unhook her bra from behind, finally releasing her breasts and sending a surge of pure X-rated longing through him. He could barely breathe. She was so dainty, her breasts exquisite and small, tipped with rosy peaks. She stepped out of the rest of her clothes gracefully and then stood there, her chest rising and falling because she was breathing so fast.

'You're so beautiful,' Abe said hoarsely. He slipped off the bed, moved to stand in front of her and rested his hands lightly on her shoulders. She looked up at him, her face open and expectant.

'So are you.'

His heart squeezed tight and unbidden words came tumbling out. 'I am really sorry, Georgie, that I was not by your side during your pregnancy and afterwards. You may find my level of duty puzzling but, of course, I would have asked for your hand in marriage then and would have devoted my life to doing whatever it took to secure the well-being of our daughter.'

Georgie noted again how she was rendered a postscript in his drive to do whatever he had to for Tilly's sake, but she wasn't going to reflect on that right now. He'd been right to say that the past, with all its bitterness, had to be put behind them so that their eventual marriage could start in good faith.

Four years ago, he would have asked for her hand in marriage, would have confessed who he really was. Would she have accepted him? Of course, she would have. She would have been hurt that he hadn't told her who he was from the start, but she would have been persuaded by his argument that anonymity had been a prize he hadn't wanted to relinquish because it was as rare as hen's teeth in his world.

'Let's not talk any more.' She skimmed her hands along his waist and then along the rim of his boxers and felt the pulsing of his hardness tenting them.

'You're right, my darling,' he growled. 'We have far more important affairs of state to be getting on with.'

They fell onto the bed, their bodies slickly rubbing together, their hands finding familiar places to caress.

Georgie wriggled her way down, pushing him still with one hand flattened on his chest. She gently licked his nipple with the tip of her tongue and then teased a path with her tongue along his body, tasting the saltiness of his skin and the tightness of muscle and sinew. She ran her fingers lightly along his inner thighs and smiled at his sharp intake of breath.

When she took his bigness in her mouth and darted her tongue along the corded sheath, she wanted to pass out with desire and longing.

Abe had to grit his teeth to stop himself from a headlong rush into release. He looked at the dark cap of her hair as she teased him with her mouth and tongue and then, when he could no longer take the exquisite torture, he manoeuvred her supple body so that he could explore her wetness as she was exploring his hard arousal, so that they could feast on one another.

For Abe, he had the strangest sensation of coming home and he knew that that was because their relationship was on a completely different footing. She was now the mother of his child and as such occupied a special position, one that could be challenged by no one. Naturally that would account for this surge of pleasure and contentment.

He could feel her moving towards a climax. He teased her core with the tip of his tongue and felt its stiffness and the way she moved against his mouth, impatient and desperate for him to go further, to send her hurtling over the edge.

She was by no means alone in this. Never had he felt more aroused.

Oh, but how well he knew her body! Like muscle memory stirring after years of slumber and roaring back into life, he knew just how long to tease her until she was so close to coming that a single thrust was enough to send her over the edge.

He eased her off him and they rearranged themselves with the ease born of familiarity.

Fumbling to locate protection was an obstacle quickly surmounted and when he sank into her, her whole body welcomed him.

Georgie was hanging onto self-control by a thread and that first thrust and then his deeper, second thrust was sufficient to hijack all hope of anything lasting longer than five seconds.

Her orgasm sent her soaring into orbit. Her short nails dug into the small of his back as wave upon wave of pleasure tore through her and she could feel his own orgasm swelling inside her, which turned her on even more.

Her body, dormant for so long, burst into life with the explosive intensity of a dam bursting its banks.

His groan of satisfaction as he came was a blissful sound and when he collapsed onto her, she relished the slickness of his body, damp from exertion.

He rolled onto his side and looked at her with slumberous eyes, then he weaved his fingers through her short hair and smiled.

'I should get dressed,' he murmured. 'My father is very much looking forward to meeting both you and his granddaughter and I have some work to plough through before Tilly and I leave.'

'And I should head to my room, think about having a bath.'

'I don't think so,' he drawled softly. 'This is your suite now. My bed is now our bed, remember? The adjoining door between our suites can be opened so that we both have quick access to Tilly at any time during the day or night.'

Georgie closed her eyes. Their room, their bed...

The sharing of their lives started now because she suspected that their formal union would not be something hastily arranged. As a prince, he would have to have everything in place and that would take time, but in the interim they would be as good as married because she would be sharing his suite, sleeping with him, entering fully into this next phase in her life.

Where would it lead? A shiver of anticipation raced through her and she tried to stifle it because she knew that she would have to bring common sense to bear on this relationship, would have to temper any bursts of optimism that the love she felt might one day be returned with the reality of knowing that they were only here, only together like this, because of Tilly.

But still…

'We'll have to discuss…well, the formal stuff,' she ventured, her voice calm and controlled and interested.

'Royal protocol?' He grinned.

'I suppose so,' Georgie said seriously.

'Life is going to be a great deal less restricted than you imagine,' he told her. 'Tomorrow, I will give you the grand tour. You've seen a section of the palace. There is also a comprehensive gym and two swimming pools, one outdoor and one indoor. The main difference is that anything you want, you will get.'

'That's not necessarily a good thing,' Georgie pointed out, 'and it certainly isn't for a toddler. Tilly will run rings around you if she senses that she can have whatever she wants.'

Abe laughed. He should be heading down to his offices so that he could get some work done before he headed over to his father's palace with Tilly, but when Georgie looked at him the way she was looking at him now, with a mixture of gravity, calm and just a touch of apprehension and self-doubt, he found that all he wanted to do was remain where he was, lying here in bed with her at a crazy time in the middle of the afternoon.

It struck him that whatever advantages he had assumed would be conferred had he married a woman versed in the way of royalty, he could very well have ended up with someone who wouldn't have given a damn about making sure a child of theirs kept their feet firmly adhered to the ground. With vast wealth at their disposal, there would have been the temptation to raise their child to assume automatic superiority and that would have been a serious error of judgement.

'Plus,' Georgie now interjected into the silence, frowning thoughtfully, 'I can't just sit around snapping my fingers and being waited on hand and foot.'

'We have a long conversation ahead of us.' Abe regretfully braced himself to face an hour of work. 'Too long to start now.'

'But we're going to have to have the conversation,' she insisted, squirming into a sitting position against the pillows and watching as he heaved himself off the bed to stare down at her for a few seconds.

The intimacy between them filled her with joy but she realised that being filled with joy because the guy she loved was standing in front of her naked, because he was going to be her husband, wasn't a reason for her to be lulled into following his dictates without question. That would be the start of a very slippery slope.

'Of course we will.' Abe returned her gaze with one equally serious. He moved to perch on the side of the bed. 'You have done an amazing job with Tilly. Do you really think I would stop you from carrying on with that amazing job once we are married? And as for your not sitting around snapping your fingers...' He grinned. 'I can't imagine anyone less likely to be happy doing that.' He stood up, eyebrows raised, but still smiling. 'I can put a time in my diary for us to have this conversation if you like,' he teased. 'Because the expression on your face is telling me that you think it is a conversation I may try to evade.'

'The expression on my face,' Georgie said, 'should be telling you that I am going to be the one giving up everything I've ever known to start a life out here with you, for Tilly's sake. I don't want to think that I'm going to end up floundering because everything I know has been whipped away from under my feet and there are no plans in place for me to have anything at all to call my own or to help me to…adjust to what's going to be a very, very different life.'

'I get that, Georgie.' He raked his fingers through his hair. 'Leave this with me. It will be sorted. There is nothing for you to worry about.'

She nodded but there was a sour taste in her mouth as she remained in the bed as he had a shower, returned to the room, got dressed.

He was so breathtakingly beautiful that she could feel her reserves of willpower slipping away as she watched him.

How easy it would be to fall completely under his spell all over again, but she would do well to remember that leaving it up to him because he would sort everything and there would be nothing to worry about was much, much easier said than done.

He had nothing to lose. She was in love with him and that was a weakness in itself because it made her susceptible to dreams and hopes that might or might not materialise. The unvarnished truth was that once they were married, she would be vulnerable in a way she wasn't now and, if she had no support network at all, she might end up lost, even if he didn't intend for it to go that way. He would have got everything that he wanted and could she trust him not to sideline her once that happened?

There was a lot inside her that stupidly *did* trust him but, for someone who craved stability, she needed to find a place for herself here, some sort of anchor to hold onto.

Dressed in dark jeans and a white tee shirt, Abe strolled to stand over her. 'You will be fetched when my driver arrives,' he said. 'And you have my cell number. Call if you want anything at all. Shall I get Fatima to bring Tilly in to you? She will need to be introduced to the fact that you and I will now be sharing a bedroom and, no later than tomorrow, we will explain the situation to her, who I am and the way forward.'

Georgie nodded her agreement, dismissing her unsettling thoughts because they weren't going to get her anywhere.

Tomorrow the way forward he had mentioned would begin, but for now she would meet his father and think optimistically about the future even though the comfort zone she had always clung to had been well and truly left behind.

CHAPTER SEVEN

LIFE CHANGED FAST for Georgie. In short order, she met Abe's father, who welcomed her warmly. She thought that again Tilly was a passport to immediate acceptance here, but she refused to dwell on the downsides of that.

If she started dwelling on too many things, then she would quickly reach the conclusion that she was little more than a spare part and she didn't want to question the choices she had made.

The truth was that Tilly was beyond happy. She adored the space, the vast acres of garden, being able to run around, and, more than that, she adored Abe.

They had told her who he was and she had accepted that she now had a dad with the joyful alacrity of a three-year-old too young to really ask any questions.

It was only a matter of days since Georgie had accepted his marriage proposal but the wheels were already turning quickly. Before long, she would meet the team who would be co-ordinating the extravagant wedding. She had also already been introduced to a select number of family members. That number would grow because she would be expected to immerse herself in Abe's world, which was one in which his company seemed to always be in demand.

She had been given a guided tour of the palace by

a member of his staff, who had walked several paces behind her as she was shown into every room and the provenance of all the tapestries and mosaic walls and paintings were explained. It had been a slightly unnerving experience.

And, of course, she now had help with Tilly. Plenty of it. More than she actually wanted or needed. She and Tilly still spent time together, but time was no longer something snatched on weekends or after a day working at the hotel. Now, their time together could meander for as little or as long as Georgie liked and then, when she wanted to disappear indoors to cool down by the swimming pool or else read a book or send emails, she could because Fatima or the other nanny would be there to take Tilly off her hands.

There was an eerie sense of limbo about her life and in this limbo, Abe had become her anchor.

He was an attentive partner, a dedicated father and an amazing lover and she knew that being at sea in a different country was playing a part in deepening her love for him.

She thought of him and the feeling of being slightly adrift dissipated.

She couldn't rely on him to sort her life out completely, but he had introduced her to people, and if she still felt lost wandering in his vast palace, then she would get used to it in due course.

The most important thing was her daughter's happiness.

It was apparent that Abe had meant every word he had said when he'd told her that Tilly was the one who mattered in the events that had played out between them.

He would do everything he could to ensure she had a stable and happy life. He was being true to his word thus far and Georgie didn't see why that would change.

But was she more than just part of the package deal?

She hoped so because they continued to get along now that the ammunition had been put away.

And the sex...

She smiled now, thinking about it.

The air sizzled between them. They stepped into the bedroom at night and the heat between them was like a burning inferno. One touch from him and her body responded with scorching urgency.

Right now, at a little after six-thirty in the evening, she was waiting for him in one of the many sitting rooms, this one overlooking the very pool where she had enjoyed a couple of hours earlier with Tilly and Fatima.

She was in a loose-fitting flowered dress with short sleeves that swished to mid-calf. It was one of many new outfits that had been provided for her. A few she had been guided into buying—such as ornate gowns for formal occasions—but she had chosen the rest, along with an assortment of shoes and accessories.

She had drawn the line at jewellery.

'I wouldn't feel comfortable wearing such priceless jewellery on an everyday basis,' she had told Abe two days previously as all manner of rings and necklaces and earrings had been paraded in front of her on beds of purple velvet by the top jeweller in the country. He had been summoned to the palace and had shown his wares with a mixture of deference to the Crown Prince and pride in his vast knowledge of every single gem he had set in front of her for her inspection.

Afterwards, over dinner, Abe had looked at her, his dark eyes amused, and informed her that she was the first woman he had ever met who wasn't interested in jewellery.

'I do love jewellery,' Georgie had responded, blushing when he had rubbed her shin with his bare foot under the table in between the courses that were being ferried out for them from the kitchens, 'but I suppose I'm a little more accustomed to the cosmetic kind when it comes to sticking something on to go to the supermarket.'

'There's no supermarket shopping for you here,' he'd pointed out.

'And I miss that,' she'd said sincerely. 'I never thought I'd miss going to the supermarket, but I do.'

Surprisingly, he had nodded and looked at her thoughtfully. 'I understand.'

'Do you, Abe?' Georgie had asked with genuine curiosity. 'How can you say that when you've never been to a supermarket in your entire life?'

'Ah, now that's where you're wrong. Don't forget,' he had murmured, skimming his foot along her shin just a tiny bit higher, knowing what her reaction would be, 'that I did go to Cambridge University so I have had some experience of what the inside of a supermarket looks like.'

'Are you sure you didn't have one of your minders running those tedious errands for you?' she had asked wryly, and he had burst out laughing.

'Admittedly it was an irresistible temptation some of the time.'

'I can't believe how spoiled you were.'

'My mother was very down to earth, despite her elevated standing,' Abe had said pensively, in a one-off sharing of confidence, 'I remember that about her, a necessity to instil discipline rather than an easy acceptance of what came with a life of privilege. Unfortunately, when she died, my father retreated into himself for a very long time. He emerged eventually but by then we were both changed irrevocably. I had grown up by myself and he... he substituted the more balanced approach to parenting that my mother had brought to the table with an abundance of material displays of affection. I think it was the only way he could think of handling me. He lacked the spirit to take over where my mother had left off and so, for some years, he replaced this with lavish spending on anything I wanted.'

'That's very sad, Abe. Losing the mother you clearly adored changed everything for both you and your father.' Georgie could empathise; after all, she had also lost her own mother young. She understood why Abe was so keen to protect Tilly and why he felt he would always need to try his hardest to hold back from falling in love himself, as though to repress certain emotions had the power to prevent all hurt. She had been able to see in his expression that it was a time in his young life he was reluctant to dwell on, so she hadn't been at all surprised when he had swiftly brought the topic back to a less emotional angle.

'The minders came as part of the deal,' he had added to lighten the tone. 'Very restricting, hence I did actually take many an opportunity when I was older to venture into supermarkets whenever and wherever I could to purchase something and nothing.'

Georgie had burst out laughing because he could be so funny with an intelligent, dry wit that was pretty irresistible.

'Maybe,' she had mused, 'having lost his wife, he was at pains to make sure he didn't lose you as well, hence the bodyguards to protect you physically and the splurging out materially to try and keep you close. Maybe he thought that, having lost your mother, the last thing you needed might have been too much discipline.'

'You could be right.' His voice had been crisp, winding up the conversation, but he had not been able to hold back from saying, with sadness, 'He could have tried just giving me his time and his companionship and his moral support though...'

He had swiftly moved on from there, back into his own comfort zone of physical contact and Georgie had tactfully not pressed him for any more information.

He was far too proud to have welcomed that approach but when he had opened up to her like that about his past her heart had nevertheless soared and wild hope for more than just 'getting along well' with him had bloomed— even more so when he had also talked to her about his brief time in Ibiza, when he had, for the first time, tasted what *normality* must feel like for most people.

Then he had laughed and shrugged and his eyes had darkened and they had made it to the bedroom mysteriously with their clothes intact because she had never wanted him so badly before.

Were things finally moving in a different direction?

She was smiling at the sound of his feet on the marble flooring and then came that familiar burst of excitement as he appeared in the doorway, knock-out sexy in a pair of linen trousers and a white shirt. The pale colours emphasised the burnished bronze of his skin and the raven darkness of his hair.

He was taking her out to dinner, which would be nice because she was keen to sample some of the different cuisines in the restaurants. As a chef, she was tasting new flavours and combinations every day and she couldn't wait to broaden her scope.

'You look...amazing,' he said softly, strolling towards her and pausing as she stood up and moved forward.

He reached out and took her hands in his.

She did look amazing. Some kind of loose, floaty dress that managed to conceal everything yet stir the senses in quite an extraordinary way. Her hands were soft in his, her eyes wide and with that guarded look that often underlined her expression.

Would she ever trust him not to hurt her again? he wondered. He had walked out on her once and now she was here and he couldn't help but think that were it not for the fact that he was a prince, she would not have been here at all. Yes, she would have told him about Tilly because she had a strong sense of what was right and what was wrong, but there was a nagging suspicion at the back of his mind that if he had been any old Mr Ordinary, she would have dug her heels in and retained her freedom.

But he wasn't Mr Ordinary and so she had been persuaded into doing what was best for Tilly, even though she had had to walk away from her dreams in the process.

He had been truthful when he had told her that they shared a child who had a right to an upbringing that would only be possible here in Qaram.

Then he had painted an alternative picture of life as it would be should she choose to turn her back on his proposal. He had spared no details and he had watched carefully as she had absorbed what he'd said. So here she was and, while he recognised the importance of making her feel that this was her home, there was no way he could ever give her the fairy-tale life her romantic heart had always craved.

He had witnessed the impact on his father of his mother's death, could remember his own heart-crushing pain at her passing. His duty now lay in running his country, for which great emotional strength was needed and, as far as he was concerned, strength was only possible if you didn't put yourself in the position where you became weak because you'd handed your heart over to someone else for safe-keeping, and it hadn't ended up being kept safe at all. After all, his father had never been the same after his wife had died, and all the pain and misery and stress had ultimately led to a heart attack. So it was up to Abe to make the sacrifices his father had been unable to, in order to be the ruler their country needed.

But within those confines, he would do what it took to make Georgie's life as comfortable as possible and it was a big plus that the chemistry between them continued to burn so strong.

He'd meant what he'd told her—sex and friendship were a better basis for a marriage than anything else.

In life, you couldn't have everything.

'Where are we going?' she asked. 'I hope it's not somewhere too formal, Abe. I'm not sure this dress would do if that's the case...'

'Extremely informal.'

'I didn't realise that princes did informal,' she said, half laughing as they headed out into the main thoroughfare of the palace and following his lead as he asked her about her day and Tilly's.

They left the palace without bodyguards.

Just the two of them piling into a four-wheel-drive Jeep.

'Are you allowed to do this?' she asked as he cruised away from the palace, covering the extensive grounds at a leisurely pace.

It felt intimate here, away from the army of staff, who were practically invisible but not quite invisible enough.

'Do what?'

'Drive alone? Out here?'

He grimaced. 'This is probably one of the safest places on the planet. True, there are occasions when a bodyguard might be a necessity but generally I save the protection for when I'm abroad. I would do without it altogether but

Jared, the head of security, worries. Between him and my father, I don't know who panics more easily.'

Georgie relaxed, stared out of the window. It was balmy outside and the windows were down, and the breeze blowing her short hair this way and that made her feel a little drowsy. She slid a surreptitious glance to him. He had one arm loosely hanging over the open window, steering with that hand, and the other casually resting on the gear stick. It was very dark out here now that they had left the palace behind and the green gave way to patchy sandy dunes interspersed with stunted palm trees and in the distance...the sea.

She gazed at the dark landscape, at the distant inky line of sea. It was a thin black strip against the night sky, which was bejewelled with stars.

Just for a moment Georgie allowed herself the illusion of romance, the illusion that she was with a guy who actually cared about *her* for who she was. They had great sex, shared a child, wined and dined together, but they had never been on a *date* with all the sizzling excitement and breathy hopes for the future that a date implied. This felt like that date.

The Jeep swerved right, heading down towards the black strip of sea, bumping along the dunes, and then banked along a track towards a villa.

'What's this?' She squinted and then, as they got closer, the lights came on outside illuminating a picture-perfect white villa with a red roof, which overlooked the sea.

'It's my bolt-hole.'

'You have a bolt-hole?'

He laughed again, killed the engine and swivelled so that he was looking at her. 'I say *my* bolt-hole. I suppose I should say *our* bolt-hole. I've brought you here because

I want you to know that the palace is not the only residence we will occupy. You find it daunting and I can't blame you.'

'I think Tilly rather enjoys it, though.' Georgie smiled. 'She thinks it's a hoot to drive that car of hers along some of the corridors.'

'She does that?' He grinned and slanted a sideways look at her.

'Stop trying to kid me; I've seen you encouraging her, Abe.'

'Why not? It is just a house, after all.' He paused. 'She gets to do what I never did, as it happens. I think this villa will make a refreshing change for you too.'

He was thinking of her. For once she wasn't the post-script following behind his concerns for their daughter, but a concern in her own right, and her heart couldn't help but warm to that idea.

He reached across to open the car door for her.

'Dinner will be here and no one will be in attendance. No one serving the food and pouring the wine. Just the two of us. I had a light meal prepared. It's waiting inside.'

'That's very thoughtful of you, Abe.' Georgie's heart squeezed tight with pleasure and as they walked towards the villa, small by palace standards but still imposing by any normal benchmark, she reached out for his hand and linked her fingers through his.

'You will find that I can be very thoughtful,' Abe murmured.

'I didn't think you were the sort of guy to need a bolt-hole. Why would you need a bolt-hole?'

It was so quiet here, a silent blackness all around them with just the faintest swish of breeze disturbing the endless sea of sand dunes that gave onto the coastline. It was majestic.

'Doesn't everyone?'

'I never saw you as a bolt-hole kind of guy,' she told him, and he laughed as he pushed open the door to let her slide past him.

Georgie stared around her. The villa had been aired and overhead fans swirled a cool breeze against her skin. The entrance hall was big, but the rich patina of the wooden floors made it feel warmer and more inviting than the cold marble in the palace. To one side, a staircase swept up to a galleried landing and, ahead, deep, patterned silk rugs led to various spaces and out, she guessed, to a view of the dunes rolling down to the sea.

He led her towards the kitchen, where the table had been set with the finest china and several platters were laid out with lids, which he ceremoniously opened with exaggerated flourish.

All this for her... Surely, whether he would admit it or not, this signalled more than a passing bout of thoughtfulness?

'Makes a change, would you not agree?' he asked, sauntering to the fridge and fetching a bottle of wine so that he could pour them both a glass.

'A fantastic change.' She sat and watched him and her heart sped up as he leaned over her, hands clasping the arms of her chair so that she was caged in.

'There is something I would like to say...'

'Is there?' Georgie cleared her throat and longed for a sip of the wine lying tantalisingly just out of reach. His fabulous eyes were intent on her face and sent a wave of colour creeping up her cheeks.

For a few seconds, Abe continued to look at her, then he moved to one of the chairs and swivelled it so that he was facing her.

'This is a first for me, Georgie,' he said seriously, while

she hung onto his every word with bated breath and rising hope.

Would this finally be the declaration of love she had been longing for?

'This villa has always been my own private space because yes, I, like everyone else, enjoy having somewhere to relax, far from the stress of day-to-day life. I have never brought anyone here but I want you to see this as much yours as mine and I would like to suggest that it become our primary residence, with the palace used for more formal occasions. We could have minimum staff and not all the time. You are not in your own home at the moment, and I realise there is a leap to make so I feel that being here might bridge that gap.'

'Ahh…' Georgie pinned a suitably grateful smile on her face and bracingly told herself that he really *had* been thoughtful in bringing her here and offering it as a place where she would certainly feel more comfortable.

But she was alarmed at how fast she had bolted towards a completely different interpretation of what she'd thought he was going to say. There was a lot to be said for taking each day one at a time. Patience was a great virtue and not to be underestimated, as her father used to tell her. *'The hare didn't win the race, the tortoise did.'*

She was a romantic at heart but being a romantic, she decided, was no excuse for being a complete idiot and she wasn't going to let her love for him, and her dependency on him while she found her feet in this strange new world, deter her from having a few guidelines of her own.

'I think it's a fantastic idea, this place for us.' She smiled warmly now. 'You're right. It's a lot less daunting than living in a palace and I've missed…well, having my own space even if that means not having help all the time. I want to get into the kitchen and do some cooking, for a start...'

'Naturally, Fatima will be on call and, indeed, she can live in with us if you'd like. There is a separate suite that would do for housing her.' He paused. 'I have never had any particular longing for the rituals of domesticity but, yes, it would be good to have fewer staff around jumping to our every need. Having a child has certainly opened my eyes to that.'

'There's also something else I should say.'

'Am I going to like it? An opener like that is never followed up by the popping of champagne corks. Talk to me. I'm all ears.'

'You've made a case for us being married, you've persuaded me that it's the right thing to do, that it's the *only* thing to do but...'

'But?'

Georgie hesitated. Was this the right place to have this conversation? The right time? Yet, she knew that she had to tell him what she thought because it was far too easy to let herself fall under his spell and be swept along by a heady combination of sex and her own foolish love.

'This relationship we have... Yes, we get along and, yes, I won't deny that I really enjoy...what we do...together...'

'Sex, Georgie.' He smiled gently. 'We do the raunchiest things in bed and yet you still blush like a virgin when it comes to talking about it. I can't deny how much I enjoy it when you do that.'

'Sex never lasts,' she said flatly.

'It can drop off, in my experience, I agree.'

'And when things change between us...when that eventually fades away, as your wife I will still expect you to remain faithful to me.' She watched him carefully, watched to see any little hesitation, but she could read nothing at all in his expression. His silence propelled her to carry on. 'I don't think I'm asking too much. You may laugh but that was the way I was brought up, to expect fidelity within marriage. I've seen so many cases of what happens when one partner or the other fools around, the damage it causes to their families. You might think that two parents living together, whatever the circumstances of their marriage, is preferable to living apart when it comes to children, but adultery undermines in ways that I would never be able to accept so...'

'You have my word.'

'Oh. Right. Good.' She breathed a sigh of relief.

'There was no need to ask,' he said quietly. 'I have always been a one-woman man.'

'I had to make absolutely sure.'

'You did.' He shrugged. 'And now let us agree that that is something we leave behind. Not only do you have my word on that score, but you also have my word that, should the time ever arrive when I feel myself tempted to stray, then not only will I tell you but I will also give you the option of bailing on our marriage.'

Georgie nodded.

'And the same, naturally, goes for you,' he added mildly. 'What's good for the goose, as you English would say, is good for the gander. What if you are the one who decides to spread your wings?'

'That's not me.'

'How can you be sure, Georgie? I know you were raised with all the right principles in place, but there is nothing in life that is written in stone. When you are surrounded by sand dunes, you quickly understand that what seems hard and fast can change very quickly, depending on the direction of the wind. I've had a lot of experience.

You have had precious little. What makes you so sure that you won't start wondering what other excitement lies out there, as yet untested?'

'You truly don't know me if you think that,' she said with conviction.

'In that case, like I said, let's leave it there and enjoy the feast that's been prepared. Afterwards, I will give you a guided tour. You'll be excited to know that it'll take a fraction of the time it took for you to become acquainted with the palace.'

Georgie relaxed. He might not love her—*yet*—the way she loved him, but he was committed to what they were doing. He wouldn't decide that boredom might be a good excuse to stray and she believed what he had told her.

They both had principles.

The food was exquisite. They camped at the kitchen table and she enjoyed every mouthful. Sitting opposite him, she couldn't help but stare at his outrageous beauty and be lulled by his anecdotes as he described his country to her and its history. The sex might fade at some far distant point in the future, but right now she was turned on just at the anticipation of being in bed with him later tonight.

He showed her round the villa. The paintings were bold and colourful, and he explained that they were all done by local artists. He reminded her of her love of painting, of the sketchbook she used to carry around with her all those years ago in Ibiza. He remembered the cloth case she had used for her charcoals.

There was an arts council, he told her, and she could get involved with it. He explained who worked on it and how she could contribute to growing it.

She'd asked him how on earth she was going to orient herself when she knew no one and he was answering that question now and just the thought of finding some kind of footing was incredibly calming.

In the relaxed, informal atmosphere at the villa, without staff, they discussed the minutiae of their arrangements.

Social engagements, the whens and whys and wherefores, Tilly's schooling, Georgie's apartment in London—which she would have liked to have kept but which he vetoed very firmly and, though she wanted to dig her heels in for some vague reason, she honestly couldn't come up with a good enough reason to argue the toss.

In the quiet of his villa, Abe tried to work out what she was thinking. He had predicted that she would like the villa, the peace, the proximity to the sea and, by daylight, the stunning views of ocean and sand.

He had used the opportunity to discuss all those things that somehow hadn't been raised in any depth thus far and she had listened and accepted what he said with surprisingly little objection.

He hadn't liked that, but he had no idea what to do about it and, from every angle, he was assailed by guilt at what she was giving up for him, even though he knew that he had nothing to feel guilty about.

He wasn't going to promise anything he couldn't deliver and all he could and *would* deliver would be a lifestyle she might enjoy in time.

'No need to tidy up,' he said, more harshly than intended, as she made to clear the dishes once they'd finished. 'It will be done when we leave.'

She blushed and shrugged and he stared at her, frowning and not quite knowing how to ease the tension that had sprung up out of nowhere.

There was one obvious way to regain their equilibrium. *His* comfort zone.

He slipped his arm around her waist and pulled her to him, and as she was teetering and beginning to laugh he swept her off her feet and began walking to the door while she clung to him, and he felt the tension ease right out of her, as he'd hoped it would.

'Time to get back to the palace.' He nuzzled her neck and she squealed and then rubbed her cheek against his six o'clock shadow. 'I have needs and talking isn't one of them...'

CHAPTER EIGHT

'TOMORROW, THE NEWSPAPERS will be running the happy news of our impending marriage.' This the following morning as they were having breakfast on the patio with Tilly between them, squirming on her chair and reeling off a non-stop battery of questions, mostly pertaining to the swimming pool and when she could get to it.

'I thought everyone already knew about us... Tilly...' No sooner had she come to terms with one staging post, Georgie thought, than she found herself confronted by another.

She had travelled to Qaram to acquaint both herself and Tilly with the country she'd thought their daughter would be visiting a couple of times a year.

Had she expected to end up sleeping with Abe? No. Had she spent years living with the bitterness of knowing that he had used her and dumped her without a backward glance? Yes!

But it felt as if the ground had shifted under her feet without her even really realising.

Abe had re-entered her life and had managed to disentangle her fingers from every single thing she had been clinging to ever since she had met him.

He had blown a hole in the little life she had built for herself and now she was due to be his wife, meeting people she would never have met before, living a life she had never dreamt conceivable.

Bitterness had been no protection for her heart. Bit by bit, she had fallen for him all over again and this time there was no sense that it might be infatuation. They shared a child and what she felt now was deep and strong. But how many more deep breaths would she have to take to face up to yet another challenge she hadn't banked on?

The thought of the town crier publicising their impending marriage made her feel like a character from a Disney movie, but this was rarefied life as few knew it.

'Protocol,' he returned succinctly. 'Tilly, are you going to eat that bread or are you going to play with it?'

'Play with it?' Tilly responded hopefully. 'I want to have a swim. I'm hot!'

Georgie looked at her daughter, so different from when they had been living in London. Now, Tilly was livelier, more energetic, more curious. Under the blazing sun, her skin had turned a burnished bronze, just like her dad's, and she looked the picture of health.

Nursery every day and snatched playtimes before bed and on the weekends…those things were gone. More than that, though, was the joy of Tilly having a father who, true to his word, geared his day towards making sure he spent some quality time with his daughter.

And wasn't that good for *her* as well? Georgie thought. Having someone there to share the responsibilities? Not just that, but having someone who found as much pleasure in the small, funny things Tilly said and did?

She loved everything about this man and yet there was still a pool of uncertainty somewhere deep inside that she had signed her life over to a guy who had not once said anything to her that might have given her any idea that she was loved.

'Lessons first, Tilly, and then pool after.' Lessons involved a lovely young girl who came in to teach and already Tilly, who was bright as a sparrow, was beginning to learn the basics of reading and the foundations of the language that would become her own in due course.

When the new term began, she would attend school, a battle easily won by Georgie because, although Abe had been home-tutored, he was far more in favour of the routine of school and the benefits of friendship with peers that it brought.

She absently watched as Tilly skipped off with Fatima, having given her a hug, but she was frowning when she looked at Abe. He tossed his linen serviette on the table, shoved his chair at an angle so that he could extend his legs to one side and looked right back at her with raised eyebrows.

'Something on your mind, Georgie?'

'No.' She looked away, out to the pleasing panorama of tended green with its distant horizon of tan sands.

'Spit it out.'

'You should get off to work.' She tried a smile on for size but he refused to buy into it.

'Work can wait.'

'So there will be no turning back once it hits the headlines,' she mused, gazing past him. 'Feels odd, I suppose. Just when I get accustomed to the thought of me and you...of *us*... I now have to gear myself up for a press conference about it.'

'Was there going to be any turning back for you?' Abe wondered if a time would come when her doubts would be banished for ever. After she was wearing his ring? How many more times would he have to persuade her into truly believing him when he told her that they had the makings of a very successful union?

He looked at her, so slender, chewing her lip anxiously, a vision of feminine prettiness in a short-sleeved pale yellow tee shirt and a light skirt. She brought out an intensely protective urge in him. She was the mother of his child so that was perfectly understandable. Frustrated, he raked his fingers through his hair and continued to gaze at her.

'No, but—'

'Then where is the problem?'

'There are still so many things to put into place.'

'You worry too much.'

'Of course I do! Can you blame me? It's a big step and now it feels…' She sighed helplessly and he reached out and threaded his fingers through hers.

'The hotel knows.' Abe decided that ticking her various concerns off the checklist might be the best way forward. It made him smile, which was odd because he had never had much time for moody female behaviour. In Georgie, it excited and challenged him; it was that simple. She would never bore him.

'Yes. I spoke to my friend there and we had a long chat about everything. It was good of you to break the news.'

'You were dithering. Your flat…that's in the process of being sold. You said you wanted the money you got from it to be transferred to your next-door neighbour who helped you over the years with Tilly? It'll be done.'

'That's a great help. I'm not sure how I would have managed it from over here.'

'We have discussed the details about Tilly's schooling. The arts council? They are ready and overjoyed to have your input when you feel you would like to go along…' He paused. 'This meet-and-greet with the press is simply a formality, Georgie. Nothing to get unduly exercised about.'

'I suppose it's the feeling that everything is rushing

towards me and I can't put up any stop signs, not that I *want* to...'

'But you feel safe as long as you think your options are being kept open,' Abe finished astutely, and she nodded. 'And seeing it in print makes you anxious.'

She nodded again.

'Like I said, it'll be a formality. The toughest part you have already dealt with and that was meeting my father, members of my family, my friends. And bear in mind that it will not be marriage overnight. I will be expected to have a lavish wedding with a guest list of hundreds, hence the fact that we won't actually tie the knot for another month or so. Trust me, by the time we exchange vows, all your anxieties will have been vanquished.'

'How can you be so sure of everything?' she asked, but she had relaxed and was half smiling.

'No one can be sure of everything,' Abe murmured, 'but it's fair to say that I usually am and I'm usually right.' He stood up, held his hand out for her. The coolness of her fingers entwined with his sent a jolt of red-hot lust through him, but he gritted his teeth and fought off that now familiar craving to take her, however inconvenient the timing might have been.

'Thank you for that reassurance, Abe,' Georgie said drily. 'It's good to know that I'm with someone who is always right.'

'Isn't it?' He dealt her a slashing sidelong grin that sent shivers through her. 'Now I have to get to work so don't tempt me.'

'Tempt you to do what?' Georgie smiled innocently.

'I'll show you tonight...'

The following morning, Georgie woke to an empty room. They had made passionate love the night before and she had obviously fallen into a deep sleep because she hadn't heard Abe leaving the bedroom and neither had she been awakened by Tilly toddling in demanding cuddles.

She glanced at her phone, realised that it was nearly nine in the morning and, with a yelp of dismay, she leapt out of bed, flung on her dressing gown and burst into the adjoining suite to find Abe and Tilly in the process of choosing clothes for Tilly to wear.

'I overslept!' She tugged her dressing-gown belt tightly round her waist and gazed at the array of outfits scattered across the floor. 'What's all this about?'

'Is it not a lady's prerogative to choose what she wants to wear?' Abe, sitting on the ground with his long legs stretched out in front of him, looked at his daughter with tender indulgence. 'She's been fed and watered, and Fatima is going to collect her in half an hour to take her to my father's palace. She's going to meet some of the children who will also be attending her school next term. We will join everyone after the reporters are through with us.'

'Oh, good heavens, I'd completely forgotten about that.'

'No need to panic. It is not for another couple of hours. Join us. We were debating which outfit might be most appropriate for meeting other toddlers. Right now, the pink ballet dancer one appears to be in the lead.' He pointed to a confection of pink lace and silk that had mysteriously appeared in Tilly's wardrobe a few days ago.

As she looked at them both there on the ground the scene could not have been more natural, more heartwarming, and only his reminder that a bunch of reporters would be congregating in a couple of hours to take photos of them signalled just how unusual her new reality really was.

Photos of them both smiling for the camera would be

published in one form or another across the world. Not only would everyone at the hotel where she had worked see them, but eventually, when they appeared in the weekly glossy magazines her friends back home read, they too would be agog to see her on the arm of a drop-dead gorgeous prince.

Oblivious to her mother's panic, Tilly was reaching to hold up the ballet tutu and Georgie marvelled that this was a world her daughter would become so accustomed to that in time the flashbulbs of cameras pointing at her would be accepted as part and parcel of the life she led.

For the first time, Georgie really appreciated what Abe had meant when he had urged her to marry him because it was important that Tilly claim a legacy that was her right by birth and was protected while she did so.

It seemed crazy that she had ever imagined that things could have been normal had Tilly moved from one country to another, from a flat in London to a palace in Qaram. She would have been utterly confused.

'Tilly.' Georgie stepped forward and smiled at her daughter, who looked at her quizzically. 'Why not go for the flowered dress and the sandals?'

'Boring,' was the immediate response.

'Argumentative like her mother,' Georgie said as Abe grinned and looked at her with lazy amusement.

For a while, Georgie forgot the stress ahead of her and got into the spirit of choosing something for Tilly to wear, and Tilly, in the thick of all the attention, was in her element.

They were laughing when, twenty minutes later, Fatima arrived to gather up a delighted Tilly, who had compromised with half the ballet outfit, sporting a tutu and ballet pumps with a flowered cotton tee shirt.

'Will you be working until…the photo shoot?' There

was still the ghost of a smile on Georgie's face as she closed the door behind Fatima and Tilly and turned to look at Abe, who was rising to his feet and stepping over the scattered discarded outfits to move towards her.

In faded jeans and a tee shirt, he was utterly casual and utterly gorgeous.

She stared and sucked in her breath when he was standing right in front of her.

Would she ever, she wondered, be able to be close to this man without her entire nervous system going into freefall? Was this all part of the package deal when you fell in love with someone? She'd thought all the disillusionment she had suffered at his hands four years previously might have stood her in good stead when it came to securing her defences against him. She'd been wrong.

'I will,' Abe said gravely. 'But just for the moment...' he lightly held the edge of her silky dressing gown between two fingers and smiled '...the glimpse of an errant breast has managed to catch my attention.'

'What are you talking about?'

Georgie stared down to see that, between her lifting Tilly up and closing the door when Fatima had come to sweep her away, the dressing-gown belt had loosened so that she was a little less decent than she'd thought she was.

He slipped his fingers underneath the thin silk and stroked the soft swell of her breasts and then gently, absently brushed a finger over her nipple, which stiffened in immediate response.

He kissed her. A long, slow and tender kiss that made her melt and, with a soft little moan, she reached up on tiptoe to return the kiss, loving the wet melding of their tongues.

His kiss deepened and she didn't have to feel the rigid

bulge to know that he was turned on—she could hear it in his roughened groan. He pulled apart the dressing gown, underneath which she was just in a pair of knickers, and it slithered to the ground in a pool of pale green and blue.

Georgie arched up into his embrace and he cupped her buttocks, driving her against him, urging her to swing up to wrap her legs around his waist.

It was an invisible communication, a barely felt touch, and Georgie automatically did just that and hugged him close as he carried her into the bedroom and laid her down on the bed, but when she would have squirmed up against the pillows, he stayed her and positioned her so that she was lying on the bed with both legs hanging off.

Heady with anticipation, Georgie looked down as he knelt in front of her. He eased the knickers off and discarded them, attention remaining firmly focused on the delicate triangle of hair between her thighs.

The gentle slide of his tongue, finding the groove that sheathed her womanhood, evinced a low moan of pure pleasure from her.

He kept her thighs spread with the flattened palms of his hands and tasted her the way someone might taste the most delicate and fragrant of morsels. He licked and delved and licked again until Georgie was going crazy with wanting more, but he wouldn't let her squirm away from his questing tongue.

Instead, he continued to lick, to tease the tight bud with the tip of his darting tongue, and when he inserted his finger deep into her, she couldn't stop herself. The slow build to an orgasm accelerated with the speed of a supersonic rocket and she came against his mouth in long, shuddering spasms of intense, exquisite pleasure.

She looked down at his dark head between her legs and reached to curl her fingers in his lush hair.

'Abe...'

'You're way too good at distracting me,' he growled.

Their lovemaking was fast and intense. Georgie clung to Abe; the feel of him filling her, the rub of his hardness against the still tender, engorged parts of her, sent waves of deep satisfaction coursing through her.

She could have stayed there with him for ever, could have held him close and lain with him while time passed by, but with less than a couple of hours to get ready she flew into preparation mode like a bat out of hell.

'I'll leave you to it,' he said. 'I have some work to get through and I will change in my offices and meet you back here in an hour. There isn't a huge amount of time, I know, but...'

'But that's what happens when you lose focus.'

'I could not have said it better myself.'

That said, Georgie thought, flying through a shower and then flinging open her wardrobe doors to inspect which of the, as yet, unworn formal dresses she would put on, hot, hard sex had certainly had the desired effect of squashing all of her nerves. She just didn't have the time to feel anything but rushed!

She opted for something that could weather the blazing heat that would confront her once she was standing outside the palace where, Abe had informed her, the photo shoot would take place.

She was becoming accustomed to the temperatures, which soared during the day and only really became comfortable once the sun had dipped away.

Dressing for the sun here bore no resemblance to dressing for the sun in London.

Thirty-five minutes later, she looked at her reflection in the floor-to-ceiling mirror in the bedroom.

The dress was modest, with loose sleeves in shades of

apricot. It was pleasingly Grecian in style and designed to repel the intense heat. Strangely, it often paid to wear loose clothes that covered you up practically from head to toe when it came to combating the temperatures the minute you stepped foot outdoors.

He had said he would fetch her and when he did, it occurred to Georgie that she'd had no idea what he would be wearing. A pair of light trousers? Linen? A shirt? One of those handmade white ones with the royal insignia embroidered in tiny letters? He had wardrobes full of them. She hadn't expected him in traditional white robes, but he was, and the sight of him took her breath away. She was vaguely aware of him saying something complimentary to her but she didn't really take it in. She was too busy staring, and in the end, embarrassed, she cleared her throat and made an attempt to focus.

'Ready?'

'As ready as I'll ever be.' She walked towards him, still blushing.

He looked what he was: a prince, a man who could change lives, who held the reins of supreme power in his hands. He held out his arm for her and she took it. Her heart was pounding as she headed out of the room and then down the sweeping staircase at the bottom of which various members of staff had gathered.

All that was missing was a red carpet. The front doors were pulled open and a waft of hot air engulfed her and she blinked at the bank of photographers waiting for them to emerge.

Her fingers tightened on his forearm and he patted her gently, completely in control of the situation.

There was no pushing or shoving. Everything was orderly and she knew that she was smiling although her nervous system had kicked into fifth gear, more than making up for the previous lull.

'Relax,' he murmured, sotto voce, and she forced herself to try and unbend a bit.

Faces behind long lenses were arranged in banks—far more than she had expected. Surely there were photographers and reporters who weren't just from Qaram? It was astonishing that she had not realised, from the very first moment she'd discovered Abe's true identity, just what a huge deal this whole situation was going to be.

Her body was as rigid as a plank of wood. His exhortation to her to relax could not have fallen on deafer ears.

She was barely aware of his arm sliding around her waist or of him turning to look down on her but then, suddenly, there were just the two of them. Everything else, the heat, the cameras, the people—all of it disappeared and became background noise because all she could see were his dark, dark eyes and the sensuous curve of his mouth. All she could feel was the warm reassurance radiating out from him towards her.

He smiled long and low and she practically melted as he bent to capture her mouth, gently inserting his tongue, tasting her and demanding a response in return, which she was all too happy to give.

She curled her hands around his neck and linked her fingers together, her body moulding gently against his. When he pulled back, she blinked, momentarily disoriented.

'Now, *that's* more like it,' he said, smiling. '*Now* you're relaxed.'

Yes, now she really was relaxed and so completely in love that she couldn't tear her eyes away from his face. She'd been nervous as a kitten and he had put his arms around her and made her feel safe. That was how he made her feel time and again. Safe. It shouldn't make sense, not when she'd spent years hating him, not when she knew that this marriage on the cards was little more than a business arrangement, and yet he still made her feel safe, as though what was happening between them couldn't have been more right.

Looking down at her upturned face, Abe, for one fleeting second, was sucked into the crazy illusion that this was the real thing. Her eyes were shining. She looked like... like the queen she would very soon become, and it was nothing to do with the clothes she wore or her physical attractiveness.

There was a kindness and a generosity there that gave her a regal aura of which she was touchingly unaware. It was a modesty that hailed from her background, Abe thought. As the daughter of a vicar, an only child and one who had lost her own mother at a young age, she had been raised to put others before herself. It was why she had told him about Tilly, why she could never be bought with money or status, why she had been persuaded into marrying him.

He had been struck dumb when she had opened that bedroom door to him. He was so used to seeing her casually dressed, to see her dressed for the part had stopped him dead in his tracks. Had she noticed? She had looked perfect for the role as his wife-to-be.

Even now, standing here, with the sun pouring down on them and the sound of cameras clicking, Abe could *feel* the warmth and benevolence of the journalists and photographers in front of them.

This was a woman who deserved the best that life had to offer and he was not equipped to give that to her.

He might be able to give her fame and fortune, and he

could shower her in jewels and grant her every material wish, but what about those other wishes? The ones she deserved? He couldn't grant those. He was a man who had locked his heart away and thrown away the key and it was only fair that he did not allow her to harbour any illusions on that score.

He'd hurt her once, four years ago and he wasn't going to hurt her again. This was a truth written on stone, as far as he was concerned.

However, uneasy with this train of thought, Abe focused on the here and now and on the crowd in front of them.

He would think things through, navigate a way forward that would be fair on Georgie. That look in her eyes as she had gazed up at him, that soft smile playing on her mouth, those things had told a story and he did not want that story to end in a place where she believed that promises were being made that he knew would never be delivered.

Their fingers were entwined and he squeezed her hand supportively before withdrawing his and was proud and pleased that she did what was expected. No woman bred for this very purpose, no woman with all the right credentials, could have done better.

After half an hour, he bowed and announced, in a good-natured voice, that that was it for the day.

Questions were posed and he answered a couple of them but was already turning away, hand moving to the small of her back, urging her back into the cool of the palace.

'Was it as bad as you thought?' was the first thing he asked when they were inside. 'I should tell you that you acquitted yourself with aplomb.'

'Thank you.' Georgie reddened with pleasure. 'I'd expected more of a scrum, to be honest.' He was heading in the direction of one of the sitting areas, a room that was less chillingly formal than most of them, tucked away to the side and overlooking the gardens at the back. 'What is the plan now? When will we leave to go and see your father?'

Fresh juice had been laid out ahead of their arrival and Abe poured them both a glass. It had been a good morning and a good photo shoot, and it would be criminal to spoil things now by launching into another heart-to-heart on marital expectations. Did he really have to spell things out for her again in black and white? Wasn't that a bit crass? He'd been very open on the day she'd agreed to marry him, that love played no part in their future, and still she'd agreed to marry him. Could he have been mistaken about that look in her eyes when she had gazed up at him?

Actions, he decided, always spoke louder than words. If she were to be travelling in the direction of expecting love and all the complications associated with it, then wouldn't it be more hurtful to give a long speech on what she shouldn't expect? She was astute. Wouldn't it be better to *show* her what he meant by how he behaved instead? Wouldn't that approach be more subtle? Less humiliating for her? Kinder?

When Abe thought about hurting her, the ache he felt deep, deep inside was almost physical, which only reinforced his decision that this was the right way forward.

'I'll change first.' He grimaced. 'These clothes feel restrictive even though they're loose.'

'Okay.' Georgie smiled. He had offered her some juice, which was very refreshing, and then he had stepped back, away from her.

Was it her imagination or was there a certain polite remoteness to him now that the business of the photo shoot was over and done with?

He had kissed her, and she had lost herself in that kiss, but it hadn't escaped her notice that he had let go of her hand immediately afterwards.

No matter. She was way too sensitive about…everything.

The bottom line was that the photo shoot had been fun. There had been no attacking questions and everyone had seemed delighted that their Prince was due to marry, that he was a father, that a love that had been lost had been miraculously restored. Serendipity. It was an assumption Abe had not denied.

'And now that the cat's out of the bag…life is going to get even more hectic, I am afraid.'

'What do you mean?'

'Parties, events, social engagements…there is one the day after tomorrow. Nothing too fancy but it will be a good opportunity for you to meet some of the people we will be socialising with.'

Parties…events…social engagements…

The pace was stepping up, Georgie thought, but she smiled and relaxed. Why would she be scared? Wasn't Abe going to be by her side?

CHAPTER NINE

TILLY WAS WHIRLING round and round the room, half dressed, pretending to be a pirate from one of the books Abe repeatedly read to her on a nightly basis. It had captured her imagination but unfortunately was a high energy game and right now Georgie needed to get her daughter dressed and ready to leave for the party Abe had told her about only a couple of days previously.

Since then she had seen little of him because he had been out of the country, but they had spoken and it seemed that the informal do was something of an official engagement party, which his father would be hosting.

It was clear that their idea of 'informal' differed greatly, because he had informed her, as a postscript, that there would be in the region of sixty people attending.

'It was hurriedly arranged,' he had explained the night before when he had called her, 'but my father was excited after the photo shoot and there was curiosity all round, if I am honest. I did try to talk him into a less rushed time schedule, but he was having none of it.'

So now here she was trying to capture the bundle of energy that was her daughter because both of them would have to get ready. They would be driven to his father's palace where she would meet Abe, who would come straight from the airport.

The thought of seeing Abe again after only a couple of days without him filled Georgie with excitement. It felt as though he had been away for months, *years*. She had chosen what she was going to wear carefully and, yes, she knew what was expected of her on the sartorial front, but she also knew what he liked and she had gone for a deep burgundy dress that framed her slender body like a glove while remaining perfectly decent, because the figure-hugging, contoured sheath was superimposed under layers of transparent, pale pink voile and silk that floated around her in an extremely flattering manner.

Two weeks ago, she would have been a bag of nerves but that was then. Now, things had subtly changed.

She grabbed Tilly, subjected her to a series of kisses and tickles and frogmarched her to the bathroom, where she bribed her into the bath with a selection of toys and her favourite bubble bath.

She chatted and sang and played but her mind absently darted across the landscape that had become her life, against all odds.

The confusion and panic she had felt when she had first arrived in Qaram had ebbed away and in its place was a contentment she had never expected to feel. She wasn't an outsider, but someone who had been welcomed into a country that was not her own. She had had to rely on Abe and he had been true to his word. He had guided her every step of the way, slowly integrating her into his way of life.

She had been dogged for so long by fear of change. Life had changed for her when her mother had died but, over time, that void had been filled by her dad, the crack in her life papered over, but then he had died, leaving her on her own, and although she had jumped ship to go to Ibiza, in an attempt to lose herself in something new and different and challenging, she had never stopped craving stability.

Having Tilly had propelled Georgie into a life where no chances were taken because someone else had been depending on her, relying on her not to guide her into unsteady waters.

So Abe, coming back into her life like an invading storm, had filled her with trepidation.

Every step she had taken had been difficult as she had been edged away from her bone-deep desire for security into a world where she no longer knew the rules.

She need not have worried because Abe had been there for her. Was it any wonder that she couldn't think of him without smiling? They were perfect together. They were perfect in bed and they were perfect out of it as well.

So there were no loud declarations of love. That just wasn't his style. She had seen enough to hope that he cared for her as deeply as she cared for him, whether he realised it or not. She was also hoping that the two days spent apart might have awakened some recognition in him of what he felt for her.

Had he missed her? He certainly seemed to show a keen interest in how she was spending her time in his absence. He had told her to do whatever she wanted to the villa, to make whatever changes she wanted, so that it would feel like home.

At the moment, they were still living in the palace, but as soon as they were married they would decamp to the villa, and he was keen that she had a hand in kitting it out. She had felt a flair of excitement at the thought of that. She had already started planning on redoing and expanding the kitchen, and maybe even putting in a studio, because the light pouring in from the ocean was fantastic for painting. Who knew? Perhaps she could resurrect her vanished career as an illustrator for kids' books... At any rate, she could illustrate for a book for Tilly, which would be nice.

Tilly would miss the vast playroom with the miniature village, but there would be a pool and walks on the beach at sunset. Like Cornwall. At a stretch.

She managed to dress Tilly in an outfit not of her choosing, the fairy confection sidelined in favour of a far more subdued dress and sandals. Fatima whipped her away to give her some dinner then, leaving Georgie an hour and a half to get dressed, which she did slowly and carefully.

A long, luxurious bath and then make-up and then the outfit. It was a little after six and the driver would be delivering them to Basha's palace for six forty-five. Abe would be there and she was fired up to see him, already looking forward to a night of heady passion after the party.

She slipped her feet into delicate, strappy sandals that elevated her height to a very respectable five eight and she and a very excited Tilly were ready and waiting for Abe's driver, Sid, to arrive for them.

She felt good. She felt excited. She felt like a woman in love, and the little voice in her head that had kept repeating that that was a very foolish way to feel had become fainter and fainter over time.

There would be children of Tilly's age there to play with. A few she had already met. Like most young kids, and perhaps because she had become accustomed to the sociability of being in a nursery from a very young age, Tilly had no qualms when it came to making friends.

They arrived at the palace and Tilly could barely contain her excitement at seeing two of the kids she had met only recently. Georgie knew what the routine was likely to be. All the young children would be proudly paraded in front of people for a short while and then whooshed off to one of the rooms in the palace where they would be supervised until, one by one, they eventually fell asleep.

The palace was decorated lavishly, especially considering the very short notice.

But then, an army of people could go a long way when it came to making sure the details were all picture-perfect even though time was limited.

There were small lights blazing on all the trees that led to the courtyard in front of the palace. The palace itself shone as bright as a Christmas tree and the front doors had been thrown open and were guarded by a uniformed man on either side. High-end cars were parked neatly to one side, disappearing into the darkness at the back, and people were entering, formally dressed, many of the men in traditional outfits.

Georgie felt a pang of intense nerves but excitement at the thought of seeing Abe overcame whatever anxiety she was feeling.

The door was opened for her and Tilly flew out but then stopped dead in her tracks at the sight of everyone and turned to Georgie to be lifted up.

So that was how Georgie entered the palace, as people fell back to let her through and one of the members of staff hurried forward to guide a path straight to Abe— with Tilly wrapped up in her arms, wreaking havoc with the dress and ruining the classy entrance she had hoped for, where Abe would turn to look at her and wouldn't be able to look away.

There was no music but there was a lot of laughter and talking and buzz. Dozens of waiters were working the crowded room, serving drinks and nibbles on huge circular platters.

Georgie was stopped so many times along the way that she lost count. She'd personally met very few of the guests but Qaram was small and, now that she and Abe were officially pronounced a couple in the eyes of the world, everyone was keen to get to know her.

She smiled and nodded and chatted and felt more at ease than she'd expected. English might not have been the first language for many there, but they were all fluent in it and they all seemed to share the same keenness to put her at her ease.

Having finally deposited Tilly on the ground and straightened her dress, she looked up and there he was, standing towards the back of the room with a drink in his hand, surrounded by a little cluster of men, who all looked like businessmen.

He was staring directly at her, and Georgie felt her heart do a little tap dance inside her, then she smiled and began weaving her way towards him.

He simultaneously moved towards her as well, excusing himself from the group of men to whom he had been chatting about a Pharma deal and what it could do for the country.

She looked stunning, he thought. Of course she did. When she'd walked in with Tilly in her arms, she'd embodied, for him, the essence of motherhood and his chest had positively swollen with pride.

Her smile, when she'd spotted him, had been spontaneous and wide and filled with delight and, remembering his resolution, he had stood firm against the temptation to smile back at her.

He had had a couple of days away from her to really think things over and the more he thought, the more he came to the conclusion that it was important not to encourage her into thinking that there could ever be more to what they had than what was there already. Good sex, friendship, and shared adoration of their daughter.

She'd told him that sex faded in time. He wasn't so sure it would in their case. It was certainly going as strong as it ever had been and if it ever faded? They would still maintain their shared warmth and camaraderie. It would be enough.

In the meanwhile, it would be important to make sure they were both on the same page.

'I tried your mobile,' he said, drawing her to one side, 'to let you know that I had arrived, but there was no answer.'

'I forgot it at home,' Georgie confessed. 'It was all very calm to start with but then suddenly it was a mad dash and I didn't think to bring it.' She was disappointed that he had not commented on her dress, on how she looked, but then it was a busy evening for him and he would be tired, no doubt, having just flown in from abroad.

'You know the routine for tonight?'

'Sorry?'

'The procedure?'

'Well...yes...' Georgie glanced around. Everyone seemed to be having a good time, which, she thought, was the main thing.

'I sent you an email this morning. Did you get around to reading it?'

'No. Tell me what it said. Have I dressed inappropriately?' She glanced around again but, no, surely she wasn't overdressed or underdressed?

'You look fine. It is about the seating arrangements for the dinner. You will be responsible for ushering everyone through to the dining hall. A member of staff will alert you to when seating arrangements have to commence.

My father will sit at one end of the table and I will be at the other end. You will be next to me bar one.'

Fine? Was that all he had to say on the subject of the outfit she had been at great pains to choose in the expectation that it would please him?

And now here he was, outlining how the next few hours should unfold, reminding her in no uncertain terms that this might be a party to celebrate their forthcoming union, but it was also an event she would have to oversee in her role as his wife-to-be.

Georgie felt her previous heady excitement cool.

'Of course,' she said a little stiffly.

'I am going to see Tilly now.' He smiled and Georgie thought that it was the first time he had really smiled since laying eyes on her this evening.

'I managed to talk her down from the fairy outfit. She's very sensibly dressed for the occasion, although she did insist on travelling with a bag of toys...'

Abe burst out laughing. 'I wonder if those toddlers in there have the faintest idea who is going to be running rings around them in the years to come,' he mused. He glanced at his watch, looked at her and she took the hint immediately.

Time to do her duty, to mingle and socialise and wait for the appointed time when she would have to usher everyone towards the dining area for the extensive sit-down meal.

There should have been some hitches. Weren't there always at an event like this, especially one that had been hurriedly cobbled together at the very last minute thanks to Basha's insistence?

Thankfully, there were none.

People chatted and voices grew louder and the nibbles that were passed round were amazing. Georgie thought about the snacks she had trolleyed up to that hotel room on the day she had seen Abe again for the first time. It seemed like a lifetime ago now.

She checked in on Tilly three times, the last time to find her sound asleep on one of the brightly coloured modular sofas that were low enough to be completely child friendly.

She managed to grab a few sentences with Basha over the course of the evening, congratulating him on organising the event in such a short space of time, and was thrilled when he responded by telling her that it meant the world to him that everyone, friends and family alike, could get to meet the girl who would become his daughter-in-law.

The food was amazing and, sandwiched between the chair of the arts council and a distant relative of Abe's, she felt that it was a successful evening.

But how much had she seen of Abe?

Virtually nothing at all. He had briefly chatted to her when she'd arrived and then he had promptly left her to her own devices for the remainder of the evening and when, eventually, she *had* seen him because he had been sitting close to her at the dinner table, he had shot her a reassuring smile, raised his eyebrows in a silent question, asking her if all was going well, and then, again, had promptly turned his attention to the attractive brunette next to him.

For the first time since she had arrived in Qaram, Georgie felt that she was getting a glimpse of what life would look like in the weeks and months and years to come. The hand-holding had come to a close and this was now her end of the bargain, to fulfil her duties as his wife, without the emotional reserves there to bolster her because underneath the 'rubbing along nicely' was a void that would never be filled. He would have her back, because she was Tilly's mother and because that was his obligation, but if she'd thought that he would be the one to offer her love and support, someone who would feel her doubts and sometimes her insecurities and ache for her because she meant the world to him, then she'd been kidding herself.

Her job would be to acquit herself well and he would be proud of her. They would have sex and, for him, everything would be just as he wanted it to be. Would he stray? He had a high libido and there was no doubt that, married or not, he would have a million women ready and willing to sleep with him, but he would expect them to continue being lovers and so why would he stray if by doing so he risked Georgie leaving him, thereby jeopardising his daughter's security?

She would have wished her dreams away on a man who was incapable of giving her the love she wanted, and for the first time she felt that fact truly hit home for her. Dreams and hopes and reading into things had turned the need for pragmatism into lovesick compliance, against all of her best instincts.

A trickle of unease filtered through her, but she kept going until the last guest had gone, at which point Abe went to fetch Tilly from where she was still sound asleep, and still sleeping in exactly the same position as she had been three hours previously. She literally hadn't moved so much as a finger.

It was a little after midnight.

Many of the relatives were staying at the palace with Basha. Others had been ferried away in chauffeur-driven cars, which had begun circling the courtyard just before midnight, waiting for their clients.

They both fell into the back seat of their car and Georgie lay back and closed her eyes.

'Tired?' Abe queried and she looked across at him. He still had Tilly in his arms and she had settled against him, her small body floppy in sleep.

'Exhausted.'

'You did very well tonight. I was proud of you.'

'Good.' She turned to stare out of the window even though there was nothing to see because it was pitch black outside now that the bright lights of Basha's palace had been left behind.

She didn't want to talk even though she didn't want the space to be able to think either. She didn't want to give house room to the hurt bubbling inside that she had been practically ignored by Abe for the whole of the evening.

Fatima had long since retired to bed so they both took Tilly up to her bedroom and Georgie began busying herself changing Tilly into pyjamas, aware of Abe hovering in the background and then, eventually, turning on his heel and heading out of the room.

She was yawning as she finally entered the bedroom where Abe, having had a shower, was brushing his teeth, completely naked but for a white towel slung low on his hips and loosely knotted.

He disappeared into the bathroom and emerged a couple of minutes later and strolled towards her.

'You looked lovely in that dress, Georgie, in case I failed to mention it.'

He ran his fingers along the neckline and she drew in a sharp breath, her body responding on cue, nipples tightening, straining against her lacy bra.

He cupped the nape of her neck and pulled her towards him so that his naked chest lightly brushed the silky fall of her evening dress. Of its own wilful accord, Georgie's hand rested against his chest, so hard, so broad and so intensely masculine with its dark hair and flat brown nipples she adored running her tongue over.

She skimmed her fingers along his waist and resisted the temptation to tug the damn towel off him.

She didn't want to do that. She didn't want her thoughts to be obliterated by the feverish, frantic pleasure of sex.

He did that, she realised. His language was the language of sex and he knew how to use it to his greatest advantage, but the unease that had sprung up during the course of the evening wasn't going away and for the first time she wasn't in the mood.

'I'm tired,' she said flatly, spinning around and making straight for the chest of drawers to pull out a nightie.

'Yes, it was a long night,' he acknowledged slowly, suddenly sounding wary.

She didn't answer. She locked the bathroom door behind her, changed into her maiden-aunt nightie and emerged to find him lying in bed with the bedside light on. One arm was folded behind his head and his eyes followed her thoughtfully as she busied herself getting her book and checking her phone before slipping into bed next to him and securing the duvet very firmly around her.

'Are you going to tell me what's wrong or will you stew in silence until the lights get switched off?'

'Nothing's wrong,' she denied curtly.

Abe rolled onto his side to stare at her with a frown. She had seemed at ease this evening, even enjoying herself, he would go so far as to say. Had someone said something to upset her?

'How do you think the evening went?' he asked, trying to draw her out.

'I'm too tired for a conversation, Abe.'

'But not too tired to read?'

'I'm too tired to have sex,' Georgie said bluntly. She shuffled to switch off the light on her side.

He stared at her as she swivelled away and he couldn't help reaching out to manoeuvre her so that she was reluctantly facing him, bodies so close that he could feel the heat emanating from her.

'Is that what I asked?'

'No, but it's what you meant.'

'I thought you seemed to be having a passable time this evening, after the nerves.' He heard the warning bells behind her incendiary statement and chose to ignore them.

'I'm surprised you even noticed, Abe, considering you didn't spend more than five minutes in my company.'

Abe stilled. 'Is that what this is about? The fact that you had to circulate on your own without me holding your hand every step of the way?'

Georgie recoiled, stung. 'I don't expect you to do that, Abe.'

'I realise,' he said, bypassing his discomfort at knowing that he had spoken more harshly than he'd intended, 'that this is all new to you and, believe me, I want to make sure you settle here and find a way of calling it your home, however long that may take.'

'To which end, you're prepared to give me my very own villa, which I can turn into the sort of house I am accustomed to?'

'You think I am being selfish in that?'

'I think you're being considerate, Abe. Considerate and thoughtful, because what other choice do you have?'

'Perhaps we should have this conversation in the light of day,' he suggested, reaching to turn off his side light, plunging the bedroom into flickering shadows and dark pools.

'You wanted to talk,' Georgie said, more calmly, 'so let's talk. This evening... I finally realised where I am in the pecking order of your life.'

'Extremely high, if you want the truth.'

'No, I'm nowhere near the top. I'm only in it in the first place because of Tilly. You're prepared to do everything within your power to make me feel comfortable here because I'm the mother of your child. But tonight... I realised that, underneath it all, this is a purely business arrangement to you. Yes, I don't doubt that you like me well enough to "rub along nicely", and I don't doubt that you enjoy making love with me, but it's still a business arrangement.'

'Where are you going with this, Georgie? Have I ever misled you on that front? I thought I'd been open and honest about our reasons for marrying from the start. Would you rather I'd lied to you?'

'No. And, no, you haven't misled me. The sad truth is that I ended up misleading myself.' She felt too close to him, his bare chest within touching distance. She sat up abruptly, drew her knees up and folded her arms around them and for a few seconds she buried her head against her knees, just trying to marshal her thoughts.

She wasn't surprised when she felt him getting off the bed and she raised her eyes to follow his progress in the dark. He pulled a chair across so that he was sitting by her side of the bed.

For Abe, she thought, bed equalled sex and this was definitely not the sort of conversation he felt comfortable having between the sheets.

He could compartmentalise brilliantly. His love for

his daughter—immediate, instinctual and without compromise—was wonderful but it didn't spill over into his feelings for *her*, for Georgie. Georgie was finally waking up to the reality that she would always and only ever be the duty he had had to take on board as part of the package deal to have his daughter.

The sex was a great bonus but, without it, he would still have offered her exactly the same deal because he would have wanted the same net result.

Georgie knew that they could carry on making love and she could continue to fool herself that what they had might actually end up going somewhere, but tonight had finally opened her eyes to a future that was much more likely. In fact, a future that was downright inevitable.

The problem was that, the more she slept with him, the more blurred the lines between fiction and reality would become.

He saw things through a filter that was purely black and white and that was why their arrangement would work so brilliantly for him.

For her, however...?

'Don't go there, Georgie.' Abe broke the silence, a roughened undertone in his voice.

'I did enjoy tonight,' she said in a low voice. She couldn't read the expression in his eyes because the room was dark, but she could sense his alertness in his body language. 'Everyone was very nice, and I met people there I hope to get to know better over time. It was nerve-racking to start with, but I settled into it quicker than I thought I would.'

'But...? Because there is a *but* this time, isn't there?'

'I looked for you now and again. I thought you might have shown a bit more interest in my presence. Abe, you were away for two nights...' she dragged in a juddering breath and her eyes locked to his and her heart skipped a beat '…and yet, when you saw me, you didn't even seem that pleased. We were there to do a job and you left me to get on with it because that's the role I've been taken on to fill.'

He sat back, shook his head and raked his fingers through his hair, his movements for once less graceful than usual.

'My apologies,' he said heavily.

'Why would you apologise? Like you said, you never misled me. The fact is that I fell in love with you four years ago in Ibiza and I never stopped. I just never stopped.'

'Don't!'

'You have no idea how devastated I was when I found out that you'd left without telling me…'

'Yes, I do. You have told me countless times but there is only so often I can apologise for the past. It cannot be changed.'

'I realise that! What I'm saying, Abe, is that I thought all that hurt and bitterness would have protected me against you when you came back into my life. I told you about Tilly and I thought that everything would be reasonably straightforward, that, whatever happened, there was no way you could get to me again, but I was wrong. You did get to me again and tonight it's struck me that everything I feel for you is misplaced because I will never be anything to you but an obligation to bear.'

'That is categorically not true.'

'Then tell me what I mean to you.'

'From what I'm hearing, it would appear not what you're hoping you do.'

'Don't worry; I'm going to go ahead with our arrangement because you're right. Life sometimes entails sacrifices and when it comes to kids, they shouldn't have to pay the price for their parents' mistakes. I can also see with my own two eyes how much you love Tilly, how hard you've tried to gain her trust and, more than that, I can see that Tilly absolutely adores you. But...' she broke out in a film of fine perspiration, knowing that what she next said would determine the course of her life for ever '...no more sex, Abe.' She breathed in deeply. 'From now on, things will have to change between us. You're right, we get along just fine, but we're no longer going to muddy the waters by seeing sex as a bonus.'

Her voice was calm and even. She was proud of herself. How much longer she could maintain the façade was anybody's guess but she knew that she had to get through this next bit, had to dictate her terms and not just go along with the flow because she was in love with him. It had been easy to justify letting her emotions take control of the steering wheel and it was frightening when she thought how long that might have continued if she hadn't had a wake-up call.

He leant towards her with urgency, his dark eyes doing all sorts of unwelcome things to her body, but she held up one hand to stop him in his tracks.

'From now on, we don't share a bed and we lead separate lives until the time comes when Tilly is old enough to understand that not all marriages are made in heaven, and then we can divorce. I know you. You're a man with... desires...but you would have to promise me that you will be discreet.'

'What the hell are you saying, Georgie?'

'I have to protect myself and that starts right now. I don't expect you to remain celibate for me. You can do what you like, and you have my word I will not object.' She looked away. Every word was a shard of glass to her heart but it was for the best. 'I need more emotionally than you have to give and, one day, I know I'll find it. I'm still really young. You do your thing, Abe, and what we have will be what it should have been from the start—a business arrangement with a timeline and a deadline. Now, if you don't mind, I don't want to discuss this any longer. I won't be changing my mind and I don't want you to try to persuade me to. I'm going to go to sleep now and tomorrow...well, tomorrow will be another day...'

CHAPTER TEN

PROMISE NOTHING THAT you can't deliver...spare her the pain of wanting more than you can give...show her how the land lies without varnishing the truth and you'll both be in a better place, where nothing is expected except what's been put on the table...

It had all seemed very straightforward. Abe was well aware that his childhood had set the boundary of his emotional limitations years ago. The prospect of an arranged married had suited him just fine. There would be no risk to his heart, no loss to destroy his soul, and so he had engineered Georgie into the position of accepting the only thing he was making available to her: a marriage based on compatibility and great sex but without love and all its unwelcome complications. He had been upfront with her from the start and then, when he had uneasily suspected that she might have been straying from the straight and narrow, veering into the dangerous, turbulent territory of wanting more than he could ever give, he had tried to pull back, for both their sakes.

Hadn't that been what he had done the night before? Shown her, in not so many words, what their relationship was all about?

Now, glowering at three in the morning in the darkness of his office, brooding over the fact that she had effectively kicked him out of the bedroom, he tried to harness his normally very obedient pragmatism.

He had slung on a pair of loose joggers and a tee shirt and, with his feet on the desk and his leather chair pushed back, he continued to glare through the huge windows out to the darkened, limitless landscape outside.

She wanted more. She wanted love. She wanted the whole fairy-tale story with the happy-ever-after ending and there was no way that he could give her that. He'd already warned her it didn't exist.

He didn't do love! Except for his daughter, his heart was sealed behind a locked door and there was no key to open it up.

Perhaps it was best that all of this had come to a head when it had. She had offered a practical solution to the situation. They would still get married as planned. Tilly's security remained the most important thing and she recognised that as much as he did. Yes, sex would come to an end but perhaps that was a wise decision?

This could be a clean start for them. They would still communicate over what was important and doubtless would remain as compatible in that area as they always had been and if their marriage ended up feeling like a business deal, then wasn't that what it was all about anyway?

She had talked about timelines and deadlines and wasn't that exactly what was needed? A projected way forward with a definite end point? He might be deeply traditional in many ways, and certainly when it came to giving his own flesh and blood the life he knew she deserved, but he was realistic enough to know that relationships didn't necessarily last for ever and if, in the end, Georgie wanted to find love with someone capable of giving it to her, then why shouldn't she once Tilly was old enough for them to work out a suitable arrangement between them?

She had told him that, in essence, he was now a free man. They would marry but he would be able to find physical satisfaction outside wedlock.

He gritted his teeth.

It made all kinds of sense, yes, so why did everything inside him rebel at the prospect?

He pushed himself away from the desk, leapt to his feet and hit the ground running, right back to the bedroom because there was no way this conversation was finished yet.

Georgie was determined to get to sleep. She'd said what she'd wanted to say and the calm of knowing that she had done the right thing had not translated into a peaceful frame of mind.

She had given him permission to stray!

How was that going to play out? How was she going to deal with that? But what other option had she had when she had withdrawn the possibility of them ever sharing a bed together again?

Rather than think about it, she'd dived into her book, but the print had been blurry and her thoughts had been way too busy playing ping-pong for her to do anything other than *think, think, think*...

Eventually, Georgie fell into fitful sleep, so when she heard the bedroom door opening, it took her a few seconds to realise that Abe was back in the room.

She saw the outline of his muscular body framed momentarily in the doorway, backlit by the subdued lighting in the wide corridor outside. He'd changed into clothes but he was barefoot and she was still as he padded across to the bed.

'I know you're awake, Georgie.'

Georgie didn't bother pretending, especially when he followed up that opening remark by perching on the side of the bed.

She flipped over onto her back and shot up so that she was sitting.

'I don't want to talk about this any more, Abe,' she said quietly. 'I've said everything I want to say and now I just want to turn over a new page in this relationship.'

His response was to snap on the bedside light next to her, which made it impossible for her to conceal her expression or fake drowsiness.

'Tell me how you can say that I am not here for you,' he demanded.

'You're not here for me in the way I want you to be. You know exactly what I'm talking about because I told you and I didn't try to hide behind lots of empty words. I want love, Abe, and I deserve it.'

In that instant, Abe realised that sitting on the fence was no longer acceptable. He hadn't even known that that was what he had been doing. He had been protecting himself by suppressing his emotions and he had thought to be protecting *her* as well.

'You tell me that I can have my freedom,' he said gruffly, badly wanting to reach out and touch her, hurting in places he hadn't realised it was possible to hurt, 'and I can't think of anything worse.'

'Well, I'm very sorry to hear that, Abe, but we're finished when it comes to sleeping together. It should never have happened in the first place. I was weak.'

'There's nothing weak about two consenting adults enjoying one another in bed.'

'There is when one of them wants more.'

'Maybe both of them want more,' Abe muttered, suddenly restless and fidgety and stumbling in untried territory.

'What are you trying to say?' Georgie asked bluntly. 'If you think that you can somehow talk me back between the sheets, then it's not going to work. I need to protect myself, Abe, and this is the only way I can do it.'

'That was only ever my wish,' he ventured. 'To protect you.'

He shook his head and looked at her with such blazing sincerity that Georgie briefly averted her eyes, but the pull of his piercing gaze was too compelling. 'I wanted to protect you from...from *me*,' he told her. 'I thought I could never love you the way you needed me to. It wasn't in my make-up, Georgie. Love comes with pain and that was something I learnt from an early age when my mother died.'

'For goodness' sake, Abe,' Georgie cried helplessly, 'that shouldn't be the way it works.' She took a deep breath. 'Nothing is going to convince you otherwise,' she said, 'but my mother also died when I was young, remember? But I didn't let that dictate how I lived the rest of my life.'

'I know.' He half smiled. 'I suppose there was also the onus on me of knowing that one day I would be responsible for running Qaram and, when that time came, there would be no room in my life for the vagaries of love to distract me from doing my duty like it did my father.'

'Which brings us right back to what I told you earlier, Abe. It's over between us. We will provide a united front for Tilly's sake but, beyond that, we will lead our separate lives.'

'I can't do that.'

'Too bad.'

Why not? Georgie was never again going to allow *hope* to determine her behaviour and she firmly squashed all rising tendrils now.

Why was he here? Yes, of course, it was *his* bedroom. It was *his* palace and he could come and go wherever he pleased, but she had asked him to go away and she had meant it and so why was he back? It wasn't as though he were the sort of heartless creep to override what she wanted. He might not love her, but he was anything *but* a heartless creep.

'You tell me that you want more than…a business arrangement for Tilly's sake. More than just sex. I find that you are not alone in this.'

'What are you trying to say? You're talking in riddles, Abe, and I don't understand.'

'I never stopped to do the maths.' He lowered his head before looking at her once again. 'When I first met you, I never thought it would ever be anything more than a fling. It was how I was programmed to think. I had duties over here and that was all there was to it. We were ships passing in the night. Not telling you who I was seemed like a good idea at the time. Why would I? We've been here before, I know, and we have talked about this, but I met you, Georgie, and I'd never felt more liberated. I outstayed my welcome in Ibiza.' He smiled wistfully. 'Got back here to face the nightmare of my father in hospital and dire warnings to brace myself for the worst. I left thinking I had done the right thing in not saying goodbye, in sparing the inevitable conversation in which I would let you down. Perhaps I even thought that if you were incredibly angry with me and hated me for it, you would recover more quickly.'

'You're right,' she said shortly. 'We've talked about this and I don't want to go over old ground again.'

'Nor do I but I find I must. After you, Georgie, there was precious little on the relationship front...' He sighed and looked at her with such uncharacteristic hesitancy that she had to fight against some treacherous softening.

'Do you honestly think that I'm interested in hearing about what you got up to after we broke up?' she demanded jerkily. 'I'm not!'

'Hear me out, my darling. Please. I'm trying to find words I've never had to find in my life before. I should have been gearing up to marry. My father's early retirement, my taking over the duties of running the country... both those things should have propelled me into the next phase of my life, which was to marry and have children, but I couldn't seem to find the impetus. I know it was a constant source of worry to my father. The necessity of finding a suitable wife was an imperative and, in his depressed frame of mind, he had visions of dying without seeing me wed.' Abe paused. 'No one appealed to me and yet I never joined the dots, never saw the shadow you had cast. Georgie, what I didn't see was that you had managed to set a benchmark that no one else could ever come close to meeting.'

Georgie flushed. Was he lying? Was this some ploy to get her back onside? Surely he couldn't be so cruel?

'Then why didn't you get in touch?' she asked. 'If I set such a high benchmark? Why, Abe?'

'Looking back,' Abe said roughly, 'don't you think I don't realise that that was one of the biggest mistakes of my life? And not because of Tilly, not because I inadvertently missed out on so much, but because of you. Because I fell in love with you over the course of those three weeks and I never recovered. Maybe if I had had some calm in the beginning, I might have sat down and drawn all those conclusions I should have drawn from the start, but I got back to Qaram and then life became turbocharged. I barely had time to sleep, far less think. Or maybe I didn't want to think, didn't want to question everything I had made sure to build into my psyche from a young age.'

Georgie found that she was holding her breath. Her brain was also foggy and the tendrils of hope she had been forcefully shoving down now proliferated at speed.

Had he just said that he had fallen in love with her? Or was her fevered imagination playing tricks?

'It terrifies me, Georgie, to think that I might have continued to sleepwalk into believing that I could be happy without you by my side. I never saw love as part of the business of being married, I never wanted the chaos of being at the mercy of my emotions, but here I am, in love with you and happy to let my emotions chart the direction of my life. I don't want us to be married for convenience. I want us to be married for all those reasons I know you've always believed in. I can only hope that you still believe in them.'

'Oh, Abe.' She smiled and half laughed and pulled him towards her and didn't try to stop her tears. 'With every bit of me, I love you, and I will love you for ever.'

Ibiza. The sun. The azure sea. The turquoise skies above but, this time, no cheap hotel on a packed beach, even though she and Abe had gone right back to the place where they had first met, that buzzing little hotel with its crowded restaurant, the very hotel that had changed her life for ever. After all, this honeymoon was all about paying their nostalgic respects to the place where they had fallen in love, even though it had taken them four years of love lost and then found once again.

Now, she looked out to the infinity pool, where Abe was having fun with Tilly. The orange ball of the setting sun bathed them in a dusky glow. In a minute, they would head inside. The villa behind her was the very height of luxury, befitting royalty. Fatima, here with them, would take over settling Tilly and she and Abe...

She smiled to herself and gazed at the ring on her finger and thought that life could not get any more perfect.

Well...maybe it just about *could*...

On cue, Abe emerged from the pool, Tilly in his arms, sexier and more sinfully striking than any male had a right to be.

'What are you thinking?' he murmured, dipping to briefly kiss her on the mouth.

'I'm thinking we should open some champagne tonight,' Georgie returned as he swapped Tilly over to her before draping her in one of the fluffy white towels.

'I agree.' He slung his arm around her as they made their way inside. 'We need to celebrate the fact that we are here, together and married, because frankly life could not get any better.'

Georgie smiled. She thought back to their wedding a mere six weeks ago. It had been a huge affair, with journalists relishing the exquisite opulence, from the renowned orchestra that provided background music to the sit-down meal, to the ten-metre-long flower tunnel, the blush-pink and ivory flowers imported from Holland. She would remember every second of it and was especially pleased that all her friends from the hotel where she had worked in London had been flown out for the event.

It had been spectacular, as was this honeymoon, which had been delayed to accommodate Tilly's schooling.

Staff were on hand to make sure every need was met but Georgie had earlier given them the evening off. They had their own extensive residence in the grounds at the back but tonight was going to be a night without the lavishly prepared meal.

An hour later, having quickly showered and read a story to Tilly before Fatima took over, Georgie was in the kitchen.

'You're cooking.' Abe smiled, moved towards her and enfolded her in his arms, hands reaching down to cup her buttocks. 'I like that. I like it when you cook. Have I told you that?'

'You have. Many times, my darling.'

They had moved into the villa by the sea, a stone's throw from the palace but light years away in atmosphere. There was none of the formality of an army of staff tending to their every need. It was normality insofar as 'normality' could be categorised as having a top chef cook as and when requested and all cleaning and daily duties done by two girls who came early and left before dusk.

It was also where Georgie had resumed her painting, when she could find time amongst the many duties she had taken on ever since they had married.

'What are we having?' He moved to lift lids off pans and this time she was the one to put her arms around his waist, to rest her head against his back, breathing in his unique smell that could still send her into wonderful meltdown.

'Paella,' she murmured, turning him to face her and looking up into his eyes. 'As befitting where we are. And, of course, champagne, although I may not partake...'

'Tell me more...' He smiled and couldn't stop smiling.

'I don't think I need to, do I?' She tiptoed and kissed

him, feeling him still grinning as she drew back, his grin matching hers. 'In approximately eight months' time... you'll be a dad again...'

Abe couldn't think that it was possible to be as happy as he was this very moment. He was with the woman he adored and now they were going to add to their family. He couldn't stop smiling.

'And this time I get to enjoy the experience from the very start. My darling love, I can't wait...'

* * * * *

THE INNOCENT'S PROTECTOR IN PARADISE

ANNIE WEST

MILLS & BOON

To three wonderful women
who are always there when I need them:
Abby Green, Anna Campbell and Michelle Douglas.
Thank you!

PROLOGUE

'I'M WORRIED ABOUT LOLA. Something's seriously wrong but she won't tell me about it.'

Niall might have scoffed and asked how Ed could be sure there was a problem since his sister refused to share any details. But he trusted his best friend's judgement. Ed didn't worry over nothing.

Niall tucked the phone under his ear, turning to hear better over an airport announcement. 'What sort of wrong?'

'I don't know. She sounds…strained. You know what she's like. The world's worst liar. She tells me she's busy at work, but it's not that. The other day I heard a police siren in the background then she hung up quickly. When I asked later she said there'd been trouble in the street but her voice gave her away. Something's definitely wrong.'

Niall frowned. 'Police? You can't seriously think Lola's in strife with the cops.' Ed's little sister was the person least likely, ever, to commit a crime.

He remembered the first time he'd gone to the Suarez house with his new friend Ed after school. Little Lola had solemnly surveyed him with big eyes as if, wisely, unsure whether to trust him. But then he did have a cut lip and the beginning of a black eye after that scuffle in the street. He'd felt as if Ed's kid sister had seen straight beneath his teenage bravado to the dark emptiness beneath.

It was only later that he discovered little Lola wasn't judging him. In fact, over time she came to treat him like another big brother. It was change she didn't like, and he, a troubled newcomer, was definitely that.

'Maybe if you were home in Melbourne instead of working away, she'd confide.' There were six years between Lola and Ed but they were close. As close as any siblings he'd known.

Niall pinched the bridge of his nose, ignoring a sudden slam of emotion.

'That's the problem,' Ed huffed. 'I *can't* get away. I'm in Antarctica for months yet. That's why I want you to check on her. You're heading to Melbourne, aren't you?'

'I'm at the airport now.' Niall stared through the plate glass window at the planes on the tarmac. 'I'll drop by to see her this evening, after my meetings.'

Niall didn't need to think twice about doing as Ed asked. He owed the Suarez family a debt he could never repay. Together they'd turned his life around when he teetered on the edge of self-destruction. If it hadn't been for them, his would have been a short journey from misfit teenager to gangs, violence and a quick end.

They'd reminded him that there were good things left in the world and encouraged him to dream big.

'I knew I could rely on you, mate. Thanks. Just…do whatever you need to look after her. She's her own worst enemy, thinks she always has to be strong and not lean on anyone.' Ed's sigh filled his ear.

'Don't worry. I'll keep the kid safe. I'm quite fond of her.'

Even if he hadn't seen her in years. Niall did a quick calculation. He'd last seen Lola when he went back to Melbourne for her mother's funeral. Lola had been just shy of her sixteenth birthday. Her sombre new clothes, bought, he guessed, for the funeral, and her bleak expression, had belonged to someone much older.

Niall had done what he could to comfort her, offering a hug and a shoulder to cry on, but she'd withdrawn into herself as if embarrassed to touch him. Her features, an intriguing amalgam of teenager and adult, had been stiff with rejection.

He'd understood. At a time like that it was family that counted. Not a stray who'd been informally adopted by her open-hearted parents. When you got down to it, he wasn't a Suarez. His past, his record with his own family, were appalling, even if he'd since made good professionally.

Niall rubbed his hand around the back of his neck, hearing his boarding call. He didn't fly south often. Melbourne held too many memories he preferred to forget. He spent most of his time in Brisbane or overseas.

He strolled to the gate. 'Leave it to me, Ed. I promise to look after her.' He paused. 'Lola's probably just got a new boyfriend she doesn't want you to know about yet.' Niall grinned, wondering what the kid looked like now. Her mother had been beautiful.

'Then I leave it to you to check him out, since that's your area of expertise. Just don't let her fob you off.'

Fob him off? Little Lola? The idea tugged Niall's mouth into a smile. The pretty airline attendant waiting for him blinked, then returned his smile with an eager grin.

CHAPTER ONE

YOU'RE JUMPING TO CONCLUSIONS. Stay calm.

But Lola's heart pounded so fast it felt as if it might take off. The heavy thrum vibrated through her chest like a helicopter rising from the ground.

She *was* certain.

Someone had been in her flat.

She felt it as soon as she entered. Switching on the light, she stopped in the doorway, trying to figure out what was wrong. Everything looked the same at first glance. Nothing disturbed.

Yet something registered as she took a deep calming breath. An unfamiliar chemical scent.

Lola stepped back out onto the landing, looking around, but couldn't see any sign of cleaning or maintenance work.

She hesitated in the doorway, contemplating calling the police again. That was what eventually drove her inside. Knowing they'd respond to her call but find nothing conclusive. The more she phoned in, the less urgent her calls would seem, like the boy who cried wolf.

That had happened to Therese.

Lola shivered, remembering her one-time neighbour.

So here she was, still in her work clothes, chilled to the bone despite the heating she'd turned on high, trying to decide how much danger she was in.

Had Braithwaite watched her enter the apartment

block? She'd seen him, she was *sure* she'd seen him in the street these past weeks, though he'd disappeared quickly.

Had he watched her come into her flat tonight? Lola was sure she'd left the lounge room curtains closed when she went to work.

She crossed her arms, rubbing her hands up and down her sleeves, trying to get warm.

She went from room to room, checking the larger cupboards and under the bed, but she was alone.

Still she felt unnerved.

The doorbell rang and she jumped, nerves jangling.

It was half past seven and she wasn't expecting anyone. Her new neighbours kept to themselves. No dropping by for a chat or to borrow something.

Again it rang, the sound longer this time, as if whoever pressed the button knew she was in.

Braithwaite?

Lola froze, even stopped breathing for a moment as fear clamped its icy grip around her lungs and throat.

Had she locked the door?

Of course you did. You always do now.

Even so, her mind raced with awful imaginings of it opening and him coming in.

She grabbed her phone and thumbed in the emergency number just in case. Then she forced herself to walk the short hallway to the front door.

Gingerly, heart pounding an uneven tattoo, she peered through the spyhole.

It wasn't Braithwaite.

A relieved sigh eased from her lips.

She saw broad shoulders in a dark suit. A sliver of pale shirt collar and the back of a man's head. Glossy, black hair. Short hair, not like Braithwaite's. And Braithwaite wasn't as tall or broad-shouldered.

The man turned. His tie was askew as if he'd tugged it loose after a long day. He was too tall for her to see his eyes through the peephole, but she registered a firm, determined chin and a sensual mouth bracketed by grooves that should look grim yet instead made her insides flutter.

Lola's hand went to her throat. Her pulse hammered there as if her heart had risen from her ribcage, leaving her chest hollow.

No, not Braithwaite.

But another man she'd give almost anything not to see.

Niall Pedersen.

What was *he* doing here?

He made a habit of arriving when she was at her most vulnerable. Last time had been for her mother's funeral.

Lola's mouth twisted with grim humour even as her belly curdled with pain and resentment. And a stubborn kernel of something else she still hadn't managed to eradicate and refused to think about.

She shut her eyes and counted to five, trying to shove down the wobbly, vulnerable feeling that everything was spinning out of control. She reached out and unlocked the door just as the buzzer sounded for a third time.

Niall filled the doorway. Had he been so broad across the shoulders eight years ago?

Lola told herself she couldn't remember, when in fact she had perfect recall.

Why did she stand, gawping up as if she'd never seen him before?

Because eight years had done more than fill out the lean promise of youth. It had given him an air of authority and assurance and etched new lines around his mouth and eyes that transformed a handsome youth into a man with serious charisma.

Lola's knees threatened to buckle and she hung onto the door handle, silently cursing.

He didn't know it but this man had blighted her life. She'd do well to remember it.

'Niall, this is unexpected.' Her voice was deeper than he'd expected and slightly husky. He felt it as a ripple of pleasure through his belly and a tingling awareness even lower.

For an instant he stared, mind blank while his hormones sped into overdrive. Until logic kicked in.

Lola. Ed's kid sister. The girl he'd come to help.

Girl no longer. She was a woman now.

Niall swallowed, amazed to feel his throat constrict.

He'd known she'd be different. He just hadn't reckoned on how different.

'Lola.' He managed, just, to keep the question from his voice. As if, even knowing it had to be her, he couldn't reconcile the sweet, serious kid he'd known with this woman. 'It's good to see you.'

His gaze skated over her dark grey pencil skirt to long legs in shimmery hose and high heels. His smile solidified as he followed svelte curves then returned to her face.

She'd grown into her nose and her wide mouth. And those eyes, that had once made her look like a serious little owl, were the lustrous eyes of a beautiful woman.

She looked stern and sexy at the same time. As if her rigidly pulled-back hair and business suit camouflaged a sultry woman who...

Niall stiffened, horrified. This was *Lola*! He did *not* think about Ed's little sister that way.

Even so, he wished his mate had warned him. All these years when he'd mentioned Lola he'd never once hinted she'd turned into a stunner.

Of course she's altered. It's been almost a decade.

Yet Niall felt sideswiped by the change in her.

'What are you—?' she began.

'Are you going to invite me—?' he said at the same time.

Her lips flattened, surprising him. For she, and the rest of the Suarez family, had always been generously hospitable. Then her expression changed, her mouth tilted up at the corners as she stepped back and waved him in. 'Please, come in.'

It was only as he passed her that he saw the phone in her hand, her thumb hovering over the call button.

'Have I come at a bad time?'

A second's hesitation then she shook her head. Yet she didn't meet his eyes as she shut and locked the door behind him.

'No, I've just got home and wasn't expecting anyone.'

'You work long hours,' he observed, trying not to focus on the movement of her hips beneath the tailored skirt as he followed her into a sitting room.

Niall looked around curiously. The place was furnished in soothing pale greens and white. Except for one bright pop of colour, a tumble of cushions on the sofa in bright orange and bronze. A bookcase was stacked full, the bottom shelves with big, serious-looking books on management and finance and the top with fiction titles.

'I've got a big project on at the moment. I'm sure you know how it is. You didn't get where you are by working nine to five.'

Niall nodded. 'True.' He'd worked hard for his success, CEO of a multibillion-dollar enterprise in his early thirties.

He waited for her to take a seat, but she stood in the entrance to the room, shoulders high and hands clasped as if not sure what to do with them.

Strange. The way she dressed, and the confident sway of her body as she'd strode down the hallway, projected an assured, capable woman. But the vibe he got was something else. His eyes narrowed. Was she biting the corner of her mouth?

It was something she used to do when nervous.

Time telescoped and for a second he was back in the Suarez family kitchen, watching little Lola fret over a school assignment. She'd been convinced she'd fail, till Niall took pity on her and checked it for her, reassuring her she'd not only pass but do brilliantly.

'I'm in Melbourne on business and wondered if you'd like to go to dinner. I don't get here often and thought it would be good to catch up.'

'Dinner?' She looked at him as if she'd never heard the

word before. Not the reaction he usually got when he asked a woman out.

'I realise it's short notice.'

'I... That's very kind of you.' She flashed a smile that didn't reach her eyes. 'Any other time and I'd love to. But it's been a long day and I have an early start tomorrow.'

'I understand.' Yet his sixth sense, alerted by Ed's call, told him there was something more than tiredness here. Which was why he didn't take the hint and leave. After all, they were as good as family. 'How about we order some food in? I can organise it while you get out of your office clothes.' His gaze strayed of its own volition to her slender legs in those heels and he yanked it back up again.

'Oh!' He could see her trying to think of a reason to refuse.

'Just a quick meal.' He reassured her. 'I've got a heavy schedule tomorrow myself.' He sweetened the words with a smile and watched her blink. The tightness around her mouth eased a little.

Warmth filled him. This wasn't just about a favour to Ed. He mightn't have seen Lola in years but he still cared about her. He saw faint shadows beneath her eyes and concern stirred.

'Thank you. But—'

'Unless you're expecting someone. A boyfriend maybe?'

'No. No boyfriend.' Her eyes widened a little as if surprised she'd let the words slip.

Niall felt a punch of something that might have been satisfaction. Because he could at least report to Ed that there was no guy turning Lola's life upside down.

'I'd like to hear what you're doing these days.' He paused. 'And I'd love company. Being in the city has brought back a lot of memories.' It was true. His spine had been stiff all day as the ghosts of the past followed him.

He spread his hands and offered a rueful smile. She didn't know his whole story, but enough to understand there were dark shadows over his early years. Not even Ed knew all the details.

Niall saw her waver, her desire to be alone fighting her soft heart.

She nodded abruptly. 'That would be…nice. I could do with company too.' Then she smiled. A genuine smile that clogged his airways for a second.

Because Niall was still getting used to this new Lola. Once the novelty wore off, he'd go back to thinking of her as he always had. Little Lola.

Not as a disturbingly attractive woman.

'Excellent. What sort of food do you want?'

'There's a great Thai place down the road. The menu's on the fridge. Help yourself.' She spun on her heel and headed towards her bedroom.

The lights were already on in the gleaming kitchen. He stood in the doorway, noting that in this at least she hadn't changed. Lola wasn't obsessive, but the difference between her space and Ed's had always been a family joke. Ed thrived on clutter while Lola had everything in its right place.

It was good to know she hadn't changed completely. She'd always been organised and thoughtful. Tender-hearted too, hence her being swayed by his apparent need for company. And determined. When she set her mind to something she didn't give up.

Here there was no clutter. The pristine white was softened by a row of potted herbs along the windowsill. Niall passed them then paused.

Something smelled odd.

He retraced his steps then leaned across, inhaling. Slowly he turned first one pot around then another and another.

Each plant was dead on the side that had faced the window. Not gradually ageing, but green and alive on one side and completely dead and shrivelled on the other. The difference between the two halves was a clear line straight down the middle.

He leaned forward and an acrid odour hit his nostrils. He jerked back, grimacing.

Something noxious had been put on each plant. But so neatly it might have been done using a ruler.

Niall frowned. Lola wouldn't make a mistake like that. She'd always had a green thumb, helping her mother in the garden.

His nape prickled as he stared at the damaged plants. Poisoned, if he guessed correctly. That was what he smelled. The lingering scent of acid.

He could think of no sane reason why Lola would half poison her plants. Especially ones she used in cooking.

His sixth sense stirred. The one that had kept him alive in his teens when he'd hung with a crowd that was rougher and more dangerous than he. That instinct had saved him more than once. Nowadays the closest he came to experiencing it was as a frisson of excitement that told him a new software breakthrough, or a new business opportunity, promised success.

He stood still, surveying the kitchen.

Everything gleamed and even the single flyer on the fridge sat precisely square. A blue and white checked tea towel hung neatly over the oven's handle. The benchtop was clear except for a blue bowl full of winter oranges, a gleaming stainless-steel electric jug and an empty, clear glass teapot.

No, not empty. As Niall turned he caught sight of something that glinted.

He stepped back and saw he was mistaken. The teapot was empty, ready for the next brew. Yet that warning niggle persisted. He swept his gaze around the kitchen, then reached for the teapot and pulled the lid off.

Niall carried it directly under the kitchen light, surveying the clear residue in the bottom of the vessel.

Every hair on his neck and arms stood up as he inspected the tiny grains. He touched them with his index finger and lifted it for closer inspection.

Not sugar, as he'd first thought.

Ground glass.

Someone had sabotaged Lola's kitchen horrifically. If she'd made tea, not really paying attention, she'd have taken the lid off the pot, added tea then water, and poured herself a cup laced with glass.

Niall shuddered. Whoever had done this hadn't just planned to scare Lola. Her tormentor meant to do serious harm. It didn't matter that, contrary to common belief, this wasn't likely to be lethal. What mattered was the guy's intent. That was more than ugly. *It was murderous.*

Niall slammed the teapot onto the bench and seconds later was pounding on her closed bedroom door.

'Lola? Are you okay?'

Silence. His imagination ran riot. If someone had sabotaged her kitchen, what about her bedroom?

Grabbing the handle, he turned it and shoved, just as she pulled it open. Niall's momentum took him across the threshold, straight into Lola.

His heart slammed his ribs, relief filling him as his hands closed around her. Soft curves pressed into him as he absorbed her scented warmth.

She was safe.

'Niall? What's going on?' She scowled up at him, eyes narrowing as she reared back.

Reluctantly he released her, fighting another instinct. This one urged him to pull her hard against him and keep her there.

Protectiveness?

Or a compulsion that sprang not from anything so pure, but from his primal response to her soft femininity in that split second of full body contact?

The insight stunned him.

Niall gritted his jaw and stepped back, putting more distance between them.

She's fine, he assured himself.

Actually she was more than fine, in slim-fitting jeans and a soft green sweater that drew his eyes to her willowy frame.

'Sorry. I didn't mean to barge in. Is everything okay here?'

He forced himself to look past her, taking in the feminine room. The antique mirror and the collection of delicate fans in custom-made glass-fronted frames on one wall. The floor-to-ceiling wardrobe. The cream-covered bed, strewn with ruby-red cushions.

'Why wouldn't it be?' Yet her voice betrayed her. Lola was nervous.

Niall's gaze fixed on her lovely features. She was too pale and once more she gnawed on her lip. 'Are you going to tell me what's going on?'

Lola's chin shot up but she couldn't look him in the eye. 'I don't know what you mean.'

Tell him!

And what's he going to do? He lives at the other end of the country. He can't protect you. He'll just fuss and tell Ed who'll then fret because he's not here.

'Someone's been in your apartment.'

Her eyes widened. Reluctantly she looked up from that sexy mouth and uncompromising chin to navy-blue eyes that even after eight years still had the power to undo her.

Something deep, deep within crumpled.

The hope she'd clung to, that by now she'd have shed this unwanted crush, faded, leaving her floundering.

Lola breathed deep, marshalling her thoughts. How could she even think about her response to Niall at a time like this?

Because fixating on all that raw masculinity was preferable to thinking about the danger she was in. The danger the police seemed unable to tackle.

She was terrified. She'd been scared for weeks and it was wearing her out.

Lola took another breath and clawed back some control. 'How do you know?' She'd been here a full five minutes before Niall and hadn't been able to pinpoint what was different about the place. Apart from the smell.

'I'll show you in a moment.' His brows gathered in a frown. 'You know who it was, don't you?' Niall's expression morphed from concerned to angry. 'Is it a man? Did you give him a key?'

No, not angry. *Furious.*

As if it were her fault that she was being stalked!

The realisation snapped her out of shocked stasis.

'No. I didn't give anyone a key.'

Black eyebrows rose and his mobile mouth pulled into a grimace that spoke of distaste. 'Okay. How about someone you invited back here. Someone who stayed the night. They could have taken an impression of your key when you weren't looking and got a spare made.'

That was a laugh.

There'd been no men in her life, not in that sense.

Not for want of trying on Lola's part. The thought mocked her. But no matter how hopeful she was when agreeing to a date, it inevitably failed to lead anywhere. For no man lived up to the ideal she'd built in her head.

Her fault, she knew. And this man's.

That, alone, was reason to hate him.

'You really don't have much faith in my judgement, do you?' If anything, she set her standards too high. It was a problem she'd tried, and failed, to rectify.

Her gaze skated across those straight shoulders, taking in his lean body that looked so athletic and potently masculine.

Lola shut her eyes, willing herself to concentrate.

'Just tell me. How do you know someone's been here?' She opened her eyes to find him canting towards her, his eyes fixed on her mouth. Heat drilled down, filling her with melting sensations she wished she could feel with some other man. *Any* other man!

Niall straightened, his expression grim. 'Come.' He stood back and led the way to the kitchen.

Relieved, she followed, eager to shift her focus. The room looked the same as ever, except…

Lola gasped when she saw her herbs. That faint smell was stronger here, strong enough that as she got close it caught the back of her throat.

Or maybe that was fear.

Her eyes widened as she saw the withered foliage. No, not withered. Burnt. He'd burnt them with acid.

Lola's hand went to her mouth as she gagged, remembering what had happened to Therese. The sear of acid on flesh. Lola's other arm wrapped around her middle as her insides cramped, stomach curdling. A cry of horror escaped before she could stop it.

It was Braithwaite. Not her imagination, as the last police officer had tried to convince her.

'Lola? Lola!' Strong arms encircled her and pulled her close. Niall was tall and taut with muscle. For a few seconds she stood stiff and unresisting, afraid that leaning on him felt too easy when she had to remain strong.

But as Niall's heat seeped into her, inevitably she sagged against him, the great shudders racking her gradually subsiding into tremors.

It felt like a lifetime since she'd let herself relax. She'd been on alert so long. How long since she'd stood this close to someone? Not since her dad took off on his round-Australia camping trip six months ago.

'It's okay, Lola.' Niall's deep voice resonated through her as she leaned against him.

She opened her mouth to say it wasn't okay. It was a horrible, frightening mess. Instead she shut her eyes and let her head rest against him. Nestled here, it wasn't acid she smelled but cedar, spice and warm male. Lola drank it in greedily.

One large hand slowly circled her back. A gesture of comfort that eased the knot of unbearable tension she'd carried high in her chest for weeks.

Finally, when the temptation never to move grew too

strong, she lifted her head. Somehow her arms had gone around Niall, circling tight as if clutching at safety. Hastily she released him, stepping back.

At least now her heart wasn't hammering in her throat. The panic had edged down to manageable levels.

'Sorry, Niall. I'm not usually so…' She shrugged, preferring not to put into words her vulnerability.

'Don't apologise.' His voice was gruff and she watched his chest rise on a deep breath. Finally she lifted her gaze to his face and her newfound sense of strength ebbed.

'What is it? Is there something else?' His expression was so grim, fear feathered her spine.

'Isn't that enough? Come on, let's get you out of here.'

'Out?' Lola frowned. 'I need to call the police. Report an intruder.'

Niall was already ushering her out of the kitchen. 'Of course. But it doesn't have to be now. Tomorrow during business hours will do. I'll make sure the place is secure so no one can enter in the meantime.'

It was tempting, the thought of walking away and leaving this for tomorrow. It had been a long, trying day, and the police interview would make it longer. She already felt exhausted.

'My car's outside. We can get you a bed where I'm staying and forget all this till the morning.'

Impossible to forget, but how she longed to escape this nightmare, even if for one night. Maybe then she'd find her usual energy and determination.

She looked into that concerned dark blue stare and was suddenly glad Niall had come. 'I'll pack a bag.'

CHAPTER TWO

NIALL WATCHED HER go to her room and released a slow breath. A shudder of frustration and fury coursed through him. Fury at what had happened and frustration that he didn't have a quick fix for Lola.

Why had Ed waited so long to help her? Her brother, or someone, should have been looking out for her!

Whoever had done this had, judging by Lola's response, been active before. He guessed she knew the intruder.

His belly clenched. Was it an ex-lover? Someone Lola had been intimate with? Nausea stirred.

He grimaced. He had trouble imagining her with a man. Not because she wasn't attractive but...

Because he wanted that man to be him?

Her slender body, sultry mouth and combination of feistiness and softness made him ache in places he shouldn't. That was wrong in so many ways. Self-disgust filled him and he told himself it was the shock of seeing her all grown up. It couldn't be anything more. He wouldn't allow it.

Yet it was beyond him to think of this as simply a protection job. The sort his staff dealt with regularly. He'd wanted to scoop Lola into his arms and tell her it would be all right. That he'd look after her.

A pang of old, familiar guilt knifed his gut. The fear that, once more, he would fail in his duty. But he ignored it. He couldn't dwell on past mistakes now.

That desire to protect had stopped him telling Lola about the ground glass. About the immediate physical threat. The intruder hadn't just wanted to scare her. He'd intended serious physical harm.

Niall had been on the point of telling her then decided against it. Even as a child, Lola had done a good job of appearing calm when she was worried. She hated admitting she was out of her depth. Yet those acid-damaged plants had undone her totally. Clearly she'd been at the end of her tether.

The sight of her dazed hazel eyes, more brown than green, and dull with distress, had twisted his vitals. The feel of her, shaking as she burrowed against him, the way she'd clung...

How could he add to her fear by revealing the cruel trap set for her?

Time enough later, when she was calm and rested.

Glancing at the bedroom door, Niall moved away and pulled out his phone. Pedersen Security's Melbourne office was staffed twenty-four hours a day, seven days a week. Securing the premises till the police arrived tomorrow was easily done.

As he issued his instructions, low-voiced, he began searching. For that sixth sense still hummed. It told him there was more to find.

What else had the bastard left? Another boobytrap?

A couple of minutes later he found it. Not a boobytrap but a camera concealed high in the hallway.

It wasn't the highest spec. Not the sort of equipment his own company supplied. But it would do the job, giving an unseen watcher a clear view of the lounge room and the bedroom and bathroom doorways.

Ice crackled along his bones. Yet it did nothing to quench the searing wrath in his belly.

How long had the camera been there?

Were there more? In the bathroom perhaps?

Pain cracked through Niall's jaw and he realised he was grinding his teeth.

He wanted to get his hands on whoever was doing this.

A noise made him turn and there was Lola, emerging from the bedroom with an overnight bag and a laptop. She looked slender and defenceless, despite her pushed-back shoulders and calm expression.

Too calm. Her eyes betrayed her as did the tremor in her hand as she hitched her shoulder bag up.

Niall strode forward and took the overnight case.

'All ready?' He forced a reassuring note to his voice and saw the tight pinch of her mouth ease.

'Yes, let's get out of here.'

He nodded and opened the door for her. He'd promised Ed that he'd keep her safe. He'd keep that promise, no matter what it took.

Niall knew the consequences of failure too well. He refused to live with another life on his conscience.

He'd protect Lola and stop whoever was hurting her.

She wouldn't come back until he knew it was completely safe.

Lola had spent the drive into the city in a fog of anxiety and anger. It was only when Niall pulled up at the entrance to Melbourne's grandest hotel that she blinked and realised where she was.

By then a uniformed staff member was opening the car for her while another stood before huge gilt and glass doors, where a crimson carpet led into a stunning atrium.

Niall's a billionaire. Of course he stays at the best.

Yet it took Lola by surprise. When she thought of him it wasn't his wealth that came to mind, or the astronomical success he'd achieved following his breakthrough, developing security software that had revolutionised the industry.

Lola knew all about it because she'd followed his success via Ed's updates and the press reports. He was a favourite subject, since his small Brisbane security firm had grown into an international success story. And because he was perfect fodder for the media, handsome, rich and with an endless supply of gorgeous blonde companions.

She tried to gather her thoughts, watching Niall speak to a porter, refusing assistance with her bag.

He was unfazed by the grand surroundings. She, on the other hand, felt rumpled and out of place. She longed for somewhere quiet and cosy to regroup, not this palatial place.

Niall had never been cowed by anything. Neither authority figures nor brute force. As a teenager he'd stood up to school bullies. For a while it seemed he was always in fights. On the other hand he'd taken time to help her with her homework and let her hang around while he and Ed tinkered on old computers or while he practised martial arts.

He'd been like another brother.

But it was a long time since she'd thought of him like that.

'Ready?' There it was. A warmth in those dark blue eyes that she recognised from years ago. When she'd hung on his every word and he'd responded with infinite patience.

Maybe he'd never noticed her massive crush. She could only hope.

'Yes.' Lola hefted her laptop case and hitched her shoulder bag, preceding him.

Instead of going to the reception desk, Niall led her towards a bank of lifts.

'I need to check in.'

The doors slid open with a discreet ping and he ushered her inside.

'There's plenty of room in my suite. You can have a shower or bath while I order dinner. That way you don't have to go anywhere or do anything until tomorrow.'

It was a sign of how shattered she felt that it sounded like paradise. Lola's protest died.

That was how, thirty minutes later, she found herself in the most luxurious bathroom she'd ever seen, staring out of the full-length window at the city lights. Niall's suite was an apartment-style penthouse with a view of the Yarra River winding through the CBD.

Her little flat and all her troubles seemed a world away.

Except for the burr of apprehension beneath her skin. Even the long, hot shower, the ruthless scrubbing of hair and skin, couldn't eradicate the taint of fear.

She tasted it still on her tongue.

With a moue of self-disgust she cinched the belt of the soft-as-a-cloud plush robe she'd found. It was crazy but she couldn't bring herself to put her jeans and sweater on again, though she'd only worn them half an hour.

Because they made her think of that ravaged scene in her kitchen. Lola shut her eyes, catching again the pungent scent of acid.

She snapped her eyes open and saw herself in the mirror. Face too pale. Scared, mud-coloured eyes. Her hair several shades darker from being wet and already beginning to curl. But she didn't have the energy to straighten it.

After all, she wasn't dressing to impress Niall.

No matter what feminine pride urged.

Sweeping up her clothes, she entered the bedroom. The door on the far side was open and through it she saw Niall, pacing the massive lounge room as he spoke, low-voiced, on the phone.

Lola didn't think she'd made any noise but instantly his head turned, dark eyes snaring hers.

It was nonsense to believe that stare stopped her in her tracks. Or sent awareness sizzling through her. Or snagged the breath in her lungs, making them tight.

She was over him. Had been over him for years.

Her mouth lifted in a rueful grimace. There was nothing to get over. There'd never been anything between them. Just juvenile hopes that should have died a natural death by now.

Besides, Niall had always been drawn to curvy blondes, never mediocre brunettes. In his teens that bias had been a bit of a joke between him and Ed. But his preference had lasted, proven by every press photo of him with a gorgeous woman at his side, and Ed's comments about his friend's predictability.

Niall only dated blondes. Glamorous, sophisticated blondes. He would never look at her and think *desirable woman*. Even if she dyed her hair, which she wasn't planning, she'd never manage the sophisticated, overtly glamorous style he favoured. Or the bombshell body.

She was happy as she was. She wasn't pining for Niall any more.

Lola turned away, rummaging in her bag for something to wear. She didn't have much choice. It was tomorrow's work clothes or pyjamas.

She reached for the long pyjamas, plain white flannelette with a sprinkling of red hearts. Plain white buttons down the loose-fitting shirt. Her grim smile turned into a husky laugh that made her throat ache. This was as far from slinky, enticing lingerie as you could get.

'Dinner's ready if you are.' Niall stood in the doorway, his expression unreadable.

Even so, Lola felt suddenly hyper-conscious of the way the plush robe rubbed against her nipples, thighs and stomach as she moved. A snaking tendril of awareness writhed in that hollow place between her thighs.

People said sexual arousal was common after danger. It was a survival instinct. And, though Braithwaite hadn't put her in physical danger, it felt that way.

That was the simplest, the only acceptable explanation of her response to feeling Niall's gaze, heavy as a touch on her body.

'I'll be ready in a moment.'

Lola refused to share a meal with him wearing nothing but a robe, even if it covered her from neck to knee.

'Very cute,' he murmured minutes later when she pulled a chair up to the table where he'd put an array of covered plates.

'Sorry?'

'The hearts.' He nodded to the collar of her thick pyjamas, visible behind the V-neck of her robe. 'They're cute.'

Lola opened her mouth to tell him women didn't want to be called cute, then realised that might invite speculation on what she did want to hear. She busied herself lifting the lids keeping the food warm.

'I hope you're hungry. There's enough here to feed an army.'

He shrugged and she fought not to stare. With his tailored jacket off and sleeves rolled up Niall looked too accessible and attractive for her peace of mind.

'I wasn't sure what you liked so I chose a variety. As I recall you have a healthy appetite.'

Which was a polite way of saying she'd comfort eaten through puberty.

Niall probably thought of her as she'd been at twelve or thirteen. Chubby and frumpy with her home-made clothes that she was always either growing into or out of. The flannel pyjamas would reinforce the image.

For a second she wished she'd packed a whisper-thin nightie and matching robe of black lace, sexy and alluring. Except she didn't look good in black and she didn't have anything like that in her wardrobe.

How nice it would be, just once, to steal Niall's breath. To have him think her impossibly irresistible.

Dream on, Lola!

Determined, she forced herself to concentrate on the food, taking a sample of everything and telling herself she needed to refuel. The last few days had been frantic at work and at home she'd been too unsettled to cook a proper meal. Maybe that was why tonight's events made her feel so weak and worried.

Or it could be because Braithwaite actually got into your flat!

If he'd been inside when you got home...

She shivered and put her cutlery down with a clatter, horror glazing her vision and tightening her throat.

'Are you ready to tell me about it?'

The words were smooth, as if Niall had an unquestionable right to know everything.

Lola was used to being the capable one. The one who looked after others, not the one needing care.

For a second she felt again that horrible sense of total helplessness, when the world had turned on its head. It had engulfed her when she was a teenager. Her mother had died and her father, lost without his other half, had numbed the pain with a catastrophic drinking and gambling binge, losing his job, almost losing the house, and heading towards self-destruction. Ed had been away at university and didn't see everything. It had been left to Lola to support her dad and help him find a way out, back to the real world.

She'd find a way out of this. She had to.

She refused to let Braithwaite destroy her.

'Lola?' A warm, callused hand covered hers. 'You don't have to tell me now. But you need to know I'll do whatever it takes to keep you safe. I promise.'

She raised her eyes and blinked to clear her vision.

Niall looked as serious as she'd ever seen him. As if the sight of her so troubled got under his skin. He'd always been protective.

But she'd learnt to rely on herself. To solve her own problems, in the process becoming a stalwart for others when things went wrong.

Yet she was weary. So tired of being strong.

Niall deserved some explanation, even if his protection could only be short term while he visited Melbourne. They said talking was therapeutic. Lola had lost track of the number of friends who, over the years, had come to her for a shoulder to cry on.

Nevertheless she hesitated. Sharing this would invite Niall

into her private life. A place she'd tried and failed to keep free of his shadow.

'Thanks, Niall. It's kind of you to go to so much effort for someone you don't even know any more.'

His eyebrows soared. 'I know it's been a while, Lola, but surely we're still friends.'

Was that a shadow of hurt in his eyes? Surely not. Niall was a tough, self-made tycoon with the world at his feet. He wouldn't fret over old ties.

Except, according to Ed, Niall was closer to the Suarez family than he was to his estranged father, his only living relative. Perhaps Lola wasn't the only one for whom those golden years when her parents had welcomed Niall into their family were special.

'Of course.'

'And you trust me.' His gaze held hers and it felt as if something powerful passed between them. Something more than shared memories. 'Like a brother.'

How Lola wished that were true. She did trust him. But as a brother? Not given the effect he had on her hormones.

Still.

Always.

Despair scoured her and she looked away, desperate for something else to focus on.

Too much had happened today. Her emotions were too close to the surface.

He lifted a bottle of wine towards her glass in silent question. Her eyes rounded as she read the label. It was an iconic Australian Shiraz she'd never had the money to order and probably never would. Another reminder that Niall Pedersen now lived in a completely different world.

She nodded. A lovely smooth glass of red would warm her against the chill still frosting her bones. 'Yes, please.'

Lola ate a forkful of steaming beef and mushroom pie, her eyes closing in appreciation of the rich flavour and the buttery, flaky texture of fresh-made pastry.

The food was delicious and, to her surprise, so was the companionable atmosphere that gradually developed. Niall gave up prodding and settled in to share the meal with her, chatting across a range of subjects that didn't require much input. Slowly she felt herself sink further into her comfortable chair.

It was as Niall poured her a second glass of the gorgeous wine that she made up her mind to tell him. Possibly because he hadn't kept pushing but respected her need for peace.

Besides, she discovered, she *wanted* to share with him. Maybe because he'd be gone soon. It would be like unburdening herself to a stranger she wouldn't see again.

She took a slow sip of the Shiraz, enjoying its mellow flavour and her burgeoning sense of comfort. How different from the stress of the last weeks.

'His name is Braithwaite. Jayden Braithwaite. He's...' she paused, remembering her last police interview and the insistence on facts '... I *think* he's stalking me.'

'How do you know him?' Instead of watching her, Niall concentrated on buttering a crusty bread roll. Because he knew it was easier to talk about difficult things without being stared at?

'He used to live next door. He was my ex-neighbour, Therese's partner.'

Dark eyes snared hers. 'Your neighbour's partner?'

Did Lola imagine the stress on the word *neighbour*? She frowned.

'Braithwaite wasn't my type.' She shuddered and took another small sip from her glass.

Niall said nothing, just nodded and turned his attention to the bread.

'Over time Therese became scared. He grew controlling, even over simple things like talking to neighbours or going to buy groceries. Things escalated and he became violent.' Lola paused, remembering the sound of screams and falling furniture. 'She kicked him out.'

'But he didn't stay away?'

Lola slanted a look into that dark, intent face.

'He stalked her. Made her life hell. She never knew when he was going to appear. He sent letters begging her to let him move back and at the same time posted flyers in the neighbourhood and to her colleagues at work, saying awful things about her.'

'And the police?'

'Said they didn't have enough evidence. They couldn't get DNA evidence linking him to the letters and posters. Even when the attacks got worse, slashed car tyres, disgusting things sent through the mail...' Lola rubbed her hands up and down her arms. 'Finally, he caught her walking to her car and threw acid over her.'

Niall swore, low and savage, and for some reason the sound eased Lola's distress.

'How is she?'

Lola shrugged. 'She survived. She turned when she saw him and the acid only hit her arm and shoulder. That was bad enough. It's not just physical scars she carries.' Lola's voice choked off.

'You were there?' Once more that firm hand covered hers and she was glad of the contact.

'I was on my balcony and saw what happened. I managed to snap a photo of him. It was one of the reasons they finally managed to lock him away.'

'So he blames you for his prison sentence?'

She nodded jerkily. 'He somehow got a lenient sentence and he's recently been released. Therese moved away and changed her name but I'm in the same place. I've seen him a couple of times. I know it's him. I just can't prove he's following me.'

'Tonight's not the first time he's bothered you?'

Lola sank back in her chair, but that lovely mellow feeling was gone. 'It's been weeks.' Fraught weeks as she wound tighter and tighter trying to anticipate what he'd do next.

Niall turned her hand over on the table and threaded his fingers through hers. His were longer and stronger, yet their joined hands felt matched. Lola looked down at them, wondering why that should be.

But then her nerves were stretched thin. Any reassuring touch would feel good.

'He's been following you. What else?'

She shivered and he squeezed her hand. Strange how that simple reassurance made it easier to gather her shredded self-control.

'I've got a list on the computer with dates, times and photos.'

'He sent you mail?'

'No. But there are other things.'

She hurried on, giving a truncated version. 'It started with phone calls at all hours of the night. Then the feeling I was being followed. Nuisance phone calls at work. Messages that my father or Ed had been in an accident, dragging me out of meetings to deal with emergencies that didn't exist.' She'd been overwhelmed with relief each time, but her stress levels had steadily built and never had a chance to reduce.

'Damage to my front door. Then a cricket ball through the bedroom window.'

'Were you hurt?' His fingers tightened around hers.

'I wasn't home.'

'What did the police say?'

She shrugged. 'I'm only one floor up. They said it could have been kids playing.'

'And the damage to the door?'

'Vandals. There was nothing to link it to Braithwaite.'

'What else?'

'A dead mouse in the letter box. Then a dead rat on the balcony.' Lola reached for her glass, swirling the dark liquid. 'My cat, well, Therese's cat, but I adopted it when she moved...it got run over. I found it on the footpath when I got home last night.'

Needing time, she sipped her wine, but now it tasted sour. She put it down and pulled her hand free of Niall's.

It was time to regroup. Be strong. Niall wouldn't be around to fight her battles. That was up to her.

'The incidents have been escalating.'

Her head jerked up, her gaze colliding with his. That was what had scared her—what came next.

'Yes. Then today…' She didn't finish. The thought of that man in her home made her sick. 'You said you'd secure the flat tonight. I should have asked—'

'Don't fret about it. Pedersen Security staff are guarding it till the police come tomorrow. After that, we'll install better locks and ongoing security.'

Niall made it seem easy.

She had no idea about security systems. All she knew was that she never again wanted to discover Braithwaite had been in her space.

'Thank you. You're very kind.'

Something flashed across his sculpted features. 'It's nothing. Easily taken care of.'

His tone told her Niall understood how serious this was. He was anything but dismissive.

Lola exhaled slowly, relieved that at last there was someone who understood. The police had varied from disbelieving to sympathetic but pessimistic about proving Braithwaite's involvement.

She hadn't given her work colleagues the full story, not wanting to be seen as a helpless victim starring in some ongoing drama. She'd worked incredibly hard to build her strong professional reputation. She didn't want to distract people from that when she stood on the cusp of what might be her big break. Her bosses would be sympathetic, but she wanted them to think of her as a rising star, not someone needing sympathy.

'Thanks for listening,' she murmured. 'It's good to get it

off my chest.' It felt as if someone had loosened a tight band around her ribs. Her breath came more easily.

'What are friends for?' He lifted his glass and took a long sip. 'It turns out my meetings tomorrow are starting late. While you're talking to the police, I'll make the necessary arrangements. We'll keep you safe until your stalker is dealt with. You have my word on it.'

CHAPTER THREE

LOLA HUFFED OUT a tired breath. The office was empty this late on a Friday and she'd worked on overdrive to wrap up everything.

After starting the day with the police, she'd been way behind when she got to work and barely had enough time to run through her part of the presentation before it began.

At least work was an antidote to her anxiety over Braithwaite. The semi-permanent frisson of anxiety rippling under her skin had eased with today's good news.

A smile tugged her mouth. She still couldn't believe it. The proposal hadn't just been approved, they'd been complimented on their innovative approach.

Her first creative project!

She might work for an advertising agency but her expertise was in administration. She'd left school early and begun as an office junior, climbing to become office administrator despite being only in her mid-twenties.

She was practical, meticulous and good with people—it had seemed like her destiny. Except over the years she'd been fascinated by the work going on around her, absorbing information, even studying on the side.

Until an account manager, short-staffed and desperate, had let her help out. That had fed her interest and she'd discovered to her surprise that she wasn't just the methodical organiser she'd always thought. She had creative instincts itching to be tested.

Lola had no illusions. She had a long way to go if she really wanted to shift her career direction, but getting approval to assist in a small way on this new campaign was a start. A chance to gauge if it really was what she wanted to do, and if she had the potential to succeed.

She'd have to work doubly hard and maybe she didn't have what it took. But after all these years, she longed for the chance to try.

Her phone rang. 'Lola?'

Niall Pedersen. His rich voice turned her good intentions inside out. Intentions to sever ties to the man who still affected her as he had when she was a teenager.

Last night she'd been sucked into the warmth of his caring, allowing herself to forget how dangerous he was to her equilibrium.

She stifled a bitter laugh. Two men in her life, both unwanted, both dangerous but in totally different ways.

'Hi, Niall. Finished your meetings?'

He'd suggested they meet after work and she'd been unable to refuse. Not after all his help.

He'd been there when the police came to the flat this morning, staying on with the key when she had to get to the office. He'd generously organised state-of-the-art security for her flat, staring down her insistence that he send her the bill, saying it would be an insult to accept payment.

'I'm waiting out the front. Whenever you're ready.'

'I'll be down in five.'

Swiftly saving the changes to her document, Lola shut down her computer and slipped on the shoes she'd kicked off. She refreshed her lip gloss and checked her hair was still in its chignon, then realised what she was doing. And that her pulse was racing.

She'd always been careful of her appearance at work, dressing for success with scrupulously straightened and styled hair. She allowed no unruly curls and dressed smartly but in muted colours. What had begun in her teens as an attempt to look older and more experienced had become habit.

There's no one to see you but Niall.

Are you primping for him?

He's not collecting you for a date. He'll never look at you that way. You're just Ed's little sister. An obligation.

Lola paused in the act of smoothing her skirt down her thighs. Her hands trembled.

She tried to tell herself it was weariness and reaction to the stress she'd been under.

But she couldn't swallow the lie. Logic told her it would be better when Niall flew back to his home thousands of kilometres to the north. Then she could focus, again, on trying to forget him. On dealing with this work opportunity and Braithwaite. Yet a needy part of her whispered that she didn't want him to leave.

It made no difference what she wanted. It never had. She'd see him, thank him, get her key and go home. Though the thought of returning to her flat held little appeal. If Braithwaite continued to target her she'd have to move. But would that stop him or would he find her again?

Rain lashed the street, a solid wall of dismal winter. But parked directly before the entrance was a familiar black sedan.

This time when Niall left she'd find a way to put him behind her. This time she'd succeed.

'Lola.' She swung around, her hand going to her throat.

Beside the entry, Niall stepped close, holding a furled umbrella. Tiny drops of moisture clung like crystals to his black hair. In jeans and a dark sweater he looked big and reassuring and far too attractive.

'I didn't see you.'

He frowned. 'You came outside without looking? What if Braithwaite had been here instead of me?'

Lola swallowed her instinctive protest. He was right.

'Usually I'm much more careful.' She bit her lip. For weeks she'd watched every step. Only tonight, thinking of Niall, she'd been distracted. Proof, if she needed it, that the sooner he left, the better.

He took her laptop, warm fingers brushing hers. Such a simple, caring gesture, yet it made her realise how rare it was. She had no one special in her life except her brother and father, and they were away for the rest of the year. Her father somewhere in the outback, her brother doing scientific research.

Lola beat down unfamiliar self-pity. She was *not* lonely. She was stronger than that.

'I'll organise some defensive training for you.' Niall's deep voice pulled her from her thoughts.

His company was renowned for its cyber security work but also provided everything from protection of premises to bodyguards for VIPs. It was rumoured that some of the most high-profile people in the world chose Pedersen Security.

'Thank you. That's very thoughtful.'

His dark gaze slanted down, capturing hers.

Something ricocheted through her, pulsing deep in her body and down her legs, making her knees tremble.

Niall's expression was unreadable. It wasn't the look of a man who viewed her as an annoying responsibility. Nor was it kind.

There was nothing soft about that intent stare. It seared, sharp enough to slice through a lifetime's defences.

Lola's breath snared as that strange sensation pulsed again, drying her mouth yet turning her insides liquid. She was aware, too aware, of how close they stood.

If she lifted her hand she'd touch wool and the hard chest she'd been fantasising about since early this morning. That was when she'd seen him bare-chested and wearing only low-slung track pants as he returned from a workout in the hotel gym. She'd been transfixed by his flagrant masculinity, the beauty of that powerful body, sheened with sweat, the play of muscles as he prowled into the suite, like a conqueror arrogantly claiming the space as his.

Her fingers twitched, the pads of her fingers prickling as if she'd actually touched him.

'Shall we?'

Lola's brain blanked. Shall we what? She was stuck on the image of him, half naked and potently desirable.

Then he nodded towards the car and flicked the umbrella open and over her head.

Of course, the car.

Her tongue stuck to the roof of her mouth and she could only hope it hadn't been hanging out as she drooled.

Ignoring the heat scorching her cheeks, she hurried to the vehicle, scrambling in before he could open the door. Seconds later he'd stowed her laptop and slid into the driver's seat.

Now she was cocooned with him, the drumming rain on the roof reinforcing the sense of being cut off from the world, alone with Niall.

Lola breathed deep, centring her thoughts, and discovered the tang of damp male flesh, cedar and spice. It was intoxicating.

'If you drop me at the station I'll catch a train. Oh, and I'll need my keys.' She'd left him in charge of her flat this morning, closing up after the police.

'You don't want public transport on a night like this. Especially with Braithwaite out there somewhere. I'll take you door to door.' Niall's voice was sharp.

Had she annoyed him? Reluctantly she turned and saw his honed features were grim.

Because she'd tried to save him a trip to the suburbs?

He turned on the ignition, the powerful car growling under his touch, then swung into the street. Lola snuggled back in her seat. 'Thanks, Niall. I appreciate you helping me out. I know you're a very busy man.'

Clearly he valued his friendship with Ed enormously. Niall was a high-flyer whose time really was money.

'How do you feel about not going back to the flat tonight?'

The words took her by surprise. Yet they resonated. She'd been thinking of her return home with dread. It was her safe place but now, despite the new security arrangements, it didn't feel safe.

Lola's head swung round. 'What are you suggesting?'

Not another night in his penthouse suite. It had been what she'd needed last night, when Braithwaite's intrusion sent her hurtling into fear. But sharing that intimate space with Niall brought its own problems.

'It's the weekend. What about a little time away from the city to get some fresh air and relax? Somewhere private. After what you've been through it would do you good to unwind. You could regroup and gather your strength.'

'It sounds lovely,' she admitted. 'But it's Friday night. Places within a reasonable distance of the city will already be booked.'

'No problem. I know a place. Private and comfortable, with glorious views over the coast. I can take you.'

She frowned. 'I thought you were wrapping up your business in Melbourne today?'

'I am. That doesn't mean I can't give you a lift. And don't worry about the return trip, that's easily sorted.'

'By the coast, you say?' Lola tried not to get excited and failed. There was something about sea views that always made her feel good. Walking on the beach would help her unwind. 'Is it very expensive?'

In the gloom she caught the flash of his smile. 'Mate's rates. I have an in with the owner so it's free.'

'I couldn't invite myself to stay at someone's place without—'

'It's no problem, Lola, believe me. The place is empty and the owner is more than happy for you to use it.'

She digested that. Putting off the return to her flat might make it even more difficult to go back. She needed to return soon, like getting back on a horse after being thrown, before the fear could build.

The trouble was she'd lived with fear so long her nerves were shot. If she went home she knew she'd spend the night listening for an intruder.

Her limbs ached with tiredness and too much stress. All day she'd struggled to concentrate, her mind constantly darting back to the flat, to Braithwaite, the police interview and, inevitably, to Niall. It had taken her longer than usual to complete the most ordinary tasks to her usual standard.

'I'd have to go home and pack a bag.'

He shook his head. 'I have it with me.'

Lola frowned. Hadn't she taken her overnight bag back home this morning? Or had she inadvertently left it in his hire car? She'd been so tense, returning to the flat and talking to the police, she couldn't recall.

She opened her mouth and found herself smothering a yawn. She'd been going to say she might need other things, but would she? There was a pair of jeans in there with a shirt and pullover, comfy pyjamas and toiletries. She imagined herself curled up on a sofa looking down over the sea and felt the tightness in her shoulders ease.

It was unorthodox, going away on the spur of the moment. Lola planned everything carefully.

But where was the harm in doing something on impulse for once? She could trust Niall's judgement. It would be somewhere safe and comfortable and she could pay him back for the return travel costs.

'I...okay. Thank you. That sounds perfect.'

He nodded and in the light from an oncoming car she saw him smile.

'It does, doesn't it? Why don't you close your eyes and rest?'

Lola didn't shut her eyes but she did zone out a little, relaxing to the swish of water on the road and the rhythmic beat of windscreen wipers. Instead of focusing on the city streets she surreptitiously watched Niall's strong hands on the wheel. His movements were economical and she felt safe with him.

Anxiety was still there, gnawing beneath the surface, but not that terrible panic she'd fought, discovering her home had been invaded.

Which led her inexorably back to Braithwaite. To the police assurance that they'd question him about breaking into her flat. Yet she didn't hold out much hope that they'd prove he was responsible.

Would this go the same way as when he'd stalked Therese? Would they only be able to prove something when he attacked her?

Lola shivered and sat straighter, rubbing her arms, trying to dispel a chill that settled despite the car's warm air.

She looked out and it took a while to recognise their surroundings.

'This isn't the way to the coast!'

'It is when we're flying.'

Lola goggled as Niall took an exit off the highway. 'Flying?' He couldn't be serious.

'Better than driving in this weather. It's only a short trip.'

The rain was even heavier now, pounding down and turning nearby lights into starbursts.

'I'm not flying anywhere!' She whipped around. It was one thing to agree to a coastal retreat. But this—

'You have something against planes? Are you a nervous flyer?'

'No. I like flying.' She'd only done it twice, flying to Sydney and back. She'd loved it. The bustle of the airport, the sense of expectation, the thrust of the engines accelerating as the plane rose. And the views. It had been wonderful, watching the world spread beneath her.

It had felt like adventure. For the first time in her life she'd allowed herself to feel jealous of Ed, heading off to far-flung places. He'd been away from home when their world imploded and it had been left to her to deal with their father's descent into grief. Since then she'd been tied to Melbourne, building her career, supporting her father and saving for the future. But one day...

'I can't fly away for the weekend on the spur of the moment.'

'Why not, when I can give you a lift?' Niall nosed the car through tall gates and she realised they were on the edge of an airfield. 'I'm going that way and can arrange for your return.'

He made it sound like a stop on a bus route! Then the headlights revealed what she guessed was a private jet.

Again it struck her how vastly separate Niall's world was from hers. All that linked them were a few shared years in the past, her brother Ed and a sexual pull that was totally one-sided. She was an ordinary working girl while he featured on rich lists and sexiest bachelor lists. He attended glamorous events and thought nothing of travelling by private jet.

He stopped the car and turned, gathering both her hands in his before she guessed his intentions. His hands were large and reassuring. It would be so easy to relax under his touch. Too easy.

Or to imagine those long fingers moving across her body.

'Come on, Lola. It will be fun. A break away, time to recharge the batteries. You don't have to do a thing. What's holding you back?'

The feeling she was being railroaded.

Niall was making plans for her as if he knew best, when Lola had been taking care of herself and her dad since she was almost sixteen. She wasn't used to ceding control.

The fact that it meant spending more time with Niall.

Something curled low in her body and she knew that was part of it. No matter what she tried to tell herself, her attraction to Niall Pederson hadn't waned and she knew she shouldn't feed it.

His thumb stroked the back of her hand, sending a tingle all the way up her arm then down to her breasts.

'Ed's worried about you. He'd be relieved to know you're having a break.'

'You haven't told him—?'

'Not yet, though I don't see why you haven't.'

Lola shrugged. 'There isn't anything he could do where he is and he'd just worry.'

Niall shook his head, his expression sombre. 'It's what big brothers do. Or they should.' His voice dipped low on a note she didn't recognise and all trace of a smile disappeared. She felt him stiffen, his fingers tightening.

Was he worried about Ed taking him to task if she went back home when Niall left?

She thought of all he'd done for her in the last twenty-four hours.

But that wasn't why she was tempted to say yes. She wanted what he offered.

'Okay. I'll tell Ed about it all.' She paused then made up her mind. Her hesitation was out of proportion with the situation. 'And, yes, I'll accept the offer of a coastal escape. Thank you.'

As the plane began its descent, Niall looked at the woman asleep in the chair beside him and told himself he was doing the right thing.

Yet alarm signals chimed in his brain.

Not because he was taking drastic measures to protect Lola. He'd do whatever it took to keep her safe. That was a given. He knew what it was to lose someone important. He'd never allow that to happen again.

The alarms jangled because of what he felt. The way his gaze clung to her mouth and those high breasts that would fit perfectly in his palms. The directions his imagination roved whenever he was with her.

And even when he wasn't.

This morning's session at the gym had been prompted by images of her looking ridiculously sexy in flannel pyjamas and an oversized robe. His workout had been rigorous to the point of punishing and he'd congratulated himself on mastering his wayward libido. Till he'd entered the suite and there she'd been, tousled curls loose around her shoulders, her cute pyjamas drawing attention to all that lithe femininity despite the fact she was covered from neck to ankle.

He swallowed some coffee, difficult over the constriction in his throat.

This was wrong. Lola was like family, or should be. Ed would have his hide if he touched her. The Suarez family trusted him. She was vulnerable and he had no business lusting after her. His duty was to concentrate on keeping her safe.

If those weren't reasons enough to keep his distance, there was the darkness inside him. The darkness of grief and grim self-knowledge.

Niall knew, had known most of his life, that he could never offer the things a woman like Lola deserved. He couldn't do long term or play happy families. The very thought brought on spiralling panic. He looked down and deliberately unfolded his fists, seeking calm.

There were women in his life—he wasn't into self-denial—but there'd never be a wife or long-term partner. Absolutely no children.

He needed, deserved to be alone.

He swallowed the last of his coffee, only to find it bitter and cold. The steward took it from him and advised they'd land soon.

Niall looked again at Lola, her face pale. She seemed younger in sleep, reminding him of their age gap and their divide in experience and character.

She was cautious yet determined, capable and feisty. And sexy. Far sexier than Ed's little sister should be. While he…

Niall slammed a steel door down. No point thinking about it. His priority was keeping her safe. End of story.

To his amazement she slept through landing and was still asleep when it was time to disembark.

How long had she been fretting over Braithwaite? Niall's chest tightened, realising she probably slept from sheer exhaustion. Helped perhaps by the glass of wine she'd accepted after they took off.

He could wake her, but he hadn't the heart. Instead he lifted her into his arms and grimaced.

Because she felt too good. She sank against him and his body seemed to sigh in relief. His tight throat turned desert dry as he strove and failed not to catalogue every centimetre of delicious femininity snuggled against him.

She murmured something as he took her to his waiting car. But instead of waking she just curled closer, so trusting that a sliver of ice spiked his heated awareness.

She spoke again, something he couldn't make out, probably because he was transfixed by the movement of her lips against his neck, her humid breath an unintentional caress that shot straight to his libido.

Settling her in the car and fixing her seat belt was a form of torture Niall had never experienced. No matter how he tried, he came into contact with things he shouldn't. The whisper slide of nylon-clad legs against his palms. Her slim waist, the gentle flare of her hips. A strand of hair caught his shirt button and it took too long to disengage himself. Doing up her seat belt, he brushed her breast with his knuckle and his groin tightened.

Instantly he straightened, the pain as his head collided with the car almost welcome.

Finally, they were on their way. It was good to have traffic and gear changes to distract him. They left the city behind and he swung the car onto the road that led into the hinterland mountains.

They were almost there when a husky voice broke the silence. 'Where are we?'

Lola shifted in her seat, turning towards the view of lights glittering along the coast below.

'That's not Melbourne. It's not familiar at all.' Her voice was sharper and she sat straighter. 'Niall?'

He tightened his grip on the wheel.

How would Lola react when she discovered he'd kidnapped her?

CHAPTER FOUR

'QUEENSLAND. THAT'S THE Gold Coast down there.'

Lola shook her head. But this wasn't like clearing blocked ears after a swim. She'd heard Niall's words. She just couldn't believe them.

One swift look at his profile in the dashboard lights revealed he appeared the same as ever. He wasn't joking. There was no sign of humour on that strong, handsome profile. He looked arrogantly sure of himself.

'Queensland?' She tested the word on her tongue, yet it didn't seem possible.

Lola swivelled back to the view down the mountain, now partially obscured as they passed through forest.

There was no mistaking the vista for Melbourne or its surrounds. There was a long, lighted urban strip with a cluster of high-rise buildings and network of streets. It trailed, like a string of glittering jewels, into the distance. Beyond it was the immense darkness of the sea. The Pacific Ocean if Niall told the truth.

Why would he lie?

'That's ridiculous! It's two states away from Victoria! Queensland is thousands of kilometres away.'

'About one thousand three hundred from Melbourne. Only a couple of hours by plane.'

'Only!' She clutched the arm rest on the door, her breath coming in shallow pants. 'This isn't what we discussed.'

Her head reeled. Again she looked out of the window but the view was the same. Stunning but unfamiliar.

How could she not have known?

How could she have slept through it all?

Because you've been running on empty for weeks. Stress at home. The new challenge at work. Juggling too much and not sleeping for fear of what Braithwaite would do next.

'I invited you to get away somewhere quiet and safe. That's where we're going.'

He sounded maddeningly calm.

Lola wanted to screech that he'd tricked her. That he had no right to do it. Instead she fought for calm, desperately sucking in a deep breath that still didn't fill her lungs. She dug her fingers into the leather of her seat. It was softer than any car upholstery she'd known. Niall swung around a rising bend and it registered that the car sat low to the ground. Some sort of sports car?

For some obscure reason the idea infuriated her. Niall with his private plane and his expensive car, walking in and taking over her life.

'Don't play that game with me,' she snarled. 'You deliberately misled me.' She swallowed, realising with shock that unfamiliar tears clogged her throat. She'd *trusted* Niall. Now she felt as if he'd made a fool of her. 'You *manipulated* me!'

That got his attention. His head snapped round and he finally looked directly at her. She stared back, furious and wounded.

He turned to the road, slowing for a bend. 'It was for your own good.'

Her hackles rose. His tone was that of an adult reining in impatience at childish behaviour.

She wasn't a child to be pacified with platitudes. Especially over something so important.

'What paternalistic claptrap! It may have passed your notice, Niall, but I'm an adult. *I* decide what's for my own good. Not you.'

'I *had* noticed. The change in you is hard to miss.' His voice ground low in a way that burred through her insides. That only added to her ire. She was furious yet he'd managed to make her aware of him in the visceral way a woman was aware of a virile man. 'Would you have come if I'd told you?'

'Of course not.'

'You've just made my point.' His voice hardened.

'Stop the car.'

'Sorry?'

'Stop the car. I need to get out.'

'Are you sick?' The arrogant so and so had the nerve to sound concerned. Maybe he didn't like the idea of her damaging his precious sports car.

It was on the tip of her tongue to say *yes, sick of you*, but she wasn't that juvenile. She knew he'd acted out of protectiveness, but she was a grown woman who made her own decisions.

She was honest enough to know part of her distress came from the fact he saw her not as a woman in her own right but an obligation, a responsibility to be organised as a favour to his friend Ed.

The car slowed and she waited for it to stop. Instead it turned off the road onto a curving private drive. Finally it halted before an elegant entrance, lit by glowing lamps.

Lola wrestled her seat belt undone and turned to open her door, only to discover it was already open, lifting up in an unfamiliar way she'd only seen in films. She shot to her feet, reeling a moment as she felt the warm road surface beneath stockinged feet. She'd lost her shoes somewhere but right now didn't care. All she cared about was putting some distance between herself and that conniving, lying—

'Lola.' His voice came from just behind her. 'Are you ill?' Hard fingers grasped her elbow till she yanked free, spinning to face him.

'Don't you dare touch me!' Her chest rose and fell rapidly and her pulse thundered in her ears.

'You need to calm down.'

Again that oh-so-patient and utterly infuriating tone.

She shoved her hands onto her hips and met his dark gaze with a fulminating glare. 'If you say I'm overreacting I really *will* lose my temper.' Childish it might be but there'd be a lot of satisfaction to be gained in slapping that confident face. 'What makes you think you've got the right to take over my life and make decisions for me?'

To her chagrin her voice wobbled and she bit down hard on her bottom lip.

Everything felt so alien. Not just the balmy, humid air caressing her overheated cheeks, or the lush, sweet perfume of night-flowering plants. This sudden uprush of strong emotion was alien to Lola. This feeling of being adrift, at someone else's mercy, when she'd spent so many years keeping her feet firmly on the ground, achieving her goals through hard work, planning and perseverance.

It made her wobbly inside to discover she was no longer in control of her world.

It had nothing to do with the intense, disturbing effect Niall Pederson had on her.

'I'm only keeping you safe and—'

'No.' She dropped her voice to the low, authoritative pitch she'd learned projected well in meetings. 'You did a lot more.' She paused, breathing down the debilitating mix of shock, helplessness and incandescent fury. 'I've already got one crackpot in Melbourne obsessively trying to control me and now I've got you, a man I trusted, doing the same.'

She saw that strike home. Niall's head jerked back as if she'd hit him. The flesh across his high cheekbones drew taut and even in this light she saw colour streak across his features.

'You can't compare me to that bastard!'

Lola didn't bother to answer, she turned back to the car, fumbling on the floor for her shoes and putting them on.

Logic told her it was an unfair comparison, but what Niall had done was unfair too. *Duping* her!

'Where's my purse?'

'You won't need it.'

'Sorry?' She swung around and took a step closer.

He folded his arms across his solid chest. He looked utterly implacable. 'You won't need money here. You're my guest.'

'*Your* guest.' She should have known. 'This is your place?'

He shrugged. 'I live in Brisbane. I bought this as a retreat but so far I haven't had time to retreat much.'

'So you lied about having an in with the owner. You made me think it was some friend.'

Niall moved his head from one side to the other as if trying to relieve a stiff neck. Yet he stood solidly before her, as if nothing so insignificant as her preferences would move him.

'I thought I'd short-circuit exactly the sort of argument we're having now.' He paused, his expression stern. 'Come inside and make yourself comfortable, Lola. It's late and you're tired.'

She shook her head. 'I want my luggage and my purse. I'll phone for a taxi.'

Again Niall tilted his head, his eyes narrowing. Did he move a fraction closer? 'There aren't taxis that come so far.'

'There must be someone who can drive me.' She lifted her chin, refusing to give up.

'I can't think who. One of the beauties of this place is its isolation. Which makes it perfect as an escape from your Mr Braithwaite. I doubt he's got the resources to follow us here, even if he could find out where you are.'

She clenched her teeth. He wasn't *her* Mr Braithwaite. Then, reading the expression on Niall's face, she wondered if he'd deliberately said that to distract her and divert her anger.

Lola looked up the long driveway, remembering how isolated the road had seemed. Perhaps there were neighbours further along but did she want to try finding out so late at night?

The cleansing surge of molten fury vied with innate pragmatism. She'd love to see Niall's face if she stomped off into the night. But then she'd be lost and alone with no money and no phone. And, knowing Niall, she wouldn't be alone for long. He was strong enough and ruthless enough to follow, toss her over his shoulder and carry her inside.

She quivered at the image that created in her whirling brain. That annoyed her too.

Swallowing her anger, she turned and marched towards the entrance of what she saw now was a magnificent house. 'I'll leave you to bring in the luggage.' And he'd better bring her phone and purse or she'd kick up such a rumpus he wouldn't know what hit him.

Niall must have unlocked the front door remotely. It was oversized, intricately carved timber in the Balinese style, finished with touches of gilding. On either side massive brass pots held glossy, broad-leaved plants that looked lush and exotic.

If the warm night hadn't alerted her that she was far from Melbourne, these tropical touches would.

The door opened easily and she found herself in an airy foyer with a soaring ceiling and polished wooden floor that led to a massive lounge. Beyond that were full-length windows that framed the starry strip of coastal lights.

Lola took off her high heels and padded across the floor. From what she could see, the place was magnificent and built on a grand scale, but with a relaxed vibe that made her think of tropical comfort and abundance.

The impression intensified as she flicked on a switch and saw sprawling lounges, beautiful fans suspended from the double-height ceiling and a display of exquisite orchids, not in tiny indoor pots, but in a glassed atrium open to the sky.

It was all sumptuous and inviting, each detail beautiful in itself and adding to a harmonious whole.

Another light, another sitting room, a glimpse of an enormous state-of-the-art kitchen, but it was the view that drew her. Even though her thoughts should be on planning to get out of here.

Maybe, she mused, pausing before sliding glass doors that led onto a wide deck, she was drawn to the view because it was easier than thinking of mundane practicalities. Of returning to cold, wet Melbourne and the threat of Braithwaite.

She shivered and crossed her arms.

Niall's right. This would be a perfect place to unwind.

Was it weak to want to hide from what awaited her at home instead of facing it?

What she hadn't realised was that the house sat high at the top of a slope. Below her she saw the inky darkness of treetops and beyond that the coastal development, glittering gemlike in the velvet night.

As she stood there, surrounded by silence, drinking in that amazing view, Lola's jangling emotions eased. It went against the grain to admit it but, though she loathed his arrogant actions, she could appreciate Niall's attempt to help.

Except he'd treated her like a package to be delivered or a child to be coaxed.

'Would you like supper? We only had a snack on the plane.' Niall's deep voice came from behind her. She'd been so caught up in her thoughts she hadn't heard him approach.

Lola huffed in wry amusement. Her idea of a snack was an apple. On their private flight they'd had blinis with smoked salmon and caviar then delicious hot savoury pastries. How the other half lived!

'I'm fine.' Even if she were hungry, she wasn't ready to share supper with this man.

Lola turned and sucked in a sharp breath.

For it hit her that she was totally alone with Niall Pedersen, the man who'd haunted her dreams for years.

This wasn't like last night in a busy city hotel. She was in his house and they were utterly alone. There was no house-keeper bustling out to welcome them.

Something about the still darkness and the lush, almost decadent luxury of this place made her hyper aware of Niall the man. Not the billionaire or family friend or would-be protector or even the outrageous kidnapper.

Warm light spilled across black hair that she knew from childhood games was soft and thick. He stood with his back to the light, so his eyes were shadowed, but there was no mistaking the strong shape of his jaw and nose or the lines of his mouth.

Her gaze flicked there and a mariachi band started up deep inside. No, not mariachi, the beat was sultry and compelling. It was a salsa. Or a tango.

Lola swallowed and fixed on a point past one wide shoulder.

'I'm not hungry.' Nor was she up to arguing with him. Despite sleeping through most of the journey, Lola felt incredibly weary. She needed her wits about her to deal with Niall. 'If you'll show me my room, I'd like some privacy.'

His head jerked up as if she'd surprised him.

Or disappointed him.

She had no idea where the idea came from. It wasn't as if he wanted her company and he couldn't expect her to want his after his high-handed actions.

If he wanted thanks, he'd get that from Ed, who probably wouldn't object to his ruthless methods.

'This way.' Niall spun on his heel and led her down a long corridor subtly illuminated with up-lights.

Lola followed, trying to work out what it was about his body language that told her he was tense. When she'd argued with him it had been like water off a duck's back, he'd been so convinced he was right.

He'd pushed up the sleeves of his shirt and his strong, sinewed forearms swung with each step. He moved easily, long legs eating up the space, yet somehow she knew he wasn't as relaxed as he seemed.

He pushed open a door and gestured her inside.

If she'd thought the rest of the house the epitome of tropical luxury, it paled before this.

Lola couldn't stifle a gasp. One wall was all windows, giving out onto that coastal view. The rest of the room, lit by the glow of small lamps, was an exotic paradise. A huge four-poster bed dominated one end, sheer curtains draping it. Its headboard was another huge gilded Balinese carving, this time of birds and flowers. Another wall consisted of an enormous mural of peacocks, shimmering in the warm light. There were comfortable chairs, occasional tables and pots of brightly flowering plants she didn't recognise.

'Your bathroom and dressing room are through there. That's where I left your cases.'

She swung around. 'Cases? There's only the overnight bag and laptop.'

He shrugged. 'You weren't prepared for a trip to Queensland so I took the liberty of packing suitable clothes before I left the flat. You won't want winter clothes here.'

Lola opened her mouth and shut it. She spun away towards the window but what caught her attention wasn't the view but Niall's reflection, watching her with the intensity of a hawk. His hands hung loose at his sides, fingers flexing as if anticipating trouble.

No wonder!

She swung back, narrowing her eyes on that handsome, imperious face.

'You went through my *things*?' She imagined him rifling through her clothes, her sensible work outfits and her casual jeans and shirts. Had he plundered her underwear drawer too?

Heat seared her throat and cheeks at the idea of Niall's hand touching her underwear.

That's as close as you'll ever get to that particular fantasy. The only way he'd touch your undies is if you're not in them. Because he's not and never has been interested in you.

She'd understood that for years. Yet still it hurt.

Because no other man had toppled Niall Pedersen from the pinnacle where her infatuation had placed him. No other guy had been as caring, as strong yet funny, as spectacularly macho yet considerate, as downright attractive as the guy who'd hung around her home in those formative years. Even now, furious and hurt, she couldn't think of a man who made her hormones sit up and beg the way he did.

Lola's pride smarted. Had he noticed the difference between her cheap, chain-store clothes and the expensive designer fashions his girlfriends wore? Had he felt sorry for her? Thought her less feminine because her underwear wasn't expensive silk and lace but cotton?

'Jayden Braithwaite could learn from you, Niall.' The words emerged husky with pain. 'He might have got into my home but as far as I know he hasn't yet stooped low enough to paw through my underwear.'

Niall flinched, head snapping back as her words lashed him.

She couldn't *really* compare him to the man stalking her! She *knew* Niall acted out of care for her.

Yet he couldn't miss her convulsive swallow or the scratchy, thickened sound of her voice as if she battled tears.

The Lola he knew hated crying, saw it as a sign of weakness. Even the day of her mother's funeral, she'd pulled away from him and not let the tears fall, though she'd adored her mother and he knew her heart was breaking.

His own throat tightened, her emotion stirring something visceral.

Niall told himself she was overreacting, trying to make him feel bad because she preferred to manage her own life—

But that's the point, Pedersen.

She's a woman, not a kid. You know that.

*She's capable and strong. She didn't ask you to come in
and push her into a solution of your own making, even if it's
what you and Ed would prefer.*

Niall tried to imagine sitting back while someone else di-
rected his life. Tried and failed.

'I'm sorry, Lola.'

Her eyebrows rose but her mouth remained a taut, flat line
that told him she didn't believe his apology.

'I keep forgetting you're not...'

'What? A kid who hero-worshipped you?'

'Hero worship?' He snorted. 'You might have tagged along
with me and Ed but, as I recall, you were pretty good at holding your own.'

'And I prefer to do that now.' Bitterness laced her tone
and her chin jutted high. Somehow she managed to look
down her nose at him, though without her shoes she barely
reached his shoulder.

'Again, I apologise. I wasn't thinking of anything but getting you somewhere safe. If you'd been any other woman...'
Of course he'd have baulked at sorting out her clothes and
especially her underwear. He took a slow breath. 'You and
Ed are like family, so I just acted. But it *was* an invasion of
your privacy.'

His apology was honest as far as it went. Yet if he were totally truthful, there was a moment when he'd grabbed a handful of her underwear, intending to pack it, and stopped. The
feel of the soft cotton had made him wonder how it would
be to touch Lola's glorious body through it.

Would she look cute and demure wearing the white bra
with its tiny red bow and the bikini panties sprigged with
clusters of cherries? Or would she be unbearably sexy, so irresistible he'd lose his battle to ignore the fact she'd turned
into a siren?

He'd held her in his arms after they discovered Braithwaite
had been in her home and, along with the desire to comfort
her, Niall had felt another sort of desire. One that shamed

him. For, even if they weren't blood relations, Niall and the Suarez family viewed him as an honorary family member.

Yet the surge of lust was real. And it was back with a vengeance.

Heat rose from the pit of his belly and his hairline prickled damply, his palms turning clammy.

Was she wearing another demure white bra? Panties dotted with strawberries this time?

His fingers twitched and his palm tingled as, unbidden, that question again filled his brain. How would it feel, touching that soft cotton when it was taut across Lola's gentle curves? He remembered the sway of her hips and beautiful backside in that pencil skirt and the memory was a grinding weight in his groin, turning and twisting.

Little Lola had changed all right. She'd become the sort of woman a man could lose his mind over. And she wasn't even trying!

She stared at him as if unimpressed by his apology. But even with a frown and her arms crossed impatiently, Lola Suarez affected him as no woman had in as long as he could remember.

Her pulse, the delicate flutter at the base of her throat, seemed like an invitation to a man who, after a sleepless night imagining her delicious body just metres away, was too close to the edge. How would she taste there? Sweet or salty? How about her lips? Her breasts, her...

'I'll be just down the hall.' His voice emerged gruff and abrupt. 'Call me if you need anything.' Then he turned and strode from the room.

Because, he realised suddenly, being here alone with Lola was the worst idea he'd ever had.

For as well as needing to protect her, Niall had one other need. One that was wholly inappropriate. To seduce Lola Suarez. To ravish her thoroughly, again and again and again, until he rid himself of this burning hunger.

CHAPTER FIVE

IT WAS HARD to stay angry after the best night's sleep she'd had in ages. Whether from exhaustion or the fact she was out of Braithwaite's reach, Lola had sunk onto that flagrantly romantic bed and been asleep before she had time to think.

For that she had Niall to thank. At home she'd have tossed and turned, on edge and sleepless.

While she fumed at his autocratic, take-charge attitude, she understood he'd done what he had because he cared.

Just not in the way she wanted.

If you'd been any other woman, he'd said. Which explained everything.

He didn't think of her as a woman, much less a desirable one. To him she was Ed's kid sister, part of the Suarez family that had informally adopted him.

He cared for her like a sister.

Lola stifled a grimace and, pulling on a summery print dress, and trying not to think of Niall's hands on it, left her room. She didn't straighten her hair or put it up as she did for the office. Nor did she put on make-up. She refused to primp for a man who thought she had the sex appeal of a piece of furniture. And she didn't need make-up to boost her confidence.

She had this. She'd be polite but firm. She'd organise a return flight to Melbourne and she'd—

Lola stopped in the kitchen doorway, all thought of grabbing toast and tea disintegrating.

Her pulse beat high in her throat as she took in Niall, hair damp and a thin T-shirt clinging to a wall of muscle. He might have just walked out of the surf with a board under his arm, but he'd probably just emerged from the shower. He looked tanned, taut and terrific and her stomach did a belly flop at the sight.

'You're up. Great. Ready for breakfast?'

His smile was easy but she saw wariness in his eyes. He was wondering what sort of mood she was in. No wonder, in all the time they'd known each other she'd never before lost her temper with him.

'I am. I'm starving.' Her gaze roved the food spread on the massive island bench. 'Are you cooking?'

Better to concentrate on food than on the fact Niall looked good enough to eat. She wasn't going to notice that any more. After she left here she doubted she'd see him again for another eight years.

'Absolutely, if you want something hot. Otherwise we've got tropical fruit, muffins, fresh pastries from the best patisserie on the coast, thick Greek yoghurt with honey and nuts—'

'That's more than enough!' She approached the array of food. 'You've been out to a patisserie?'

He shook his head. 'My housekeeper dropped them off. Her husband is a pastry chef.' At her querying look he added, 'They live further along the mountain. Now, coffee, juice, tea or maybe a Mimosa?'

'A Mimosa?'

Niall opened a massive fridge and produced a foil-topped bottle. 'Champagne and freshly squeezed orange juice. Not recommended on a workday, but I thought you might like to celebrate being on holiday.'

'I'd hardly call it a holiday.'

Niall shrugged and loaded a wicker basket of pastries onto

a vast tray along with a colourful selection of tropical fruit. 'You're not working and it's a glorious day. Why not relax and enjoy it? Ed tells me you haven't taken a holiday in ages.'

He did, did he? Lola's eyebrows twitched into a frown. What else had Ed told him?

Then she looked in the direction of Niall's outstretched arm towards the broad deck and her annoyance died. The view of rainforest, sea and city was even more magnificent in daylight. One end of the deck was taken up with a sparkling infinity pool where light danced on crystal water. As she watched, a flock of birds with iridescent plumage, lime green, blue, red and orange, darted across to a nearby tree, so stunningly bright they didn't look real.

'Rainbow Lorikeets,' Niall murmured. 'If we sit outside we can watch them.'

For a moment Lola hesitated. But she was no fool. How often did she get the chance to enjoy such surroundings? Her time here was limited so she'd make the most of it.

'Yes, please, to eating outside.' Her gaze strayed to the wine bottle; she was about to ask for plain juice when something stopped her. 'And yes to the Mimosa.'

She'd never had champagne at breakfast. It felt daring and decadent.

Her life was devoid of extravagance as she worked to build her career and her savings to afford her own place. Certainty and safety were important to her.

That was why there'd been no holidays away and no fripperies. Why her life was, in many ways, empty of excitement. But Lola wasn't going to look a gift horse in the mouth. She'd enjoy this while she could. In a couple of hours she'd probably be boarding a sardine-packed economy flight to Melbourne.

The temperature outside was balmy compared with the icy rain they'd left behind. Was it the warmth that made her relax, or the stunning surroundings, high on this mountain surrounded by birdsong and the fragrance of blossoms?

Even her interaction with Niall was different. Neither

mentioned their reason for being here or their argument. Instead they chatted casually, as if the years had telescoped and they were still in the habit of sharing a table, not needing to fill every silence.

Finally, Lola leaned back and sipped her drink. The tang of fresh juice and the tingle of bubbles made her smile. It really did make the meal a special occasion.

In other circumstances she'd love to stay here. But she had to reclaim her life.

'I slept late. I haven't had a chance to look at return flights. Do you know when they leave?'

Niall put down his glass, his face suddenly serious.

'I don't think that's a good idea.'

'Nevertheless, I need to organise a flight.' She kept her voice even. Last night she'd been furious but she wasn't making that error again. She didn't like scenes and hated losing control. All she had to do was treat Niall like a colleague. As if he didn't get under her skin.

'Lola...'

It was unlike Niall to hesitate. Plus there was something about the gruff note in his voice that made her do what she'd avoided all through the meal. She looked directly into his eyes.

What she saw made her breath hitch. His navy gaze was intent and sombre. With his knotted brow and grimly set jaw, he looked like the bearer of bad tidings. Or a man about to try to change her mind.

'I know you're concerned for me, Niall, and I appreciate it. You were wonderful, looking after me on Thursday when I needed it—I can't thank you enough for that. And this getaway...' she shrugged. 'I know you planned it with the best intentions. But I need to get back.'

Not because she really wanted to be in her flat but because it would be a mistake staying here under the same roof with him.

She might have slept the night through but she vividly

remembered fragments of her dreams and they frightened her. She didn't dream of Braithwaite. Instead, it was Niall who'd featured in her imaginings, Niall, bare-chested, his hard hands skimming all over her body, making her feel...

Heat swamped her and she reached again for her glass, gulping down the cool nectar.

'There's something you don't know.'

'Sorry?' It took a moment to surface from last night's fevered imaginings. How real Niall's touch had felt as his hand dipped over her belly and down between her legs while he lowered his head to her breast and sucked her nipple.

'I didn't tell you everything in Melbourne.'

She blinked. 'What do you mean? What's wrong?' She tried and failed to imagine what he might have withheld. Horror widened her eyes and she leaned closer. 'Is it something about Ed? Or Dad?' Her father wasn't the best at keeping in touch, especially when he was camping somewhere remote in the Northern Territory. 'Has there been an accident?'

'No! They're both okay.' Niall shook his head. 'I'm sorry to scare you. It's nothing like that.'

She slumped back, hand to her chest. Anything else she could handle. It might be almost a decade since her mother had died and Lola's world had shattered, but she remembered the devastation as if it were yesterday.

'It's about Braithwaite. He didn't just poison your plants.' He paused. 'I was about to tell you that night in your flat, but you were so upset when you discovered he'd been there. I thought it better to wait till you were calmer. But there never seemed a good time.'

Lola straightened, hands gripping the table. She remembered how desperately she'd clung to him that night. No wonder he'd hesitated before giving more bad news. 'Go on.'

'I found glass in your teapot.'

It took a moment for her to process his words. 'It's made of tempered glass.'

His mouth tightened. 'Ground glass. The pot itself wasn't

damaged so it didn't come from that. It was put there delib-erately.'

For a second it didn't make sense, then Lola found her-self on the brink of nausea. The sunlit scene wavered as she imagined what might have happened.

But it hadn't happened, because Niall had noticed and saved her. Yet horror darkened the edges of her vision.

She reached out and closed her fingers around his hand. 'Thank you. I mightn't have seen it and then—'

'Don't think about it!' His sharp voice told its own story. He appeared calm but he wasn't unmoved. His hand turned beneath hers and squeezed.

'I always knew he was dangerous, and he seemed to be getting closer and closer to me.' She just hadn't realised how close. Another wave of sickness threatened and she beat it down. It was okay to be scared but she needed to be strong. 'You told the police?'

He nodded. 'We had a long discussion.'

Lola's eyes narrowed, reading his expression. Her nape prickled in premonition. 'There's more, isn't there?'

Niall drew in a slow breath. 'I found a surveillance cam-era in your flat.'

'What?' She was on her feet, adrenaline shooting through her blood.

'A miniature camera in the hallway. It would give a view of the living room and the bedroom end of the hall.'

The bedroom end...

Her stomach churned at the thought of Braithwaite gloat-ing, watching her when she didn't know. Maybe watching her undress or shower.

'Just one?'

'Yes. The police were going to go over the place with a fine-tooth comb.'

The bright blue sky dimmed and she shivered, her bare arms pimpling as if from a blast of arctic air.

Lola's mouth worked but no words formed. She stumbled away from the table then stopped.

A laugh escaped, a sharp crack of sound that held no humour but spoke of despair and shock. How long had Braithwaite spied on her? How pointless her caution and her reports to the police when he knew her every move?

'Ah, Lola.' Niall was before her, a blur seen through stinging eyes. 'Come here.'

She heard the ache of sympathy in his voice and shook her head. Better not to touch him. She felt weak enough as it was. Her whole body trembled and her knees wobbled alarmingly.

'I'm okay. Just surprised.' She lifted her chin.

But that only brought her gaze on a collision course with Niall's. His handsome features softened in sympathy as he closed the gap between them. Lola felt his heat warm her all the way down her body, but she resisted the urge to sway closer. It would be a bad idea.

A large hand slid under her hair to cup her cheek. Niall's touch was firm and sure. How she craved some of his strength and certainty.

Fearing he'd read that yearning, she let her eyelids drop, sighing. For no matter how strong she told herself she was, she didn't have the willpower to step back.

Lola was torn between wanting more and hating herself for this vulnerability. So she stood, concentrating on sucking air into oxygen-starved lungs and trying not to move closer.

Her mind should be full of fear and worry about Braithwaite but somehow that dimmed when Niall was near.

His thumb moved, stroking her cheek, and her breath shuddered out.

'Lola.' His voice sounded different. Deeper. Thicker. She felt it like a slow-moving, searing-hot channel, carving through her insides.

Reluctantly she opened her eyes and he was closer. If she took a deep breath surely their bodies would brush. Instantly and, she told herself, without intending to, she drew in just such a breath.

Her nipples stroked his hard torso and sensation shot through her. It was electric and powerful.

His other hand grabbed her upper arm as if to support her. But strangely, now, her knees were rock solid. She wasn't wobbling.

Before her eyes Niall's mouth, that sculpted, sensual mouth, drew back hard as if he clenched his teeth. Lola saw a muscle tic at the corner of his jaw. Something about that quickened her own pulse and her lips parted.

'Lola.' Deeper again and gruff, so unlike Niall's usual smooth voice. She watched his Adam's apple dip and rise in that bronzed throat and something new shuddered to life deep inside.

Lola fought it. She really did. But a lifetime's yearning wasn't easily denied.

She swallowed too, then licked her lips, her mouth dry.

'Yes, Niall.' It didn't emerge as a question, urging him to finish whatever it was he intended to say. Instead it was an affirmation. An invitation.

She heard the roughened sound of his breathing, felt the thud of his heart as she put her hand to his chest, fingers splayed, the better to absorb the feel of hard muscle and taut flesh beneath fine cotton.

She'd never touched a man that way and it felt elemental as no kiss or exploratory caress on a date ever had.

Because those guys weren't Niall.

There was something incredibly arousing about holding his heartbeat at the centre of her palm. As if he let her capture and absorb his life force.

Which was crazy. Lola was the one overcome by the need for more. Not Niall. Never Niall. He was just being kind, comforting her when she was stressed.

Yet even as she tried to convince herself she imagined

things, he bowed his head lower, his breath feathering her forehead.

His hand slipped from her cheek, back into the wild waves of hair she hadn't bothered to tame. His fingers speared up her scalp, making it tingle with delicious sensation. She sank her head back against his supporting hand.

That left her face raised and open to him. Through half-closed eyes she tried to read his expression. His eyes glowed, appearing almost cobalt to her overwrought senses. His nostrils flared and his expression looked grim.

But then, instead of drawing away, he did the impossible, pulling her head back further and taking her mouth with his.

Everything stopped. Her breath, her heart, the sounds of birds in the trees. Even the whispery morning breeze seemed to die away as every nerve she possessed adjusted to his kiss.

It wasn't tentative. It wasn't a mere brush of lips across lips.

It was deliberate and sure. Like the man himself. His mouth opened over hers, his tongue sliding across her lips as of course she opened instantly for him.

After that came a dizzying, wild plunge akin to dropping off the top of a roller coaster and down the other side. Except there was no fear, only an urgent, rising delight. A hunger that had her shuffling closer, flattening her breasts against him and hooking both hands up over his shoulders.

Niall looped an arm around her waist, pulling her in as their mouths fused. It was bliss.

Lola's eyes closed. Not because she didn't want to see him, but because the sensations bombarding her demanded all her attention. Everything was heightened, her body sensitised so she felt even the slightest touch acutely.

Sparks ignited where her breasts crushed against him, his arm around her back was deliciously heavy and the things he did with his tongue... She pressed against him, meeting those druggingly deep forays into her mouth with urgent demands of her own.

No kiss had ever felt like this. So utterly right. So much more than a meeting of mouths.

Niall kissed with his whole body and she revelled in it. The hard strain of bunched muscles against her body that made her feel flagrantly feminine. The heat, that had started as a transfer from his body to hers but which now flamed from an ignition point low in her pelvis. The taste of him, unique, indefinable and addictive, filling her head with the promise of so much more.

And when he moved, dropping his encircling arm to settle his palm on her buttocks and draw her higher... Lola gasped as she came in contact with a hard ridge.

That felt so good. *He* felt so good.

Because this was *Niall*, the man she'd fixated on more than half a lifetime ago and yearned for ever since.

Lola tilted her pelvis, accentuating the contact, and was rewarded with a deep-seated growl that reverberated from his throat into their fused mouths.

Swallowing that utterly primitive sound felt even more intimate than the urgent press of their bodies.

Sizzling arousal shot through her, making everything soften, especially that sweet spot between her legs, where he'd hitched her high against his groin.

'Niall.' It was only as she heard the word that she registered the pressure of his mouth easing. His open lips brushed hers as he breathed deep, his chest pushing out against her.

Then his mouth was gone and she opened dazed eyes.

Cobalt eyes, impossibly bright, snared hers.

Her pulse thumped as something passed between them. A primal message that made her body tremble in anticipation.

Yes! At last!

She read the reflection of her own need. The wonder and the hunger that could no longer be denied.

A smile trembled on her lips as sweet tenderness vied with urgent arousal. Finally Niall recognised it too, the force binding them together. The compulsion so strong she hadn't been able to bury it or break it or batter it into submission through years of trying.

Now she didn't have to, because Niall's eyes, and his taut, eager body, revealed this was no longer a one-sided attraction.

'Niall.' Her voice was softer this time, but no less sure. Because this, the pair of them together, was meant to be. At last he realised it too.

Large hands firmed around her arms, pulling them down and holding her steady as he stepped away.

For a second, bereft of his supporting frame, she wavered, unable to balance on her feet. Till he spoke and abruptly Lola was no longer floating in bliss but back on brutal, unforgiving ground.

'I'm sorry, Lola. That was a mistake.'

CHAPTER SIX

NIALL TRIED AND failed to quell the wild hunger within him. The urgent compulsion to taste her again, haul her close and explore every part of Lola's delectable body.

Hell! Those eyes! Wide and disbelieving. No longer hazel but a saturated green with only flecks of brown.

Hungry eyes.

Wounded.

Accusing.

His gaze dropped to her lips, plump and reddened from that no-holds-barred kiss. From *him*, devouring her as if he'd never get enough of her sweet taste and yielding softness.

No, not yielding. She'd kissed him back ardently, pressing against him, turning a gesture of comfort into a frenzy of need.

A shudder passed through him. Niall told himself it was horror at what he'd done.

Yet the fact he had to fight the urge to tuck her in against him again, devouring not just her mouth but every inch of that supple body, told its own tale.

He wanted Lola.

He *craved* her. The last couple of days had been a nightmare, trying to protect her while at the same time wanting her for himself. Every time she got close he found himself inhaling her fresh, enticing scent. His heartbeat spiked whenever she was around. Sleeping had been close to impossible the last two nights, knowing she was lying just a room away, while he burned with unfulfilled longing.

Niall had told himself he'd imagined things. That he exaggerated a natural reaction to a gorgeous woman. That the danger she was in, and their heightened emotions, confused the issue.

He wasn't confused now. He knew with every pulse of rushing blood in his body that he wanted her.

But it was wrong.

Lola was vulnerable. She was under pressure, scared by her stalker. She hadn't thought through what she was doing.

More, she was Ed's little sister. The Suarez family had opened its arms and home to him when he was a troubled teen, flirting with danger. It had never been stated aloud but it was understood that Lola would be safe with him, despite the negative reputation he'd begun to acquire. They'd trusted him and he couldn't, wouldn't betray that trust.

'I'm sorry,' he said again, wishing he meant it.

Because even knowing it was wrong, he had to shove his hands in his pockets to stop himself reaching for her.

Those huge eyes met his. Surprisingly now he couldn't read Lola's expression. It was as if she'd brought down a shutter to hide herself from him.

Niall frowned. He didn't like the notion.

Because you want to see desire in her eyes. So you have an excuse to ignore your conscience and take what you want.

'Why?' She wrapped her arms around her middle and a chunk of something hard broke off inside him at the sight of her hurting, even if her face remained calm. 'Why was it a mistake?'

She had to ask?

Niall shook his head. 'I'm your brother's best friend.'

Her mouth turned down at the corners. 'What's that got to do with you and me?'

Niall pinched the bridge of his nose, squeezing his eyes

shut for a second, hoping when he opened them her lush
mouth wouldn't still be in that sultry pout.

No such luck. That explained his harsh tone. 'There *is* no
you and me. It was a spur of the moment impulse.' Which
made a liar of him. Oh, he'd acted on impulse, but he'd been
thinking about kissing Lola since two nights ago when she'd
opened her door to him. 'Because I wouldn't betray Ed like
that. Or your father. You're off limits.'

Her head angled to one side. By the jut of her chin he'd
guess she was angry rather than hurt, except her face had
paled. That made him feel about an inch tall.

The last thing he wanted was to hurt her.

'Betray? Did Ed tell you not to kiss me? Or my father?'
Before he could answer she pressed on. 'Do you usually let
other people tell you who you can kiss and who you can't?'

Niall swore under his breath. 'Stop trying to twist this,
Lola. We both know they wouldn't like me messing with you.'

Slowly she shook her head. 'Maybe years ago when we
were young. But not now. They both think the world of you.'

Niall flattened his mouth.

That's because they don't know everything about Niall
Pedersen. There's one secret not even Ed knew. One that
would destroy his faith in his mate.

Because when he and Ed met, it was the last thing Niall
had wanted to talk about. And later he'd feared that sharing
it would kill their friendship. He'd learned to hug the past
close and never speak of it.

'And...' She paused, licking her lips. To his horror, that
small movement tugged a white-hot wire of need straight
through his groin. 'I'm all grown up, remember? I decide
what men I kiss. It's no one's business but mine.'

Niall understood the point she was making but part of
him was still back with her deciding what men she kissed.
It was unreasonable and appalling, but he didn't want her
kissing any man.

Any man but him.

He swallowed, the movement grating his throat.

How had this happened? This wasn't just inappropriate desire. It was all-consuming.

Niall had never been proprietorial about any woman, except perhaps for a brief time in his teens when hormones had triumphed over common sense. His relationships were exclusive but time-limited. Never before had he felt sick to the gut at the idea of his current lover eventually going off with someone else.

And Lola isn't even your lover!

This had to stop.

'The point is, I made a mistake. I shouldn't have kissed you, that's all that matters.'

'Even if you enjoyed it?'

Especially because he enjoyed it.

'Call it a conditioned reflex. I'm not proud of it, but holding a woman in my arms, an attractive woman…' he added as he saw her frown gather. Then he lifted his shoulders in a shrug as if it was some simple mistake. 'I just—'

'Got curious? Couldn't help yourself?' Her voice rang with something Niall couldn't identify. Outrage or hurt? She laughed, and the sound, so utterly lacking in amusement, made him shrivel inside. 'Is this like all cats looking the same colour in the dark? You're telling me that holding a woman, any woman, in your arms, would make you try your luck with her?'

Nothing could be further from the truth. Niall was nothing if not discriminating. But he didn't defend himself. Better she think that of him. It was sure to kill any hint of desire she felt.

He waited for her to slap him or shout at him. Instead Lola watched him steadily, as if cataloguing him for future reference. That stare was so coolly assessing he had to resist the urge to shuffle his feet and look away.

Her eyes had changed, the brilliant green less pronounced now. Her mouth was prim and tight, not the cupid's bow that had been an invitation to kiss.

His heart sank. He hated seeing her hiding hurt and disappointment. He hovered on the brink of saying he'd lied. That he wanted her.

But it was vital he convince Lola that was somewhere they couldn't go.

How could he protect her if he was distracted by sex?

Niall knew the consequences if he failed her. His stomach churned in a nauseating roil of regret and pain, flashes of the dark past exploding in his vision so that Lola's beautiful face blurred before him.

The cost of failure was too high. He refused to have yet another death on his hands.

That alone gave him the strength he needed. 'Trust me, Lola, this leads nowhere. What we need to concentrate on is how to keep you safe until Braithwaite's caught.'

He's lying.

She sensed it. Felt it in her bones.

Despite the years apart, she knew Niall. There was something he wasn't telling her. Some reason he changed the subject.

Unless he's just not into you.

Unless it's just as he said. One female body might be as good as another to him. You have no idea what sort of life he leads now.

Ed definitely wasn't going to tell her about his best friend's sexual activities. And who was she to judge with her vast inexperience?

Lola's heart jammed high behind her ribs as some of the fight bled out of her. Perhaps Niall really was programmed to respond sexually to any woman in his arms. Her mouth rucked up in a bitter smile. He'd only added *attractive* woman as an afterthought. Trying to spare her ego. Maybe she didn't even qualify as passably attractive in his rarefied world.

A sharp, sour tang filled her mouth.

Disappointment? Disillusionment?

She didn't stop to investigate. She did what she'd learned to do when her mother died and her world had shredded around her, focusing on one, tangible thing at a time and working out a way to deal with it.

'So you want me to stay here till Braithwaite's caught, is that it?'

Some of the rigidity eased from Niall's frame at her words.

One thing she couldn't fault him on. He really was concerned to keep her safe.

'It makes sense, doesn't it?'

Not if it meant sharing a space with Niall. Not when she wanted to shrivel up in a foetal position and nurse her bruised ego instead of talk with him as if what they'd just shared meant nothing at all.

She shook her head. 'That would only work if Braithwaite's caught soon. I can't put my life and my job on hold permanently.'

'You can work remotely for a while, can't you? Surely your manager would support you if you explained the circumstances.'

Niall was right. Her team was dedicated and hardworking but flexible too. She had a good boss and he'd support her if he could. But it could only be a short-term solution.

'Possibly,' she admitted reluctantly. 'But I can't stay here indefinitely. And until the police arrest Braithwaite, nothing's changed.'

'Call them. Talk to them about whether it's safe for you to return home.'

He looked so sure of himself, Lola guessed he'd already had such a conversation. Heat flared. Anger, she discovered, was a great antidote to sexual frustration and hurt pride.

'I'd planned to, straight after breakfast.' She glanced at her watch and nodded. 'I'll do it now.'

What followed left her feeling enervated. The good news was the case now seemed to be a police priority, something she hadn't been sure of before. The bad news was that there was no proof it had been Braithwaite in her flat. They'd searched his room in the boarding house where he lived but discovered nothing. Their best guess was that he'd monitored her from somewhere else.

Lola suggested coming home as a way of enticing him to overstep the mark, though her stomach cramped with anxiety at the thought. But the officer was against it. Particularly as Mr Pedersen had already offered an alternative plan.

Lola frowned. Surely this was between her and the police, not Niall?

It turned out he'd offered to have one of his security staff stay in her home. An experienced female operative who'd dress like Lola and return to the flat after dark with a suitcase like Lola's. The hidden camera had been disabled so Braithwaite couldn't watch the flat's interior. It was hoped he'd think the woman was Lola and make a move against her.

'But he might hurt her!' Lola protested.

There followed a long conversation about professional qualifications and experience. The extra surveillance equipment installed in the block of flats, which would give the resident and the police early warning if Braithwaite approached. The concerted effort to catch him red-handed in the very near future.

'Frankly, Ms Suarez, with this very generous offer of assistance from Mr Pedersen, it would be a relief knowing you're safely out of harm's way.'

Lola ended the call feeling flat. It wasn't that she wanted to catch her stalker herself. She'd be happy never to lay eyes on the man again. But she felt…useless. She counted her practical problem-solving skills as her main asset. Now she felt helpless.

That was what made her feel so terrible. She'd spent eight years doing everything she could to avoid feeling that way again. Building a safe, certain future, being capable, independent and in control.

That nightmare time when her mother died and her father

spun out of control still haunted her. She'd felt rudderless, terrified of losing her dad too, and their home. She'd been determined never to feel that way again.

Lola shot to her feet, pacing her bedroom. What was she thinking to resent professionals protecting her? She was grateful.

The problem, apart from feeling adrift and horribly powerless, was being beholden to Niall. She hated that. Hated the way that made her feel. Hated that he felt sorry for her.

Hated the way he'd rejected her!

She felt first hot then cold at the memory of him gently but inexorably pushing her away.

Lola wasn't an object of pity. She refused to be.

So she did the sensible thing and contacted her boss, explaining her situation and getting approval to work remotely for the next week.

Twenty minutes later, her bag over her shoulder, she went in search of Niall.

'I've got approval to work remotely for a week.'

'Excellent.'

He didn't look surprised and suspicion surfaced. But surely even take-control Niall wouldn't have interfered by contacting her employer. Lola shoved the notion aside.

'I'm going out for the day. I'll see you later.'

'Sorry?' That wiped the smug expression off his face. Was it petty of her to be pleased? She was sick of him setting limits for her, even if they were sensible. His intentions were good but when he hovered protectively it made her feel weak and vulnerable, exactly what she strived to avoid.

'There may not be taxis, but I've discovered there's a bus to the city from a couple of kilometres down the hill. If I go now I'll catch it easily. While I'm here I want to explore.'

Niall frowned. 'That's not a good idea.'

The coil of brooding antagonism in Lola's belly tightened. 'You said yourself that Braithwaite's unlikely to follow me here, even if he had any way of discovering where

I am, which he doesn't.' She paused and gave him a cool smile. 'There's a return bus late in the afternoon. I'll see you around six.'

She'd only taken a couple of steps when Niall was before her, blocking her way.

'Why not stay here? Enjoy the pool and relax in the sun?'

It sounded tempting but Lola felt claustrophobic. She shook her head. 'I need to get out. For weeks I've felt hemmed in by the threat of a stalker. Now I've got away for a little, I refuse to hide here. I need to get out and enjoy my freedom.'

Especially as this freedom might only be fleeting. Niall and the police spoke confidently about catching Braithwaite and proving a case against him. But Lola knew how difficult it would be. And even with proof, how long would he be off the streets?

Maybe that was why she was so edgy.

Maybe it didn't have anything to do with Niall pushing her away after turning her inside out with that stunning kiss.

And if you believe that you've suddenly gone weak in the head.

'You're serious about this?'

'Oh, come on, Niall!' She jammed her hands onto her hips. 'I'm talking about a day on the Gold Coast. Broad daylight. Holiday makers. A little shopping, a little sightseeing. I'm perfectly capable of managing that.'

'It's not that.' He looked discomfited as if he belatedly realised he was overreacting.

'What's the problem, then? Afraid I'll sneak off and rent a car and go somewhere you don't know about?' She read surprise in his features and realised that for once she'd come up with something he hadn't anticipated. Her lips tugged up in a smile. 'Sadly, I can't because I don't have a driver's licence.'

She lived in a city with good public transport. And, when her friends were busy learning to drive, she'd been too occupied, devoting herself to saving her father from self-destruction.

'But I'm used to public transport.' She sidestepped and headed to the door.

'Wait.' Long fingers encircled her wrist. Shock ran through her. Tiny rivulets of effervescence as if her capillaries fizzed with electricity.

A scant second later Niall's hand dropped away as if burnt.

Lola swallowed. She'd swear her wrist bore the imprint of his fingers. Not because his touch bruised, but because she craved more. Yet he couldn't bear even that contact. Was he afraid his earlier rejection wasn't enough to keep her at bay?

'I'll drive you.'

Niall cursed the impulsive offer all the way down to the city. It had been bad enough last night, cocooned in the sports car with Lola from the airport, every sense on high alert. Not just because of possible external danger but because of the danger she presented to his self-control.

Today was worse. Barely an hour ago he'd held her in his arms, ravaged her sweet mouth and gathered her luscious body close.

He wanted more.

Despite what he'd said about it being wrong.

He had a responsibility to protect Lola, not seduce her.

Tell that to your libido, Pedersen!

His body felt stretched, rigid with the force of control he had to exert. Because, instead of taking another swooping curve down the mountain, he wanted to coast off the road into a secluded lay-by and kiss her again. Find out if she really did taste as delicious as he remembered, like succulent summer fruit.

He wanted to discover if their bodies locked together as easily as he suspected they would.

'Have you told Ed?'

Her words sliced through his thoughts and the wheel wobbled in his hands.

Tell his best friend he lusted after Ed's kid sister? Not likely!

'Did you tell him about Braithwaite?'

Niall breathed out slowly. Braithwaite. Of course. 'No, I'll leave that to you.'

Lola snorted and he flicked her a sideways look. 'What's so funny?'

'The fact there's something you think I can do for myself.'

He frowned and shifted down a gear. 'If there's something behind that pointed remark you'd better explain.'

Because his thought processes were slowed by insistent fantasies that featured Lola wearing a lot less than that button-through dress.

What on earth had possessed him to pack a dress for her with a line of buttons from top to bottom?

It was nothing short of an invitation to flick them undone. Slowly, savouring the delectable sight of her gradually revealed body. Or quickly, tearing it wide, because his patience wore thin and he couldn't wait a second more.

'I mean—' no missing the edge to her voice '—ever since you walked back into my world you've done your best to take over.' She raised a palm. 'I know it's because you care and I thank you for that. But I need to feel I've still got some agency in what happens to me.'

Niall scowled. 'I'm sorry you feel that way. It wasn't my intention to upset you.'

From the corner of his eye he saw her wave her hand. 'I know. Nevertheless, you need to remember I'm used to looking after myself. I make my own decisions. I have done for years.'

Niall nodded but kept his mouth shut. Blurting out that he was the one with security expertise wouldn't help, nor reiterating the fact that her stalker was precisely the sort of obsessive, violent man who posed the worst sort of threat to a woman.

He wanted Lola wary, not scared witless.

Which meant he'd have to give her some space, let her pretend this was a holiday. Back off a bit, even if he intended to stay hyper-vigilant.

Two deaths on his conscience was enough. There wouldn't be a third. Especially—his breath caught—especially not Lola.

So for the rest of the day he set out to lift her burden of fear and turn this into a holiday.

First the beach, for a stroll along the long flat, sandy strip. Then morning tea at an outdoor café where they could watch the passing parade. Then shopping.

But there again, Lola's bolshie independence disrupted his plans. Niall was happy, more or less, to accompany her into most of the boutiques. But she had other ideas. They were passing a store window filled with filmy, decadent night-gowns and underwear that alternated between minuscule and see-through.

Without pausing, Lola sashayed inside, he'd swear with an extra sway to her hips. Not by a single backward glance did she acknowledge she was gauging whether he'd follow, but he knew she'd gone there deliberately. Instead of pointing to a lacy, low-cut bra in the window as she spoke to the shop assistant, she made a production of touching it, her fingers skimming the crimson lace that surely wouldn't even cover her nipples when she tried it on.

Niall knew when he was beaten.

Stiff-legged, he walked across the road and ordered an espresso, his eyes never leaving the shop. He'd monitor her from here. If there was even a hint of threat he'd be at her side in seconds.

He could have followed her. In other circumstances he'd have revelled in it. But those circumstances would be when he was with a lover. Niall wasn't shy about sex or about a beautiful woman wearing erotic clothes. He might have chosen some items for her to try on. He'd definitely have asked to see her model them.

But not with Lola.

He'd been on the edge of arousal ever since that kiss. It was a wonder she hadn't noticed, except she'd been too busy keeping her nose in the air, indignant at his attempts to look after her. Then later, once they reached the Gold Coast, too wrapped up in the sights and sounds, like a kid on a once-in-a-lifetime treat.

But Lola was no child. He almost wished she were. Then things would be easy. They'd be friends. There'd be no disturbing sizzle of sexual awareness. No hunger biting at his belly and undermining him.

Niall hadn't built a multibillion-dollar business through hard work alone. He was the public face of his company. He mixed with people all the time, he socialised, encouraged, persuaded and negotiated.

Yet with Lola he could never find the right words. His brain and his tongue disconnected. If he ran his business as badly as he'd managed his relationship with Lola he'd be bankrupt in a week.

Because beneath every interaction was that inconvenient hunger. The urgent need to do more than protect her. To ignore what he owed her family, and all the reasons he was the worst possible man for her. To bed her.

He pinched the bridge of his nose.

Bed? He'd take her on the front seat of his sports car given half a chance!

'Niall. It *is* you! I thought you weren't going to be in Queensland this week?'

He looked up into the inquisitive eyes of Carolyn Meier, doyenne of the Gold Coast social scene and formidable organiser. Quickly he surveyed the boutique, making sure Lola was still there and safe.

'Carolyn.' He got up and kissed her cheek. 'Good to see you. And you were right, I thought I'd be away.'

'But things changed?' She clapped her hands. 'Excellent. That means you can attend my party tomorrow after all.

Now, don't say you can't. I need all the bidders I can get for our charity auction.'

Niall was about to shake his head when, past Carolyn's shoulder, he saw Lola through the shop window holding a negligee that consisted of a few wispy panels of lace.

Niall gulped, his throat parched. He turned to Carolyn. 'I'd love to come. If I can bring a friend.'

Because he sorely needed distraction. Attending the sort of society function he usually avoided was preferable to fighting a losing battle against his libido and Lola Suarez.

CHAPTER SEVEN

LOLA ENJOYED HERSELF ENORMOUSLY.

Despite Niall's presence.

No, she admitted, *because* of Niall.

Her words must have had some effect because he stopped hovering so obviously like the bodyguard he'd appointed himself, though he was always near enough to protect her. Which, she admitted wryly, was reassuring, despite her earlier protests.

When he relaxed and stopped trying to manage her life he was good company. So much that her hurt at his rejection eased to manageable proportions.

After all, she'd spent years berating herself over her onesided weakness for him.

Her lips twitched as she remembered the frozen look on his face as she'd sauntered into a lingerie shop. As if it had never occurred to him that Ed's little sister was woman enough to wear such things.

Who'd have guessed the mighty, powerful Niall Pedersen would be cowed by a little silk and lace?

She'd been pleased with her tactic, she'd splurged on some sexy underwear, simply because it appealed and she needed a boost.

She'd almost laughed at Niall's taut expression as she'd emerged from the shop carrying a petite black bag embossed with gold and tied with a gold ribbon. She'd felt feminine and carefree and she liked it.

Lola also liked the lunch place he chose. Magnificent views of the endless ocean and the best seafood she'd ever eaten. The ambience of refined opulence and the attitude of the staff, discreetly eager to please, reminded her yet again that the Niall she'd known now inhabited a completely different world from her. One of wealth and privilege.

She had another reminder when he told her they'd been invited to a party the next night. A society party, likely to be flamboyant and definitely requiring something other than the summer clothes Niall had packed for her.

Lola didn't go to lots of parties and definitely not glittering society events. Her life was humdrum as she worked hard and saved her money. She regularly told herself her turn for adventure would come when she was financially secure. But here, now, was a little adventure and she intended to enjoy it to the full.

The low point of the day came when Niall insisted he buy her a new dress for the party. If it had been anyone but Niall, the man she'd been in thrall to for years, she might have accepted. But pernickety pride got in the way.

In the end she accepted his card, had a fantastic time trailing from one exclusive shop to another and finally bought a fantastic dress at a discounted bargain price using her own money, before returning Niall's card unused. Let him find out she hadn't spent his funds when he got his card statement.

Then, to top off the day, they'd visited an iconic wildlife park. A place she'd heard about since she was a child. They'd watched huge flocks of lorikeets swoop in to feed. Unafraid of the crowd, the birds settled everywhere, including on her arms, as they sipped the sweet nectar provided for them. Their vivid colours were a feast for the eyes and once more the difference from her own world, and the dreary end of winter in Melbourne, was stark.

Dreamily, Lola looked out across the deck of Niall's stunning retreat towards the high rises on the coast, glittering in the late afternoon light. She was in the infinity pool, her arms resting on the edge, and it felt as if she were in some fantasy world, far from mundane reality. The warmth, the scents and sounds of the forest, her buoyancy in the water, all produced a mesmerising effect that made her wish she could stay here for ever.

Not just to avoid Braithwaite, but because she hadn't felt this relaxed in ages.

Their day out yesterday had been fun in so many ways, marred only by disappointment that as soon as they returned Niall, after checking the premises' security systems, had excused himself for a conference call that must have lasted hours. She'd made herself a salad for dinner and ate alone before whiling away a few hours watching a film she'd missed at the movies.

Today, her second day in Queensland, Niall had taken her out again, this time exploring the spectacular rainforest on the edge of his mountain. But they weren't gone long, and as soon as they returned he'd headed to his office after warning her again about not answering the door. Every so often she heard him talking, presumably on business calls.

It was a reminder that, but for her, he'd be back in Brisbane, no doubt with PAs and executives in attendance, even on a Sunday.

'Have you got sunscreen on? With that pale skin you'll burn easily.'

His deep voice trawled across her bare shoulders and wound down, deep inside to the secret place that still had a weakness for Niall Pedersen.

Lola ignored that shivery feeling and rolled her eyes, telling herself he was back into big brother mode.

'I'm twenty-four, Niall, not four.'

She turned and raised her hand to shade her eyes against the afternoon sun. She could make out his tall figure on the deck but not his expression. No doubt it was concerned or disapproving. Because, despite the camaraderie they'd shared yesterday and briefly today on their bushwalk, Niall seemed borderline grumpy today.

Maybe he regretted the need to stay here with her. It would be easier to do business at his firm's headquarters. Or maybe he'd had a date lined up for the weekend and had to cancel to babysit her.

Lola's breath snagged and her feeling of well-being dimmed. Was there some fascinating woman waiting for him in Brisbane? Was that why he sounded terse?

She plastered on a smile and spread her arms wide on the edge of the pool behind her, leisurely kicking out and enjoying the caress of warm water on bare flesh.

That had been another impulse buy yesterday. A bright red bikini, as different as possible from the modest navy one-piece in her suitcase. The thought of Niall handling that serviceable but dull swimsuit, and the memory of how he'd regretted that amazing kiss, had galvanised her into recklessness. He might see her in a bikini and think of sun protection, but *she* felt feminine in it. She lifted her chin higher.

'Coming in, Niall? It's a lovely temperature.' He'd been closeted in his office for hours. But she didn't mention that. It would sound as if she'd been keeping tabs on him.

'No. Not today.' He sounded brusque, his tension reaching her from the other side of the pool.

'Niall? What's happened? Have you heard from the police?'

She swam across the pool so she could see him properly.

'No. There's no news from Melbourne.'

But something bothered him. Lola read it in his clamped-down features. 'Bad day at the office?'

His mouth tucked up at the corner and instantly heat drilled down right through her core. She wished he wouldn't do that. Melt her insides with the merest hint of a smile.

'Something like that. I came to tell you we'll leave in an hour for this party.'

'I'll get out then.' It wouldn't take long to get ready but she'd promised herself a soak in her huge tub. The bath oil smelled heavenly and she wanted to try it.

Niall should have moved back. He hadn't expected her to pull herself straight out of the pool at his feet. But instead of swimming to the steps, she vaulted out, rising in one supple movement before him.

He should definitely have moved back *then*.

Except she stood there, all sweet, streamlined curves, gleaming wet and so desirable his mouth dried.

Surely that bikini wasn't legal?

Says the man whose lovers swim topless or naked.

But this was different. This was Lola.

It wasn't her status as Ed's sibling that made the difference. It was that he was within a hair's breadth of cupping those pert breasts with their pebbled nipples in his eager palms. Or sliding his thumbs under the side strings of her bikini and dragging the bright red fabric down her legs.

Red for passion.

For danger.

Niall's groin tightened with a heavy rush of blood. He hefted a mighty breath but couldn't fill his lungs. He tried again and only managed to take in the scent of her, wet woman and something tangy like ripe fruit.

'Excuse me.'

Lola moved, reaching for him, and hectic heat hammered in his blood.

He waited for her touch but it didn't come. Because she grabbed the towel slung over the chair beside him. The movement brought her so close he swore he felt a current of air brush him at the movement.

Finally he shuffled a step back, giving her space while she dried her shoulder-length hair.

This was why he'd kept to his study last night and today. Rousting staff from their rest in order to discuss the Asian expansion and the difficulty getting enough top-quality staff for the VIP protection teams.

To distract himself from thoughts of Lola.

Much good it had done. Whenever he looked out from his study to check on her by the pool he'd lost his train of thought. And when he didn't immediately see her he'd gone prowling, silently seeking her out to check she was safe.

How many times last night had he stood in the doorway of her bedroom, checking on her?

Of course, in his sinful thoughts, he did far more than check on her.

'You're looking forward to tonight?' His voice grated.

'I am.' Her smile lit her face, banishing the slight shadows of worry and tiredness as she wrapped the towel around her, tucking in one corner at her breast. 'I've never been to a glitzy society party. It *will* be glitzy, won't it?'

Her enthusiasm eased his tension a little. At least she had no idea of his battle with his baser self.

'It sure will.' The sort of thing he usually avoided. 'Carolyn loves to put on a show and the more publicity, the more money to her charities. There'll even be a red carpet.' Seeing Lola's eyes light up, he hurried on. 'But we won't use it. We'll take the lift from the basement.' Photographers weren't allowed at the event itself so Lola should be safe from public attention.

'Of course.' Her smile dimmed and something crushed inside him. 'Because we don't want Braithwaite finding out where I am.'

Niall nodded. He'd take no chance of Lola being snapped by paparazzi and her photo widely published, even if it seemed unlikely Braithwaite could reach her here. 'Don't worry, Lola. There'll be enough glitz to satisfy you even without the red carpet.' He paused. 'Frankly, I didn't think that would be your thing.'

She tilted her head to one side in that way she'd always

had, as if considering his words closely, and trying to read his expression.

He sure as hell hoped she couldn't tell what was going on in his mind.

'It's not. But it's been ages since I've done anything more exciting than Friday drinks after work or catching a meal and a movie with friends. I've been studying and working full-time so all my leave is used for that.' She hitched her towel higher and Niall fought not to stare at the plump, creamy skin of her breast before she covered it again. 'You know what they say, about all work and no play.'

'So you want to play tonight?' The words spilled before he could stop them. Then it was too late because all he could think of was the games he'd like to play with Lola. In private.

His body responded with predictable enthusiasm.

'A little.' Her cheerful expression slipped and he realised, belatedly, that she'd had to work at it.

A rush of sympathy hit him. Of course she had to work at it. She had a dangerous maniac out to get her. She was making the best of a bad situation, looking for distractions, and who could blame her?

Niall conjured a smile and stepped aside, gesturing for her to precede him into the house. 'Shall we? I have a feeling it's going to be a memorable night.'

Tonight would be all about Lola, not just her safety, but giving her some much-needed fun. Carolyn's party would be perfect for that.

Nothing, he assured himself, could be simpler.

CHAPTER EIGHT

LOLA ZIPPED UP the dark red dress but delayed looking in the mirror. She'd loved it in the boutique. But could she carry it off? The vivid colour, the sexy cut?

It was so not her. She dressed conservatively, partly because it suited the image she wanted to project at work. Partly because it suited her looks.

Lola was ordinary. Medium. Average.

She had dark brown hair but not as dark and lustrous as her mother's. Nor did she have her mother's flashing ebony eyes or stunning hourglass figure. Lola's eyes were an indeterminate shade of browny-green. Or was it greeny-brown? As for curves... She smoothed her palms over her hips. She had curves, just not spectacular ones.

Everyone hearing her name before meeting her expected Lola to be a stunning Latina bombshell. They were always disappointed.

Just once she'd like to live up to the promise of her exotic name.

Lola shook her head, her mouth compressing. Since when did she think like this? Not since her teens, surely. She had a healthy, fit body and that was a blessing.

Niall. He was the reason.

Not that he'd ever given her cause to be uncomfortable about her body. He'd never commented on it.

But she'd seen photos of the glamazons he dated. Curvy, blonde and beautiful.

Just once, she'd like him to see her not as little Lola who was like a sibling to him, but as a seductive woman. She'd imagined she'd succeeded yesterday when he kissed her, until he pushed her away so fast she almost got whiplash.

She frowned, remembering his stare just now as she'd got out of the pool in front of him. He'd looked so stern it was hard to read his thoughts. She'd told herself she'd bought the bikini for herself, for the fun of it, but part of her had wondered if Niall might see her in it and...

What? Suddenly decide she was his sort of woman?

Lola snorted and reached for the stiletto sandals she'd bought with the dress. Slowly she looped the narrow leather straps once, twice around her ankle then tied them in a bow before doing up the other shoe.

One good thing about the nightmare her life had become. It had brought Niall back into her world, giving her the chance to put him behind her.

What had begun as a schoolgirl crush had turned into something problematic. Because in a severe case of arrested development she hadn't grown out of it. Partly, she realised, because her mother's death had made her cling harder than ever to what she knew and what felt safe.

No one had made her feel safer than Niall. Well, her father had, until he turned into a stranger, going into a tailspin when he lost his wife. Everything Lola knew had wobbled on its foundations.

Then, while Lola had become more and more cautious, her friends had started dating. She, as the sensible one, the good listener, had been the recipient of so many confidences about sexual experiences gone wrong, dating disasters, predatory and dangerously aggressive boyfriends, it had fed her natural caution in ever-diminishing circles.

Till she'd been almost afraid to date.

By the time she did, she was primed to expect disaster.

All the time, at the back of her mind, was the mirage of Niall Pedersen. Not the real man but the fantasy she'd built him into in her head. She'd extrapolated on his kindness and his phenomenal looks and turned him into an ideal man against whom no one could compete.

Was it any wonder her love life was non-existent?

The time had come to do something about it.

When she'd bought this outfit she'd wondered if it would alter Niall's view of her. He wasn't as immune to her as he pretended. Inner muscles clenched as she remembered being clamped against his erection when they'd kissed.

Maybe, wonder of wonders, she'd end this ridiculous crush with a night in his bed. From what her friends said, he wouldn't seem nearly so amazing after that. And it would be a chance to burn off the sexual frustration that had reached dangerous heights.

Lola shook her head. She was determined not to think about Niall. They had no future. He'd made that clear. Instead she'd enjoy her glamorous party and test out her underdeveloped flirting skills on a stranger or two.

She'd turn over a new leaf. When she got home, and when she got free of Braithwaite, she'd start dating seriously. She'd relegate Niall to the past and get on with life.

Swinging around, she surveyed herself in the mirror.

She looked...different.

Lola hadn't straightened her hair or put it up. She told herself the unbound waves suited the look.

The dress clasped her body close down to her hips before flaring a little around her thighs. She wore no bra since the dress was cut so low at the back but she liked the narrow double straps, just wide enough for a row of diamantés, that rose over each shoulder and crossed on her back. And the shoes... Lola smiled at the spiky, sexy heels.

She didn't look like ordinary Lola Suarez any more.

Lifting her chin, she met her eyes in the mirror. It didn't matter that she wasn't Niall's type. She was her own woman and intended to enjoy herself.

* * *

'I'm ready.'

Niall swung round and Lola repressed a shiver of nervous excitement.

So he looked a million dollars. So what? He wasn't for her. Nor did it matter if he approved of how she looked.

Yet her gaze lingered on the blue shirt that matched his eyes, and the pale jacket and trousers that made the most of his tall, lean frame, accentuating the dark gold of his skin.

Tropical dressy and pure gorgeousness. That was how he looked.

Lola ignored her suddenly erratic pulse, telling herself it was excitement about the party. She also tamped down a wriggle of discomfort, imagining all the women who'd cluster around him tonight. Good! That would leave her free to enjoy herself. She didn't need a babysitter.

'You look...' He stopped speaking as she moved from the dim hallway into the light.

She saw the hint of a frown pinch his forehead and all at once he looked stern, the angles and planes of his face hard and angular.

'Glamorous?' she prompted, jutting one hip and posing with her hand at her waist as if she hadn't a care in the world. 'Just right for a glitzy party?' She spun on the spot, her skirt twirling around her bare legs.

'Very nice.'

Nice! Lola's mouth tightened. Even Ed could do better than that and he rarely noticed anything without feathers or fur.

For a second she wondered if she'd made a mistake, buying this dress. But only for a second. She liked how she looked. She didn't need Niall's approval.

'Have you got a cardigan? You might get cold.'

Lola blinked. It was like hearing a voice from the past. In her teens, her father had expected her to carry a cardigan in case it got cold, an umbrella in case it rained and a tissue. Beside him, her mother would just smile and tell her to enjoy herself. After her mother died, Lola's outings were curtailed and for a long time her father hadn't noticed her, much less what she wore.

'I'm sure I'll be fine.' She moved towards the door. 'Shall we go?'

For a long moment Niall said nothing. She even wondered if he'd changed his mind. Then, abruptly, he stalked towards her.

Despite her determination not to be affected, her heart fluttered as he approached, his stride all fluid power. Then she turned and preceded him through the door.

The drive down the mountain was different. Niall drove with the same ease and focus but something new simmered in the air between them.

'Are you having trouble at work?' she asked eventually.

'What makes you think so?'

'Surely even a self-made billionaire has Sundays off.'

He shrugged. 'A few issues needed personal attention.'

Lola shifted in her seat, hating the way her wayward imagination linked the shiver-deep voice with the words *personal attention*.

With luck she'd spend the evening chatting up some gorgeous, fascinating guy. Someone who didn't remind her of Niall. Though if he had a rich, deep voice it wouldn't hurt. And a hard, powerful body.

She shifted again. The upholstery was even softer than she remembered, possibly because her dress was so short she felt the leather against bare skin.

It was a relief when they reached the city and, as they skirted a block where a crowd had gathered on the pavement, Lola was glad they weren't making a red-carpet entrance. She intended to enjoy herself but wasn't sure she had the confidence for that.

As Niall ushered her into the lift from the basement carpark, he finally spoke, breaking her thoughts.

'You look more than nice.' His words yanked her face up

towards his. A shot of blue fire blasted through her. 'You look fabulous.'

Lola waited for that indefinable something in his expression that told her he exaggerated, probably to boost her confidence after his earlier, lukewarm response. It didn't come.

Instead there was just his bright stare and a steady burn of admiration that warmed her from the inside out.

Her breath snagged behind her ribs and her lungs felt too tight. She drew in a quick breath, hyper-aware of the sharp rise of her braless breasts against thin silk.

'Thank you. So do you.' She licked her lips, her mouth suddenly dry.

Niall's gaze dropped to her lips and something shifted inside. That heat settled low in her abdomen and—

The lift doors opened and they were no longer alone.

They stepped straight into an amazing apartment, and into the heart of a flamboyant celebration.

The place was packed. There were people and movement everywhere and the lavishly decorated setting made Lola's eyes widen as Niall led her forward.

A huge atrium extended up over three floors with a curving marble staircase and a vast, shallow pool at its base. The enormous space was decked out like an exuberantly decorated circus tent. But more lavish than a real tent. There were swathes of silks, satins and bling everywhere.

Wait staff wended their way through the throng on unicycles, balancing trays of bubbly and incredible cocktails adorned with fruit and fizzing sparklers. Tightrope walkers danced overhead and acrobats, dressed in lavish outfits that seemed to consist mainly of sparkling crystal, performed amazing feats. There was even a fire-eater, ankle-deep in the sapphire-tiled pool.

'He's probably in the water as a safety precaution,' Niall bent close to murmur, his breath warm on her ear. 'Last year Carolyn insisted on lighting Catherine wheels inside and there was a slight problem. She doesn't do things by halves.'

'It's amazing.' Lola breathed, trying not to notice the way her cheek tingled from the caress of his breath. Instead she focused on the throng of guests, some in casual clothes and others dressed to the nines in stunning displays of wearable wealth. 'It's…'

'Gaudy? Over the top?' She turned to find a blonde woman beside her, her trim form spectacular in a beautifully tailored ringmaster's outfit. Instead of a bow tie, she sported the most amazing necklace Lola had ever seen. If they were real diamonds… 'I hope so, darling. I wanted something people wouldn't forget in a hurry. Though I did have my heart set on having an elephant too. But Ted, my husband, made such a fuss about trying to get even a baby elephant into the lift, and then I remembered we don't support animals in circuses any more, so maybe it wasn't such a good idea.'

The woman grinned, her gap-toothed smile so warm Lola forgot the fortune in gems she wore. 'I'm Carolyn. You must be Niall's friend.'

'Lola.' She smiled back. 'Thank you so much for inviting me.' Automatically she put out her hand as she did at work, then wondered if rich people air-kissed instead.

But Carolyn's handshake was firm and friendly. 'I'm pleased to meet you.' She darted a look at Niall that Lola couldn't read. 'Absolutely delighted. Anything you want, just ask. Meanwhile, let me introduce you…'

They were swept up into a round of introductions that made Lola's head spin. The guests included a raft of VIPs she knew by repute. International movie stars and directors, on the coast for filming. Famous authors and artists. Billionaires and philanthropists. A naturalist documentary maker whose face was famous the world over. He knew Ed's work and monopolised her until Niall interrupted, saying there was someone she needed to meet.

That someone was Jake, an advertising executive, way above Lola's paygrade, but personable and pleasant, and happy to talk about building a career in the industry.

Niall moved away and Lola was glad he didn't hover. Though time and again she'd look up from a conversation to find his dark eyes on her.

Was he in bodyguard mode? Or making sure she didn't feel out of her depth? He needn't worry. She was having a great time.

Lola turned back to Jake, who asked her about her career plans. He really was very nice. Handsome too, with his surfer blond good looks, and thoughtful, snagging her a fresh glass of wine from a passing waiter.

She just wished she couldn't still feel Niall's eyes on her. Or the betraying kernel of tension deep inside that had nothing to do with the party or Braithwaite and everything to do with the crush she was determined to end sooner rather than later.

So when Jake asked her if she wanted to dance, she gulped down a mouthful of crisp white wine and put her glass aside, smiling her assent. 'I'd love to. Thank you.'

Niall had made plenty of mistakes in his time but none as significant as this one.

He should never have brought her here.
Never have introduced her to Jake Sinclair.

Bad enough to watch Jake dance with Lola earlier, when the music was loud and upbeat. But now, hours later, the music had changed and the dancers moved slowly, in what looked more like slowly savoured sex than dancing.

Pain shot up Niall's jaw and he realised he was grinding his molars. Again.

Breaking away from the knot of people around him, ignoring the clutch of feminine fingers on his arm and the invitation in a pair of bright blue eyes, Niall shouldered his way through the throng to a relatively quiet spot where he could watch the dance floor and brood in peace.

Except there'd be no peace, not with Lola, gorgeous in that red dress and come-take-me heels that emphasised the slender shape of her legs and drew the eye up to her ripe peach of a derriere. Not when she was plastered against a grinning Jake Sinclair.

Multiple times tonight Niall had intervened, steering Lola towards new acquaintances he thought she'd enjoy. Staying beside her during the fundraising auction and enjoying her enthusiasm when he'd won various items. He'd found any excuse to remove her from Jake and that appreciative glint in his eye. But whenever he left her Jake turned up again.

Yet Niall had been compelled to give her space.

Lola hated being reminded of the reasons for his protectiveness and he'd vowed tonight would be about her enjoying herself after the stress of recent days. More importantly, if he stayed beside her he might give in to the desperate urge to touch her himself.

His belly clenched as he watched her move sinuously, every slim line and curve revealed by the tight, short dress that had lit a hungry flame inside him.

Back at the house he'd been on the verge of telling her the party had been cancelled and they had to stay in. Except that would mean an evening alone in her company. An evening with a temptress dressed to party…and seduce.

Niall was strong-willed. Apart from that one kiss, he'd stood firm against his baser instincts from the moment he'd walked into Lola's apartment a few days ago. But there were limits and he'd reached his.

The voice of his conscience, reminding him that he owed her a duty of care—that he couldn't, shouldn't, mustn't touch her—had been silent since she sashayed out of her bedroom looking like a sexy angel from a wet dream.

He hefted in a draught of air that did nothing to cool the deep-seated pulse of need throbbing through him.

Niall knew what Jake Sinclair wanted. Because he wanted the same. Lola, naked in his bed. Or, his temperature spiked, still in that dress, as she rode his erection while he held her hips and feasted on her tantalising breasts through the red fabric. Niall swallowed hard and gulped down the whisky he'd moved on to when beer failed to slake his thirst.

Nothing would slake his thirst but Lola.

His only consolation was that Jake wouldn't get her either. Not on Niall's watch.

Lola was safe tonight from Braithwaite, given the tighter security arrangements he'd arranged for the building. Even so Niall was on constant alert for any hint of danger.

He'd also make sure she was safe from casual philanderers. This was the first time she'd danced with Jake in thirty minutes. It would be the last. But he'd wait till the music stopped before intervening. He had that much control, just.

Jake's hand slid down her hip, drawing her closer, and a growl built at the back of Niall's throat.

'If you don't like it, do something about it, darling.'

He turned to find Carolyn at his elbow, looking at Lola and Jake.

'I will. Soon.' When this never-ending song finished. 'She deserves a chance to enjoy herself.'

'At your expense?' Carolyn slanted him a curious look. 'From what I saw she'd be happier dancing with you.'

Niall turned back towards the dancers. 'She looks happy to me.' His voice hit a rough note and he swallowed a little more whisky, easing his dry throat.

'Ah, but you haven't seen the way she's been looking at you all night. Funny that you haven't noticed. But then you've gone to such trouble not to stare at her all the time. Till now.'

Could it be true? Would Lola prefer to be with him?

Niall reminded himself it wasn't possible. It wouldn't be right.

But his body had other ideas. The music ended and he strode forward, thrusting his glass into Carolyn's hand, the sound of her chuckle in his ears.

He wasn't in the habit of revealing weakness. But right now he didn't care that his hostess had read him like a book. All he cared for was...

'My dance.' No please. No hesitation. Just his hand on Jake's shoulder, pulling him away, and his other hand on Lola's. Her eyes met his and the fire in his belly dropped straight to his groin.

Carolyn had been right. He saw excitement flare in Lola's eyes, her lips parting as if she drew in a sudden breath.

Jake said something Niall didn't hear as he pulled Lola towards him and, miracle of miracles, she settled against him, her slender body fitting close.

Niall sucked in a shaky breath as his brain struggled to catalogue all the many ways this felt good. Finally he gave up and simply basked in the rush of pleasure. After a moment he noticed the music and remembered to move. It was no more than a shuffle, but it brought Lola against him in new and delicious ways.

Was that a sigh? He gathered her nearer, tilting her head against his shoulder and bending his head to inhale the summer sunshine scent of her hair.

Another wash of desire filled him and he slipped his hand to her hip, wondering if she'd object. Instead she moved closer and his thigh insinuated between her legs as they turned.

Niall's hand slid further, lower, till he claimed her buttock and then a new heat blasted him. The heat of her sex rubbing against him.

Need jolted through him so hard he forgot they were supposed to be dancing. He stood, rock hard, his leg pressing between hers, his hand drawing her to him in a movement that was purely, overtly sexual.

He had to stop this. Had to remember why he couldn't—

'Niall? Don't you want to dance any more?'

She looked up and he was drowning in soft green. It was like looking into the rainforest, greens and darker flecks of shadow beckoning him closer.

He opened his mouth then shut it again. He didn't trust

himself to speak. If he vocalised he feared it might be an utterly feral roar of possessiveness.

Then he saw her mouth turn down at the corners and some of the light dim in her lovely eyes.

'No,' he said at last, his voice thick. 'It's not dancing I want.'

Her lips, the lips that had been so soft against his, formed into an O of surprise.

Not rejection or distaste.

She lifted her hand from his shoulder and raked her fingers through the hair on the back of his head. Instinctively he tipped his head back into her touch as tingling ripples of pleasure cascaded from her fingertips.

If it felt that good when she merely touched his scalp...

'Nor me,' she murmured in a throaty voice that untied another row of knots in the web of his self-control.

Niall frowned, trying to make sense of her words. Then she moved against him in a suggestive sway that blasted everything else into the background.

'Hold that thought,' he growled. Drawing together the tattered fibres of his self-possession, he stepped back, ignoring his body's silent scream of protest. He was strung so tight it was a wonder he could even make the move.

The only positive was seeing his own distress mirrored in Lola's eyes.

He threaded his fingers through hers and led her to the edge of the room. He felt clumsy, his gait stiff-legged because of the hard-on he could do nothing about.

Not yet. But soon. Meanwhile his body felt as if it were stretched on a rack, taut to the edge of pain.

Faces blurred as they passed. People spoke but he didn't stop. Then, near the lift, he spied a familiar blonde, her top hat tipped at a jaunty angle, a cocktail in one hand and her finger on the button for the lift.

'Darlings! I'm so pleased you had a good time.' Niall read a mischievous twinkle in Carolyn's eyes. 'I had a feeling you might be leaving. Ah, here it is.' She turned and, with a flourish, gestured for them to step inside.

'Thanks, Carolyn. It's been…memorable.'

Lola added her thanks before the doors shut, enclosing them together. Instantly his tension ratcheted from extreme to the catastrophic. His pulse thundered and her perfume in his nostrils threatened to short-circuit his senses.

Niall punched in his private access code with an unsteady hand, then leaned forward for the iris scanner he'd insisted on during the building phase.

He kept his attention on the display panel because he feared if he looked at Lola the security staff monitoring the cameras would get an eyeful of their boss having unbridled sex with the temptress beside him.

But he kept tight hold of her hand.

Niall swallowed hard. When had holding hands become an erotic experience?

Touching Lola's soft palm, her slim fingers threaded through his, felt like a promise of what was to come. Soon he'd feel her smooth body against him as they melded together completely.

He swallowed again, his skin steaming despite the perfectly stable temperature.

'We're going up, not down.'

He had to concentrate on making his voice work. 'I had more to drink than I intended.' Because the sight of Lola cosying up to Jake Sinclair drove him to ignore his usual limits. 'I won't take a chance on being over the limit. We'll stay here the night.'

'You have an apartment here as well as on the mountain?'

Ridiculous how tough it was to concentrate on conversation.

'An investment.' The whole building was, but he kept the penthouse for himself. He'd rent it out now he had the house in the hinterland. The doors opened and they stepped into the penthouse.

A swish of sound as the doors closed, leaving them cut off from the outside world. The air rushed from Niall's lungs and some of the corded tension in his tortured muscles eased.

At last.

He turned to the woman beside him. The woman who drove him to the edge of reason. Sure enough, one glance at those wide eyes and parted lips, and something slammed down inside him.

The voice of caution smashing into oblivion?

Because nothing, not conscience or good intentions or even guilt, could make him release her now.

He'd gone past the point of no return. Unless…

'Lola.' His tongue was thick and his voice husky. 'If you don't want me, say so now. Then choose a bedroom and shut the door and you won't see me till tomorrow.'

How he'd find the strength to deliver on the promise he didn't know. But one thing at a time.

She shook her head and his hand tightened, dismay filling him. Had he misread—?

Lola's gaze locked on his. The impact was a pulse of energy straight to his groin. 'I want you, Niall. So much.'

CHAPTER NINE

HE TOOK HER mouth so fast he tasted his name on her lips.

No, that was the taste of Lola. Once experienced, impossible to forget.

The sweet tang had haunted him.

How often had he woken from fitful sleep to the memory of her flavour on his tongue? Hungering for the full banquet of her luscious body instead of a mere taste?

He hauled her close, softness against hard, needy flesh, and felt the vibrations as his last reserves of caution crashed down. Her lips were soft, her mouth accommodating yet demanding, everything he remembered and so much more.

A shudder shot from his nape, down between his shoulder blades to the soles of his feet. Her smoky, seductive voice still echoed in his ears.

She wanted him.

The way she slid up against him, as if trying to meld herself to his erection, was better than any fantasy. Stars exploded at the corners of his vision but putting any distance between them was impossible.

One hand cradling her skull, Niall leaned into the kiss, bending her backwards so she clung. His might be the dominant position but there was nothing submissive about Lola. She devoured him with a hungry fervour that catapulted his need higher. And that low humming sound in the back of her throat—part approval, part demand—ignited his blood like a flame touching oil.

The kiss deepened, became a mating of mouths, mirroring the sex act they both needed so desperately.

Niall couldn't remember a kiss ever being like this—the most erotic foreplay. And the most devastating.

His chest cramped as he lost oxygen and forgot to breathe in more.

Frantic to touch, he dropped his hand from Lola's waist to mould her buttock, pulling her in even harder. She circled her pelvis against him and he froze, clawing at the ragged remnants of his restraint.

'Wait,' he groaned. 'Stop.'

Clamping her with both hands now, he held her still. One more undulation and she'd undo him. Heart hammering, he eased away just enough to suck in air.

'But I want—'

Another time he might have triumphed at the sulky pout in her voice, and on her kiss-swollen mouth. Now all he could do was pray he didn't embarrass himself.

'I know, sweetheart. Me too. But give me a moment.'

Another first. He'd never teetered on the edge of climax after just a kiss, and fully clothed at that.

He pressed a kiss to her neck, to that fragrant curve, and felt her shiver as she tilted her head to give him better access.

Niall slid his hands possessively and frowned. He felt only taut curves and slippery silk but no underwear.

Snapping open eyes he hadn't realised he'd closed, he looked beyond her to the full-length mirror on the opposite wall of the entry. Saw his hands on the shimmery red dress, hauling it higher and higher until it was no longer silk he touched but even softer flesh. Bare, pale flesh bisected by the tiniest line of dark red lace.

G-strings were nothing new. Once a lover had come to him wearing nothing but a raincoat and crotchless knickers.

But that memory was blurred. Nothing, ever, had looked as sexy as Lola's pert bottom with that suggestive sliver of lace.

There was a galloping sound in his ears and a rushing pressure driving down between his legs. Niall was on the verge of spilling himself like an over-excited schoolkid.

'Wait,' he said again, nipping the curve where her neck met her shoulder and feeling her tremble.

Before she could object, Niall stepped back, putting a whole centimetre of space between them, even though the savage beast inside him howled a protest.

Dreamy green eyes opened, catching his gaze, but refusing to be snared, and ruthless with the need to make this last, Niall moved her up against the wall.

Then he dropped to his knees.

In her high heels she was just at the right height.

Anticipation sizzled as he yanked her teasing little skirt up at the front. Past slim thighs that trembled, till he found the V of scarlet lace.

He exhaled on a rush of pleasure. Then saw her twitch as his breath warmed her skin. Her hand appeared, making to cover the treasure he'd found.

But she didn't resist when he took her hand and pulled it away. One palm still pinning her skirt against her belly, he raised her hand to his mouth as he lifted his gaze.

Her mouth was open on a sigh of pleasure. When he licked across her palm and up the length of her index finger she swallowed convulsively, her wide eyes narrowing under weighted lids.

He'd barely started and the mere sight of her undid him.

She looked sultry and inviting, yet something about her made him think of some goddess, alluring but untouchable.

Except he *was* touching her. He intended to brand himself on her body so thoroughly that she couldn't think straight.

Taking his time, he laved the next finger and the next, drawing each into his mouth and sucking.

A small, keening sound reached his ears and he felt her tremble.

'Niall.'

The way she said his name was like a prayer and a demand, urgent and reverent at the same time, making him feel like some sort of conquering hero. He wanted to hear Lola say his name like that again and again. He wanted to hear her scream it as she came, convulsing around him.

His erection throbbed against the confines of his clothes but he did his best to ignore that, focusing on Lola.

Releasing her hand, he leaned forward, pressing his mouth against red lace that was already gratifyingly damp, drawing slowly against that intimate heat till she shook even harder. Her scent was more concentrated here, sweet and tart with a hint of womanly musk.

Niall's hands were unsteady as he peeled the tiny strips of lace from her hips, rolling them down her legs. She tried to step out but the lace caught first on the sexy leather bow at her ankle, then on her spike heel.

He heard a muffled sob and offered soothing words as he helped her free.

Then his fragile patience ended. Pushing her thighs apart, he leaned forward, breathing in her rich perfume and sinking his face against dark, downy curls.

Lola clutched him, one hand to his shoulder, the other in his hair.

One exploratory flick of his tongue and she cried out, greedily bucking her hips. He smiled, licking again, slower and further, and felt her shudder.

Lola's breathing fractured and he felt her thigh muscles tense. He barely had time to delve with first one finger, then a second, when she screamed. Her frantic convulsions squeezed his fingers as her thighs pushed against him.

Remarkably, Niall almost came with her. He was so ready that feeling and tasting Lola's climax, the first he'd given her, almost sent him over the edge.

Fingernails scraped his scalp and he welcomed the sting, giving him something to concentrate on other than the urge to lose himself.

Lola wilted and he uncoiled, rising and lifting her into his arms in the same movement.

She was limp and delectable.

Nudging her hair aside, he slid his lips across her cheek to her mouth and was rewarded with instant entry. This time their kiss held a new element. A languorous welcome from the woman he'd pleasured to screaming point. Did she taste herself on his lips?

Niall had to move. Despite the fact that walking was near impossible because his body was so primed. Because he wanted Lola horizontal and naked.

Somehow, mouth still fused with hers, he navigated past the reception rooms to the bedrooms, guided by the low lighting that had switched on when they entered.

He veered into the first bedroom, stopping before the bed to put her on her feet. He needed to be out of his trousers and wearing protection before he lay against her.

One easy glide and her zip was down, but those crossed shoulder straps...

'Let me.' Lola's voice was a throaty purr and he actually took a half-step back as he peeled off his jacket and ripped at his shirt. Because any more incitement would be too much.

His wallet was in his hand, fingers freeing a condom, when Lola's beautiful dress slid to the floor.

All the air left Niall's lungs in a rush of appreciation.

'You're gorgeous.'

He'd known it from the first. The moment in Melbourne when she'd opened her door to him he'd seen she'd grown into her early promise. But knowing and seeing every bare inch—they were two different things.

His gaze skated down then lingered, slow on the way back up. Her fingers twitched, hands moving as if to cover herself. Then her chin lifted and her hands dropped to her sides.

Wasn't she used to being naked with her lovers? With her beautiful, streamlined curves, she had a body any man would desire.

'I want to touch you but I don't dare.' His voice was like hot tar spilling across gravel and the constriction in his throat tightened when Lola's lips curled at the corners.

She was bewitching. Tantalising. Effortlessly sexy and yet once more he was struck by the idea of an untouchable ideal. A woman far removed from the normal run.

'I want to touch you too.'

She made it sound like a husky invitation and Niall had to stop himself from moving closer. Instead his hands went to his belt, fumbling with the buckle and fastening as if they were unfamiliar puzzles. Toeing off his shoes, he stripped off clothes and sheathed himself. He did it with his eyes closed because the sight of Lola's direct gaze as his hands moved to his penis was temptation overload.

When he looked again it was to see her slick her tongue over her bottom lip, her attention still on his groin. On cue, his erection bobbed higher, rampantly eager.

Lola chuckled and for a moment he thought she sounded nervous as well as amused. But she didn't look nervous. She looked *hungry*.

Niall grabbed her hand and led her to the bed, careful not to touch her anywhere else. Despite the way his eyes kept returning to those tip-tilted breasts.

'What did you say?' Her voice was barely audible.

'Nothing.' His mouth must have moved as he mentally ran through his thirteen times table, trying to focus on something other than Lola's bare body and the ecstasy that beckoned.

He didn't get past twenty-six. Because then she lay down on the bed, all lean muscle and sinuous, elegant curves. Her raspberry-crested breasts wobbled as she shuffled across to make space for him.

Niall didn't need space. He had no intention of lying anywhere but between her thighs.

He joined her, kneeling above her with his hands planted near her shoulders. It was like having a banquet set before him and not knowing where to begin. His lower body was taut and heavy with need, ready to take. But he summoned a little finesse, wanting her eager for him again.

Keeping his hands on the bed, he lowered his head to her breast, exploring the satiny, scented skin with his lips and tongue, till she was twitching beneath him, her breath coming in rough pants. Smiling, he moved to her other breast, teasing that ripe nipple with his teeth, to be rewarded with a cry of muffled desperation.

Lola's thighs fell open between his knees and her hands clamped his head to her breast, as if fearing he might leave before finishing what he'd started.

No chance of that.

Shoving her legs wider with his knees, he settled in the cradle of her hips, his smile turning to a grimace as the impact of their bodies touching blasted through him.

Desperate, he slid his hand between them, down that dainty cleft and up into moist heat. Instantly she lifted, seeking more, and his last restraint snapped.

One elbow on the bed, he guided himself to her, delaying only a second to appreciate the moment as her forest green eyes ate him up. Then, with one sure, hard thrust, he took her.

He thought he'd known. Thought he was prepared.

But nothing had readied him for Lola. So incredibly tight, so slick and—

'Niall!' It wasn't a scream of ecstasy but a whisper of shock.

He was shocked at the unexpected impediment that turned out to be no barrier at all as his momentum took him into Lola's sweet, mind-numbing heat.

He knew a momentary impulse to stop. Actually withdrawing was impossible. But by then it was over and he nestled right at her core. They fitted together so snugly he couldn't but savour it.

A shudder racked him so deeply it seemed to start in his bone marrow and work out.

Lifting a hand that trembled because of the effort it took to remain still, Niall brushed the hair off her face. He tried to read her expression. Her shock had faded and thankfully he saw no sign of pain.

Had he hurt her?

'Are you all right, sweetheart?'

Her skin was flushed and damp and her eyes veiled, as if hiding secrets.

But her biggest secret was out.

Lola had been a virgin!

Finally his thinking brain caught up with his physical instincts and guilt smote him.

Lola, a virgin.

He was rearing up when her hands clamped to his shoulders. A silky calf slid up and over his backside and everything inside him shouted hallelujah.

Niall gritted his teeth, torn between guilt and desire.

Her beautiful eyes held his and just like that his internal struggle ended.

Who did he think he was fooling? Pulling back was impossible.

He lowered his head, nuzzling her neck, down to that most sensitive spot that made her gasp and wriggle beneath him.

That was all it took, the sound of her breath, and that tiny shimmy of her hips, and he was gone.

Niall captured her lips, claiming her mouth as his body took hers, pumping smooth and fast, each slide into her untried depths producing the most phenomenal joy he'd ever known.

Seconds later he was beyond thought.

Primitive instinct, not conscious decision, made him bite gently at her neck, his fingers slipping between her legs as the firestorm exploded in his blood. He rammed his body into hers, all control lost.

Through the blurring haze, Niall felt Lola's muscles contract and caress him, as urgent and heedless as his own bucking spasms.

'Lola.' It was a silent cry of triumph against her lips as ecstasy dragged him under.

CHAPTER TEN

LOLA HEARD MOVEMENT, water running, but was still riding high on adrenaline and sexual satisfaction.

She smiled into the downy soft pillow.

Making love with Niall was beyond anything she'd imagined.

Hot and urgent, but even a novice could appreciate the effort he'd put into ensuring her pleasure.

When he'd gone down on his knees before her! Her heart rolled over at the thought and muscles deep inside, muscles she'd barely been aware of before tonight, tightened.

A shiver of voluptuous reminiscence shook her.

It had been worth the wait. She understood instinctively that sex with anyone else wouldn't have been like this.

Did Niall feel this indescribable wonder too?

It was unlikely. Surely her response was amplified because all this was new to her.

And because it was Niall. The man she'd fixated on for half her life.

Her heart felt overfull, as if the emotions she'd bottled up so long were bursting out and bubbling over. The enormity of merging her body with his had untied something locked tight within her. Something she'd strived half her life to hide.

What they shared had seemed momentous, far more than a physical act. So profound, it was as if the earth tilted around them. Lola felt undone by the enormity of her feelings and at the same time strengthened by them.

But she knew better than to mention them to Niall. He didn't feel the same. A shadow dimmed her pleasure but she ignored it. She refused to pine for the moon tonight when Niall had taken her to the stars. She still felt the glitter of that pulsating white light deep within.

He'd been so passionate. He hadn't been taking pity on her, the poor victim of a stalker. He'd been with her every step of the way.

Tonight Lola had been excited to discover that the particularly grim expression Niall wore from time to time, when those chiselled features turned stone-like and the pulse at his jaw flicked hard, betrayed arousal.

Her lips curved at the thought of how very aroused Niall had been. Enormously aroused.

A giggle escaped, the sound loud in the quiet room.

She opened her eyes and saw the rim of light around the bathroom door.

Surely he was taking a long time to dispose of a condom?

But then, with that water running, he must be showering.

Lola rolled onto her back, minutely conscious of the cool sheet beneath her heated skin, the slide of her thighs against each other, and the wet, swollen feeling of fullness between her legs.

Yet, even sated, she felt the tiniest lick of heat in her belly as she thought of Niall, naked, with water sluicing down his strong back and over those tightly curved buttocks.

One hand had grabbed him there as he'd powered into her and it had been phenomenally exciting, feeling the bunch of taut muscle as he thrust deep inside.

The little flicker of heat grew to a flame.

How would he react if she joined him in the shower? If she caressed him the way he'd caressed her?

There was only one complication. She didn't think her legs would move. Her bones had disintegrated when he took her to the stars a second time and now her limbs were heavy. The only parts of her that still worked were her buzzing brain and that gently throbbing spot between her legs.

The door opened and Niall stood there, broad shoulders and tapering figure outlined by the light.

Lola's mouth dried. He looked so good.

She couldn't read his expression with the light behind him and wondered if he could see hers. Did she look dreamy-eyed? She didn't care. Not when he was striding across to her and the yearning she'd never been able to suppress swamped her, stronger than ever.

This man.

Only ever *this* man.

Whatever the reason, it had only ever been Niall Pedersen for her.

But he didn't join her in bed. Instead he bent down and lifted her, his arms cradling her naked body as he straightened.

Lola registered again the exciting, teasing prickle of his chest hair against her skin. Flesh to flesh, held close in those powerful arms, was a potent reinforcement of his maleness and her femininity. Of how perfectly they matched.

This was blisteringly, fiercely real. Far beyond her previous, pallid imaginings.

She shivered and his hands tightened.

'Are you okay? Did I hurt you very much?' Niall's voice sounded curiously stretched.

'No.' Not enough to complain about and the discomfort was swiftly gone. Lola leaned into him, her palm against his neck, breathing in the fresh scent of citrus soap and damp male flesh. 'You showered.' Disappointment stirred.

She felt his breath shudder out.

Because of her? Because of her touch?

There was so much she didn't know, so much she wanted to learn about him, about them.

'I've run you a bath. It might relax you after... It might help if you're sore.'

Never in her life had Niall sounded anything but certain. Even as a rangy, spiky teenager, wary of trusting others, he'd always projected an air of self-assurance.

His thoughtfulness touched her.

But then it always had. Right from the first, she'd sensed she could trust him.

'Thanks, Niall.' She leaned her face against him, breathing him in. Wishing she could stay exactly where she was. But a moment later he was lowering her feet into water.

'How's the temperature?'

'Perfect. Thank you.' The warmth caressed her soles, making her aware of small aches and the kernel of tenderness between her legs.

Seconds later she was shoulder deep in the huge bath, her eyelids riding low as the last, lingering tension left her body. Bliss!

Movement caught her attention, made her sit up.

'You're leaving?' Usually she was good at hiding her feelings from him, but even she heard the hurt in her voice.

'I thought you'd like privacy.' Niall's features were unreadable, his eyes watchful.

What she'd like was for him to join her. To hold her in his arms while they shared the aftermath of the single most remarkable experience of her life. To prolong that profound sense of oneness.

Caution stopped her blurting all that out. If she couldn't have the fantasy, she could come close.

'Won't you keep me company? Please?'

Finally he moved, but not, as she'd hoped, into the bath with her. Her body might be limp but her mind was very, very active when it came to Niall.

He settled on a low padded chair she hadn't even noticed in the opulent, mirrored and marbled bathroom. It was at the far end of the bath and he sat facing slightly away from her.

Over the rim of the high bath she could only see his head and chest, and she felt a pang of regret at the distance, the lack of physical contact.

His black eyebrows crunched down in a frown. 'How do you feel?'

'Terrific!'

His eyes widened and she almost laughed at his patent surprise.

'Well, worn out, but in the most delicious way.' She shivered, remembering how they'd been together, and felt internal muscles twitch. Water lapped around her shoulders like a caress.

Niall's gaze, almost ebony in this light, held hers as if he sifted her words. What was going on in his head?

He swallowed, his Adam's apple bobbing hard in his throat. It was all he could do to stay here, pretending he was glued to the seat, and not climb into that oversized tub and expand Lola's sexual experience a whole lot more.

His skin prickled tight despite the warm fug of steamy air.

He'd just had raw, lusty sex with Lola.

His best friend's little sister.

The woman he'd vowed to protect.

For days he'd repeated that mantra. Hoping reinforcement would prevent him acting on urges a better man would resist.

The prickle turned to a shudder as he tried and failed not to notice her glistening pink-washed skin. The bob of cherry-dark nipples cresting the surface of the water as she sat higher.

There'd been cherries on her cotton knickers in Melbourne.

He blinked, trying to divert his thoughts from ripe fruit and cherries in particular. And what he'd just done. But there was nowhere to go. Just into the swamp of self-disgust at ravaging her innocence or straight back into lust, as if he hadn't just taken his fill.

Yet now he was ready for more.

Niall swung his gaze away and found himself staring through the open door at the rumpled bed, surrounded by a spray of discarded clothes.

It had been no tender wooing. Yes, he'd ensured she climaxed. The first time with his face between her legs, jammed up against a wall barely one step inside the apartment! The second with him rutting, hard and fast, more animal than civilised man. The flesh at his nape crawled.

'I wish I'd known you were inexperienced.'

Without intending to, he turned his head, his gaze snagging on hers. His heart pounded so hard he felt it rise in his throat.

'Then you wouldn't have made love to me.'

Niall sucked in air. He'd like to believe she was right. Yet he had an unedifying suspicion even that wouldn't have stopped him. He'd been driven by a primitive force so compelling nothing short of the building falling around their ears would have got in the way.

'You're not going all quaint on me, are you, Niall? Everyone has a first time.' Her nipples crested the water again as she took a breath. 'I'm glad mine was with you.'

Then she gave him that smile. The one that sent his brains corkscrewing down to his groin. It wasn't a deliberately sexy smile, but her pleasure and her honesty undid every knot and frayed rope in the barrier he'd been trying to cobble together since leaving the bed.

The trouble was, he was glad too. Because he couldn't stomach the idea of her with any other man.

Yet inevitably guilt cast its shadow.

Her smile faded, drooping at the edges, and he realised she'd read his silence.

'I feel honoured, Lola.'

She shook her head, dark waves swishing around her shoulders. 'You *are* going old-fashioned on me. I can see it in your face.' In one sudden movement she sat up completely, baring her beautiful breasts, her hands clutching the sides of the tub. 'Don't spoil it by going all poker-faced, Niall.'

Despite himself that dragged a huff of laughter from him. 'Poker-faced? Is that what I am?'

Good thing that, where she sat she couldn't see his erection stirring.

'I know you feel responsible for protecting me, but you're not my keeper. I choose who I share myself with.'

That airy wave of her hand would be more impressive if she hadn't been a virgin thirty minutes ago.

And if he didn't feel such a strong connection to her. Not just to a memory of the girl she'd once been, but to Lola, the woman he'd begun to know in recent days. The woman who intrigued, tempted and disturbed him.

With her he was alternately out of his depth or attuned at a gut-deep level that didn't require explanation or conversation between them. Both worried him.

Niall mightn't be her keeper but nor was he some passing stranger.

'Yet you didn't choose to share yourself with anyone until tonight. Why is that?'

Lola gnawed the corner of her mouth, a habit she'd had as a kid when nervous or cornered in an argument. 'I've been busy and the time never seemed right.'

Niall surveyed her minutely, knowing there was something she wasn't saying. Sensing it was something he needed to know. He was about to press her then paused.

Who did he think he was? The virginity police?

Was it really his business why she hadn't had sex before?

Like a searing streak of lightning, realisation hit. *He was glad he was the first.* Even if it did make him feel ridiculously possessive. Ants crawled beneath his skin at the idea of Lola doing with anyone else what she'd done with him.

He told himself he should be grateful Lola was okay, taking it in her stride. Almost as if it were just another holiday experience to tick off her list, like attending a glitzy party.

Niall frowned. Was that what had happened? Was he a passing diversion, helping to turn her enforced seclusion into a fun break?

He was stunned by the white-hot blast of rejection he felt at the idea. And the swift urge to close the space between them and claim her, imprinting himself in her pores, in every nerve and pleasure receptor in her body. So that in future, whenever Lola thought of desire and sexual delight, she thought of him.

Why? It wasn't as if he wanted her imagining tonight was anything more than an overflow of pent-up sexual frustration. Imagine if Lola, like some previous lovers, started thinking in terms of a long-term relationship, wedding bells and families!

That doused the stirring heat in his groin as if he'd dived under an iceberg.

Because the one thing Niall could never do was become a family man. The thought of being responsible for a wife and kids stirred old nausea in his gut and dark shadows in his mind.

'Are you okay, Niall?'

He grimaced. 'I'm the one who should ask that.' He'd never been with a virgin. He didn't know what he'd expected. Blood and tears? 'Are you sure I didn't hurt you?'

Again she chewed her lip. Niall wanted to lean in and stop her, kissing her mouth into ripe softness before plundering her sweetness. He shuddered and tried to rein in his galloping imagination.

'Briefly. So briefly I barely noticed.'

Yet the wash of pink covering her breasts, throat and cheeks was a reminder of how new this was to her. It made him want to beat his chest in primitive triumph at being her only lover. Or hang his head in shame at betraying the trust she and her family had placed in him. The betrayal of his own code of conduct. Sex with a woman under his protection, a vulnerable woman in hiding.

'In fact…' She paused, slanting him a look under long, veiling eyelashes that he felt as a tightening in his groin. 'I feel so good, I'd like to do it again.'

'Again?'

Tomorrow. She meant tomorrow or maybe the day after. When she was no longer tender—

'It's not that odd, surely.' Her attention dropped to somewhere around his collarbone, the pink on her cheeks deepening to rose. 'But maybe it's too soon for you. Do you need more time?'

As if he weren't fighting a losing battle against arousal! He pressed his lips into a flat line, rather than blurt out the truth.

She looked adorably hesitant and devastatingly provocative. Everything from the dark curve of her long eyelashes to those reddened lips to her luscious body beneath the water called to him.

Her chin hiked up but still she didn't meet his eyes. 'But I'll understand if you don't want to. If you prefer more experienced partners.'

Niall opened his mouth to tell her it wasn't a matter of experience, and that it wouldn't happen again. Because he wasn't right for her on so many levels.

Even if it would be torture, holding back.

Shock grabbed him by the throat when he heard himself say in a gravel voice, 'You're the sexiest woman I've ever known, Lola. That's why I stayed here and showered. Because I worried if I went back to the bedroom I'd persuade you into sex again when you need time to recover.'

It was a relief to unleash the truth. Despite the self-disgust stirring in his belly. But he was only human, and resisting Lola, naked, enticing Lola, was futile.

Already he was on his feet beside the bath, towering over her.

Yet she was the one with the power. Her wide-eyed stare at his erection set his body flaming. It was an effort not to leap into that massive tub with her and drive himself hard between her thighs. She reduced him to raw, unvarnished hunger, stripped of finesse. It was a frightening experience for a man used to controlling his life, his environment, and his libido.

'I'm so glad,' she murmured, kneeling at the edge of the bath.

Niall was bending forward to help her up and into his arms when she planted her wet palm on his thigh, another on his bare buttock, and leaned in, delicately touching the tip of his arousal with her tongue.

Arrows of fire scorched their flaming way through his body. He froze, his body refusing to step away and the voice in his head telling him only a fool would deny her.

Serious as an owl, her forehead furrowed in concentration, she touched him again, this time bending lower and laving right along his length.

A shudder buckled his knees yet stiffened his sinews. He found his hands clutching at her dark hair.

Niall swallowed, the sensation like the scrape of shattered glass. He croaked, 'You don't have to do that.' Maybe she thought it was expected, since he'd gone down on her. Yet instead of gently pushing her away, he held her where she was.

'I want to. I'm curious.' Another lingering lick, this time ending with her lips drawing on him, and he shuddered.

Sensations bombarded Lola, delicious sensations. The taste of Niall, spice and salt. The inferno heat of him against her face. The texture of silk over his iron-hard erection that was unlike anything else. She lifted her hand from his thigh, tentatively circling her fingers around him, and he pressed forward into her caress. She caught a groan over the rush of her pulse in her ears.

Then there was the taut muscle of his backside, trembling and bunching beneath her hand, more proof that Niall was no longer in charge.

The thought excited her. Aroused her. Heat forked in a

fiery slipstream from her breasts to her belly, to that needy place inside where only Niall had been. Where she wanted him again.

Slowly, carefully, she leaned closer, drawing him in. She was rewarded with a hiss of shock from Niall and a buck of his hips, pushing deeper, demanding.

Lola paused, despite her excitement, a little stunned by his raw response, the desperate way he thrust against her and the way his hands held her captive.

He was so big, so strong. She was at the mercy of that strength.

Except, looking up through slitted eyes, she saw Niall watching her, his face pared back to lines of stark arousal. That was when she registered the tremor in his hands and the lost look in those remarkable eyes.

Slowly she drew on his engorged flesh, delighting in his heavy shudder. His head dropped back, his mouth open on a gasp that told her it was the other way around. Niall was at her mercy.

Carefully, alert to his responses, she slid her hand along him, squeezing a little, learning from each jolt and sigh what he liked.

And what he liked, she did too. Lola felt privileged and powerful, bringing this strong, ardent man, if not to his knees, then to a point of shaking neediness. She wanted—

Firm hands moved her back. Glittering eyes held hers as he tilted her chin up.

'Later.' His voice ground low and husky, but there was no mistaking who was taking the lead now.

Lola considered protesting. She had a lot more experimenting and exploring to do. But something in Niall's heated stare told her she wouldn't regret it.

'Is that a promise?'

Niall's sudden bark of laughter made her smile.

'If you think I'd try to prevent you you've got rocks in

your head. But right now there's something I want more.'
The smile on his lips turned hungry. 'You, Lola.'

He stepped back, ransacking the cupboards and finally
pulling out a box of condoms.

'Shall we?' Sheathed, he held out his arm to help her out
of the bath.

Instead Lola eased back away from him, supremely conscious of the warm water eddying around her sensitised flesh.
'Why don't you join me? There's lots of room.' The bath was
constructed on a decadently generous size.

For one beat of her heart Niall paused. Then he lifted
those long legs over the side and sank down, arms splay-
ing out along the rim of the bath. He leaned his head back,
watching her with dark, beckoning eyes, like some sybaritic
pasha, eyeing a favourite concubine.

Lola blinked. Clearly she'd kept a lid on her sexuality
for too long, judging by tonight's surprising impulses and
imaginings.

'What are you thinking, Lola?'

She moved nearer, reading the rapid tic of his pulse at his
throat and the lines of taut tendons and bunched muscles. It
cost Niall to appear relaxed.

He wanted her. Niall Pedersen, the man she'd fantasised
about for years, wanted her that badly.

'I'm thinking sleep is overrated.'

His arm snaked out, long fingers taking hers and drawing her to him. Lola expected him to reverse their positions
so she sat against the end of the bath. Instead he planted his
hands on her hips and pulled her across him, his erection
bobbing against her belly.

A twist of need spiralled through her.

'On your knees, Lola. Hands on my shoulders.' With the
words he nudged her legs open so she straddled him, knees
tucked behind his hips.

Long fingers parting the flesh between her thighs made
her hiss and slide against him.

'You *are* eager.' But he didn't sound smug, more relieved. 'How about we go at your pace this time, sweetheart?'

Lola nodded yet hesitated, not quite sure.

Then Niall smiled. The sort of smile that dug right down under her heart and squeezed. His hands went again to her hips, gently tugging her up onto her knees.

'Now, gently down.' His hand was there, and something else, nudging her.

A tiny movement and she felt pressure, delicious pressure. Another movement and Niall grimaced, his fingers branding her hips but she didn't mind because everything felt so perfect. Shuffling a little further forward, she let herself sink, let her breasts slide against his hard chest as their bodies melded.

The sensations were an intense variation on what had gone before. Exquisite fullness, sensitivity that bordered between pleasure and something even more intense.

But best of all wasn't the physical, it was, again, the feeling of oneness. Niall's gaze held hers, infinitely gentle, infinitely hot, as he urged her back up and she sank down again, faster, harder.

Excitement shuddered through her.

Niall's hands went to her breasts and her breath seized. She leaned in, and one big hand cupped the back of her head, bringing her down for a slow, open-mouthed kiss that was all the more erotic because it imitated their bodies mating.

Lola clutched Niall's damp hair, holding him still as the kiss deepened and her rhythm quickened. Kaleidoscope sparks fizzed in her blood and flickered behind her closed eyelids. Then Niall held her to him as he thrust up, pinioning her, groaning her name, and the world shattered.

As she came spinning slowly back to earth, dazed and not sure where she ended and he began, Niall cradled her close. She sank against him, spent and exhausted, knowing there was nowhere on earth she'd prefer to be.

That was when full realisation hit and she understood the appalling fix she was in.

She'd told herself reality could never measure up to the idealised man she'd built in her head. Now she learned that real life Niall far outstripped her fantasies. Making love with him felt...

That was just it. Even she, newly inducted into the mysteries of sex, understood her euphoria wasn't just about spectacular physical gratification.

It was as much about how she felt, emotionally.

Because her crush on him hadn't merely survived the years of separation.

It had grown and expanded.

Into love.

Her breath snagged.

She'd made mistakes in her life. Was this the biggest yet? What on earth was she going to do?

CHAPTER ELEVEN

NEXT MORNING NIALL found the resolve to leave the bed before dawn and go for a long run on the beach, rather than wake Lola for sex. Then, after checking she was still asleep, he showered in another bathroom and went out to buy their breakfast.

He should have been pleased when he got back to find her up and dressed, because in theory it made it easier to keep his distance. No matter how enthusiastic she'd been, he was pretty certain she'd be sore this morning.

Plus his conscience was finally working, reminding him of all the reasons Lola was taboo.

Should have been taboo.

A pity his body didn't get the message. Just looking at Lola aroused him. And Lola in that slinky dress was torture to a sinner who'd already crossed from right to wrong and wanted to indulge himself again.

If Lola had given him the slightest encouragement...

But she hadn't. Today she'd been different. Self-contained.

She'd eaten a hearty breakfast and said what a good time she'd had at the party. For a second her eyes had glowed with warmth and he'd wanted to wrap his arms around her and hold her close. Even if they didn't have sex, he wanted to hold her. His arms felt empty this morning. He'd never before experienced an ache for one particular woman.

He'd watched her mouth as she sipped her coffee and

chewed on a pastry and remembered those lips on his. And on other parts of his body. Want had turned to blazing, biting hunger. If she'd given any hint she desired him again...

Instead she'd worried about getting back to her computer and her job. As if what they'd shared had been fun but forgettable.

Niall hadn't been sure what to expect but it wasn't that. She'd pulled the rug from under him in more ways than he could count.

He couldn't even complain that she treated him with easy-going friendship when for days he'd been trying to do the same.

Now, in his study, back on the mountain, Niall felt that familiar tremor of need. It hadn't abated one bit, though he'd worked all day to repress his lust.

Which was the right thing to do. Belatedly.

Especially as Lola had kept her distance all day. There'd been no flirting. No eager invitation back to bed.

Niall had learned that though she was inexperienced, Lola wasn't shy about sexual desire. She was generous and demanding, not afraid to ask for what she wanted, or to give.

Another shudder racked him as he remembered how wholeheartedly she gave.

Inevitably Niall's gaze lifted from the computer screen he'd stared at blankly to Lola, set up in a shady spot next to the pool with her laptop.

It was late afternoon and she'd been for a lunchtime swim. Instead of dressing fully again, she'd spent the afternoon wearing a work shirt over that skimpy bikini.

From the waist up she looked all business for her online meetings.

But from there down she was tantalising temptation. The streamlined curves of her calves, thighs and hips mesmerised him, killing his ability to concentrate.

Shut in his study, Niall had got no work done, apart from checking fruitlessly for news of Braithwaite. He'd spent half the afternoon imagining being naked with Lola and the other half watching her through the window or finding excuses to talk with her. He'd made them a salad lunch. Then coffee. He'd shared the update his Melbourne staff had provided, that there'd been no sign of Braithwaite at her flat. Lola had reciprocated with a similar update from the police.

That had sent Niall back to his study where he'd spent an hour scoping further options to draw her stalker out, discussing them with experts, and going back to the drawing board.

Now she was smiling as she talked with someone online. A man or a woman? Threads of jealousy that he had no right to feel wove through him, tangling in a knot in his belly.

What the hell was happening to him?

He'd never expected any woman's undivided attention, except in bed.

Niall shoved his chair back from the desk and paced the room, trying to wrangle his thoughts into line.

He'd been ready this morning to tell Lola the sex had been terrific but couldn't happen again. Not just because she was Ed's sister and he was responsible for her safety. But because he knew, deep in his bones, that Lola wasn't a woman for a short affair. She was a woman for keeps. One who deserved a solid, loving relationship. The sort of relationship he simply couldn't provide.

Niall wasn't arrogant enough to think she'd want that with him. She'd made it clear she was enjoying the chance for sexual experimentation. But he couldn't take the chance of blurring the lines between them. Not when it could mean hurting her.

But she'd undercut him, treating him with the easy familiarity of an old friend, all trace of the lover gone.

He should be grateful.

He should be pleased.

Instead he was wound so tight with frustration and pique he didn't know what to do with himself.

Except take his lead from her and be what she wanted, an old friend.

Even if it killed him.

'Stir-fry okay for dinner?'

Lola looked up from her laptop to find Niall, seriously scrumptious in a black polo shirt and pale cotton trousers, standing in the doorway. Her insides gave an all too familiar shimmy and she had to work at sitting still and not throwing herself into his arms.

Powerful arms that had held her safe when the world shattered in a fire burst of ecstasy and her heart welled with all the emotion she couldn't dare share with him.

'That sounds great. Can I help?'

It wasn't as if she'd achieve anything here. It was late and she'd only kept the computer open, trying to work, because the alternative was to do something stupid like fling herself at the man who'd avoided her all day.

He couldn't have made it clearer that last night had been, if not a mistake, then a one-off.

He'd left her in the early hours, while it was still pitch dark, presumably to sleep in another room. That had extinguished her glow of well-being and put an end to her sleepy musings about a lazy morning in bed. Forget any hopes Niall would consider an affair, even just for the length of her stay in Queensland.

Disappointment had seared through her. Last night had been remarkable. Astounding.

Her heart dived.

The only intimacy she'd ever share with the man she loved.

How naïve she'd been to think he couldn't hurt her more than he already had.

She'd spent the day acting as if it hadn't happened. As if they were just old friends. It was the only way she knew to salvage her pride and stop herself from doing something stupid like kissing him.

He'd only reject her again.

'It's fine. I'll manage.'

Lola closed the laptop and rose, pinning on a smile. She was stiff from sitting for hours. That was why she moved. Not to be closer to Niall.

'It'll be easier with two.'

Because, despite everything, she couldn't stay away. Her weakness for this man ran blood deep.

What would it hurt to indulge herself and be near him? He wasn't going to bridge the chasm between them. She'd only be here another couple of days. After that she mightn't see Niall again.

Lola ignored the sudden ache in her middle and concentrated on trying to look relaxed.

It was only as she followed him into the beautifully appointed chef's kitchen that she realised he wasn't relaxed either. His shoulders sat high and his hands were bunched at his sides.

'Is something wrong, Niall? Do you need to get back to Brisbane?' He'd only come here because of her. 'You don't need to stay and chaperone me. I'll be fine alone.'

Lola faltered as he swung around to face her. To her surprise she read something like anger in his strong features. Banked heat in his eyes and repressed emotion in the taut line of his lips.

Energy ripped through her in a jagged strike, like lightning hitting earth. Her whole body vibrated, her fingertips tingling.

No, not anger. Not totally.

'Eager to be rid of me, are you, Lola?' His jaw firmed. His arms folded over his chest, muscles bulging and rippling beneath dark gold skin. 'Am I cramping your style? If I left you could invite Jake Sinclair here. Or would you rather have the passcode to the Gold Coast apartment? That might be more convenient.'

Lola frowned up at him, her hand planted on the vast

granite-topped island bench for support. For suddenly her head felt swimmy. Or maybe it was her knees.

'Niall? What are you talking about? Why would I invite Jake Sinclair here?'

His gaze locked on hers, not dark navy but bright cobalt. How could a cool colour look so hot?

He blinked and his expression changed. A tremor passed through him and Lola watched his shoulders drop, his fingers stretch as he unfolded his arms.

For the first time she could remember Niall seemed reluctant to meet her eyes. Instead he stared past her, as if the kitchen cabinetry held him enthralled.

'Sorry.' He shook his head, then raked his fingers through his hair. 'Ignore me, I'm talking nonsense. It's not been a good day. I shouldn't take it out on you.'

He moved towards the refrigerator but her hand on his arm stopped him.

In slow motion he tilted his head down to stare at her fingers, as if no one had ever had the temerity to touch him.

Lola told herself to drop her hand but instead her fingers gripped harder, digging into taut, hot flesh, its smattering of dark hair tickling.

She was about to ask if she'd done something wrong when her synapses fired and she made sense of his words.

'You think I have an assignation with Jake Sinclair?' The idea was ludicrous, but she read the truth in Niall's face.

Now she had no trouble yanking her hand away. She cradled it against herself as if stung.

'What are you saying, Niall? That I planned a sexual liaison last night with a man I'd never met before?' She hefted a quick breath but still felt short of oxygen. 'Right before I spent the night with you?' The words rushed out, so fast they tripped over each other.

She backed up a step, her mouth crumpling at the horrible, sour taste on her tongue.

'Lola, no! I don't. It's not like that!'

No trace of anger on his face now. Niall looked as if she'd kneed him in the groin, his face a strange pasty colour. She wished she *had* kneed him in the groin. Instead she'd spent the day daydreaming about making love with him!

'Or do you believe sex with you magically turned me from virgin to vamp? That I'm now so desperate for sex I'd ring up a virtual stranger and offer myself to him?'

Red mist filled her vision. What they'd shared last night had felt special, transcendent even. Niall's words made it seem tawdry.

'No!' Hard hands grabbed her above the elbows. 'Of course not!'

'You know,' she said, spurred by hurt and fury, 'it's not a bad idea. I liked sex.' *With Niall!* But she ignored that scream of outrage in her head. 'Why don't you go to Brisbane and I might consider calling Jake?'

She didn't hear what Niall said. Or she heard but couldn't make sense of the growling undercurrent of oaths over the thrumming of her pulse.

But she saw the fierce light in his eyes. A light so savage it made every cell in her body tingle with dangerous excitement.

'You won't call him.' Niall ground the words out with slow emphasis. 'Not for sex.'

Lola had never tossed her head in her life. She did now. 'I can do whatever I like. *Be* with anyone I like.'

Niall inclined his head. 'But you want to be with *me*, don't you, Lola?' His gaze challenged and she couldn't look away.

Did she imagine desperation in those stark features? Surely not.

Niall trailed the tip of his index finger across her open lips then down, by torturously slow degrees, to her throat, her collarbone, the open collar of her shirt, lingering there, just above where her heart thundered.

Exquisite sensations bombarded her. She was torn between wanting to slap his hand away and hooking it into her shirt so he could rip it open.

'Why should I want a man who thinks I'm...?' Words failed her.

'I don't. Of course I don't. I took out my frustration on you. I'm sorry.' His palm flattened on the upper slope of her chest and she felt it like a brand of possession. 'I've spent the day going crazy, keeping my distance because it's the right thing to do. When all I want is to be buried deep inside you, feeling you climax around me.'

Shock smacked her.

'You want me? You're...jealous? There's nothing to be jealous of!'

'Pathetic, isn't it? I know you haven't got a thing with Jake. I don't know where the words came from. It was a despicable thing to say and I only did it because I'm in a foul mood. I apologise.' Niall slid his hand up, back to her face, but this time he cradled her cheek with infinite tenderness, his own features rigid with what looked like pain.

Lola had never seen him hurt like this. Never known him to lash out.

'I want you, so badly,' he admitted. 'I know I shouldn't. I know all the reasons I need to keep my distance. All the reasons I'm wrong for you. But they don't help.' He sucked in air like a drowning man about to go under. 'So tell me that you despise me, and I'll walk away.'

'And if I don't?'

The world stilled, her heartbeat slowing as, amazed, she read vulnerability in Niall's proud features. Regret, shame and arousal.

For about a second Lola contemplated stepping away. Making good on her self-talk about severing the bond with Niall.

But after last night it was impossible. Especially now when she saw pain in his eyes.

As a teenager, Niall had been reckless of his safety but

he'd never come close to hurting her. She'd have taken her oath that he'd do anything rather than harm her.

He might not love her but he cared for her. And he wanted her. He looked tortured. Whether by the fact he'd hurt her or by the force of his desire, or both, Lola couldn't tell.

She strove for pride but couldn't hold it. She loved him so much she'd take what she could get.

Lola took his hand and placed it on her breast, rejoicing in his hissed intake of breath and the convulsive way his hand tightened, making pleasure sing through her.

'Really?' He shook his head. 'After what I said you should—'

Lola put her hand over his mouth. 'I'll decide what I should and shouldn't do.'

He opened his mouth against her hand and licked her palm, slowly, as he gently squeezed her breast. A shaft of glowing heat tunnelled down to her pelvis, making her shake.

Niall gathered her close and she was never more grateful for his strength.

It was wonderful to discover he shook too.

Lola moistened her dry lips and stood on her toes to whisper against his ear. 'What I want, Niall, is you buried deep inside me, so you can feel me climax around you and I can feel you.' She felt him jolt with surprise, and triumph slashed through her. Emboldened, she nipped his earlobe. 'And I want it now.'

Instantly Niall spanned her hips with his capable hands and lifted her up onto the island bench, pushing her knees wide.

Dark eyes held hers.

'You're sure?' He sounded gruff, as if the words stuck in his throat. Lola understood the feeling. She didn't even try to speak, just nodded, watching his mouth curl in a slow, sexy grin that turned her to mush.

'I love a woman who knows what she wants.'

Love. For a second her thoughts snagged on the word. Except Niall slid his hand down inside the front of her bikini bottom, fingers carefully yet ruthlessly probing, and Lola forgot about everything but the need for more.

She wasn't just damp there, she was wet, and the slide of his hand...

'Niall! Please.'

She shoved the fabric down her hips, wriggling to free herself, while he pulled his hand away and reached into his pocket.

Her eyes rounded as he lifted a foil package and tore it with his teeth.

Seeing her expression, he smiled grimly. 'No, I don't usually carry condoms wherever I go. But today I hoped...' He shook his head. 'I shouldn't. I kept telling myself you need space. But you undo me, Lola.'

The idea that she messed with his head appealed. It evened up things between them because that was exactly what he did to her.

She smiled and pressed a light kiss to his lips. Niall caught her to him and turned it into something long and soul deep. Her body was on fire for him but so was her heart.

When they pulled apart, gasping for air, Niall shucked his trousers and underwear and put on the condom. Seconds later they were both naked.

Niall ate her up with glazed eyes. 'One day we're going to take our time, Lola. We might even do something unconventional like start making love in bed.'

It was a tiny thing, but her heart sang at the implication they'd do this again. That this wasn't, after all, a one-night thing.

She reached for his shoulders. 'But not now.'

'Definitely not now.' He positioned himself between her spread thighs.

For the longest moment they were still, staring into each other's eyes, absorbing the feel of their bodies just touching, and the anticipation shimmering between them. Then, with one slow, smooth movement, Niall pushed home, right to the heart of her.

Her mouth fell open on a gasp of astonishment. She'd learned what to expect last night yet this felt so profound. With his grave gaze pinioning hers, his heavy grip holding her in a way that was both possessive and caressing, it was easy to believe Niall too experienced more than sexual arousal. That he also felt the emotional bond.

But inevitably arousal won.

Lola grabbed his shoulders as he leaned forward till she lay back on the cool countertop. His bare chest covered her breasts and she arched as his chest hair tickled her.

Niall urged her legs up high over his hips, sinking even deeper, and Lola welcomed him with a circle of her hips and a squeeze of muscles that made him judder.

Then there was no time for thought, just the quick tempo of their bodies rising and joining, the rhythm that became a runaway pulse, urgent and deep. More urgent. Deeper. Quicker. Hungry and hungrier. Her fingernails scored his smooth shoulders and he responded with a powerful thrust that seated him impossibly tight as stars burst and they climaxed together, clinging, eyes locked and, she'd swear, hearts pounding in tandem.

Ages later, when the world came back, Niall gathered her close and carried her to his bedroom. No words were spoken. Lola wasn't sure she was capable of speech. Besides, their bodies spoke for them.

He didn't let her go, even getting into the bed he cradled her near and she revelled in the bond between them.

For the rest of the night there was barely a moment when Niall wasn't touching her. Either making love, or just holding her.

They remembered to eat around midnight, but only on snacks they fed to each other. That turned out to be deliciously messy, necessitating a long soak in the bath till the water turned cold and their flesh pruny, and Niall insisted she needed sleep. They slept tangled together, then saw the dawn in making love again.

Lola knew, whatever happened in the future, she had this one night of profound joy to treasure.

The question was, could she have more?

CHAPTER TWELVE

THE ANSWER WAS YES. She could have more.

Because after that night things changed.

Niall never spoke about keeping his distance or her family's expectations. He was with her all the time, except for the hours they both worked.

They got into a routine, each working in their own part of the sprawling house, totally alone but for the housekeeper who appeared every couple of days to clean and bring supplies. Lola and Niall did everything together, eating, bathing, swimming, sleeping.

Not sleeping.

Her mouth tugged into a reminiscent smile as she thought of the hours they'd spent last night, making love.

They should both be too exhausted to work, given how little sleep they got. Instead Lola seemed to fizz with energy. When she did sleep, inevitably in Niall's arms, it was a deep, restful slumber that left her feeling rejuvenated.

As for the rest, work was going surprisingly well, despite her being isolated from colleagues, and her relationship with Niall had grown into something new. It wasn't just sexual attraction. The easy intimacy they'd had years ago was back, but coloured by a new awareness and respect.

It was over two weeks since they'd arrived here and their relationship had grown into the give and take of a well-matched couple.

It surprised her how fast and easily they'd become a couple in much more than sex. Maybe their history together, the fact that they'd known each other so well for so long, was part of it.

Lola knew who Niall was at heart, his strengths, like determination, generosity and kindness, and his weaknesses, like keeping problems to himself and automatically taking charge. The latter, at least, she saw changing as he stopped trying to manage her.

She reached for her coffee and sipped. The only dark cloud was the fact Braithwaite was still at large. There'd been no further attacks on her home and it looked unlikely the police would prove anything against him.

Lola dreaded returning to Melbourne. Partly because it meant facing Braithwaite. She wasn't optimistic or naïve enough to believe her tormentor had seen the error of his ways and decided to leave her alone. More likely he'd sussed that the woman in her flat wasn't Lola, and he was biding his time.

But what she really fretted over was leaving Niall, whose home and business were here in Queensland.

What they shared was more than a fling. She *hoped* they had a future together. It felt that was where they were headed. And yet…

She looked up from her coffee cup. Niall was shaking hands with the business acquaintance he'd spotted in the doorway of the elegant restaurant. It seemed they were saying goodbye.

He turned back into the dining room, heading for their lunch table. He didn't seem to notice the eager looks turned his way or the whispered comments. Instead his gaze was fixed on her with devastating intensity.

A woman could get used to Niall looking at her that way, disregarding every other woman, including quite a few beautiful blondes, like the sort she'd seen him with in press reports.

'Is everything all right, Lola?' He pulled out his chair and sat, immediately reaching for her hand. She loved the way Niall touched her frequently. Those tiny, tender caresses that spoke not just of sex, but of caring. 'You looked pensive.'

'Did I?'

Niall watched her straighten, her mouth curving into a smile that looked, not wary precisely, but not as easy and open as usual.

He'd grown accustomed to her open pleasure in everything they shared, from cooking to discussing business trends or books. From watching a movie, snuggled up together, to sex.

He wasn't just accustomed but hooked. He could no more keep away from Lola than he could walk on the waves that lapped the beach outside.

Even knowing this was wrong. That in the long run, he couldn't be the man for her.

Niall's penance was the torture of knowing this must end. Lola deserved better than him. He should never have touched her.

With luck she'd tire of him soon. Realise he wasn't the sort of man she should waste her time on and move on. Though the thought filled him with dread. He wasn't ready to say goodbye to sweet, sassy Lola, her seriousness and her sexy ways.

'Were you thinking about Braithwaite?' He rubbed his thumb over her wrist, noting its heavy throb. 'I'm sure there'll be news soon. We just have to be patient.'

It frustrated him, the way her stalker had dropped under the radar. Naturally Braithwaite had backed off when his spy camera was found. But sooner or later he'd try something again, and the police and Pedersen Security would be waiting for him.

'I know. But for how long? Three weeks? Three months?' Lola looked at their clasped hands, her mouth flattened. 'I'm in limbo. It feels like Braithwaite has won, driving me from my home, disrupting my life.'

Pressure built in Niall's chest. 'I know it feels like that at the moment but, believe me, we'll put an end to his harassment.' Niall and his team were pursuing every avenue to make that happen. 'But there are compensations.'

A moment ago he was thinking about how it would be best if Lola left him. Yet he couldn't bear to think of her unhappy here. 'Your work's going well, isn't it? It sounds like the new project is really progressing.' He offered a winning smile. 'And this isn't a bad place for a break.'

Surely it wasn't just the place, but the company too, that she enjoyed. But Niall refused to fish for compliments.

He *knew* Lola was happy here with him. He'd felt it, seen it in her smiles and enthusiasm. Read it in their avid sex life, but more, in the contentment and ease that had grown between them.

He'd never experienced anything like it. A unique and stimulating combination of full-on sexual attraction that showed no signs of abating, melded with friendship and a level of understanding that sometimes made words superfluous because they were so attuned.

'Not a bad place at all.' She smiled and Niall felt the unfamiliar tightness behind his ribs ease. 'Sometimes I wish we could continue like this for ever.' Her eyes locked on his and a fizz of intense pleasure filled him.

Till reality, that cold, unwelcome guest at the table, muscled its way in again.

There could be no for ever for them.

He could give Lola what she needed for now but she was too precious, too special to waste on someone like him long term.

He drew in a sharp breath to match the sharp pain lancing his lungs.

That was his punishment for breaking the rules and giving in to his lust for her. Even now the clock was ticking.

'The best holidays are like that, aren't they? You want them to continue indefinitely.' He managed to sound upbeat but couldn't summon a smile this time.

No matter how right and sensible, he wasn't ready for this interlude to end. Inevitably it must, but every instinct screamed *not yet*!

Which was why he forced himself to continue. 'But even Paradise would pall after a while, don't you think?'

Lola tilted her head in that assessing way she'd always had.

Sometimes it felt as if she saw deeper inside him than anyone ever had. Further than the business competitors who searched for his weak points. Deeper than the father he hadn't seen in years. His dad had seen the bleak, damning darkness inside Niall and he'd chosen to turn away, focusing his energy on his new family, pretending his first son didn't exist.

Who could blame him?

'Niall? Did you hear me?'

Lola leaned close, looking concerned.

He sat straighter, giving her a smile that he hoped covered his disturbing thoughts.

But he was shocked at the force of those thoughts. The piercing regret that he couldn't be the man for Lola. And the suspicion Lola saw at least a little of his inner turmoil. Niall had spent years masking that, in his teens behind an overtly don't-care attitude and as an adult with rigid self-discipline.

Looking into those warm, hazel eyes, Niall felt his self-discipline waver.

'Sorry, I missed that.'

'I asked if there was time for a walk on the beach before we head back to your house. I know we spent the morning in the surf, but the weather's perfect.'

He smiled. He loved the fact Lola was just as enthusiastic about a walk by the sea, or seeing brightly coloured birds up close, as she was about attending a glittering society party or being superlative at her job. She made him appreciate pleasures he often took for granted in his high-demand, high-profile world.

'Whatever you like, Lola.'

Her eyes danced wickedly and she leaned in, her summery scent teasing him. 'Well…there's something else I'd like to do, but we need privacy.' Instantly Niall's libido revved into life. 'We can do that when we get home,' she purred as she rose from the table.

For a second he basked in a glow of well-being. The sensual promise of her words and suggestive glance, the way she referred to his place as *home*. As if it could eventually be more than a place to retreat for brief periods. As if together they could—

Niall clamped down a barrier against such thoughts. A shared future was impossible.

He'd have to settle for what they had now, enjoy it to the full, because, he realised with shocking clarity, it was probably the best he'd ever have.

'Niall?' She paused, looking back over her shoulder. 'Are you okay?'

Lola didn't know his secrets but she had an uncanny ability to read his mood. Something he'd do well to remember.

'Never better, lover.' He put his arm around her on the pretext of guiding her from the plush restaurant. In reality he was determined not to miss a moment of touching her.

Leaving their shoes in the car, they strolled along the beach, down on the wet, white sand, where shallow waves curled around their ankles. By mutual consent they headed away from the red and yellow flags marking the safe swimming zone.

Hands linked, they didn't talk much. It was enough to enjoy the beach, the day and the company. Lola skipped, yelping, when a higher waved raced in, splashing her skirt, and Niall swung her up into his arms, revelling in the simple pleasure of holding her.

'Swing me too?'

At first Niall didn't know where the voice came from. He was too attuned to Lola's laugh and her blinding smile. Then he felt something touch his leg and looked down.

There, her hand on his knee, was a little girl, auburn curls dancing in the breeze, dark eyes turned up to him.

'Please, mister. Me too?'

Niall's breath backed up.

The little hand patted his leg and a hopeful smile filled her face.

Niall found his breath and expelled it in an audible whoosh. For a second the resemblance had been uncanny, but now he saw the differences between that eager face and the one he'd known.

Yet pain still knifed his chest.

Slowly he moved away a step, then another, till he could put Lola down on dry sand.

The child followed. He turned his head. Where were her parents?

'Swing me, please?'

Niall shook his head, telling himself no parent would want a stranger, especially a male stranger, cuddling their little girl.

From the corner of his eye he saw Lola shoot him a look. Then she crouched down in front of the child. 'Hello, my name's Lola. What's yours?'

The girl shook her head. 'I'm not allowed to talk to strangers.'

That almost jerked a laugh from Niall's frozen vocal cords. She couldn't talk to Lola but she could beg him to swing her through the air? Her parents had their hands full getting the stranger danger message through to this little one.

'Where's your family?' Lola persisted. 'They might be worried about you.'

Niall scanned the family groups scattered along the beach. None seemed to be frantically searching for a lost child.

He felt again that little hand paw his leg and flinched.

'Plee-ee-ase?'

She was a cute little thing and he saw the soft light in Lola's eyes. Did she want kids? The idea stabbed him.

'No swings unless your parents say so.'

His words emerged brusquely but they had their effect. Seconds later the child was racing up the beach to where a woman was busy helping two other children built a giant sandcastle.

Even from a distance Niall saw her shock as she registered the little girl race towards her, pointing back to them. The shock of someone who hadn't realised their charge was in potential danger.

Something rippled deep in the icy depths of his belly and curled around the back of his neck. Fellow feeling.

Beside him, Lola waved her hand and the woman acknowledged it with a nod as she gathered the child close.

Seconds later they heard a wail. Not of pain but frustration. Clearly the girl's mother had said *no*.

Relief settled in Niall's belly as he clasped Lola's hand. They turned back the way they'd come.

Lola slanted a look at him and shook her head. 'She'll keep her mum busy.'

'But you liked her.'

'She has character. Don't you think?'

Niall shrugged. 'I'm no expert on kids.'

'No.' He sensed her gaze on him. 'You didn't seem comfortable. Haven't you been around children at all?'

The ice inside spread, crackling up his spine, making him shudder. 'Only a bit.'

Liar. But that was way in the past. A past he tried never to visit.

'I spent years getting extra money babysitting. I enjoyed it.'

Niall slanted a look at her. 'You'd be good at it.' She had the patience and focus. And a great sense of humour. He could imagine her on her hands and knees, playing games with the kids she looked after.

'I'm sure you will be when the time comes.'

'Sorry?'

She turned away, apparently fascinated by a board rider. 'If or when you have children.'

Familiar coldness blanketed his shoulders, despite the bright sunlight. 'That's not going to happen. I won't ever have a family. You know I'm a loner.'

Lola couldn't get Niall's words out of her head. It wasn't just the words but how he'd said them. With such iron-clad certainty. Each word hard and definite. As if he could know for sure what the future held.

For some reason the joy went out of the day.

She tried to tell herself Niall didn't mean it about never having family, and always being alone. But she couldn't convince herself.

On the way back up the mountain, conversation was desultory and Niall left her almost immediately after they arrived, saying he needed to return a call. Lola had taken a call herself, from the police, saying Braithwaite had been spotted near her home and that they were hopeful he might be planning something that would incriminate him.

The news didn't cheer her. Her thoughts kept circling back to Niall and those dismissive words.

She'd spent years pining for this man. Now she'd made the mistake of falling in love with him.

Bad enough that there was a huge gulf between them. They moved in completely different circles as well as living in different states. If he truly believed he'd face the future alone, that meant he saw this as a short fling without a chance of it becoming something else. The idea caught at her ribs, stymying her breathing.

She wanted that chance.

Wanted a future with Niall.

Which was why she couldn't let it rest. She rapped on the door to his study and pushed it open. He stood looking out at the gathering dusk, birds wheeling over the trees in a swirl of colour.

'Niall…'

'Lola.' He swung around and she tensed. His expression didn't bode well.

'I wondered if you wanted dinner soon.' Coward! But suddenly she wasn't sure she wanted to know if he'd been serious about being a loner. About how he saw their relationship or whether there was any tiny chance in the future of him returning her feelings.

'In a while.' He paused and she saw his chest rise with a deep breath. As if he too girded himself for bad news. 'I wanted to talk with you. It's important.'

She didn't like the sound of that. Yet she needed to know. So she crossed the room, let him take her hand and pull her down to sit on the long leather sofa beside him.

Yesterday they'd made love here. They'd still been wet from the pool and they'd laughed as the leather squeaked against their slick, bare skin. Until rapture took them and they'd lost themselves in each other.

Their body language was different now, despite their clasped hands resting on Niall's thigh. There was tension in the air and rigidity in his big frame. Lola tried to slow her breathing, pushing her shoulders down.

'It follows on from our conversation on the beach,' he began and she nodded.

'I wanted to talk to you about that.' Lola smoothed her fingers over his knuckle. She'd spent years hiding her feelings and she was tired of it. She shot him a look, catching his gaze and feeling her pulse race. She wasn't naïve enough to think he'd fallen in love too, but she needed to know there was a chance for more.

'What we've shared has been wonderful, Niall. I've always cared for you, but these last weeks—'

'Please, Lola.' His finger touched her mouth, stopping her words. 'There's something I have to tell you first.'

Did he guess what she'd been going to say?

Did he know she loved him?

He didn't look like a man about to sweep her close and tell her he felt the same for her.

He looked like a man about to deliver tragic news.

Lola found herself watching their clasped hands, twined tight together, as if they each took strength from the other, knowing this was going to be bad.

'Say it, then.' She looked up and wished she couldn't see how hard this was for him. His features were drawn, his expression grim. Instinct told her she wouldn't like this, yet at the same time she wanted to smooth the frown from his brow and ease the pain she sensed in him.

It was easy to love a man who was strong, sexy and bold. Yet the tenderness welling inside her was no less, as she braced herself for the worst.

'You deserve someone better than me, Lola. I've always known it, and I suspect your family did too.'

She opened her mouth to protest that her family had loved him but his expression stopped her.

'What happened on the beach brought home to me how selfish I've been.' He turned his head slowly from side to side as if releasing stiff neck muscles, then rolled his shoulders. 'I knew from the start that I was no good for you. But I stopped thinking about it because I wanted you.'

His voice dropped to that low, resonant note she felt deep inside. Time and again he'd seduced her with his voice as much as his body. Yet now she heard pain, not seduction.

She lifted her hand to his jaw and he flinched. 'Don't, Lola. I don't deserve your tenderness.'

Yet for a moment he leaned into her palm before pulling away and setting his jaw. She dropped her hand, her heart falling too.

'You deserve a loving partner. Someone who'll always be

there for you. Who can look after you and protect you and give you children if you want them.' His eyes locked on hers and she felt it like a flash of lightning striking to her heart. 'You want children, don't you?'

She nodded. 'One day, if I can.' She wasn't in a hurry, but she'd always imagined herself with a family.

'I can't. Or,' he said quickly when she went to speak, 'I *won't*. It wouldn't be right. I'm not cut out to have a family. I couldn't trust myself with a family.'

Lola frowned. 'I don't understand.' Niall was the most caring, protective man she knew. 'You'd make a wonderful husband and father.'

His shudder told its own story.

'Don't!' His voice was thick with distress. 'I'll never be that. I couldn't trust myself, or ask others to put their trust in me.' His eyes met hers, inky dark and stark with pain. 'My sister and my mother both died because of me.'

CHAPTER THIRTEEN

LOLA STARED AT HIM, trying to make sense of the words that fell between them, as searing and heavy as drops of molten lead.

'You had a sister?'

Had Ed known? Her parents? She'd never suspected. But then Niall had never spoken about his family. Even when she was little, Lola had learned never to ask about his home life because he withdrew into himself.

Why had she never wondered about that? Never questioned Ed? It was just something she'd taken for granted.

Niall inclined his head, his throat working as if he had as much trouble swallowing as she did.

'Catriona. Younger than me. She had bright red hair and a cheeky smile.'

Lola was instantly reminded of the little girl on the beach. Was that why Niall had frozen? For a second she'd imagined she saw panic in his eyes, though later she'd told herself she imagined it.

'You spent a lot of time with her.' It was there in his voice, in the curve of his mouth when he mentioned his sister. So much for his supposed inexperience with children.

'My parents were busy. I looked after her most of the time when I wasn't at school.'

'In Melbourne?'

He shook his head. 'I moved there with my father. After.'

Niall's jaw set like stone, as did the big thigh muscle beneath their joined hands. Yet she felt the tiny tremors running through him.

'How old was she, Niall?'

'Four. I was nine.' He breathed deep. 'It was late afternoon. We were playing in the hall when Dad told us to go outside because we were too noisy.' He paused. 'I think our parents were arguing again and didn't want us to hear. So we went out and Catriona asked me to show her how to ride the scooter I'd got for Christmas.'

Lola's heart dipped at his expression.

'We had a long driveway running down the side of the house so I taught her there, where I'd learned. She got the hang of it quickly and kept wanting to go further and faster. But she was a good kid and listened when I said she couldn't go out of our garden onto the footpath.'

Niall stopped then finally continued. She could see how much it cost him. 'I got distracted, just for a minute, I swear. I thought Mum called me and I turned around to check. When I turned back it was too late. All I can think is that Catriona intended to stop when she reached the footpath but there was a bump there and instead of stopping she careered out of control straight onto the street. Just as a car came past.'

'Oh, Niall!' Lola leaned against him, her arm going around his back, tears of horror and sympathy glazing her vision.

'Some nights I still hear the sound of those brakes. And Mum screaming.'

Lola tugged her hand free of his and looped both her arms around him. It didn't matter that he was bigger and stronger than her. She held him close, whispering words of comfort. Nonsense words, probably, but it didn't matter. All that mattered was the raw hurt he still felt and the need to ease it.

Eventually Niall lifted her up and settled her across his lap. They clutched each other tight, rocking together.

'It wasn't your fault, Niall. You were just a child. It was an accident.'

She felt him shake his head. 'It's no excuse. It was my job to look after her. That's what I always did. But because I wasn't paying attention, Catriona died.'

Lola opened her mouth then snapped it shut. Would it really help to tell him that if there was fault anywhere it was with his parents, who'd set a nine-year-old to watch his little sibling so they had privacy for an argument? It was the sort of awful accident no one could foresee.

Did this explain his protective attitude to her? From the first Niall had looked out for her. Yet she suspected it was a trait he'd carried before Catriona's death.

She felt him take a deep breath. 'After that my parents barely spoke and when they did it was to argue. Finally they separated. Mum got the short straw and took me with her. Dad moved to Melbourne.'

The short straw? Surely a bereaved mother would cleave even closer to her remaining child?

'Things weren't good. She blamed me for Catriona, naturally.' He broke off but Lola heard his ragged breathing, felt it in the rough movements of his chest.

'It *wasn't* your fault, Niall. Surely someone, a counsellor or other family members, made that clear?'

It was horrible to think of his mother blaming him. Was that why he still felt guilty? Anger swelled that a little kid should be made to carry that burden.

'Looking back now, I realise she was severely depressed. I was a reminder of what she'd lost and she couldn't move on. I could never be enough for her. I wasn't a solace but a torture to her.' He paused and Lola felt a horrible anticipation of worse to come. 'When I was eleven I came home from school to find her on the floor, dead from an overdose of prescription drugs.'

'Oh, Niall. That's appalling. I'm so sorry.'

To have a parent inflict such an experience on their child! He held her tight and Lola nestled into his embrace, hugging him, trying to provide physical comfort when words were insufficient.

The way he spoke, the carefully neutral tone, was at odds with his rigidity and his tight embrace.

This, she realised, was the Niall she knew. Who hid his deepest feelings from the world. Just as, in his youth, he'd hidden them behind a spiky, combative attitude, and later, in his absorption with computers and passion for martial arts.

'If Catriona hadn't died, if I'd kept her safe the way I was supposed to, my mother wouldn't have killed herself.'

Lola pulled back in his arms, unable to sit still any longer. Hands cupping his face, she looked into his wounded dark eyes.

'You're *not* responsible for her death, Niall. You're not responsible for either one.'

His mouth lifted in a crumpled curve that hollowed her insides. 'You look so fierce, Lola. But it doesn't matter. It's too late now. I'll always carry that guilt.'

'Don't say that!'

It couldn't be too late for him. She refused to think it.

Lola leaned in and kissed him hard. So hard her teeth mashed his until he opened his mouth enough to let her in. She leaned in, kissing him with all the love in her heart, as if somehow she could undo years of misguided guilt.

Finally, breathless, she pulled back, planting her hands on his shoulders.

Lola felt furious with herself, forcing a kiss on him. As if that could magically change things! Furious with his mother, who'd taken her grief out on her little boy. Furious with his father, who hadn't been there to support them.

But what was the point of so much anger? How could she understand the grief that had torn the family apart?

Lola knew grief. It had taken over her life when her mother died. But to lose a child, or in Niall's case, to lose his family…

She looked into his eyes and read sorrow and regret. And knew, with a leaden heart, it wasn't only for the past, but for *them*. Because he believed his past made it impossible to share a future. He felt himself unworthy of love, of family.

Words formed in her head but none were the right ones. None would convince this wounded, caring, stubborn man that he deserved a future with someone who loved him. How could any platitude of hers convince him?

'What happened to your father?' It wasn't what she really wanted to know. But it was better than the silence.

'I moved in with him till I left school. By then he had a new family, a wife and the first of their babies on the way.' He shrugged. 'We don't see each other now.'

There was finality in his words, as if warning her not to go there. Had they drifted apart or had his father pushed him away when he started a new family, rejecting his grieving son?

Fury roiled inside her at the way Niall had been turned into a scapegoat, made to pay for a tragic accident by adults who should have known better. She pushed it down. Giving vent to fruitless anger wouldn't help the man she loved.

'So, you see, Lola, I'm not cut out for a family. I'm not good at it and I'd never trust myself, or ask someone to trust me in that way. Do you understand?'

She nodded, her throat constricting as if caught in a noose.

'You're special.' His smile cut through her, because it held no happiness. 'You deserve to have the best life can give you, with the right man.' He breathed slowly. 'I needed to tell you, so you understood. I feel closer to you than I've felt with—' He shook his head as if regretting the words, leaving Lola to wonder what he'd meant to say. Closer than to any other woman? Her yearning heart beat faster.

'I always make it clear from the start that I can only do short-term relationships. Except with you.' He pushed her hair back from her face and her insides twisted at the tenderness of the gesture. 'I should never have touched you. What we've shared has been wonderful, but it can't go anywhere. You need to know that. I've never shared this with anyone else.'

Lola blinked up at him.

All this time and he'd never shared this?

Pain filled her as she thought of him bearing all this alone. The backs of her eyes turned gritty and hot but she refused to cry. He'd probably blame himself then for hurting her!

Niall carried an impossible burden. He was scared of hurting those he cared for. The only saving grace was that he *did* care. He'd cared for his family, far more than his parents deserved, she couldn't help feeling.

He cared for her, if not in the way she wanted. She'd seen him interact with friends and acquaintances at the party and occasionally elsewhere in the last couple of weeks, and he'd revealed himself to be generous and warm-hearted.

It was a tragic waste that a man like Niall couldn't move on and trust himself as he deserved.

'Thank you for telling me, Niall.'

Was it imagination or did he relax a little at her words?

'Though I disagree with you.' She lifted her hand when he would have interrupted. 'I hear what you're saying. I understand why you think the way you do. But I don't believe for a second that you're unworthy of love or can't be trusted with a family of your own.'

'Lola.' His voice held a warning and his hands moved to her hips as if to dislodge her from his lap.

'Hear me out, Niall, just once.'

For a long moment he didn't respond, then finally nodded his head abruptly.

'We all blame ourselves when things go wrong. When my mother died I fretted about all the things I might have done differently that would have saved her.'

'You can't—'

She pressed her fingers to his lips. 'I know. It's madness to think that way, but for a while I circled back to it again and again.' Just as she'd wondered if she could have prevented her father's gambling. 'With time, and support, you'd have realised that. But you didn't get that support.' She swallowed the bitter words on her tongue. 'Instead you suffered a second tragedy, not of your making.'

Niall's mouth tightened but he said nothing.

'I know you, Niall. My whole family knew you and trusted you. Do you really think my parents would have given the run of the house to a boy who might endanger me? If anything, you've always been more protective than Ed.'

'Because I know how easily things can go wrong.'

Lola nodded. 'Exactly, don't you see? Things *go wrong*. It's not always a matter of blame. You did the best you could. You thought your mother called so of course you turned around. You're not to blame for what happened. To think that you don't deserve happiness is just plain wrong.'

For a second Lola wondered if she'd got through to him. But this mindset was ingrained. He was just being patient and polite while he heard her out.

'Thank you, Lola. I know you mean well.' He paused. 'I'll always be available if you need help. Either you or Ed. So long as you understand that this, between us, was a mistake. We should never have become intimate.'

Her chin jerked up. 'Because you can't trust me not to become needy and dependent?'

She shot to her feet, torn between hurt that he was so obstinate and anger at herself for falling for a man so determined to dwell in the past. She *did* feel needy and dependent.

'I did my share of seducing,' she snapped. 'Promise me that you won't add *Seducing Lola* to the list of things you feel guilty about. You're already burdened with enough.'

She sounded grumpy but couldn't help it. They'd found something special but Niall was hell-bent on self-sacrifice.

'Lola, listen, I—'

'If you don't mind, let's postpone the rest of the lecture on why you're no good for me till later. I've got a bit of a headache and want to lie down.'

She turned away, fearing he'd reach out and stop her, which would be disastrous because he'd see the tears she fought, clinging to her lashes.

But he didn't say a word. Nor did he follow.

Niall expected that from then on Lola would keep her distance.

He'd underestimated her.

An hour later she joined him in the kitchen, where he'd been staring into the fridge, telling himself he should organise a meal for them, but unable to focus.

His thoughts were a jumble. Taken up with the past, but, more importantly, with the sight, sound, scent and feel of Lola, sitting on his lap, holding him tight and telling him it wasn't his fault. That he wasn't the damned soul he'd always believed. That he had a right to expect more.

His chest ached and there was a hard, tight nugget of something lodged behind his ribs that wouldn't shift.

Then she walked into the kitchen, as if nothing had happened, and took over organising their meal.

Almost as if nothing had happened, because her gaze never quite met his and her smile was a dim facsimile of her usual one.

That was when Niall discovered he was a coward. For he didn't force conversation back to their earlier discussion. Instead he fetched the spices she demanded for her marinade, searched out a white wine to accompany the chicken, and fired the charcoal barbecue.

A stranger would have thought the scene companionable as they worked together, her preparing a spicy salad while he cooked the marinated meat, then sat, eating and looking out into the dusky evening.

But Niall felt the difference. There was a new constraint between them and Lola's eyes looked different. As if the light had gone out behind them.

He'd done the right thing, warning her of his true nature

and setting boundaries that should have been spelled out long before. Yet that didn't make it any easier.

He was weak where she was concerned. The fact he'd given in to his physical craving for her, despite the dictates of his conscience, was proof. How could he entertain thoughts of a future with Lola, or trust himself to care for her as she deserved, when he couldn't even summon the strength to resist her?

He'd been so tempted to believe her persuasive words. Because he wanted, badly, for them to be true. No one had ever shown such absolute trust in him personally, not just in his business acumen. She had such faith, even admiration. He'd wondered if maybe redemption were possible. Could Lola's belief in him make a difference?

The thought was short-lived. It would kill him if he again lost someone he cared for through his own neglect. He couldn't take that risk, not with Lola.

They washed up together, utterly rational, polite companions, but Niall couldn't take any more. Being close to Lola, but not close enough, knowing he'd never be close enough again, was too much.

He excused himself, saying he had to finish some work prior to a meeting he had to attend in Brisbane tomorrow. Yet when he got to his office he couldn't settle. Didn't even open his computer. Just stood, staring into the night.

That was where Lola found him. She didn't say anything, just walked over and curved her hand through his arm, pulling him towards the door.

'Lola, I can't—'

'Shh.' Her fingers skimmed his mouth and that tantalising touch made his throat convulse. 'Don't overthink this, Niall. We both need company. That's all.'

Minutes later they were in bed, bodies tangling and breathing heavy, their eyes locked as they used hands and mouths to give each other pleasure and eventually release.

Then Niall played the coward again, closing his eyes and

pretending to sleep because he feared what he might let slip if he spoke to Lola in this unguarded state. That he might forget what she needed and deserved and think only of his selfish desire to keep her close.

Lola woke in the early hours. Even in sleep it was as if Niall protected her, cradling her against his chest. She shifted her weight and he must have been awake, for he lifted his hand in a slow caress.

He brought her to arousal so fast her head would have spun if she weren't lying across him.

Lola blinked back searing heat and tried not to think about anything but the moment. The simple joy of carnal desire. They made love again silently, with the ease of long-time lovers, yet with an urgency that made it feel like the first time.

Or the last.

Niall's touch was infinitely tender yet devastatingly arousing. Within minutes they were locked together, bodies melding, hearts beating in unison, as if they'd been made for such moments.

The thought didn't bring its usual magic, instead awakening her impatience at this stubborn, stoic man who'd made self-abnegation an art form. She clawed at his shoulders, biting down on his neck, feeling his powerful body jerk in response.

Their lovemaking changed. Became less perfect, less easy, turning into a wild, no-holds-barred plunge of two beings driven by desperation.

Her orgasm came hard and fast, almost before she realised. Niall's came at the same time. She saw him arch, head flung back as he pumped into her. His mouth moved, silently forming her name.

That was when Lola broke, closing her eyes against the tears she couldn't let fall, holding tight to the man she loved, knowing he would never let her be his.

CHAPTER FOURTEEN

'Ms Suarez?'

Lola yawned and pushed her tangled hair off her face. She'd had too little sleep, fretting over Niall and his determination to end their relationship. He'd left at dawn this morning, driving to Brisbane for a day of meetings, his demeanour telling her nothing had changed.

'Yes? Speaking.'

'Inspector Corcoran here.'

Lola stiffened, leaning against the kitchen counter where she waited for her tea to brew. She'd *thought* she recognised the voice.

'Inspector.' She swallowed. 'You have some news?'

'Yes, I do.' He paused and she wondered what was coming. 'There's been an incident. Jayden Braithwaite is dead.'

'Dead?' She blinked, trying to get her mind into gear. 'Braithwaite is dead? You're sure it's him?'

'Yes, his identity's been confirmed.'

The rest of his words blurred as her legs gave way and she slid down to the floor.

'Ms Suarez? Are you still there?'

The voice sounded far away and she realised belatedly that the phone was on the floor, grasped in her white-knuckled grip. She shook all over and it took conscious effort to lift the phone to her ear.

'I'm sorry, Inspector. I missed that. Would you mind repeating what you said?'

Twenty minutes later, phone still gripped in her hand, Lola got to her feet. She tipped out the cold, stewed tea and boiled the kettle again.

She felt calm now, almost unnaturally so. After that first wave of reaction, her emotions had flattened out completely. It felt as if everything were happening a long way away, or to someone else.

It seemed Niall's insistence on posting someone in Lola's flat had finally borne fruit, luring Braithwaite into action. Last night another attempt had been made to get into her home, but the security Niall had organised, and the alert presence of her body double, had foiled that.

The police had arrived just too late to catch Braithwaite and he hadn't returned to his boarding house. Instead, hours later, the police had been called to an explosion in a supposedly derelict warehouse. The theory was that, angry at his close shave trying to enter her apartment, Braithwaite had grown impatient and careless. Experts said he'd been planning a letter bomb that had accidentally detonated. In addition to the remains of the explosive device, they found an envelope addressed to her, plus the equipment he'd used earlier to monitor her flat.

No, the inspector said, there was no doubt it was Braithwaite. There was no doubt he'd been planning more harm. And there was no reason now for her to remain in Queensland.

No reason except Niall was here and she feared that if she left she'd never see him again.

The kettle clicked off and she busied herself, making tea. Ignoring the splintering cracks in her unnatural calm as shock started to wear off. A shaft of pain pierced her and she sucked in her breath, trying to stifle it.

She loved Niall. What she felt wasn't infatuation or a crush. Once upon a time, perhaps, but not now.

But he didn't feel that way about her. Worse, he'd believed in his guilt and unworthiness for so long, she feared she'd never convince him to take a chance on them as a couple.

Her mouth twisted as she added milk to her tea and took a sip.

A screech sounded outside and she looked up to see lorikeets squabbling in the trees, their colours blurring. It took a moment to realise the hazy focus came from the moisture welling in her eyes.

So much for feeling numb!

Lola cradled her tea and looked out at the view she'd come to love.

What could she do? Stay here and try to persuade Niall that he was wrong, and that what they shared was worth keeping alive? She wouldn't talk in terms of permanency because he'd shut her down instantly. But if she could persuade him to keep going as they were…

Then what?

Give up your job and your life in Melbourne in hopes Niall might one day see sense?

Live on a knife edge, waiting for the day he decides it's not working and you need to separate?

Lola gulped down tea, feeling it scald her throat.

She was tired of feeling vulnerable around Niall. It had to stop.

She'd spent years pining for the impossible. Hoping Niall would one day notice her, or that some stranger would live up to the impossible ideal she'd built in her head.

Niall wasn't the hero she'd imagined. He was close to it, so very close, but he was flawed like everyone else. His vision of himself was so skewed he didn't dare believe he could be happy with anyone. Which meant he couldn't offer her even a hope of a future together.

Lola didn't expect promises of for ever straight away, but she wanted the chance for that. She wanted to love a man who might one day love her back.

Niall cared for her. He wanted to protect her.

But he didn't love her. Chances were he never would.

Which meant she only had one choice.

Turning her back on the riot of colour and sound in the treetops, she carried her tea to the bedroom and her packing.

During his early drive to Brisbane Niall received a report that Braithwaite had tried to enter Lola's flat the previous night but got away.

Blood chilling, he'd demanded details. Disappointment at the man's escape vied with relief that Lola's body double was okay. And that Lola was safe here in Queensland.

The thought of losing another person he cared about, someone he was responsible for…the idea was unthinkable.

About to do a U-turn and head back to Lola and the mountain house, he stopped. Logic decreed she was safe since Braithwaite believed her to be in Melbourne. Yet the urge to be with her was strong.

Except she'd be hurt and annoyed at what she'd see as Niall's overprotectiveness.

So he forced himself to keep going, arriving early for the negotiations that had been months in the planning. Yet he couldn't dispel the disquiet gnawing at his gut.

Mid-morning, during a break in the negotiations, came the information that Braithwaite was dead. At first Niall couldn't believe it. The news of the planned letter bomb curdled his gut. If Lola had been there, defenceless…

But she hadn't been. She was alive and well.

Relief slammed into him, an overwhelming wave, rocking him back on his heels.

Lola wouldn't have to look over her shoulder worrying about a malevolent stalker.

He called her but went straight to her message bank.

She was probably busy, talking to the cops.

There was nothing to worry about. She was safe.

Yet, behind the crashing wave of relief loomed something

else. Something exacerbated by the fact he wasn't able to talk with her. An overwhelming sense of—could it be?—anxiety.

'Mr Pedersen? We're resuming in the conference room now.'

Niall nodded but stayed where he was, staring at the phone in his hand, trying to identify the reason for his unease.

He should be celebrating. He'd kept Lola safe from Braithwaite. Yet he didn't feel triumphant or even mildly satisfied. Instead a cold weight filled his belly.

Lola has no reason to stay now.

Why would she stay with a man like you? She knows the truth about you now.

You could never be right for a woman like her.

A woman who deserved and, he guessed, wanted, more than a short affair. He could imagine Lola with children. With a stellar career and a doting husband.

Pain spiked in his jaw at the thought of her smiling at some nameless, faceless man. Being with him in the ways she'd been with Niall. Sharing her future.

He swallowed and somehow the pain in his jaw transferred to his throat. It felt as if it were studded with nails.

Niall couldn't allow himself to think about a future with anyone. He knew his limitations. Knew that eventually he'd let her down. Catastrophe followed him as night followed day, which was why he kept his personal relationships short. The idea of losing Lola through some mistake he'd made, some error of judgement or fleeting distraction...

So why did the thought of her leaving fill him with dread?

Not just dread, but a terrible ache as if from a physical blow.

Fear of abandonment?

Not likely! He'd come to terms years before with the loss of his family, two dead and one uncaring of the severed bond between them. His father had been eager to forget the son responsible for destroying their family unit, concentrating on his new wife and children.

Niall was used to being alone.

He didn't need anyone. Just as no one needed him.

Keep telling yourself that, Pedersen.

'Niall?' It was his chief legal advisor. 'We need you.'

'Coming.'

He thumbed in a text to Lola and returned to the conference room.

Never had a meeting dragged so much. Especially a negotiation that promised a significant and lucrative expansion of business.

Yet Niall couldn't concentrate. More than once he caught his team frowning at him, wondering at his abstraction. Fortunately they were well prepared and the discussions proceeded as planned.

In the next break, Niall dragged out his phone before anyone could accost him. Still Lola didn't answer. Nor had she returned his text.

Fear skated down his spine.

He rang his housekeeper, only to discover she was out of the area for the day. He was on the point of ringing Pedersen Security staff on the Gold Coast, to ask them to...

What? Drive up the mountain and check she was okay? Braithwaite was dead. Lola wasn't in danger.

Yet instinct told him they needed to speak.

Not just to hear how she was doing with this news about her stalker, but because of what he'd told her yesterday.

He'd revealed his history, waiting for the moment she'd shy away from him, horrified. But she hadn't. She'd held him and kissed him. Kissed him! As if *he* were the victim, not the one responsible.

Niall had come to think of Lola as practical and clearsighted, but he'd reckoned without her soft heart. Her response had thrown him, almost made him forget his vow to keep her safe. Safe even from him.

Instead of keeping her distance, she'd led him to bed! And he, weak where Lola was concerned, had taken everything she offered, losing himself in her sweet body and generous loving. Not once but several times.

Was it any wonder he'd left while she was barely awake, using his Brisbane meeting as an excuse?

Because in the grey, dawn light he knew he'd have to find the strength to walk away from her. For her own good.

Another call straight to message bank. Another text she didn't answer.

Pinching the bridge of his nose, trying to ease his rising panic, Niall searched out the head of his legal team, instructing him on the rest of the deal. Then, before the lawyer could do more than gape, Niall took the stairs to the basement car park at a gallop rather than wait for the lift. Minutes later he was in his car, heading to the mountains.

He was too late.

The house was empty. Lola was gone.

Yet it was Niall who felt empty, standing before her empty wardrobe. Completely hollow, as if a slight breeze might knock him off his feet.

He'd known grief and loss. Yet he hadn't been prepared for this. Niall told himself it was for the best but it was no consolation.

He found her note on the kitchen bench. The island bench where, more than once, they'd made love because they couldn't bear to wait to get to a bedroom.

Holding his breath, he opened the folded page.

Niall scanned it rapidly, searching for a reference to seeing him again. But his eyes snagged on phrases that made the hair stand up on the back of his neck and his breath stop.

...care for you deeply...
...move on with my life. It's been on hold far too long, because of my feelings for you.

He'd had no idea. Could it be true?

Lola, caring for him all this time? Lola hoping...

His heart hammered as he thought back over everything she'd said and done, how she'd looked and acted, but already he was reading on. What he read made his heart stutter then plunge in a descent that didn't seem to stop.

...understand you're scared of losing someone you care for.

He'd always known Lola was insightful. Even as a kid she'd seen more than many of the people around her. But the simplicity with which she named his fear stunned him.

Niall braced himself on the granite countertop, vaguely aware of his laboured breaths and the hard pump of his lungs.

He *was* scared of getting close to someone and letting them down. Because of him Catriona had died. Because of that his parents split up and his mother killed herself. In her final years, whenever she looked at him he'd seen blame and despair in her eyes.

Yet Lola made his fear sound like cowardice, not prudence or the need to protect others from his flawed self.

He swallowed hard, pain scraping his gullet.

Could she be right?

He couldn't think like that. It was the sort of wishful thinking that could undo him. Or endanger someone special, like Lola.

You deserve more from life and I do too. So I'm moving on.
Goodbye, Niall.

There was no signature. No trite words about seeing him later.

Goodbye.

She meant for ever.

Lola was doing what he'd hoped, severing ties. Leaving him so he couldn't harm her any more.

His head spun with the idea that she'd had feelings for him all this time. That because of him, she'd held herself back from being with other men.

Stupidly, he felt a leap of excitement that it hadn't just been primal sexual attraction for her. That she cared profoundly.

Until he recalled what that meant. Caring equated in his experience with vulnerability. Love with death and grief. He couldn't be selfish enough to want her...*attached* to him in that way.

Could he?

Of course not.

Yet as he held the paper her words blurred and he felt an ache behind his eyes and at the back of his throat that he hadn't felt since he was eleven. When he'd watched them lower a coffin into the ground and grieved the mother who'd no longer loved him.

This was for the best. Lola would be safe now, without him.

CHAPTER FIFTEEN

THREE WEEKS LATER, on a sunny spring Saturday, Lola moved into her new flat. It was further out from the city centre but the neighbourhood had a good vibe and there were no bad memories to send a shiver down her spine when she came home late from work.

Bending at the knees, she lifted a box of books for the big bookcase. Once she put her pictures and books up it would feel more like home. She ignored the inner voice that told her she was kidding herself.

How could any place feel like home when she'd left her heart behind in Queensland?

It sounded corny, but it was true.

She just had to close her eyes to see Niall's face when he'd revealed his past. His pain as he told her he was to blame for what happened to his family, impressing upon her that she deserved better than a man like him.

There was a gaping hole where her heart had torn open.

Shc'd wanted to help him. Encourage him to understand he wasn't to blame and that the future could be bright for them both if he'd only take the risk and trust himself. As he'd insisted she trust him when she was in danger.

But life wasn't that easy, was it? Even for a man who was scarily clear-sighted in other things, like building an internationally renowned business in a decade, he had a blind spot about his past.

If it had been easy, Niall would have believed her. Lola imagined him reading the note explaining her feelings and realising he felt the same. He'd have jumped on his private jet and beaten her back to Melbourne.

Foolishly, when she'd arrived she'd scanned the arrivals hall for his tall figure. She'd half expected to hear him calling her name, because he couldn't let her go.

The last weeks she'd gone through the motions. Her friends and colleagues hadn't seemed to notice. Maybe they thought she was shaken up by what had happened with Braithwaite.

She worked hard, even managed to contribute sensibly to her new team project. She'd organised a new place to live in record time because she no longer felt comfortable in her old one.

Lola had told herself that was why sleep proved elusive. But it was a lie. She'd lain awake thinking of Niall. Wanting him and wishing he could move on from his past. But she didn't have the professional skills to help him understand he was a victim in his family's tragedy, not its cause.

She'd always seen his drive and determination as strengths but now she cursed his obstinacy. He was so wedded to guilt he couldn't move past it.

Putting the box down, Lola sighed and stretched, forcing her thoughts from Niall. New place, new start. No more foolish dreams. No more—

The intercom from the building's main entrance sounded and she frowned. She'd turned down a couple of offers from friends to help unpack because after a week at work she was tired of putting on a front. Smiling made her face sore and it was tough pretending everything was okay when she wondered if she'd ever be okay again.

'Yes?'

Silence for a second that made her wonder if someone had keyed in the wrong flat number.

'Hello, Lola.'

Shock pressed her back against the wall, her hand to her throat as if to hold down the pulse leaping there.

'Niall?' Her voice sounded scratchy.

'Can I come up?'

No, no, no!

That's the last thing you need. How are you going to forget him if you...?

Lola pushed the button that opened the main entrance. So much for listening to caution!

'I'm at number—'

'Twenty, I know.'

He knew? How?

Did it matter? With his resources it would be child's play to discover her address. The easiest way would have been to ask her. But he hadn't. He hadn't been in contact. She'd assumed he didn't intend to see her again.

Yet now here he was.

Lola smoothed down her shirt, a little grimy from hauling boxes, then realised she was primping.

She set her jaw. No more. She couldn't cut off her feelings for Niall as if they'd never been, but she wouldn't go back to hoping for more than he could give. She'd spent too long doing that and look where it had got her. With an aching heart and a dead feeling inside, as if part of her had been amputated.

Drawing a deep breath, she went to the door, opening it just as Niall appeared, striding up the stairs two at a time, the picture of lean energy.

Her pulse thrummed and a boulder lodged in her throat. She swallowed. 'Is there a problem with the lift?'

He lifted his head as he took the last couple of steps, his gaze cutting straight to hers. Lola was glad to lean against the doorjamb because her stupid legs turned wobbly.

'It was slow.'

Part of her wanted to see that as proof he was eager to see

her. The new, saner Lola said Niall had always had energy to burn. It was nothing personal.

'Can I come in?' He was before her now, looking obscenely delectable in faded jeans that outlined his powerful thighs and a dark shirt the colour of his eyes, the sleeves rolled up.

It was one thing to tell herself she was strong. An entirely other thing to feel it when that dark blue gaze snared hers.

'Why?' She stood straight, folding her arms across her chest. But her determination wilted as she took in the sharp set of his features. He looked as if he'd lost weight, those beautiful, pared features edging towards gaunt.

Lola blinked. No time now for imaginings.

Yet as she stared, she noticed tiny vertical lines above his nose that she'd swear hadn't been there before, and the grooves bracketing his mouth surely scored deeper.

'It won't take long, but it's important.'

His expression revealed nothing, a reminder that when it came to negotiating and getting his way, Niall was in a league of his own.

He probably wants to check you're fine so he can report to Ed then finally wash his hands of you.

Because they had nothing else to say to each other. Lola's mouth twisted and pain corkscrewed down through her middle.

Finally, because she probably owed him her life, Lola nodded. 'Come in.'

He moved swiftly. He was in her flat, moving down the hallway before she could blink.

In a hurry to get this over. Well, that suited her.

The lounge room was full of boxes and there was nowhere to sit but she wasn't going to invite him into her bedroom, the only room she'd finished, right down to fresh sheets on the bed.

'Nice place.'

Her eyebrows rose. The place looked a wreck at the moment and the whole flat would fit inside just one of the elegant sitting rooms in his mountain retreat.

Lola narrowed her eyes and saw the jerky movement as he swallowed. Could it possibly be that Niall was nervous? Now she really was imagining things.

He watched Lola cross her arms, reinforcing the barriers between them.

Even so he had the devil's own job not eating her up with his eyes. The press of her breasts against the thin white shirt alone threatened to undo him. He saw the outline of her white bra. Was that a familiar tiny red bow between her breasts?

Instantly he wondered if she wore the cute panties dotted with cherries beneath her close-fitting jeans.

Heat smothered his skin as erotic images bombarded him, but he squashed them with the devastating knowledge she didn't want him here. It was branded in her stance, the hitched-high shoulders, the tilted chin and downturned mouth. She didn't even bother to break the ice by offering refreshments, which in her family was tantamount to a deliberate insult.

Niall swallowed again, pain scouring from his throat down to his abdomen.

Had he really expected a welcome?

'What do you want, Niall?'

'I had to see you and—'

'Of course,' she interrupted. 'To check I'm okay. It's what you do, isn't it? Because you promised Ed. And, presumably, to check I was satisfied with your firm's service before you sign the task off as completed.'

She laughed and his nerves jangled at the note of bitterness. He'd never heard Lola sound like that.

'You can put your mind at rest. They, you, did a sterling job. If ever anyone I know needs protection, I'll be sure to recommend Pedersen Security. I might even write an online review.'

She reduced what they'd shared to a *job*?

Out of the all-consuming blur of pain and doubt, made more terrible by the tiny bud of hope that had begun to form, indignation flared.

The likelihood of him getting what he wanted was minuscule. Niall knew coming here was a triumph of desperation over sense. But he refused to let Lola relegate what he'd done to a mere job.

'I'd try to help anyone who found themselves in that situation.' He watched her stiffen. 'But don't ever pretend, even to yourself, that I protected you as a job or solely out of a sense of obligation to Ed.'

He sucked in a searing breath. 'Yes, I owe your family a debt I can never repay. Yes, Ed's my best mate and there's not much I wouldn't do for him. But I *care* for you.'

It wasn't the way he'd planned to say it. He'd practised a softly, softly approach, slowly winning her over, not arguing.

'Oh, you *care*, Niall, just not enough.' She uncrossed her arms, shifted her weight and recrossed them. For a second he saw vulnerability in her shadowed eyes and taut mouth, and that tiny bud of hope grew a little.

He closed the space between them in two strides, watching surprise freeze her features.

'I care more than I can say.' His voice hit a gravel rumble and he had to pause as feelings, all those feelings he'd once strived to suppress, bubbled up in a churning, confused mass.

Niall touched her arms, his hands closing gently on her elbows. Then, discovering how she trembled, he ran his palms up to her shoulders with some vague idea of soothing or supporting her. Which would have made sense if his hands weren't unsteady too.

'I can't...' He shook his head impatiently. 'I'm not good with the words, Lola. Not about emotions.' For most of his life strong emotion had equated to pain and regret. To self-disgust. And because whatever words of love his parents had ever bestowed were long forgotten under the weight of guilt.

She didn't say anything to help him, just watched mutely. But as he stared back Niall saw her hazel eyes glitter brighter. Her breasts rose high with each shallow breath as if she, too, found breathing difficult.

'I'm scared,' he confessed and saw her frown. 'Scared that I'll let you down, or that your feelings have changed. But even so I couldn't keep away. I need you, Lola, in ways I'd never imagined before.'

The strength of that need stunned him. He'd spent three weeks battling the urge to follow her, trying to find a way to shore up his determination to keep away.

But with Lola he'd tasted Paradise, not just in bed, but in her loving warmth. And he found that, after all, he was a weak man, too weak to stay away.

'Oh, Niall!' Her hands gripped his arms and another tiny tendril shot out from that bud of hope.

Except she didn't sound happy. She sounded torn.

'Lola.' Even her name was a benediction. 'I don't want to hurt you. If you don't want me any more I'll go and you'll never see me again.'

'Don't you...dare.'

It was a whisper, barely heard over his rushing pulse. Niall tilted his head closer, reading the glow in her eyes.

'You still want me?' Despite every hope it seemed impossible. Niall had been alone so long, all his life it seemed. So the idea of this one, marvellous woman believing in him, trusting him, seemed unfathomable.

'For a very clever man you can be so blind, Niall Pedersen. I've wanted you since I had braces and puppy fat.'

Disappointment vied with elation. 'Lola, whatever pedestal you once put me on, I'm not that man.' Surely he'd made that clear? 'I'm deeply flawed.' Much as he wanted her, he couldn't let her throw her future away on a mirage. 'I shouldn't have touched you but I'm weak where you're concerned. I delayed telling you the truth about my past because I was selfish. I couldn't bear for you to turn away from me, even though I knew you should. Because being with you made me...'

Her eyebrows rose. 'Happy?'

He shook his head, lifting his hand to stroke her cheek. 'Far more than that, lovely Lola.' He drew a trembling breath. 'Happy. Content. Fulfilled. *Hopeful*. For the first time I felt...' he shook his head '...right. As if all these years a part of me was missing and I'd found it again.'

'Oh, Niall.' Her mouth worked and she blinked.

'Hell! Lola, I'm sorry. Don't cry, please.'

'I'm not crying, I'm happy. And before you warn me off again, I know full well that you're not perfect. Neither of us are.'

Niall scowled down at her. He couldn't recall any of his girlfriends crying with happiness. Maybe it was the nature of the emotion that made the difference.

His emotions were all over the place, hope and excitement vying with fear and wonder.

'The problem is,' he made himself go on, needing to say this, 'I can't guarantee to make you happy.' Or to protect her as she deserved, but Niall had learned enough to know she didn't want to hear about him protecting her. 'I'd like to try though.'

He ignored the prickling between his shoulder blades, the reminder of past mistakes. It was the hardest thing he'd done in his life, trying to forge a new path, telling himself maybe Lola was right and he could find love. Putting the past behind him.

She opened her mouth then closed it again. Finally she spoke, her eyes locked on his. 'You'd like to make me happy because I make you feel hopeful and *right*?'

Niall's hopes dipped. It didn't sound enough, did it? He yanked in more air, wondering why his lungs wouldn't fill.

'I'm not much of a catch, I know.' Not with his emotional hang-ups. At her raised eyebrows he shook his head. 'Well, except for the money.'

Suddenly she was smiling and it was the most wonderful thing he'd seen in weeks. 'That's a lovely compliment, Niall. That you know I'm not interested in your money.'

He tried to think of something else to entice her, but all the smooth words he'd practised on the flight south had deserted him. There was just the truth, raw and unvarnished.

Soft fingers brushed his cheek, feathering to his jaw then lower, to splay around the back of his neck. He revelled in her touch.

'As for not being good with words—' she shook her head '—I disagree. Do you *really* feel like you've found a part of you that was missing?' Her eyes shone and gradually Niall's anxiety disappeared.

He cupped her face in both hands. 'I do. With you I feel hopeful. I feel…*love*.' That was the only possible explanation. 'I've tried to explain away my feelings for weeks but they wouldn't be explained away. I love you, Lola Suarez. I want to be with you. Long term.'

After years of telling lovers he was only interested in time-limited affairs, he needed to spell that out, and it felt good, far better than he'd expected.

He read excitement in Lola's eyes and the upward curve of her lips. 'You really mean it!'

Niall could no longer resist. He pressed a kiss to the corner of her smiling mouth. Then to the other corner. Somehow his arms were around her and she was kissing him back with a tender passion that was unique to Lola.

It felt wondrous.

Niall teetered on the brink of fear. Loving this woman made him vulnerable in ways he'd planned never to be vulnerable again. But it was too late for fear. Too late for anything but holding tight and trusting in their love for each other.

He pulled back, just enough to look into her hazel eyes. They sparkled like green gems and his heart thudded with pride and humility.

This woman loved him. Really, truly loved him.

The tender buds of hope branched out into a green garden, where once there'd been only wasteland.

'If you trust me, I'll do my best to be the sort of man you deserve.' It wouldn't be easy, he had so much to learn, but he was determined. With Lola, Niall had the best possible incentive.

'You already are that man, my love.' Her words carved their way through his very soul. She gazed up at him and what he read in her expression unshackled the last chains around his heart. 'And I promise to do my best to be the sort of woman you deserve.'

'Sweet Lola,' he groaned. 'You're everything I want and need and far more than I deserve.'

He bent to kiss her again when she whispered, 'Did I mention that the only room that's finished is the bedroom? There are fresh sheets and...'

Lola never got to finish. His mouth found hers. Right now talking seemed like such a waste of time.

Still kissing, Niall swung her up into his arms and carried her into the bedroom, where he demonstrated his feelings for her in more tangible ways.

EPILOGUE

THE DOORS OPENED with their usual discreet hiss. With Niall's hand warm at her back, Lola stepped inside.

Awestruck, she gazed around her. 'Carolyn's outdone herself this time.'

She'd thought that after two years she was used to their hostess's wild extravagance. But the profusion of colourful silks and glittering, overflowing treasure chests dazzled the eyes. The multi-storey atrium was dominated by an enormous ship's mast, complete with bright sails and a sequinned pirate flag. The rigging was made of golden chains studded with faux gems and the sails and flag billowed in the breeze created by concealed fans.

Niall chuckled. 'Do you think she could have fitted in any more bling?'

'I doubt it, darling.' Their hostess's amused voice came from nearby. 'Poor Ted's been wearing his sunglasses inside since we set up.' Her throaty laugh engulfed them as she hugged Lola. Then she kissed Niall on the cheek and with a wink at Lola added, 'Any excuse to kiss your delicious man, darling.'

Lola smiled as Niall reached for her hand, threading their fingers together. That familiar jolt shot through her.

The thrill of being with the man she loved hadn't worn off. She doubted it ever would. Especially when he gave her that special smile he reserved just for her. The smile of a man who loved her and was no longer afraid to admit it.

She heard a sigh and turned back to Carolyn, taking in for the first time the full impact of her costume.

'You approve?' Carolyn batted her eyelashes as Lola grinned and Niall laughed.

'It's truly memorable,' Lola offered. 'Only you could carry it off with such style.'

Anyone else would look comical wearing a ruby studded eyepatch, skin-tight black silk trousers tucked into high-heeled boots and a white silk shirt that fell in enormous flounces and ruffles. But Carolyn had the necessary panache to carry off even the sequinned, toy parrot on her shoulder. The rubies at her throat and the jewel-studded sword by her hip only added to overall effect.

'Thank you, darling. But I'd trade it all for that glow of yours. You look gorgeous.' She looked from one to the other. 'As for you, Niall, settling down suits you. It's a delight to see you both so happy.'

A man in a satin frock coat and breeches called and Carolyn turned. 'Sorry, my dears. I'm needed. Catering, you know. I'll see you later.'

They stood for a moment taking in the throng of pirates and women in corseted, long-skirted dresses mixing with others, like themselves, in more conventional dress.

'Not sorry you came?' Lola murmured. Society parties weren't really Niall's thing.

'Never.' He drew her through the vast space till they found a relatively quiet oasis from which to watch the revelry. 'Not when I'm with the most beautiful woman here.'

If anyone else had said that, Lola would have known it for flattery. But as Niall's hungry gaze traced her figure in her metallic green dress, she knew that he meant it. To him she was beautiful, just as to her he was the sexiest man on the planet. As well as the most loving.

A shiver of happiness passed through her.

'Cold?' He wrapped his arm around her and she leaned in.

'Not at all. Just thinking how lucky I am.'

His heated gaze morphed into something else. Something serious yet incredibly tender.

'That would be me, darling Lola. Lucky to have you.'

He lifted her left hand, a look of satisfaction on his face as he took in her gold wedding band and the deep lustre of the square-cut emerald on her engagement ring. He lifted her hand to his lips and joy fizzed in her blood.

It had been a year since their wedding on a secluded tropical beach, attended by her father and Ed and a handful of her friends and Niall's. In that year she and Niall had grown ever closer, dealing with the inevitable challenges two strong-willed people would face, joining their lives.

Yet they'd been willing to adapt and learn. Lola had sought counselling after the trauma of being stalked and Niall had finally done the same, finding a level of peace with his difficult past.

Nor had he tried to take over her life or make her decisions. She'd been dumbfounded when Niall moved to Melbourne to be with her, rearranging his business to achieve that. He could oversee his company from almost anywhere, he'd said, whereas she needed to be with her team while she pursued her new direction.

With her career taking off, she'd recently scored a promising junior advertising job in Queensland and they'd moved north. They spent weekdays in the city and weekends in Niall's mountain retreat or on the island hideaway he'd bought as a wedding gift.

'Life just gets better and better,' he murmured as he kissed her wrist, sending squiggles of delight through her.

'Really?' He seemed happy, but now and then she wondered if, despite his excitement, this week's news might be a step too far for the man who'd once thought himself destined to stay alone.

'Really.' Niall's other hand skimmed her abdomen, his

smile so tender Lola forgot to breathe. 'It's true I'm nervous about becoming a father. I'll have to work hard at doing it well, but with you I feel up to the challenge. Together we make a great team.'

Lola placed her hand over his where it rested protectively over the new life inside her. 'My thoughts exactly.'

There it was again, the spark of emotion in his cobalt eyes that felt like a caress.

'Excellent.' He gathered her close in his arms. 'Now dance with me before I'm tempted to spirit you away.'

They had a wonderful evening, catching up with friends and making new acquaintances, enjoying convivial company and lavish entertainment.

But to Lola the best part of the night was the love in Niall's eyes and the joy of going home with him.

He was her friend, her lover, the father of her unborn baby. He was the light of her life and whatever the future held she knew they'd fight to make it good for each other and those they loved.

* * * * *

COMING SOON!

MILLS & BOON

THE HEART OF ROMANCE

A ROMANCE FOR EVERY READER

MODERN

Prepare to be swept off your feet by sophisticated, sexy and seductive heroes, in some of the world's most glamourous and romantic locations, where power and passion collide.

HISTORICAL

Escape with historical heroes from time gone by. Whether your passion is for wicked Regency Rakes, muscled Vikings or rugged Highlanders, awak the romance of the past.

MEDICAL

Set your pulse racing with dedicated, delectable doctors in the high-pressure world of medicine, where emotions run high and passion, comfort ar love are the best medicine.

True Love

Celebrate true love with tender stories of heartfelt romance, from the rush of falling in love to the joy a new baby can bring, and a focus on the emotional heart of a relationship.

Desire

Indulge in secrets and scandal, intense drama and plenty of sizzling hot action with powerful and passionate heroes who have it all: wealth, status, good looks…everything but the right woman.

HEROES

Experience all the excitement of a gripping thriller, with an intense romance at its heart. Resourceful, true-to-life women and strong, fearless me face danger and desire - a killer combination!

To see which titles are coming soon, please visit

millsandboon.co.uk/nextmonth

MILLS & BOON

Coming next month

ONE SNOWBOUND NEW YEAR'S NIGHT
Dani Collins

Van slid the door open and stepped inside only to have Becca
squeak and dance her feet, nearly dropping the groceries.

"You knew I was here," he insisted. "That's why I woke
you, so you would know I was here and you wouldn't do that.
I *live* here," he said for the millionth time, because she'd always
been leaping and screaming when he came around a corner.

"Did you? I never noticed," she grumbled, setting the bag
on the island and taking out the milk to put it in the fridge.
"I was alone here so often, I forgot I was married."

"*I* noticed that," he shot back with equal sarcasm.

They glared at each other. The civility they'd conjured in
those first minutes upstairs was completely abandoned—probably because the sexual awareness they'd reawakened was still
hissing and weaving like a basket of cobras between them,
threatening to strike again.

Becca looked away first, thrusting the eggs into the fridge
along with the pair of rib eye steaks and the package of bacon.

She hated to be called cute and hated to be ogled, so Van
tried not to do either, but *come on*. She was curvy and sleepy
and wearing that cashmere like a second skin. She was shorter
than average and had always exercised in a very haphazard
fashion, but nature had gifted her with a delightfully feminine
figure-eight symmetry. Her ample breasts were high and firm
over a narrow waist, then her hips flared into a gorgeous,
equally firm and round ass. Her fine hair was a warm brown
with sun-kissed tints, her mouth wide, and her dark brown
eyes positively soulful.

When she smiled, she had a pair of dimples that he suddenly
realized he hadn't seen in far too long.

"I don't have to be here right now," she said, slipping the coffee into the cupboard. "If you're going skiing tomorrow, I can come back while you're out."

"We're ringing in the new year right here." He chucked his chin at the windows that climbed all the way to the peak of the vaulted ceiling. Beyond the glass, the frozen lake was impossible to see through the thick and steady flakes. A gray-blue dusk was closing in.

"You have four-wheel drive, don't you?" Her hair bobbled in its knot, starting to fall as she snapped her head around. She fixed her hair as she looked back at him, arms moving with the mysterious grace of a spider spinning her web. "How did you get here?"

"Weather reports don't apply to me," he replied with self-deprecation. "Gravity got me down the driveway and I won't get back up until I can start the quad and attach the plow blade." He scratched beneath his chin, noted her betrayed glare at the windows.

Believe me, sweetheart. I'm not any happier than you are.

He thought it, but immediately wondered if he was being completely honest with himself.

"How was the road?" She fetched her phone from her purse, distracting him as she sashayed back from where it hung under her coat. "I caught a rideshare to the top of the driveway and walked down. I can meet one at the top to get back to my hotel."

"Plows will be busy doing the main roads. And it's New Year's Eve," he reminded her.

"So what am I supposed to do? Stay here? All night? With *you*?"

"Happy New Year," he said with a mocking smile.

Continue reading
ONE SNOWBOUND NEW YEAR'S NIGHT
Dani Collins

Available next month
www.millsandboon.co.uk

JOIN US ON SOCIAL MEDIA!

Stay up to date with our latest releases, author news and gossip, special offers and discounts, and all the behind-the-scenes action from Mills & Boon...

 millsandboon

 millsandboonuk

 millsandboon

It might just be true love...

MILLS & BOON
Desire

Indulge in secrets and scandal, intense drama and plenty of sizzling hot action with powerful and passionate heroes who have it all: wealth, status, good looks…everything but the right woman.